1 1

J. M

FREEDOM

BY
JOHNSTONE J. MCGUCKIAN

Copyright © 2015 Johnstone J. McGuckian
Cover Image Copyright © 2015 Steve Thornhill

All rights reserved.
ISBN: **099346100X**
ISBN-13: **978-0993461002**

PROLOGUE

Most people never care how Freedom feels and why should they? No one would ever want to feel that way. Freedom was in a constant state of tiredness but he never knew it, the drugs blocked that out and then the booze blocked those out the best it could. And then at three, Freedom's drugs, booze and tiredness all seemed to increase their various effects and the result was anything but Freedom. More to the point, for the majority of the time, Freedom was a prisoner, an irony not lost on him as he stared down through the glass at hundreds of other people. Stupidly enough, they wanted to be there and as they danced another dance and drank another shot, they didn't care about Freedom as long as it all sounded good and they could maintain their state of euphoria for the duration of another queue at the bar.

Freedom didn't want to do it that night, he didn't want to do it any night really but he had to anyway and this night was the same as ever. And it really was, the same again. Same sounds, same drinks, same drugs, even the same people. That one girl sat across a table from her friend and whatever guy she'd picked up that night, really she was too good for him but after a pill or two those things never seemed to matter. Perhaps that's why Zoë had stuck around for so long. One advantage Freedom had over other guys was good drugs at low prices. Freedom knew everyone and had to pretend to like most of them.

Looking out of the glass window again, the one that separated him from the happy people, Freedom saw the same scene play itself out repeatedly. It was getting late now, only an hour to go, or was it two? There was always someone to tell Freedom when he was to be released and he never thought to note what time that was. They'd usually turn up with a glass of water to wash away the lingering effects of the drugs and booze, so that, as he quietened everything down, his tiredness could fully kick in. That time hadn't come yet though.

Looking down over the crowd and somehow still grinning, DJ Freedom whispered to himself. To him, these people were his to command. For the immediate future their destiny and any hopes that they may have were his. They were his slaves. With just the

2

pressing of a few buttons, these people would stop dancing and maybe even leave the building. But why would he do that? As soon as they left, they'd really have their freedom and his control would no longer have an effect. Freedom had an empire that stretched as far as the exit and the only thing that stopped anybody leaving was the large bouncer, clad entirely in black and wearing an earpiece. They called him Tony, that might not even have been his name but that's what Freedom was told to call him. Tony suited him either way.

Another song was about to end and Freedom couldn't even remember what he had lined up next but it was all ready to go. He waited for the right moment, the right beat. It was only a few seconds away and if he were to mistime it then the night could be over. But it wasn't allowed to be over, he hadn't been told yet that he was allowed to end it and the fallout of ending even a second early could be fatal to his career. He tried to think hard but he couldn't remember the next song, even when he listened to it through his headphones he couldn't remember its name. Everything had faded into one consistent noise but everybody in the room seemed to be entertained. How did he get everything so right? How were people enjoying this, how was it correct? DJ Freedom had lost control of his life once more, the pills ruled it now and the women followed those. Zoë might be different but she could just as easily be another in a long line of people who were only interested in DJ Freedom and not his life outside of clubs.

She'd even met him when he was working. From the dance floor she waved at him to catch his attention, she wanted to join him in the booth. He never normally let that happen bar a few rare occasions but the way that she smiled gave him no choice. A quick signal to one of the Security staff ensured that she was allowed to climb the stairs to him. She only wanted to request a song at first but the smile persisted and Freedom found himself inviting her to stay with him and before long she was taking as many pills as he was.

Zoë stayed until the end that night and returned to Freedom's apartment with him. It was a magnificent night and the next morning she asked if she could join him in the DJ booth again. His answer was an immediate yes. He didn't know what it was but something made her different from all of the other girls on the

3

island. Her smile continued to captivate and she actually seemed to show an interest in the person that he was as opposed to the DJ personality that the entirety of Corzones Island professed to love so much.

For a while the Isle Club became a fun place to be. DJ Freedom was happy because Zoë was with him and somehow it all came together with the drugs and the music perpetuating a magical summer. Crowds seemed happier and Freedom just wanted to carry on every night. He didn't wait for the signal to end the night but instead he dreaded it, hoping that it would never come because all he wanted to do was continue for as long as he could. Zoë returned to his room with him every night but as the days passed she seemed less enthusiastic. She wanted to leave sooner and even questioned some of his musical choices. His first rule however was not to let anybody influence his choice of music, not even somebody that made him feel as good as Zoë did. She never complained too much though and Freedom would much rather have her there than not.

The right moment arrived and Freedom perfectly transitioned from one song to another and was rewarded with a cheer from the crowd, this was one of their favourites. It always was and had become the keystone of his set, despite the fact that Freedom didn't particularly like it. He'd stopped playing songs that he liked some time ago. He never let one member of the crowd influence his musical choices but the entire club needed pleasing and with every record he chose he knew that he was taking a risk. It was extremely rare that a risk didn't pay off but when his choice was wrong it was immediately clear. The population of the dance floor would significantly decrease and usually move towards the bar, working to the logic that if they drank more then the song would be more enjoyable. Sometimes it worked and other questionable choices were appreciated later in the evening.

Another mix, another song and another shot of something; probably tequila. Freedom could feel sleep trying to drag him over the edge. He couldn't go yet. He had to wait until he was told, until he was released from his glass prison. His mood changed slightly when a tall, blonde girl wearing nothing but a bikini top and a barely existent pair of denim shorts came running past the bouncers and towards him. She flung herself at him and planted a

4

kiss on his cheek. This was Zoë, the only thing about the island that made things bearable for Freedom. She probably didn't really care about him and she was on the wrong end of a handful of pills but her smile was one of the few things that would get Freedom out of bed in the morning.

Morning. DJ Freedom was now Franko Young and as he'd slept, all of the mystique and legend surrounding DJ Freedom had faded away. On this island, DJ Freedom was a celebrity but in his tiny apartment at eleven in the morning, Franko was just another wasted twenty-something. He looked over towards a small plastic bin in the corner, five bottles of beer surrounded it and another one was inside. Only six, surprising really as the inevitable headache made it feel like it had been so many more. That was just in the apartment though, he would never know how much he had consumed in the club.

Franko rolled over, expecting to see Zoë next to him but as soon as he noticed her absence he remembered what had happened. She'd walked up to him in the club and kissed him and then repeatedly apologised for going early. And she'd left. DJ Freedom had been trapped in his own empire and the one person he wanted to be there with him had gone. But there was more, they'd made an arrangement. 12:00 by the pool. Franko smiled at the realisation that the day would be just him and Zoë, truly free together. He'd not admitted it to her but Franko really did enjoy their time together. As he climbed out of bed, he groaned as the full force of the headache hit him, and walked over the kettle, he wondered if perhaps she felt the same. Probably not, nobody came to the island to find true love, such a thing could never be found amongst the inhumane number of drugs and drinks that scattered its hotspots.

Franko looked through his cupboards, knowing that he had to have some filter paper somewhere. In the evening when he was DJ Freedom any old substance could enter his body but in the daytime when he was Franko, not even instant coffee was allowed. The more he searched his inadequate kitchenette however, the more he came to realise that instant was his only option. Not only had he run out of filter paper but not a proper coffee bean was in sight. He'd gone to the supermarket the previous day and met up with Zoë as he arrived there. He'd left with a bottle of vodka and nothing to make coffee with. Franko decided to explore his next-best option and was relieved to find that there was orange juice left in the fridge. That and a paracetamol (the cupboard was always well stocked with them) would put him on the right track to recovery.

He looked at his clock: 11:54. The evening felt so far away and Franko had all of those hours to enjoy before... 11:54... He was meeting Zoë in a matter of minutes! And she'd be there, she was always there on time, something else that Franko liked, it made her seem more reliable than the others and he'd always try to return the gesture. The idea of somebody actually finding him reliable was laughable but he felt as though he'd better make some effort.

The orange juice was drunk almost as quickly as Franko pulled on his shorts and an extortionately priced shirt. He'd been there months now and he was being paid a stupid amount for what he did. As a result he'd been prone to expensive online shopping, not just for himself either, Zoë and all of the others before her had benefitted from the generous amounts paid by the Isle Club. There was no reason for it though as they'd probably stay with him as long as their holiday lasted regardless. Being close to Franko, for any amount of time, resulted in free drinks, entry and a VIP pass if nothing else. Perhaps he was just being nice.

He grabbed his wallet, phone and keys and dashed out of the door, with two minutes to reach the pool and Zoë, who'd be waiting for him by now, getting more and more impatient at every passing second. He locked the door, quickly, despite the key sticking as usual and dashed away from his apartment. Franko was in one of the larger hotels scattered across the island and it was supposedly the best, with Franko's room being one of the more expensive in the area. One of the many disadvantages of this was that it was some distance to the pool, simply due to the size of the complex.

Franko found himself running, his headache reminding him of its existence with every step. He probably looked ridiculous, he'd put on a considerable amount of weight since arriving on the island and even before then he could have been healthier. Still, Zoë was at the end of this run and she made it worth it. Images of what they could do with the day played out in his head: a nice relaxing day by the pool, a bit of shopping or even a day by the beach. The island had numerous small coves and caves and, despite the number of people, it was very easy to find a spot to claim as your own. It was a kind of unwritten law that you move on if one was taken up by a couple already, Franko had taken advantage if this a number of times but never with Zoë.

Out of breath and red as a tomato, Franko reached the pool. It was already quite busy with most people looking as hungover and out of shape as he did, if not worse. That lightened his spirits but not nearly as much as the sight of Zoë, lying on a lounger in that bikini that Franko liked so much, the one she'd been wearing when they had first met. Next to her another lounger was already prepared and it had Franko's name on it. Upon seeing him, she sat up. 'I thought you weren't coming.' She said it jokingly but her voice was sounding divine. Franko got on to his knees so his face was level with hers. They kissed. Franko couldn't help but smile as they were doing so. It was a long kiss, a happy kiss. All the things Franko had thought and feared were confirmed: Zoë was indeed as wonderful as DJ Freedom thought she had been. It was DJ Freedom who saw her the most, not Franko and he wished that the opposite was the case. DJ Freedom was a self-destructive dickhead, while Franko was just Franko. The women loved DJ Freedom but Franko, they never quite got to know him well enough. Zoë would be different.

Franko smiled again before sitting on his lounger and removing his expensive shirt, discarding it on the stone floor next to him. It was then that he looked to his side and saw the two shot glasses containing a clear liquid on a tray next to him. They were accompanied by a slice of lemon and a healthy pile of salt. Zoë indicated towards the glasses.
'These are on me.' She promptly took her glass and her helping of the salt. She suggested that Franko should do the same. Hesitantly, he did so. Zoë clearly thought she was meeting with DJ Freedom at 12:00 and unfortunately, Franko had come in his place. All he could do now was become DJ Freedom, eleven hours before he needed to.

Freedom held the shot glass in one hand and the salt in the other. 'Now!' shouted Zoë, excitedly. Freedom threw the salt into his mouth, closely followed by the tequila. Desperately holding back the wish to vomit, he grabbed the slice of lemon and stuffed it into his mouth. Willpower was the only thing keeping him dignified.

7

Why had he done such a stupid thing? He looked up and saw his reason, cool as anything, lying back in her lounger and casually discarding the lemon. Freedom did the same, placing it back on the tray. They both lay in silence for a moment.

'What the hell is wrong with you Franko?' At least she thought she was speaking to Franko, Freedom thought.

'What do you mean?' He replied, knowing exactly what her answer would be. Late nights and drugs were always a problem in the end. 'You are the most wonderful guy I have ever met but you just get lost in what you do. Look at you, you're twenty-five and going through a midlife crisis! You arrived here out of breath, I bet you've not even been out of bed for fifteen minutes, have you?' Freedom checked his watch, she was wrong, it had been almost twenty minutes by now but he wasn't going to raise the point.

'You're supposed to entertain people that are too smashed to know better,' she continued, 'not to get too smashed yourself in the process.' She didn't know how demanding his job was. He did it every night, apart from some Saturdays when they'd wheel in some B-list celebrity to entertain the crowd and it was hard. He was a prisoner in that place but he was also addicted to it. There was no getting out, not as far as his career was concerned. He'd left school at sixteen and had no real qualifications to speak of. No diplomas and no degrees. Working as a DJ was all he had and this job was the best he'd ever get.

'I know.' His reply was pathetic and he knew it but what could he say? Zoë was right.

'Listen Franko, I really like you but I don't want to see you destroy yourself.' Freedom smiled, just a little bit. Zoë really did seem to care and perhaps there was hope for Franko Young after all.

Part One - The Island

One

'Never go on holiday with your older brother.' A phrase that
William Brey had repeated to himself uncountable times over the
last two days. Harry was understanding, he always had been but
his friends, Royce and Jason had arrived on Corzones Island to
drink as much and sleep with as many women as possible. Three
days in and none of them had lived up to their own expectations
and 'desperate measures' had to be taken. Will wanted no part of
that and decided that, instead of hanging around them and being
the butt of every other joke, he'd go and explore the island on his
own. Harry had offered to go with him but Will knew that really
his brother wanted to go after women just as much as his friends.
Will spent fifteen minutes persuading Harry that he didn't mind
and after all he'd been telling the truth. Up in the hills somewhere
was an old temple and that was just the sort of thing that interested
Will, it was even the thing that made him agree to come on the
holiday in the first place. He had intended to have the lads' holiday
that Harry had always wanted but he always knew that he'd never
last long. It was impressive that he'd managed two nights of it.
Nightclubs weren't the sort of places he liked to be and it was very
rare that he'd drink anything but beer. However, in the last couple
of days he'd drank it all: Whiskey, Tequila, Gin and some horrible
variation of Vodka. The latter had made him sick and provided
ammunition for Royce and Jason's continual bating.

Will was fed up on the third day and the eleven that lay ahead were
going to be mercilessly long. It had been fine when he'd first
arrived and climbed off the boat. Corzones was so small that there
wasn't an airport so upon your flight arriving on the mainland you
were guided to a coach which took you to the nearest harbour and
then you boarded the legendary Corzones ferry. After the plane the
travelling time was about three hours and that's when the drinking
had started. The coach was loud, boisterous and constantly filled
with the chants of rival football fans. Will was hoping to get some
sleep after a long and uncomfortable flight but within seconds he'd
realised that rest of any kind would be an impossibility. Eventually
he succumbed to the peer pressure and decided to open a beer. By

this stage, Royce had produced a bottle of whiskey and the shotting had started. Will decided not to join in with that, he wasn't sure how he'd cope with the ferry and wanted to be relatively sober as he unpacked. Towards the end of the coach journey he found himself joining in with the football chants. Jason in particular had been impressed by this so Will didn't admit that he'd only picked up the words throughout the course of the journey.

The ferry seemed to be a quieter affair. The sense of anticipation was mesmerising and, yet again, Will found himself succumbing to the excitement of it all. He was going on the holiday of a lifetime! How could this week be anything but perfection? He was slightly annoyed by Jason's promises to 'get him laid', that certainly wasn't why he was going to the island but he wasn't going to let on. To Will, this week was about enjoying himself in a way that he chose to and he had to admit that it seemed he was becoming far more enthusiastic about the whole thing than he'd expected to.

After arriving reality started to set in for him. When you're not on Corzones Island it is simply a myth, a place that many dream of going to for the ultimate twenty-something holiday experience. Upon arrival, Will realised that it lived up to that myth far too well. People were drunk all of the time, drugs were abundant and all but ignored by the authorities and the constant thumping of music rang across every inch of the island, to the point that Will had stopped noticing its presence on the second day. The only time that it did seem to be noticeable was annoyingly when he was trying to sleep. However, nobody else seemed to be affected by it. Will hadn't really anticipated the impact that the various combined cultures would have on everybody. This island wasn't about rest and relaxation, it was about pushing yourself to your physical and mental limits in the name of fun. Unfortunately, fun was far from what Will was feeling and, after twenty-four hours of it, irritation started to kick in.

It was on the second night that Will concluded he needed some time to himself. He knew that Royce and Jason (and even Harry, for that matter) could be excitable but this place seemed to amplify the negative points of their personalities and, during a drinking game, Will broke. He left the club and went back to the flat. He had half-hoped that Harry and the others would follow him to make amends, however this wasn't the case and Will had spent the majority of the night in the apartment alone. Harry, Jason and Royce staggered in much later on and all managed to pass instantly into sleep. When they awoke the next morning and attempted to piece together the previous night's events, Will's departure wasn't even mentioned.

They seemed to spend a long time trying to connect a series of non-events and it appeared that the most memorable thing to happen all evening was Jason's drunken attempt to kiss a girl who was there with her boyfriend. Will's immediate reaction to this was to question why any couple would come to this island, it was hardly a romantic getaway and mistakes such as Jason's must be commonplace. For the same amount of money, you could travel to any of the great romance spots around the world and have a far more exciting time. Nevertheless, that particular couple had chosen to come to Corzones, and as a result, Jason had come very close to getting punched.

Choosing to ignore their hangovers, Harry, Royce and Jason had decided to find themselves a fabled poolside club that was open all day. They wanted to arrive there as early as possible as Royce had reasoned that this was an essential move in their quest for women and the other two had agreed with him. Will checked his watch and realised that it had been two hours since they'd left the apartment. By now they would probably be drunk and not so subtly ogling women in bikinis. As Will pondered this thought he inadvertently found himself doing the same thing as two women walked past. He quickly averted his gaze.

He was sitting next to a fountain in what was referred to as the 'town centre'. Despite Corzones' reputation and location there was an extensive shopping area in the town. The centre was a large, square area surrounded by various shops, cafés and bars. A large melting-pot of cultures. One prominent culture was that of the island itself. Up until a few years previously, Corzones had been a small island community, consisting of mostly over fifties but then business tycoon Giorgio Corzones had come along, bought up the entire island and turned it into a 'holiday community' for eighteen to thirties. As a business move, Will had to admire it. Corzones was world famous for his various business ventures, despite not being one to appear in public all that often beyond the odd charity event. It was a logical move for him to make, he owned a ferry

11

company and an airline so why not give the people somewhere to go to as well as a means to get there?

The town centre was busy, most people did their shopping at this time in the morning (it wasn't actually morning but anything before five in the evening was considered to be so) ready for the alcohol fuelled antics of the evening. Will found that the cafés and restaurants did look appealing but he knew that he probably wouldn't get a chance to sample them. Harry, Jason and Royce were on a strict diet of bacon butties for the fortnight and persuading them to try anything else would be a challenge. Will was tempted to go alone but decided against it when he saw they were full of groups of people. Lonesome dining was something Will was used to at home and he didn't want to repeat the experience while on holiday. He didn't imagine for a moment that very soon, he'd have somebody to go with.

Two

Lucy was pissed off. She didn't want to tell Sofia this but there was no getting away from it, she wasn't happy. She and Sofia had always been very different when it came to men. Lucy avoided them where possible whereas Sofia couldn't do that even if she actually tried to. Lucy was ready for it to happen and she expected to have to put up with Sofia not coming home on most nights but she'd assumed that at least in the daytime her friend would have some time for her. But of course, Sofia had fallen in love. They'd been in the Isle Club for the third night in a row and Lucy was bored of it, she wasn't enjoying herself, the music was loud and repetitive and the whole place stank. Hundreds of sweaty people all gathering in a relatively small space on a night when it was over twenty degrees outside did not make for a pleasant experience. But Sofia had wanted to go and Lucy had little choice but to join her.

She and Sofia had been friends for a long time, ever since they were very young. Her own father and Sofia's had worked together for years but then he moved to Spain when he'd married Sofia's mother. Sofia had been born and only ever lived in Spain but once a year would come and visit so her family could catch up with old friends. As a result, Lucy and Sofia had grown up becoming just as great friends as their parents. This year no trip to Spain had been planned but Sofia had the great idea that prevented them from missing out. She promptly suggested Corzones Island to Lucy and made it sound like a tropical paradise. Lucy jumped at the chance to see her friend and get away and two months later they were on the Corzones ferry and ready to begin their holiday.

So far, Sofia had been very restrained and spent most of her time with Lucy. There was the odd occasion where she'd succumbed to male interest but this had only lasted a few minutes as the male in question would buy her a drink and she'd then return to Lucy having saved another few dollars. The cycle would repeat itself every couple of hours with a different guy but essentially Sofia had stuck by her friend, a fact of which Lucy was very grateful.

Lucy could see why Sofia was so popular with the lads - her Spanish accent was very appealing for a start and her grasp of English was incredibly good but clearly not her first language. She had long, blonde hair which she took the utmost care of and a suntan that seemed to be a permanent fixture. She was tall and athletic and her smile could make any guy bend to her will in an instant. She also did something that Lucy could never bring herself to do, Sofia consistently wore incredibly short and revealing dresses that often turned heads. Lucy was wearing shorts and even in those she didn't feel particularly comfortable.

Sitting in the Isle Club, Sofia and Lucy had been fairly happy, they were both drinking identical cocktails from overly-large glasses and admiring the male clientele, something that Lucy found herself doing more and more over the course of the holiday. Objectifying was something she usually disagreed with but she figured that everybody else on the island was probably doing the exact same thing and that on this occasion, with her best friend, it couldn't do too much damage. They were sitting in a booth and looking across at the dance floor. The club was big and as promotional literature so often reminded everybody, it was the biggest club on the island and famous for its history of attracting celebrity DJs. Not tonight however, looking up at the DJ booth, raised above the ground and requiring an elevator to reach it, all Lucy saw was a skinny, pale man who must have been about her own age. He looked tired and drunk, but then again so did everybody. The dance floor was below the DJ booth and currently full of people dancing, or at least trying to. Lights scattered around a rig on the ceiling illuminated the entire place in numerous different colours. A few dance cages lined the edge of the floor but Lucy had seldom seen them used. Occasionally somebody who had drunk one too many had the confidence boost necessary to try one out but after a minute or two of dancing and the novelty of having their friends cheer them on had died, they gave up and rejoined the masses. Lucy watched the attempt of one particular girl end in a falling over, which Lucy did have to laugh at slightly as she stood at the bar. She had to admit that the bar was the most impressive part of the club, it stretched the length of an entire side wall and behind it were hundreds of different kinds of alcohol, including exotic liquors and flavours of vodka that nobody would consider even trying in any other place. This was different though, this was Corzones Island.

Lucy had returned from the bar holding another two drinks. Sofia had remained behind in the booth to save it as they both knew that the moment it was vacated, it would be taken by somebody else.

14

As she approached the booth, she saw that her spot already had been taken by a tall, muscular, blond man who was coolly chatting away to Sofia. They were both drinking the same drink, which led Lucy to believe that he had been surveying the club for a girl on her own, while holding two drinks so he could easily make his move. Sofia had been that girl and naturally she was receptive to the attractive man and the free drink. Sofia waved at Lucy and beckoned her to her place. The blond man moved up and gave Lucy a small part of the seat to perch on. As she'd sat down, she noticed that the blond man had cleverly managed to use himself to separate Sofia and Lucy, he turned to Sofia and virtually ignored Lucy's existence. 'It's ok,' she thought to herself, 'Sofia will drink the drink and then this one will be on his way like all of the others.' That didn't happen and after less than fifteen minutes, they were making out, leaving an awkward Lucy to look in every direction but theirs.

Lucy had managed to get a moment of conversation out of the blond man while Sofia went to the toilet but the enthusiastic conversation that he'd had with Sofia had turned into disinterested one-word answers for Lucy. She'd established that his name was Karl and that he was here with friends but he'd decided to come out alone that night. He commented that the island was a very unique and interesting place before burying himself in his phone. Lucy looked at the screen and saw that his text featured the word 'wingman'. At this point, Lucy realised that she no longer featured in Karl or Sofia's evenings and that any chance of enjoying herself had evaporated. Sofia returned from the toilet and after a half hearted 'Are you sure you don't mind?' from her friend, she left.

The Isle Club was located on a long, straight road known somewhat unimaginatively as 'the strip'. It contained about fifteen or so different clubs and a selection of smaller bars, all of which contained illuminated signs. The strip itself was quite busy and people moved from club to club, waving the pass they had bought that allowed them entry to everywhere as opposed to paying on the door each time. Tucked into a corner and slightly away from everything else was the taxi area. They weren't real taxis, just large quad bikes and buggies manned by various island reps. Lucy walked to the one at the front of the queue and simply said which block of apartments she was staying in. The driver gave a smiley nod and beckoned for Lucy to jump into the back of the buggy.

They moved fairly slowly up the hill and away from the strip and very soon the lights had faded into the distance, unlike the music which still thumped equally as loud. At first the driver had attempted to make conversation but Lucy was too grumpy to respond properly. Not wanting the driver to think she was rude, she apologised and cited tiredness as her reason for not being as chatty as she might be.

They drove through the town centre, it was empty, too early for hordes of people leaving the various nightspots but too late for the last stragglers to be arriving. Lucy was close to sleep, she'd drunk more than she would usually and her annoyance had given way to apathy. She couldn't be in her bed soon enough and she knew she'd sleep instantly. She struggled on the first night, as everybody does because of the music but she was used to it by the second. The last few nights she'd been playing catch-up.

After a short amount of time, the buggy arrived at her apartment and she made her way inside. She turned the light on to find that the place was even more of a mess than she'd remembered. She and Sofia had a pizza each (there was a very good takeaway nearby) and a few drinks before they went out and they'd decided to leave the remains to tidy up later on. The only problem with this was that in the small apartment, a little mess left not much space at all, Lucy decided that it would wait until morning and went straight to the bathroom.

After removing her makeup and brushing her teeth, Lucy changed into her pyjamas, poured herself a glass of water and went into her room. Most of the apartments had separate rooms, however they were separated by very thin walls and were cramped to the point that once a bed and table were placed in there, there was no other space whatsoever. Lucy climbed into her bed and lifted the thin sheet over herself. Corzones Island was very warm, especially at this time of year but Lucy liked the comfort of the cover. She knew she could sleep comfortably and that it'd be morning before Sofia was home. They'd both agreed that if they were to end up with somebody, it would be at the other person's place and not their own.

Sleep came to Lucy very easily and she didn't awaken until late the next morning. Lucy's room had a small window on one side and the sun became so strong that even the curtains couldn't maintain the darkness. Lucy had a large gulp of her water, which had been resting all night on the bedside table and was now too warm to be enjoyable. She grudgingly rolled out of bed and opened the curtain, admiring the concrete nightmare that was the surrounding apartment buildings. She could see a figure staggering towards her building and realised that it was Sofia, her dress not quite straight having been clearly put back on in the dark. Lucy decided that she would take the dignified high ground and quickly dressed herself. She filled the kettle and set it boiling before starting to brush her hair. It was at this point that Sofia arrived home, having clearly drunk too much the night before. She did however have a huge smile on her face, Lucy took this as a bad sign.

'I'm so bloody tired.' Sofia croaked, her Spanish accent now not seeming as seductive as normal. Lucy just smiled.
'You had a good night then?' Sofia grinned and went slightly red, it wasn't like her to seem embarrassed.
'Yes, it was very good.' She said, the positivity in her voice made it clear to Lucy that Sofia would be meeting Karl again. 'I need coffee.' Sofia walked to the kettle, which was now almost boiled. After rummaging in the cupboards, she produced two mugs. 'You want a drink too?' Lucy nodded and muttered a "yes please" and Sofia produced tea bags along with the jar of coffee beans. Sofia made the tea for Lucy first and passed it to her before going to make her own drink.

'Lucy, can I ask you a question?' Lucy had a very good idea of what this question would be and she was correct. 'Karl has asked if we can spend the day together and I'd would really like to...' Lucy knew Sofia well and the next sentence would be insincere apologies and an assurance that she was a great friend. She chose to interrupt.
'Go with him. That's fine. I'd like the day to myself anyway.' Sofia smiled and hugged her friend. 'Thank you. He's nice, I really like him.' Lucy returned the hug although she wasn't happy. This was supposed to be their holiday, their only chance to see each other this year. Sofia had let her usual hunger for male attention take over. Lucy knew that if she didn't let Sofia go however, she'd be in a bad mood for the rest of the holiday. All she could do was hope that Karl was just a passing fancy and that any interest in him ceased within the next day.

Sofia had a shower and some toast before leaving, she and Karl had agreed to meet for lunch before going to 'somewhere special', Lucy decided not to attempt to find out more and instead began to plan her own day. The problem was that she didn't manage to concoct a plan of any kind and eventually decided that she would try out the shops. After a shower and another cup of tea, she decided to venture out and headed immediately for the town centre.

It was another incredibly hot day, hotter than Lucy had ever experienced, she was glad that today she had chosen a casual dress instead of her usual shorts and top combination. It was by far not what she'd normally wear but everybody else was in a dress so why shouldn't she be too? Lucy managed to place the other people that were around into two categories: people who genuinely were out of bed and ready to start their day and people embarking on the well-known custom that was the 'walk of shame'. At this stage in the day, more people seemed to fall into the latter category. They were the people who had ended up staying in a bed that wasn't theirs the previous night.

Lucy was too hot within minutes of walking and although the island wasn't particularly big, it felt she'd walked a great distance. Luckily, she reached one of the various shacks set up around the place. They were a series of small shops selling snacks and drinks (both alcoholic and otherwise), Lucy had no intention of drinking alcohol yet and wasn't sure if she would at all that day. An ice-cold can of lemonade was more than welcome however. The man behind the counter was cheery, as all of the reps seemed to be and Lucy couldn't help but notice that he was quite attractive. He seemed to have bags under his eyes, clearly the result of having had a late night, as so many others on the island had done. After paying for her lemonade, Lucy continued her walk into the town centre.

Corzones Island was very much a jungle and had remained that way up until recently. When it was just a small ageing island community, only a small corner had been used but after Giorgio Corzones had bought the island an army of developers moved in. A few environmental campaigners had expressed concern but Corzones Island's strange lack of any real animal population didn't

18

give them enough ammunition to stop the project going ahead. An agreement was reached to protect as much of the island as possible and Corzones had taken this more seriously than he actually needed to. As a result Lucy found herself venturing into some thick vegetation, the only man-made aspects were the path and the chain of lights that ran alongside. It wasn't a walk deep into the jungle but the trees provided some much welcome shade to Lucy for the few minutes she was under them.

She emerged from the trees and walked past another apartment complex, this one seemed to be much nicer than Lucy's and bigger too. She could hear loud music coming from nearby and at one point saw over a fence that there was a large swimming pool at the centre of the buildings. It was starting to fill up considerably more than the rest of the island and even the bar was starting to get some custom. One person was holding an all-day breakfast sandwich in one hand and a bottle of lager in the other. It was just after twelve now and Lucy could see two people, a man in expensive shorts and a woman in a revealing bikini, shotting something that Lucy assumed was Tequila. She shook her head in disbelief and continued on her walk.

As she neared the town centre, Lucy saw that she was the only person alone and that everybody else was either with a friend or at least someone they'd hooked up with the previous night. She was lost for words and began to think about Sofia, who would be off somewhere now with Karl, probably enjoying breakfast along with his company. That wasn't what the holiday was supposed to be about, not for her anyway. The more she thought about it, the more she realised that Sofia's motives for bringing her here weren't for a girly week, but were actually so she'd have somebody she could return to when the latest man had lost interest. Perhaps she was wrong but as she slowly walked into the town centre, she very much doubted it.

Lucy was pissed off with Sofia, but not half as much as she was with the scene before her. She'd rounded a corner just in time to see a group of large laddish guys, wearing shorts and vest tops for the most part, walk up to a small and younger man who was sat at the side of the fountain at the centre of the square. He seemed to be alone and in a world of his own up until the point when one of the group of guys walked up to him and without a word pushed him into the fountain. The group walked away, muttering things about the hilarity of his face and 'banter'. Nobody seemed interested in helping the poor victim and were more concerned with ignoring it completely or in some cases, laughing. Lucy was furious and dashed towards the fountain. Standing in front of her was a guy with longish dark hair that was now dripping. He was wearing an orange T-shirt that was slightly too large for him and a pair of long shorts. He had also worn flip-flops however, only one of these was now attached to his feet, the other was floating in the centre of the fountain. Lucy helped the wet man out of the fountain before taking her own flat shoes off and climbing in herself, hoisting up her dress slightly to keep it dry, and retrieving the wayward flip-flop. She handed it to him. He smiled, 'Thank you,' he said. Lucy looked and noticed that the group had gone and that everybody else had lost interest. Lucy felt another surge of anger.

'I don't believe that! We're all here to have a good time and they...' Lucy realised that her anger wasn't the priority and something else had to be addressed first, '...are you alright?' He nodded and smiled as he brushed his hair out of his face.

'Yeah fine, just a bit cold.' Lucy could see him shivering slightly but then looked towards the sun.

'Don't worry, you'll warm up soon.'

He nodded in agreement.

'I will, it's supposed to be thirty five degrees today.'

Lucy detected a hint of pomposity in the way that he had spoken before realising again that nobody had been there to help him.

'Are you here on your own?' Lucy asked, finding it very unlikely that somebody like him would end up on this island unless persuaded to by somebody else. He must have been very much like her in that respect, she'd taken some convincing and Sofia had been very persistent before she'd caved.

'I'm here with my brother and a few of his friends, they've already started drinking though and I really don't want to.' Lucy nodded but then wished she'd said something as there was a momentary awkward pause. 'What about you?', he asked, eventually.

'I'm here with my friend Sofia but she's shacked up with some guy, Karl.' He finally introduced himself as William Brey, Will for short. He was dripping slightly less now but suddenly sneezed quite violently.

'Are you sure you're alright?' Will nodded in response, struggling through his sneeze. It quickly wore down, although he continued to shiver slightly. Lucy decided that this conversation was best moved to somewhere else. Will seemed to be quite harmless and he'd also been abandoned by friends so Lucy concluded that this could be a friendship worth pursuing. He was also quite nice. Lucy bit her tongue and just found herself saying it: 'Come on, we can get some lunch, if you'd like?' Will smiled, although he was clearly surprised by the offer.

'I... I don't even know your name?' Lucy smiled.

'It's Lucy. Now come on Will, I'll show you my favourite café on this island.' The truth was that she'd only been to one café but it seemed to be quite nice and was located on a street just off the town centre. Will stood up, still soaking wet but with a smile on his face. Having done her good deed for the day, Lucy wasn't quite as annoyed.

Three

Karl knew the island well as this was his third year here in a row and on his past two visits he'd managed to work out where the best breakfasts were. Sofia had thoroughly enjoyed hers, a proper European style spread, far nicer than the bacon sandwiches that everybody else on the island seemed to prefer. Their breakfast conversation had been rather predictable and covered the topics of how good last night was and where they'd both come from. It turned out that Karl had been to Spain within the last year as part of his work and had even stayed in Barcelona, not too far from Sofia's home. The agreement had already been made to meet up again on his next trip, whenever that would be.

After their breakfast they decided not to walk around the shops or to start drinking yet. Sofia's intention was to go and spend some time with Lucy. Karl had other plans though and promised to show her 'the most wonderful spot on the island' and Sofia decided that this was an offer she didn't want to refuse. Lucy had said she wanted some time to herself anyway. Karl paid for their breakfast, despite Sofia offering to do the same. He'd bought all of the drinks last night in the club, as well as the expensive wine they'd drunk back at his apartment. He insisted that he was paying and Sofia eventually accepted and rewarded his generosity with another kiss. There had been a lot of those and Sofia was enjoying it so much. She hadn't expected to find a man like this on Corzones.

Karl wouldn't tell her where they were going once they'd left the café but promised her a wonderful surprise. Romance was another thing that was hard to come by on the island and she wasn't going to let such an opportunity go by. As they walked along the jungle path and towards the beach, Sofia reached out for Karl's hand. It just felt right. He accepted and together they walked along the path. As the path started to go downhill, Karl pointed into the foliage.
'It's this way.' He said, smiling. She allowed him to lead her through the dense greenery for a few minutes when she noticed that all signs of civilisation were out of sight. The light thudding of some music could be heard in the distance, probably from one of the all-day pool clubs but that was it.

'Where are we going?' Sofia asked again. Karl's answer was just as mysterious as the last time, though he did stop walking and kiss her again. The whole time their hands never became separated. Not until the trees cleared and they were standing on the edge of a cliff, looking straight out over the golden sand and the glistening blue sea. It looked perfect.

'Down there.' He said, with a smile. Sofia immediately worried.

'I can't climb down there!' She was wearing flat shoes and a dress, not very practical for climbing.

'I'll help you.' Karl kissed her again before letting go of her hand and starting to climb.

Sofia had to admit that the climb wasn't a difficult as she'd first anticipated and the beach wasn't very far down from where they started. Nevertheless, Karl kept his promise and assisted her with every step down. When they reached the bottom, Sofia could see clearly the full beauty of the place she'd been brought to. It was a small cove that was completely isolated by cliffs, on top of which there was nothing but jungle. It was virtually silent, the calm waves breaking on the shore being the only sound and they even managed to expunge the distant sound of music that Sofia had registered until the moment she'd touched the sand. She had to kiss Karl again, this place was wonderful.

He beckoned her around a bend in the cliff, which revealed a cave that she hadn't been able to see at first, even in her direct line of vision it was still hard to spot in the cliff face. Its mouth wasn't particularly big but inside was a fairly large chamber, just about entirely lit from the sun that was flowing in.

'Wonderful, isn't it?' Sofia looked at Karl and nodded in agreement. Unable to contain herself she kissed him again. Together they walked back out on to the beach. Sofia sat down on the sand and replaced the sunglasses she had removed upon entering the cave. Karl sat next to her and placed his hand upon hers. 'They call this place Lovers' Cove,' he said, 'it's the most romantic place on the island. Very few people know how to find it. We probably won't be disturbed here.' Sofia smiled again, she'd done a lot of that throughout morning. She turned to Karl and they started kissing and they just didn't stop. Sofia lay down and Karl rolled on top of her. This was going to be a wonderful afternoon.

What seemed like hours passed and every second was perfect for Sofia. Her thoughts did divert to Lucy for a brief moment but she was having too much fun to really worry about her friend. Karl, who was lying next to her, suddenly sat up and tapped her shoulder.

'Someone is coming.' He said it hurriedly.

'And?' asked Sofia, she was surprised that they'd been left alone as long as they had.

'It's bad luck to be seen in Lovers' Cove by anybody else.' Karl smiled as he said this, of course it was nonsense but it was romantic nonsense and Sofia couldn't help but join in.

'We should hide in the cave,' she said with a cheeky grin, 'Nobody will find us there and we can continue as we left off.' Karl smiled, Sofia knew that she'd said exactly the right thing as Karl grinned back. They both jumped up, grabbed each other's hands and ran into the cave. A moment later another couple climbed down the cliff, unaware that anybody else was around. Inside the cave, Sofia and Karl continued their perfect afternoon together.

Four

Steve enjoyed his job, certainly more than most of his colleagues did. He'd worked in a club back at home so his hours there had been inconsistent too. If a night was late then inevitably it would end with many free drinks as they cleared the bar, ready to restock for the next day. If a night wasn't late then he'd find himself in the Isle Club or Sinners anyway, probably drinking even more than he would have normally but he didn't care. This wasn't just a job, it was a holiday, one that lasted the whole summer and Steve was going to treat it like the holiday it was and not a job. There was only one real rule that made him cautious on some nights: if you were driving the next day then don't drink too much to do so the night before. Today, Steve was driving and he'd made the decision not to go out at all the previous night, instead he'd stayed in his apartment and caught up on some TV, taking full advantage of the fact that reps got free internet access. The result was that today, Steve felt far more refreshed than he usually did.

He was sitting on a buggy by the jetty, the grand entrance to the island. It was always the first place that everybody saw as they left the ferry and therefore it was the most well-kept part of the island, just one of the specific areas that any potential investors were able to see. It wasn't official of course but Steve noticed that the areas around the jetty, Security complex and main offices were always the tidiest. The jetty itself was decorated with large and colourful signs containing the 'Corzones Island' logo, which featured a picture of a parrot and a cartoon Aztec style temple. Three wooden piers stretched out, numbered 'one', 'two' and 'three', each one corresponding to a ferry. Most days, only two of them were active but at the height of the season when it was busiest, all three would be in service. To Steve's dismay, it was a busy day and all three ferries were bringing people to, and taking them away from the island. This of course meant that Steve had more work to do than usual.

His job was simple enough: meet people at the jetty and make sure that they get to their accommodation as quickly as possible, along with their luggage. Steve sat and waited, knowing that ferry number three was due at any minute. He looked around and noticed that every other rep in the fleet of buggies had the same anxious expression. The ferry had radioed ahead and warned them that they were at capacity, meaning that this was going to be a horrible free-for-all once the boat arrived. It was always the same, people would get off the boat and due to their inability to contain their excitement, would all rush to their luggage and grab it as quickly as possible before piling it onto the trailers that were attached to the buggies and excitedly telling the rep where they were supposed to be staying. In theory, Steve should have somebody at the right place within fifteen minutes of their arrival. However, on days like this, that never seemed to happen. Too many people wanting to be the first to get their luggage, the first to be on their buggy and the first to be by the pool. Some people even asked Steve to wait for them as they went to a shop and would then get annoyed when he wasn't able to. It was made clear to him every morning that his job was to get people from the ferry and to where they were staying and be ready for the next bunch, picking up anybody that was due to leave, while on his return trip.

An army of buggies were in a line, Steve was towards the end which made it even harder as all personnel were expected to be back on time, regardless of when they left. He didn't care, all accommodation blocks were within an easy six or seven minute radius so it was never difficult to make the journey and be back with a few minutes to spare.

Ferry number three emerged from behind a rock, a large catamaran painted in the Corzones colours, with the logo taking pride of place on each side and a slightly smaller number of identification underneath it. Steve looked at the disappointed faces of the people leaving, who were currently penned in an entrance that in a moment, the boat would be lined up with. As people exited the near end of the boat, this poor bunch would enter via the far side. People were never happy to leave and most of them were hungover from that crazy final night and some were in tears after their holiday romances had been cruelly swept away from under their feet by the passage of time. Steve had known this feeling himself a couple of times, it was suggested that reps don't become involved with people visiting the island but there was no real rule against it. Steve did attempt to avoid it at first but soon realised that Corzones Island would always have its way.

The ferry was moored up perfectly next to pier number three and the gates were opened. People began to pour off the boat and rush straight to the luggage area, the crew of the boat managing to have half of the bags and cases unloaded before anybody had reached them. Steve watched the people that were leaving the boat, it was the usual mix of people, all in their teens or twenties. Some were already down to swimming gear, some of the girls wore white, summery dresses. There was the odd hat. Steve knew that in this heat they never lasted for very long before they were cast into a corner of the apartment, not to be touched again until the end of the holiday.

Most people had left the boat when Steve saw something that he wasn't expecting: a smallish man who must at least have been in his forties, wearing a colourful knitted jumper and some brown trousers. He calmly stepped off the boat and walked around towards the luggage area, getting some funny looks from his fellow passengers. He couldn't quite believe what he was seeing, who was this man and could he honestly not feel the heat? People had passed out while wearing less due to the intensity of the sunshine. The man in the jumper was the last to reach baggage collection, he wasn't in the same hurry that everybody else was and even gave way to a group of people, something that Steve had never seen before.

The man in the jumper collected his luggage, four large cases was far more than the maximum allowed but that was what he possessed. He must have paid a fortune to get those through. Steve looked along the row of buggies and realised that he was the one that would be transporting this man. He decided to leave his buggy and walk down to him, offering to help with his luggage. The man smiled at Steve and thanked him, picking up the smallest of his bags and leaving the other three for Steve to carry. He didn't mind and should have known better when he offered, the three cases however were large and weighed more than Steve had anticipated.

After lugging the cases on to the trailer attached to the back of his buggy and formally introducing himself to the man, who in turn identified himself as Professor Julius Loch, Steve began to drive towards where he would be staying. The Professor was to stay in a beachside bungalow, the most expensive form of accommodation on the whole island. It was also a longer drive than normal so

Steve made Karen, the head rep, aware that he wouldn't be back for the next ferry. After calling in the Professor's arrival, Karen told Steve to stay with him and assist until he was set up. This was unheard of and Steve had no idea what she meant by 'set up' but he continued anyway. In truth, he was grateful for the slight break that the assignment would provide.

Steve was also happy to be driving to the bungalows, it was a very hot day and the drive was mostly covered by jungle. He decided that he'd better talk to his passenger, sounding as professional he possibly could, he began.

'You're a bit older than the usual crowd we have here.' The Professor looked at Steve for a moment, studying him.

'Yes, I suppose I am, aren't I? That isn't a problem is it?' Steve couldn't tell if this reply was polite conversation or defensive, judging by his passengers mannerisms, he decided that it was the former. The Professor confirmed this when he continued, 'I suppose my being here is somewhat anachronistic compared to what you're used to?' Steve had to agree, he nodded.

'To tell you the truth Professor, it's very rare that we get anybody over thirty here.' The Professor nodded.

'Yes, I'm sure it is. But then again I don't imagine you'll get all that many people here for the same reason that I am.'

'What's that? You're not just here for a holiday?' the Professor shook his head.

'No, not at all. I'm an archaeologist and there are some very interesting ruins in the hillier part of the jungle. The remains of a temple, left by an extinct culture that once inhabited this island.'

'I think I know where you mean,' chirped Steve, who had read something about that area but never actually visited it, 'There's a bar there, owned by a local named Amerigo, I think.' The name seemed to make the Professor sit upright.

'Is it really? I once knew a man on this island named Amerigo.'

'You've been here before?' Steve asked.

'Yes, before most of the island was converted into the resort. They wanted an archaeologist to have a look around before they developed it. Giorgio Corzones was very adamant that he wouldn't damage anything of historical significance. The only thing I really found was the temple and he promised not to allow the ruins to be damaged.' Steve was fascinated, this was far more interesting than the usual 'booze and tits' reason that drew people to Corzones.

'Amerigo must have insisted on looking after that area.' The

Professor's conclusion made sense, that bar had always been there but had the reputation of being quiet. It seemed that there was an ulterior motive for its existence.

'Why are you back now?' Steve decided to keep the conversation going and learn as much as he could, if nothing else it would make for interesting conversation at rep HQ later on.

'Those cases that you helped me load on to the trailer?' Steve nodded, 'New equipment. Oxford has developed a few new things they want me to try out on the temple.'

'Why? Did you not complete your survey last time?'

'Well, I did the best that I could but the ruins and anything around them seemed to resist analysis, it was almost as if something didn't want me to know the exact details. Amerigo tried to fill in the blanks but unfortunately his explanation of things was far too superstitious.'

'Like ancient gods and stuff?'

'Exactly Steve. Amerigo's theory is that there were indigenous tribal inhabitants on this island up until the late eighteenth century.'

'That sounds unlikely.'

'It is, in fact it's impossible and there's no evidence to suggest anything later than what is usually referred to as pre-history. Admittedly, the evidence of the temple suggests that they were fairly advanced for their time but it isn't unknown.'

Much to Steve's disappointment, they had reached the bungalows and the conversation came to an end. Steve helped the Professor carry his heavy cases into the bungalow and showed him around, pointing out all of the usual things such as the minibar and the phone.

'So if you need anything, you just have to press three and you'll get straight through to accommodations. You've got a pretty nice setup here really, priority treatment and stuff.' The Professor smiled.

'Thank you. I was told that you'd also help me get to the temple site?' Steve nodded, suddenly understanding what was meant by getting the Professor 'set up'

'That's right.'

'Excellent. I'll take some equipment with me now, will you help me load the buggy?'

Steve found himself carting two of the four cases he'd just moved into the apartment back to the buggy. They were heavy and in the heat Steve's sweating increased with every step. When the bags were loaded, Steve fired up the buggy again and began to drive into the hills. In truth, they weren't very large hills at all but they were almost at the centre of the island and the area most densely populated by jungle. It was the Professor who started the conversation this time.

'Tell me Steve, what is the nightlife like here?' Steve was surprised, in his brown jeans and woollen jumper, the Professor didn't seem like the kind of person to enjoy a night out.

'It's what the island is famous for, Professor.'

'Of course it is, a scene of archaeological interest gets ignored for the nearest source of alcohol, it reminds me of the university field days I used to do.' That explained the Professor's interest in the nightlife. Steve had never been to university but had heard that lecturers enjoyed their nights out just as much as the students.

'Although I have to admit that I will be sampling what this island has to offer while I'm here.' Steve grinned.

'Well I know all of the bouncers Professor, I'll tell them that you're alright for an old guy.' It was the. Professor's turn to smile.

'Thank you. And it's good to know that I'm "alright for an old guy."' Steve immediately recognised his faux pas.

'Sorry Professor, I guess that's what comes from only seeing people about my own age for the last six months.' The Professor waved, as if to brush it aside.

'Think nothing of it Steve, I can in fact hold my own with your generation, probably better than you might think.' Satisfied that he was off the hook, Steve continued with the conversation in the same vein for the remainder of the journey.

Five

Will was enjoying himself immensely, he was sitting in a café with a girl, something that his brother would never have expected. More than that though, this girl was in fact very nice and pleasant company to boot. She'd told him all about her friend, Sofia and why she had been left to her own devices. They were in Café Solar, a surprisingly English-looking place, with plastic tables and chairs spread about the room and a modest looking counter in the corner. It was staffed by a charming man who must have been in his sixties and appeared to be a native. In the corner of the room was an old-looking TV, although Will suspected that it was simply vintage design as opposed to a genuine model. It was showing a series of promotional videos for the island. Pictures of sun, beaches, bars and so on with an overly-enthusiastic voice in the background:

'Corzones Island! A community established only six years ago by billionaire entrepreneur Giorgio Corzones that has grown immensely! Thinking of booking a holiday? Then this is the place to come for the ultimate experience.' Will and Lucy both found the advert amusing. Neither of them would have chosen Corzones as their first holiday destination and neither of them were expecting to enjoy the rest of the week. Will did hope though, that Lucy would want to spend some more time with him.

He'd dried off very quickly and by the time that they'd reached the café he was hardly even damp. It was the first time since arriving that he'd been grateful for the intensity of the heat. Even the café was too warm for Will, who had chosen to have an orange juice and ice, rather than a coffee. Lucy however, had decided to have a cup of tea and she drank it slowly as they both chatted. They spoke about where they were from, what they did and so on. Within ten minutes, Will had learned that Lucy was from Manchester and normally worked in a clothes shop, hoping to use her fashion degree at some point. Will gave her the exact same information, his family came from Reading but he'd chosen to stay in Oxford after he'd completed university there. She was just over a year older than him and her twenty-fifth birthday was only a couple of months away. Apart from that, the conversation wasn't particularly meaningful but it did establish one thing; they were now firm friends.

The man that was in charge of the café shuffled from behind a curtain behind the counter with a bowl. He walked to Will and Lucy and placed the bowl down on the table.

'Your chips,' the bowl was almost overflowing with them, 'would you like anything else?' Will shook his head and politely said that they were fine. The old man smiled and went back behind the counter and produced a magazine. Will pushed the bowl of chips to the centre of the table so that he and Lucy could share them. After adding salt and vinegar, they started to eat.

The chips were quickly devoured and it was only when half way through them that Will realised that this was the first time he'd eaten that day. They left the café and when stood outside Lucy looked at Will and asked:

'What next then?' Will was unsure.

'It's up to you.' He was just happy that she still wanted to spend time with him.

'I haven't seen the hill properly yet, perhaps we could go that way?' Will nodded and they began to walk, chatting away as they went. Will had hoped to do something other than looking at shops but he was convinced that his choice would cause Lucy to immediately lose interest.

The hill was the main shopping street on the island and just off the town centre. Lucy looked around a few shops, mostly at clothes, but she soon decided that there was nothing there to really interest her. Will had to admit that the selection didn't seem to be particularly varied. He looked idly around and spotted a wristband that he liked at a reasonable price. He bought it but felt like he only had for the sake of doing so. Other shops on the hill included a tobacconist, a chocolatiers (which Will thought to be a bit pointless as chocolate would instantly melt in this heat) and a few shops selling different kinds of alcohol at prices far higher than the island's central supermarket. Will noticed that as they walked further up the hill there seemed to be more jungle and fewer buildings.

Lucy gave up on shopping, concluding that there wasn't anything she wanted to buy. She'd visit the gift shop towards the end of her holiday but otherwise it was all just a waste of time. Again she turned to Will for a suggestion of what to do, only this time she insisted that he made the choice.

'Well you don't have to do this if you don't want to,' he said, 'but there's some ruins in the jungle that I'd like to look at. One of my old archaeology lecturers did a study on them once and said that they were really interesting. I'd like to see them.' Lucy smiled and replied immediately.

'Alright then.' Will hadn't expected this, he'd always thought that he'd be visiting the ruins alone. 'Where are they?' Will was surprised to hear that Lucy even sounded enthusiastic when she'd asked.

'I'm not entirely sure.' This was only half true as he knew exactly where they were, just not how to get to them. Apparently there was a bar nearby but it wasn't listed on any of the island maps that he'd seen. 'They're in one of the hillier parts of the jungle, near the centre of the island I think.'

Roads and paths on the island were minimal so Will and Lucy figured that finding the bar shouldn't be too difficult. They kept walking up the hill, passing the final few shops as they went, one of which sold more detailed maps of the island. After looking for a moment, they found where the bar would be. Will was quietly glad that they'd found the map as his own assumption was quite a distance away from the actual location. They passed the final shop and were suddenly in a thick area of jungle. There were two paths in front of them, both of which led uphill, Will consulted the map and they took the path on the right.

It was a much longer walk than either of them had expected, the fact that such a comparatively small part of the island had been developed meant that most people thought there was less to it than there actually was. The fairly wide road thinned into a muddy path, by the tyre tracks Will could tell that they still managed to get buggies up there but it must have been with difficulty. No buggies were visible then though so Will and Lucy continued to walk.

'I wish I'd brought a bottle of water.' Lucy had a good point as they didn't know how far the walk would be and if the terrain became any less friendly then their footwear would be rendered completely inadequate. Getting lost in the lush vegetation without anything to drink wasn't advisable. They pushed on and were walking for the best part of an hour when suddenly some calypso-style music could be heard.

'This might be it.' Will hoped that it was as he was certain that Lucy was now regretting her decision to join him.

Through the trees emerged firstly some rocks that once made up a temple, closely followed by coloured lights and the sight of tables and chairs. They were eventually able to see the bar clearly, it was mostly covered by a marquee and was nestled in between various piles of rocks, some had cave painting-like images on them. In the corner of the marquee and up against one of the largest pieces of stone was a bar that contained an impressive number of bottles. Standing behind it was a well-built man with leathery skin and long grey hair. He sported a long moustache that was slightly darker than the rest of his hair and he wore a brown cowboy-like hat.

'Hello there!' He spoke in a thick accent that Will had never heard before, he assumed that it must be local. Will and Lucy took a moment to look at each other, silently communicating their amusement at the figure that stood in front of them. 'Welcome to my bar, I am Amerigo!' The man had a wide grin, revealing a large set of tobacco-stained teeth. Will and Lucy both politely and somewhat nervously said hello.

Amerigo seemed intimidating at first but it only took a moment's conversation for Will to feel at ease with him.

'You're the first people I've seen today!' Whenever he spoke, Amerigo beamed with an excited smile. 'Please, your first drink is on the house. I make the best cocktails on the island, what do you want?' Will and Lucy pondered for a moment, it was Lucy who replied first.

'I'll just have lemonade.' She smiled nervously, clearly she didn't feel as comfortable with Amerigo as Will did.

'Nonsense!' Amerigo was clearly determined to show off his cocktail making skills.

'I'll have a Mojito then.' Will's request made Amerigo's wide smile return, the barman returned his attention to Lucy.

'Your friend is having a real drink, please do the same. I promise, it'll be the best drink you have on your entire holiday.' Lucy looked to Will for a moment, he nodded encouragingly.

'Alright, I'll have the same. Thank you.'

'Very well, I'll join you if I may!' Will smiled and waved his hand to indicate that Amerigo was welcome to.

The drinks were excellent, just as Amerigo had promised and the three of them conversed while drinking. Will and Lucy, who was now warming to the local, introduced themselves properly.

'It is a shame, this is the most fascinating part of the island and it is rare for somebody to come here and have a look.' Amerigo clearly did his job for the love of it, apparently he was paid a great deal by Giorgio Corzones to keep the bar running so his profit margins made no difference.

'That's a shame,' replied Will, whose enthusiasm was running away with him, 'these ruins are amazing. They must have been here for thousands of years. I can't work out the civilisation though.' Amerigo smiled.

'You're an archaeologist,' it was a statement of fact, not a question, 'many like you come here and they all say the same, nobody identifies who did this. It amuses me that nobody can.' Will's curiosity was now uncontrollable, he was now hooked and the expression of keen interest on Lucy's face told Will that she was also interested. Amerigo continued, 'it fuels the legend of the Velza.' Amerigo paused, clearly wanting a member of his audience to respond, Will obliged.

'What are the Velza?'

Amerigo gave a deep and mysterious grin as he continued.

'Well, this is somewhat of a subject I hold close to my heart, one I have investigated a number of times. The Velza built this temple to worship their gods. For hundreds of years they sacrificed the occupants of any ships that found the island, meaning that this entire place went undiscovered for centuries. However, as with all things, their good fortune did not last. The Velza were tricked by an explorer. He had read stories and done research, he worked out that so many ships had disappeared in this one area and correctly theorised that there may be an island here. By this stage, Great Britain was a magnificently large empire. The explorer Jasper Willow, convinced the royal court to give him some troops and a ship so that he may claim this dangerous part of the world for his homeland. The ship traveled here, armed to the teeth with the latest weaponry. If this was to be just another savage island, then they were prepared. However, their arrogance was to cost them this time.'

Will and Lucy were hooked, it was more in the way that Amerigo described the events than the story itself. He must have heard this story hundreds of times from when he was young and loved telling it. Will also suspected that he'd embellished events a little to make it a selling point for his bar. It was working though, they were both enthralled. Will and Lucy occasionally sipped at their drink as Amerigo continued. 'The expedition wiped out almost all of the Velza but lost a great many of their own men. Willow and the survivors of his expedition fled back to England for reinforcements and a year later returned to the island. Willow was killed along with all of his second expedition, bar one soldier who, when found some time later, had been driven completely insane. The ship, its crew and the Velza had never ever been seen of heard of since.'

It was a good story, thought Will. But that's all it was, a story. No historical or archaeological evidence and all-round impossible. Somebody seemed to agree with him.
'Absolute nonsense!' Will and Lucy span around and Amerigo looked up to see a man in a knitted jumper. Will recognised the man from somewhere and after a moment's pause for thought, he realised where.
'Professor Loch!' The Professor studied Will for a moment.
'William Brey, isn't it?' The Professor walked towards the bar and studied Will more closely. 'Yes, I do believe it is.' Loch turned his attention to the barman, 'and Amerigo! I haven't seen you for years. Looking after the old haunt I see, but still filling people's heads with that nonsense.' Amerigo grinned again and then walked around the bar to stand close to the Professor. He held out his arms and hugged the archaeologist.
'It has been far too long, old friend.' The hug lasted for what seemed like some time. Will and Lucy turned around to their drinks.

After a while, they were joined by somebody else, wearing a reps' uniform and struggling to carry two large cases.
'This is Steve, a representative of this island who has been selected to assist me.' Loch walked over to Steve and took one of the cases. He placed it on a table that was nearly large enough and opened it. From his seat at the bar, Will peeked inside and saw an impressive set of scientific and archaeological equipment, some of which even he didn't recognise. He explained to Lucy in a whisper what it was and she gave a nod of understanding. The Professor began to unpack.

After a minute or two, Loch, Steve and Amerigo walked towards another part of the ruins with a couple of pieces of equipment, leaving Will and Lucy alone at the bar.

'You know him then?' Will nodded,

'He was one of my old lecturers, I'm surprised to see him.' Will looked curiously at the Professor and noticed that he hadn't changed much. Perhaps he'd put on a little bit of weight and had gained a small scar on the side of his neck but otherwise all was the same.

'He just suddenly disappeared. One day a lecture was cancelled and the next week he'd been replaced. The uni just said they couldn't get in touch with him. Everybody just seemed to forget him after that.'

'He seems like a pretty unforgettable person.' Will smiled to himself, Lucy was right and now Loch was back here. Interestingly enough, Will had noticed the Oxford insignia on Loch's cases so he must be affiliated with the university still.

'You're right,' Will said, 'but they said he just disappeared.' Will hadn't noticed the Professor return to his cases and that he was now in earshot.

'You're a bright lad William, you should know better than to believe university gossip. Let me guess, there were rumours that I'd slept with a student and had to leave hurriedly? Or perhaps that I'd been sacked for alcohol and drug problems?' Loch tutted to himself. Will had to admit that he had a point. 'Student gossip, it'll never change.'

Loch fiddled around in his case and found a piece of equipment. 'You don't think the Velza legend is true then, Professor?' It was Lucy who asked the question, Will was relieved that she was still interested, he'd never want to lose a new friend to boredom, especially this one.

'I'll admit that aspects of it are true. For example, they did find somebody here who'd been driven out of his mind. But the accepted theory is that he'd been washed up after his ship had sunk. There were no signs that anybody else had been on the island, or that a ship had actually made anchor here.' Will knew that the Professor was right, but he could see the disappointment on Lucy's face and a small part of him longed for the myth to be reality. The ravings of one man found driven out of his mind on an empty island was certainly not a credible historical record however.

'Anyway, I have a lot of work to do, I'm hoping to finally discover who these temples were built by.' The Professor began to walk away but then turned back. 'I don't suppose you two would like to help would you? It's always excellent to have a research team.' Will turned and looked at Lucy, he was expecting this to be one request too far and that she'd want to leave now, however she turned to him and nodded enthusiastically.

'I haven't a clue what I'd have to do.' She said this as though it would be a problem but Loch immediately resolved the situation. 'That doesn't matter, I can teach you a few things. I'm sure William here can too.' Will and Lucy finished their cocktails and made their way over to where the Professor was starting to set up his equipment. This afternoon had turned out to be far more interesting than either Will or Lucy had anticipated.

Six

Sofia still hadn't returned, goodness know where she and Karl had ended up. Lucy wasn't too concerned however, she'd had a wonderful day and for the first time, she may actually enjoy an evening on the island too. She lay on her bed, relaxing for just a short time so she'd be awake and good company later on. Another cup of tea lay at her side and she found it to be so refreshing after a fun yet work-filled afternoon. She loved doing new things and her time with Will had proved to be far more interesting than anything she'd ever expected.

Lucy and Will had started to help Loch at about two and were there until five. In those three hours she'd learned a lot more than anybody could expect to on this island. Loch had explained the use of most of the equipment to her and even though they spent most of the afternoon comparing readouts, she'd enjoyed it immensely. Will had taken on a slightly more hands-on approach and it was clear to Lucy that he was incredibly knowledgeable in his field. The person who'd had the hardest afternoon seemed to be the rep, Steve. He was given a full list of tasks by the Professor but most of them had involved fetching and carrying. He didn't seem to mind though and at one point when the group had decided to take a little break, he'd confided in Will and Lucy that it was far easier and more enjoyable work than what he'd being doing before the Professor had arrived.

Not long after, Loch had given Steve the option of becoming his assistant for the entire duration of his study on the island. Steve happily agreed and after a quick phone call in which he'd agreed to pay for Steve's time, the Professor had his assistant. Steve seemed overjoyed, mostly because he was told that he wouldn't ever be needed earlier than midday. Lie-in's were a rarity on the island, especially for the staff and reps. Loch had indicated to Will and Lucy that they were also candidates for assisting him, however he didn't want to interrupt any holiday plans that they may have. He'd made it clear that they were more than welcome to join him whenever they wished to though. Will had seemed overjoyed by this, giving Lucy the impression that despite not educating Will for very long, the Professor had made quite an impact.

Amerigo had provided another cocktail each for Will and Lucy, and with his trademark grin, told them that yet again it was on the house. Will had speculated that Amerigo's role as local custodian of the temple took great priority over his bar. When Will and Lucy were the majority of the way through their cocktails, the Professor had dismissed Steve for the day and refused a buggy ride back to his bungalow, stating that for now he and his equipment would remain with Amerigo. Steve had then offered a ride down towards the town centre to Will and Lucy and after confirming with the Professor that they also were no longer needed for the day, Will accepted. Lucy had been grateful for the offer, the walk up to the bar had almost destroyed her footwear and she had made a note to pack something more practical into her bag before the next day.

Once they had arrived at the town centre, Steve had offered to deliver Will and Lucy to their apartments but after a small discussion, they decided to stay and get something to eat together. It was about six in the evening at this point and the town centre was considerably quieter. Most people were probably beginning the almost ritual-like pre drinks. People would return to their accommodation and prepare for their night on the strip by drinking as much as possible before leaving, the logic being that more alcohol consumed before leaving the apartment would result in less money being spent later on.

Most of the cafés around the town centre had given up and closed for the night, however many of the bars remained open. Will and Lucy had found a small, quiet place that also served food. It wasn't the cheapest place ever but they had decided to treat themselves. Will ate a pasta dish that contained numerous kinds of fish with a sauce that Lucy found to be slightly salty when she'd tried it. She had decided to keep it simple and went with a pizza topped with various vegetables and some ham. While choosing drinks, they had both learned that they liked wine and ordered a bottle of white. Both the food and the wine were easily consumed and enjoyed greatly. Lucy was happier than she'd been for a long time, something that she hadn't expected to feel on Corzones Island.

After their meal, Will had suggested that they went for a walk along the beach to help their food settle. They paid up and left the bar, following the signs towards the beach which was only a short walk away. On the walk down the path, they chatted about the afternoon that they'd had and when Lucy had mentioned that the afternoon hadn't been the kind you'd expect on Corzones Island, Will seemed worried that she hadn't enjoyed it. She assured Will that she had done and it was far better than her other options of wandering the shops on her own or reading a book beside the pool all day. Will smiled at her, unsure of what to say next.

'I guess that I don't like this island as much as I should.' Lucy bit her lip before she replied.

'I like it now I'm spending time with you. How about we go out tonight?' She had surprised herself, she actually did want to spend the evening out. Her next thought however that Will would refuse this request, they'd both been talking about how much they hated clubs for a good part of the afternoon.

'Yes,' Will replied, 'although I don't really do clubs normally.'

'Me neither, but I want to try and enjoy it. Maybe I will if I'm with you.' Will didn't find a reply after a short moment of trying so Lucy quickly continued. 'What time shall we meet?'

'I suppose I can come and meet you at your apartment and we could walk there together?' Lucy nodded. 'I'll get to you around 11 then.' Lucy checked her watch, it was nine already but she probably had enough time to prepare herself, for some reason she felt that she needed to for Will.

'Eleven is good. Just along the beach is a path that leads straight to my apartment block, we can walk there now if you like so you know where to go later?' Will agreed.

It wasn't long after that they had reached the beach and were surprised to find that it was quite busy. The sun was starting to set and a lot of people were sitting in the sand, watching as it began to fade away. Other people had decided to bring their pre-drinking to the beach and were already getting quite rowdy. There was a group was sitting around a small fire that they'd made out of driftwood, one of their number played a guitar while the others sang.

'I want to paddle!' Lucy had said suddenly. She dashed towards the sea, removing her shoes as she went and holding them in her hands as she ran into the water. Will followed her and did the same and the two of them continued along the beach, allowing the waves to break over their ankles.

Realising that it was getting late, the two of them had decided to go back to their apartments and prepare for their unexpected night in the club. Lucy still didn't know why she wanted to go out, it felt like there was an invisible force coaxing and persuading her to go. The only thing she was sure about was that she'd enjoyed her time with Will and wanted it to continue, regardless of where they ended up. It had been a strange day and Lucy hadn't anticipated any of it but as she lay in her room, she realised that the night was only just beginning.

She glanced at the time and realised that she didn't have all that long to get a shower and prepare herself for Will's arrival. She didn't want to go straight to the strip and decided that she'd offer him a drink before they left. She had a bottle of white wine and decided to place it in the fridge so that it could chill before Will arrived. This could be a perfect night, the kind of night Lucy hadn't had for a long time and hadn't really expected to ever have again. She began to choose an outfit, skipping over various items of clothing. She reached the end of the pile and nothing seemed right. She had dresses but were they right? Would Will like what she was wearing?

She backed on to the bed and sat down and began to chew her nails, stopping herself before any real damage was done. Lucy didn't know how she felt or how she even should feel. She looked into the small mirror that was hung on her wall and placed her head in her hands. She breathed deeply for some time, she didn't know exactly how long.
'Now come on,' her reflection said to her, 'pull yourself together, don't do *this* again.' Lucy bit her lip and closed her eyes in a battle to control her breathing. 'He's kinda nice and just what you need.' She didn't know if she was speaking out loud or not. 'Just be normal!' The voice was strict now and without sympathy, giving her a clear instruction. 'It really isn't that difficult Lucy. All you have to do is...' The voice was interrupted by a sudden knock at the door. Was he here already? Lucy looked at her reflection, she was a mess. She jumped up and dashed to the door, consumed with an inexplicable fear. What would Will think if he saw her like this? She forced a smile as she swung the door open. It was Sofia.

Lucy had never felt such relief and became instantly. Sofia was alone, her and Karl had gone their separate ways to prepare for the night out. They were going to meet again soon, which meant that Sofia demanded the first turn in the shower. There were a few more hollow apologies for leaving Lucy alone but she just didn't care. Lucy realised that she was happy Sofia had chosen male company over her, that was the reason that she'd made such a wonderful friend. Sofia was quick in the shower and had started to apply makeup almost the second she'd come out. It was Lucy's turn to prepare for the evening.

Lucy had her shower and wrapped a towel around herself. She emerged from the bathroom to see Sofia, who had climbed into her best dress, brushing her hair with one hand and eating a piece of toast with the other. Lucy smiled at her as she walked past and into her room. She shut the door and flicked through all of her clothes again but still nothing seemed right. Another inspection drew her attention to a black dress. It was shorter than comfort usually allowed for but Lucy was being brave this evening. She tentatively put it on and looked in the mirror. After a moment's pause for consideration, she smiled. All she hoped now was that Will would like it.

Lucy emerged from her room and walked back into the bathroom with her makeup bag. Sofia said a brief goodbye and grabbed her shoes. She walked back in through the door almost as soon as she'd left, remembering the need to pick up her purse. After another hurried goodbye, Sofia was gone and Lucy again found herself on her own. She looked at the clock and was surprised at how much time had passed. Will would surely be on his way now. Lucy returned to her makeup and after a few minutes, inspected herself in the mirror again. She was happy with what she saw and for the first time in over a year, her reflection smiled back at her.

Seven

The Temple Bar was the busiest it had been for longer than Amerigo cared to admit. The rep, Steve, had brought a group of his friends up when they'd gone off duty and Loch was still there, chatting away. As soon as Amerigo had seen the Professor his curiosity had been raised. He wasn't here for pleasure, that wasn't the sort of thing the Professor would do but his excuse of re-examining the temple hadn't felt right either. Certainly the equipment that he had was right and far more advanced than what he had arrived with last time but Amerigo knew who the Professor really was and why he'd really be here. The truth was, Amerigo had been considering contacting Loch for some time. The development of Corzones Island had never sat as well with him as it had with many of the other locals. At the time when the plans were first unveiled, there had been some opposition but those who weren't happy either moved away or chose to adapt. Anybody that had accepted the changes had benefitted from it greatly, there was more money on the island than ever as well as a real sense of community. Giorgio Corzones had always been good to the locals and sought their blessing before attempting anything new. Despite all of this, Amerigo was the one person left on the island who felt unhappy.

He wasn't unhappy with the development of the island, nor with the quiet nature of his bar but other things concerned him. Corzones seemed to have developed an interest on the history of the island and the legend of the Velza. Amerigo didn't know how many times he'd told that story despite not fully believing it, but his interest wasn't as developed as other members of the island community. Amerigo knew he wasn't the only person who presented a false view of the Velza legend, Loch believed in it too, or certainly far more than he was willing to admit. If he didn't, he wouldn't be here.

Amerigo had chatted away with the Professor for a couple of hours after Steve had left with Will and Lucy. They covered almost every subject under the sun except one: the Professor's work and real reason for being on the island. As soon as the conversation had reached a more serious point, Steve and the other reps had arrived and started to order drinks in vast quantities. After that, Loch had clammed up but promised that they would 'talk later'.

Amerigo began to make drinks for the reps, Steve had brought him quite a crowd to cater for and they seemed to keep arriving in increasing numbers. Before long, the bar seemed to be full and Amerigo found it difficult to keep up with the orders that were being placed. Loch offered to help and Amerigo gratefully accepted. The Professor was surprisingly good at mixing cocktails and between them, they managed to work through the queue at an impressive speed. Just as they both thought they had a break, a group of reps walked over from their table and ordered their second round. Business was fantastic but Amerigo just wanted these people to leave so that he and the Professor could talk seriously.

Hours passed and it had gone dark without Amerigo really noticing, the drinks just continued to be poured and drunk in a non-stop cycle. Eventually it quietened down as the reps, most of whom were now under the influence, decided that it was time to make their way to the strip. Loch also took the opportunity to leave.
'We shall talk soon,' he said when activity at the bar had ceased, 'I think I'm going to need your help. Meet me in the town centre at half past three, I need to investigate something first.' He left, concluding that before anything else he needed a shower.

The final reps left and Amerigo was alone in his bar, peace at last. He'd had a busy day and made a lot of money but for some reason he couldn't feel happy about it. Professor Loch was far more than he appeared, Amerigo knew that but he never expected Loch to return. There was more happening on Corzones Island than the Professor knew and Amerigo didn't like it. He produced a laptop from under the bar and logged on. The whole island was covered by a wifi network and being a resident, Amerigo benefitted from unlimited access. This was of course another gift from Giorgio Corzones to sweeten the deal six years ago. Amerigo began to log the day's profits and as he suspected, he was at the end of the best day that he'd had all year. He then checked his emails. He'd been looking for somewhere to live on the mainland and had finally made an offer on somewhere. The confirmation of this offer had arrived and on reading it, Amerigo felt a great deal of upset. He loved this island but it had changed and his fellow islanders had changed with it.

'A busy day I hear, Amerigo?' Amerigo jumped and looked up, it was Svoros, a café owner in the town centre. He was usually seen in a white apron but on this occasion he was wearing a suit and tie. 'One of the reps discovered this place in the day and brought his friends along for the evening.' Svoros smiled, revealing his yellowed teeth.

'That's good to hear. This must be the rep that is assigned to this Professor?' Amerigo knew the next part was coming. 'What is he studying?'

'The Professor? He's an archaeologist.' Svoros smiled again and shook his head. 'He isn't of any concern.' Svoros sighed.

'If you were part of the order then you would be concerned. Things are changing on this island Amerigo and I'd hate for you to be on the wrong side.' Amerigo smiled, he and Svoros were old friends so he had no fear of speaking plainly.

'My friend, the legend is simply that, a legend.' Svoros shook his head.

'To you maybe. Nobody knows the truth about Corzones Island, nobody except me and those I choose to share it with.'

'You don't choose to share it with me.'

'Amerigo, I wish I could. Something big is coming my friend, if you aren't with us then please don't be here when it arrives.'

With a regretful last look behind him, Svoros left the bar and walked away along the darkened path. Why this warning? Why now? Amerigo was worried, he needed to speak to the Professor. He checked his watch but saw that it was only just past midnight and he knew straight away that the next three and a half hours would pass very slowly indeed.

They did. At half three in the morning, Amerigo was rushing towards the town centre, he thought that he'd be late for his appointment but when he arrived he found the whole place dark and abandoned. He took a seat next to the fountain and waited, staring into the surrounding blackness. More time passed and there was still no sign of the Professor, could he have been caught up with whatever else he was doing or had something else happened? Amerigo was worried and began to pace around the fountain. As he reached the other side, he noticed something and at first concluded that what he thought he saw was impossible. He moved in closer to inspect and within moments his absolute worst fear was confirmed.

Eight

Why couldn't he just keep his big mouth shut? He didn't need to prove anything at all, yet Will had allowed his need to impress his brother, Royce and Jason get in the way of what was sensible. An hour later he was thoroughly regretting it. Admittedly Harry's response was positive and even encouraging but he'd provided the other two with a great amount of ammunition to take the piss. It was made worse by the fact that for the third day in a row, they had all failed to 'get laid'. Emergency measures had failed Harry, Royce and Jason, none of them had even shared more than a few words with a girl the whole day whereas Will had spent some time with Lucy.

Royce's immediate reaction to Will telling the rest of the group about his day was, 'are you gonna shag her?', Will had turned bright red and seemed to go back to the 'girls are disgusting' phase that most people experience when they're ten. Harry hadn't joined in with the ensuing 'banter' but Jason managed to surpass himself by giving Will the nickname of 'pussy slayer'. His peers' attitude made Will wonder if meeting Lucy for a night out was a good idea after all. If he ran into these others it could end in disaster. What if Lucy turned out to be more interested in one of them? Will took another shot and forced such ideas from his head. The last thing he needed at the moment was to torture himself. It had been a rollercoaster of a day and suddenly, Will was enjoying his holiday.

He'd left Lucy at her apartment, which was about fifteen minutes walk from his own. As they parted company he'd considered leaving her with a hug and fantasised about even planting a kiss on her cheek. Neither had happened and as he'd walked back to his own place a thousand 'what if?' thoughts had raced through his head. He decided to ignore them and concluded that Lucy had only invited him for the night out because he was the only male on the island who hadn't tried to sleep with her the moment they had met. Will decided that it was best to banish all of these thoughts and that his priority was to try and enjoy his night. It was true that Lucy's presence was probably going to improve his evening tenfold but they were going as friends, no matter what Will felt otherwise.

He'd got back to his apartment to find that his holiday companions were already half a bottle of vodka into their evening and trying to work out what their best plan of attack would be. All kinds of ludicrous suggestions were being thrown around including terrible chat-up lines and even Jason pretending to be disabled so that the other two could play what Royce described as 'the carer card' in front of the women that they met. Will prayed that this was a joke, chose not to join in with their conversation and announced that he was going to get a shower. He did so quickly, taking a beer with him at Harry's insistence. He was under instructions to drink as much as he could and catch up with them. The truth was that after the constant stream of mojitos provided by Amerigo and the bottle of wine that he and Lucy had shared, he was already beginning to feel the effects of the alcohol. He wasn't exactly experienced at prolonged drinking and decided to have a pint of water in an attempt to rehydrate while the others weren't looking.

After his shower, he got dressed into jeans and his most expensive shirt and decided to join his friends. They were playing a game of 'I have never', a simple game where one member of the group would describe something that had never happened to them and anybody who experienced such an occurrence would have to drink. There seemed to be a theme of ganging up on Royce, which Will had to admit was amusing. It was Harry's turn.
'I have never had sex in a car.' There was a moments silence before Jason laughed and drank. Royce sat still with his arms folded.
'Come on R once, I thought there was Thirsty Kirsty?' Royce grinned and shook his head.
'Only fingered her, we didn't have sex, did we?' Harry sighed and admitted that Royce was right.

It was Jason's turn next. He made a joke about none of them meeting any women yet on the holiday and Will couldn't help but grin. This was noticed by Royce who pressed him further. At first Will had refused to say anything but after a flurry of questions and even an 'I have never spent time with a girl while on this holiday' from Jason, Will had decided to tell the group about Lucy. He'd been as vague as possible and played down the fact that they'd shared a meal and were due to meet for a night on the strip but this hadn't stopped a series of further questions. From the moment he said anything, 'I have never' ceased and had been replaced with a very uncomfortable half an hour for Will. The more evasive he was

49

and embarrassed he became, the more intrusive and awkward the questions were. He'd spent time with women before, why were they so interested? As he pondered this, another thought entered Will's head: Why was he so interested?

Will drank too much while sitting in the circle with the others. He'd had shots again which really wasn't the right thing to do. He began to slow down, hoping that the others didn't notice. He didn't want to meet Lucy while drunk but the overwhelming feeling of nervousness caused him to drink more, for some reason it just felt right to do so. Royce and Jason stood up and walked over to get themselves a bottle of rum. Harry stayed with Will and while the others weren't looking, placed an encouraging hand on his shoulder.

'Just be yourself and don't worry,' he said with a smile, 'you'll have a good night.' Will smiled at Harry and was about to reply when Royce shouted across the room.

'Oi pussy slayer, you want a rum and coke?' Will refused but he was given one anyway. He drank it in the knowledge that this would be his final drink before leaving.

Harry had calmed Will down slightly but he was still more nervous than he had felt for some time. Will had to admit to himself that he did like Lucy but he'd really only just met her. His feelings seemed to become more prominent as he continued to drink. Will dwelled on the thought that it was Lucy who invited him out. It was even Lucy who had spoken to him first, although she was helping him out of the fountain at the time. He decided not to let Jason and Royce bother him and that the night would lead to wherever it was meant to. Either way, Will was happy to have a friend like Lucy on the island.

To a symphony of whoops and cheers, Will left his apartment and began the walk to Lucy's. It was almost eleven and most of the island was beginning to move towards the strip. Some were walking and some were sitting outside their accommodation, waiting for a taxi to pick them up. Will noticed that most people were in large groups, singing songs and drinking more as they walked. Will was alone but he didn't care, he knew that he wouldn't be soon and that he would be meeting Lucy. There was something about her that he couldn't describe, something that seemed to move further away from him the more he considered it.

He concluded that this was because of the amount that he had drunk, it had been more than he was used to and somehow he had to continue until much later into the night.

The walk seemed far longer than it had when he was returning to his own apartment, perhaps that was an effect of the drink too. Will was surprised by how dark the island seemed at night. There were lights but they seemed to be few and far between, always leaving Will in their beam but creating an eerie surrounding of shadows. When walking to his own apartment earlier in the evening, Will had taken a shortcut across a large patch of grass, in the daytime it was used for games of football and rugby. In the dark, Will stuck to the path and in the light. He had nothing to fear as large groups were passing the same area but the incident with the fountain had made Will wary of the other people on the island. He knew that nobody meant any harm but didn't wish to be the victim of another cruel prank.

After another few minutes' walk, Will could see Lucy's apartment block illuminated in the night. He stopped for a moment and took a deep breath. This was it, a night out with a girl, something that Harry and his friends envied. He still couldn't quite believe it but he was now having a better holiday then they were, although not for the reasons that they'd cite. He took a moment to observe the apartments, tall tower blocks that had been lit with a dark green and orange tint to make them seem exotic. Lucy's apartment was on the first floor and Will counted the number of windows until he worked out which one it was.

As he reached the building itself, an attractive blond girl in a dress bumped into him. She muttered an apology in a Spanish accent as she rushed away. She had made Will jump but it only took a short moment for him to regain his composure. He continued walking and reached the concrete stairs that led up to where Lucy was staying. He reached the top of the stairs and walked along towards her door. There it was, apartment D32. Will took a deep breath as he stood looking at the door. Lucy was on the other side. Will knocked on the door and waited for a moment before the door was thrown open. Lucy was standing on the other side of the threshold in a dress and with her hair perfectly straightened. She beamed at Will and invited him inside.

Lucy's flat was of a similar design to Will's but slightly smaller. Three doors lead off to a bathroom and two separate rooms (as opposed to the four doors in Will's) and Will noticed that Lucy's sofa didn't convert into a bed as his did. Harry, Jason and Royce had quickly commandeered the bedrooms in their apartment. Lucy went straight to the kitchen area and produced a bottle of wine from the fridge. Will thanked her as she poured a glass and passed it to him. She then poured a glass for herself and directed Will towards the sofa. He didn't know what to say and after a moment of searching settled on telling Lucy that she looked nice. She smiled and thanked him but dismissed the compliment. There was an awkward silence and Will didn't know how to break it. Luckily, Lucy found something to say.

'Sofia's gone out again. She was going to meet Karl so we can stay here as long as you want.' Will smiled and nodded.

'I don't mind when we go out,' he said, 'it's up to you.'

'How about we finish the wine and then go?' This sounded good to Will. He'd drunk a lot already and Lucy hadn't seem to notice, Will suspected that she'd had about the same amount, a theory that was confirmed when Will looked towards the bin and saw a few empty bottles of alcopop. Lucy had spotted him looking.

'I don't normally drink that. Sofia had some in the fridge and it's all there was apart from the wine. I was saving that for when you got here.' Will told her that she should have started without him but Lucy insisted that she wanted to share it.

The bottle of wine evaporated very quickly and Will was feeling decidedly tipsy by the end of it. He tried as hard as he could to not show that fact to Lucy and it seemed to work.

'Do you want to walk or am I getting a taxi?' Lucy produced her phone and began to look for the contact number of the Corzones taxi service.

'I don't mind.' Will was happy, he was with Lucy and he didn't mind leaving the night's arrangements to her. She concluded that a taxi was the best option as it had passed midnight and she wanted to arrive at the Isle Club before they reached capacity.

Will sat alongside Lucy on the back seat of the buggy that rushed them towards the strip. He wasn't sure if continuing the night was a good idea as he'd already drunk more than enough. However he was with Lucy, who seemed happy to be with him. It had been a far better day than Will had ever expected: the temple had proved to be interesting, he'd got to use his archaeological skills to great effect and most of all he had met the most wonderful person that had crossed his path since his arrival. As they approached the strip, Will couldn't imagine this being anything but a perfect night.

Nine

Steve wasn't having the day that he'd expected. From the moment that Professor Loch had stepped off the ferry, he had found himself involved with something that was entirely different from the normal routine. Steve had to admit that the normal duties of a rep weren't very entertaining and like all of his colleagues, he was only there for the free four month-long holiday. After the day's events he now answered to the Professor, who had already let him go early and told him to 'turn up at any point' the next morning. Deciding to not abuse the Professor's generosity, Steve had promised that he would arrive 'early' and while this time hadn't been defined, he decided that this would be about half past ten.

Steve had given Will and Lucy a ride into the town centre and left them to find something to eat. They seemed to be a nice pair if not a little different from what the island would call normal but then again, nothing was normal in this place. He'd taken his buggy back to island HQ and signed off for the day. Karen had managed to catch him as he was about to leave and began to ask questions about why the Professor wanted him. Steve got the impression that she wasn't happy with losing one of her staff and that the order had clearly come from somebody senior to her. Steve made the work sound as difficult and tiring as he possibly could and for a moment, it even looked like Karen believed him.

She kept him talking for quite a while and just as he was released, he saw that some of his friends were finishing for the day. He went to catch up with the group, who were full of questions about where he'd vanished. There was apparently a rumour going around that he'd been sacked but nobody quite knew why. After setting the record straight, Steve and the other reps began to make plans about what they'd do for the evening. The majority of the group weren't working the next day and wanted a night on the strip. Plans for what activities would occur before their arrival at the strip began to be thrown around and Steve found himself suggesting that they go to Amerigo's bar. Having been on the island for quite some time, the reps had been to almost every pub and bar on their various nights out, yet surprisingly none of them had been to the one at the temple. After a short conversation and a few questions about what it was like, the first venue of the night had been decided upon.

They caught taxis up into the jungle, Steve had to feel sorry for the drivers of the buggies, they had a long night ahead of them and had to watch a large group of their peers going to get drunk. Words of thanks and coins were exchanged when they reached the temple and the buggies sped back down the hill and into the darkness. Steve walked into the bar area, leading a group of about fifteen or so. He was surprised to see that nothing had changed at all since he had left. He knew that the bar had a reputation for being quiet but he'd expected somebody else to have arrived. The Professor was sitting on a bar stool, talking to Amerigo, who was standing behind the bar idly polishing a glass. The conversation seemed to be serious at first but upon noticing the group of reps arriving, the Professor sat up suddenly and from then on, things seemed to be less formal.

'Steve!' Amerigo shouted happily, in his booming deep voice, 'It is good to see you again!' Steve walked to the bar and took a place next to the Professor, followed by the rest of the group. He ordered his drink and was about to pay when Loch waved a hand and insisted that this one was on him. Steve appreciated the gesture but assured him that it wasn't necessary to no avail. Steve took his free drink and found a table in the centre of the bar. The light began to fade and Amerigo switched on the bars lighting, which mostly consisted of fairy lights wrapped around bits of ruined temple and the surrounding trees. Steve also noticed a change in the music, the calypso sound quickly faded into something more modern and danceable. Steve found himself hoping that Amerigo didn't expect the group of reps to start dancing, they weren't nearly drunk enough and it didn't seem like the right place.

After a short time, more reps arrived and the bar began to fill up, apparently the taxi driver who had brought the group there was recommending it to the other reps when they asked where everybody else had gone. The buggies kept coming with other groups of reps and even a few Security Officers. The general response was positive and there were even talks of making the Temple Bar the unofficial official hangout of island staff. It made sense as everywhere else they were surrounded by people on holiday who either had a constant flow of questions to ask or expected an off-duty rep to help them when they were too drunk to look after themselves. The fact that reps had to wear their badges at all times, regardless of whether they were on duty or not, wasn't particularly popular and coming to somewhere out of the way was a good method of avoiding having to work on their night out.

Amerigo was clearly not expecting such an influx of customers and not long after, the Professor was helping him make cocktails. Steve was impressed at how well he was doing but over the course of the day he had learned not to underestimate Loch in any field. The queue for the bar started to shrink and Steve took the opportunity to line up for his second drink. The Professor made his second cocktail and offered to pay for it again, however this time Steve insisted that he would pay for himself. The last thing he wanted to do was to abuse Loch's generosity.

Steve found his seat again and a moment later a vacant seat next to him was taken up by Sarah, another rep who was tall, attractive and blonde. Needless to say many of the other reps considered her to be a 'target' and as a result she was showered with free drinks and compliments almost every evening. Steve hadn't really spoken to her before apart from the odd polite 'hello' while at HQ. On this occasion however, she started the conversation.
'So coming to this place was your idea?' Steve answered with a smile. She seemed to be impressed that he had discovered the bar. She went on to ask about the Professor and what Steve was doing while working for him. It was a pleasant conversation but Steve was surprised at how interested Sarah seemed, it wasn't that exciting after all.

They continued to talk about the same subject for quite a while until another rep, Luke, brought them both back to the group by starting a conversation about moving on to the strip. By this time it was getting late and the drinks had already started to take a hold on the group of now over fifty people. The taxis were summoned and everybody readied themselves for the buggy journey down the hill. 'We'll get a buggy together.' Sarah had told Steve. He wasn't going to complain, she was attractive and almost every male in the reps office fancied her. Most people were already jealous that Steve had been given different work (which was deemed to be easier), so why not make them more jealous. Steve sat back in his chair and smiled, he'd had a great day and it seemed that the night was going to be even better.

The buggies arrived and most people left, Steve and Sarah decided to stay until the next group of taxis arrived as they both had a bit of drink to finish. There were only about ten people left in total now and the wait would only be a few minutes. The Professor left also, apparently walking as no taxi arrived for him. He said a quick goodbye to Steve before walking away into the darkness. Steve noticed a worried look crossing Amerigo's face as the Professor left, he was going to ask the barman what was the matter but the next round of taxis arrived and Sarah grabbed his hand, leading him to the first taxi in the queue.

They had the buggy to themselves as it sped down the hill. Sarah seemed to be enjoying her evening almost as much as she enjoyed flirting with Steve. The innuendos and smiles seemed to keep coming for the whole journey. When they reached the strip, Sarah insisted on paying for the taxi, saying that Steve had arranged such a great evening that she wanted to thank him. Steve swore that he saw her wink at that point and decided not to tell her that all he'd done was simply suggest a location. Steve had drunk a fair bit by this point and his night was in full swing.
'I've had an idea.' announced Sarah, suddenly.
'What?'
'Why don't we get the Professor?' Sarah smiled as she made the suggestion. Steve nodded, concluding in his own mind that the Professor was good at everything else so why shouldn't he be the same when it came to being a wingman.

The Professor's bungalow was a surprisingly short walk from the strip, Steve and Sarah had held hands the whole way. When they reached the door, Steve hesitated for a moment, knowing that if Karen found about him knocking on the door of a visitor to the island in such a state, he'd be sacked instantly. Steve decided that he could trust the Professor and threw caution to the wind. He knocked on the door. After a short moment, Loch answered. He had replaced his cardigan and brown trousers with a light grey suit, under his blazer he wore a yellow and red striped jumper.
'Hello Steve!' He turned to Sarah, 'and hello...'
'Sarah.' She introduced herself with a smile.
'We thought you might like to come to the club with us, Professor.'
Loch smiled.
'Well, I was going to have a look at the legendary strip myself, I don't see why I shouldn't accompany you.'

The walk to the strip seemed to be even quicker than the walk away from it. Sarah and the Professor spoke about why he was on the island and what his work involved, things that Steve already knew. He seemed to zone out as the other two chatted but noticed that Sarah occasionally threw him another smile. When they arrived at the strip, Loch took his time examining the various clubs. They walked past quite a few, all decorated with neon lights and all blasting loud music of various genres through their doors. Steve had to admit that the clubs weren't the most imaginatively named places in the world, there was Sinners, Touchdown (a sports bar) and a Mexican-themed place named La Bamba. The theme was consistent along the whole of the strip yet there was no denying that the dullest sounding place was in fact, by far the most popular. This was the Isle Club, the first place that had opened on Corzones Island six years ago. Steve had spent many a night in there, far more drunk than he should have been but shamelessly enjoying himself. It was home to the legendary DJ Freedom, who had apparently appeared from nowhere. There was one night a week where Freedom was given a night off to be replaced by somebody who had been in the charts recently but those nights seemed to be the quietest. For some reason, DJ Freedom had a far greater effect on the people of Corzones than anybody else ever did. Whenever he decided to leave the island, he'd have a promising career ahead of him.

Long queues of people stretched away from the entrance of each club, there wasn't any real reason for checking people as they went in, everybody on the island was of legal drinking age (that was checked before everybody boarded the ferry to the island) and any hope the island's Security staff had of keeping drugs out of the clubs had been abandoned a few years earlier. It was done for appearances' sake, just in case some kind of inspector was on the island. The only time door staff had ever come in useful was when they'd discovered a group of people who hadn't paid to be on the island and were sneaking on via a boat that was moored just off a mostly-isolated part of the coast. It was revealed that they'd stolen the boat and were using it to get a free holiday. When asked by Security for their proof of identity, they were flagged by the computer as not in the database of people staying and investigations went from there. They'd also managed to catch a few people who were enjoying their holiday so much that they'd decided not to go home when they were supposed to.

Steve didn't have to queue, it was the privilege of an off-duty rep to gain immediate entry. He and Sarah said hello to Tony the doorman as they walked in. He was tall, in his forties, bald and covered in tattoos. Steve stepped around a corner and into the club, Sarah linked his arm as they went. It took a moment for Steve to realise that the Professor wasn't with them and guessing what had happened, Steve made his way back to the entrance. As he had suspected, Loch was speaking to Tony who was hesitant to let him enter.

'I'd say you were a little too old for this place, wouldn't you mate?' Loch eyed Tony up and down.

'I would say that you seemed a little too old to be a bouncer, yet each to their own, eh?' Tony frowned, the Professor's joke had clearly failed to land with the doorman.

'Are you being funny?' Steve had never seen Tony look so annoyed.

'Well this group behind me seem to be laughing,' the Professor was right, a young group behind him were giggling away at the exchange, 'but perhaps they're just laughing at my jumper. Current styles are so difficult to keep up with, wouldn't you agree?' Tony struggled to find a reply, eventually he decided to play the heavy doorman, a role that Steve knew he didn't fit particularly well despite his appearance.

'I don't think this is your place tonight pal, if you know what I mean?' The Professor shook his head.

'Nonsense! I was a university lecturer for years and I assure you that I can keep up with anybody.' Tony seemed to be going red so Steve decided that the time had come to intervene. He stepped forward.

'Professor! There you are.' Both Loch and Tony looked straight at him.

'He's with you?' Tony looked surprised and even a bit disappointed, he was probably looking forward to dismissing the Professor.

'Yes, Professor Loch is carrying out some important survey work on the island.' Tony looked at Loch and sighed.

'In you go then mate.' The Professor gave a cheeky grin as he walked past the doorman and into the club.

'Thanks.' He said to Steve as they crossed the threshold. Behind him, Steve heard some laughing stop as Tony shouted, telling them to settle down or they wouldn't get in.

The Professor seemed to adapt to his surroundings very quickly, clearly his stories about spending plenty of time in clubs was true. He, Steve and Sarah joined a large group of other reps, most of whom had been at the Temple Bar earlier on. The group had at least thirty people in it and most of them gave the Professor some funny looks until Steve introduced him properly. One rep even complimented him on his cocktail making skills that had been demonstrated beforehand. Steve was relieved that the Professor fitted into the group so well, there was a moment upon first entering the club where he'd wondered if bringing Loch along was a good idea due to the slight altercation with Tony. Steve knew for certain that he'd made the right choice when Loch had returned from the bar with a tray full of shots, exactly the right number for one each in the group, including himself. After that any awkward looks and sly comments seemed to vanish. A few of the reps even ended up including the Professor in their rounds. Steve was impressed at how sober he seemed to be, even after far more shots than Steve would consider having in one night.

The hours went by and Professor Loch continued to enthral the group. As well as his impressive constitution when it came to drinking, he also appeared to be an impressive dancer. At one point he took Steve to one side for a talk.
'Thank you for inviting me Steve, I'm having a marvellous time. Although I have to admit that I'm struggling to recognise a lot of this music.' Steve smiled.
'This one's from the nineties Professor, you should know it!'
'I had little time for clubbing in the nineties. Although I think I did go to Ibiza at one point.' Steve, fuelled by the alcohol he'd consumed was impressed.
'Ibiza in the nineties? That must have been amazing.'
'It was. Although I was on a study there so I didn't have all that much time to enjoy the nightlife.'

Steve looked up at the raised DJ booth to see if Freedom had arrived yet but saw somebody else working away at the decks instead. This was normal, DJ Freedom didn't start until the club had reached a certain capacity and looking around, Steve could tell that it probably wasn't at the right number yet. Time passed and he noticed that the numbers did begin to increase, particularly after midnight. He spotted Will and Lucy with two other people, they were sitting in a booth. Lucy looked over at him and waved, he returned the gesture.

Eventually the music silenced and an exaggerated English accent boomed through the sound system.
'Ladies and gentlemen!' The room fell silent. 'Tonight you are here for one thing. For one man! Continuing his summer residency here at Corzones Island's number one hotspot, The Isle Club, we give you the master of the mix, the dominator of the decks himself! Let's hear it for DJ Freedom!' Steve joined in with the ear-shattering cheers that rumbled around the club. A path seemed to part in the middle of the dance floor and a door opened at one side of the club. A bright light was shining through it, so vibrant that most people had to shield their eyes. A slow electronic drum beat began to pulse in the background and smoke began to billow through the open door. Two Security staff emerged from the light and stood at either side. The drum beat grew faster and faster and the crowd began to clap along with it. There were cheers and whistles as the beat became louder, the sound of the bass began to make the club vibrate. After a few more agonising seconds of clapping and cheering, he emerged. DJ Freedom walked out of the doorway and slowly along the path that had been cleared through the dance floor. The cheers and whistles continued and there was even an 'I love you!' from somewhere in the crowd. The DJ walked towards a platform that was next to the raised DJ booth. He stood on it and turned around to face the crowd and it was only at that point that he showed any form of emotion. He allowed a little smile as the platform began to raise and take him up to his stage for the night. He disappeared into a cloud of smoke and after a moment, reappeared in the window of the booth. Music began to accompany the drum beats and Freedom's DJ set had begun. The path through the centre of the dance floor was filled in and the night had truly started.

Sarah grabbed Steve's hand and they rushed into the middle of the floor and joined in. This lasted for quite a while and Steve noticed that the Professor had started to talk to another group of reps. He decided that Loch would be fine and that he could fully divert his attention to Sarah. She looked stunning as she danced and he

61

couldn't help but join in. As they danced, they seemed to move closer and closer together until she grabbed his hand and placed it around her waist. He moved closer to her still to the point where their noses were almost touching. Steve didn't know if he initiated it or if she had but they kissed there and then. It seemed to last forever but for Steve, that wasn't long enough. She broke away from him and smiled before blushing and looking to the ground. Steve grabbed her again and the kiss resumed, just as wonderful as the first time.

After a while, Steve and Sarah decided that they would rejoin the main group. Hand in hand, they left the dance floor. Things seemed to be as they had left them, Professor Loch was talking to the main group of reps while holding a glass containing a blue cocktail that Steve wasn't able to identify.
'There you are!' The Professor still seemed entirely sober, he looked at Steve and then at Sarah. 'I see that you're enjoying yourself.' Loch gave a cheeky wink and Steve looked to his right to see that Sarah was blushing again, he gave her an encouraging squeeze of the hand which he noticed had made her smile.

The Professor provided another round of shots which were quickly consumed by the group of reps. Steve considered for a moment how much this evening must be costing Loch and checked with him that he didn't wish Steve to give him some money towards what had been drunk. He insisted that it was fine and that the money that he was receiving for his work on the island was very substantial indeed. It was getting late now, it had passed three in the morning. Steve spotted that Will and Lucy were leaving, apparently in a hurry. A moment later the Professor produced his phone from his pocket, it was of course the most up-to-date model that money could buy. Loch looked at it for a moment before replacing it in his pocket. He walked over to Steve and Sarah.
'I'm very sorry but I have to leave. I shall see you tomorrow Steve, don't worry about starting early.' He smiled at them both. 'I hope you enjoy your evening.' Steve and Sarah both muttered their goodbyes and the Professor left.

It was half past three in the morning and Steve was beginning to feel tired. He'd been drinking for quite a while and the effects were becoming more than apparent. One of his friends back in London had always told him that once you start drinking heavily, you have six hours before you crash. Since arriving on the island, Steve had come to realise that what his friend had said was true, despite his best attempts to continue beyond that. He turned to Sarah and dropped a hint that he wanted to leave and luckily, she agreed. They left the club together and decided to go to Steve's apartment.

Ten

They'd queued for ages to get into the Isle Club but at about half
midnight, they were finally allowed to enter. Lucy immediately led
Will towards the bar, insisting that she would buy the first drink as
a way of thanking him for such a wonderful day. Will smiled and
thanked her, promising himself that he would get the second round.
The queue for the bar was almost as long as the queue to enter but
Lucy managed slyly to push her way forward and got her order in
much more quickly than Will had anticipated. Will didn't know
what he'd ended up drinking but it was light blue and in a large
cocktail glass. As he looked around, Will could see that a lot of
people on the dance floor were drinking the same thing so he
decided to try it. The drink was very sweet but he didn't find it
disagreeable, he thanked Lucy and they both walked away from
the bar.

Lucy had spotted her friend Sofia, she was with a tall blond man,
who had his arm wrapped around her. Lucy decided that they
would join them as they had managed to occupy a booth. Will
followed Lucy over to her friend and they took a seat.
'Will, this is Sofia,' she said, 'and this is... Karl?' Will gave Karl a
polite nod, which was returned.
'It's good to meet you Will.' Sofia smiled as she spoke and offered
her hand, Will shook it and smiled back. Lucy was distracted, Will
looked over and saw that she was waving to Steve, who was in a
large group of people that included Professor Loch.

It didn't take long for Sofia and Karl to get bored of conversation
and start kissing. Lucy tapped Will on the shoulder and suggested
that they leave them to it. Will, who was beginning to feel slightly
awkward, agreed with Lucy and they went to the bar again. He was
buying this time and asked Lucy what their previous drink was.
Apparently it was a Baby Blue and was on offer due to its
popularity. Will took a lot longer to reach the front of the queue
than Lucy had but finally he managed to place his order. Once he
had the drinks, Lucy grabbed him by the arm.
'I want to dance,' she said, before dragging him to the dance floor.

Will wasn't normally a dancer but he had become used to it while
at university and somehow he'd managed to retain his questionable

moves over the two years since he had finished. He'd never been a dancer until one night when there had been a coach to London and a hotel for the night. Will had been persuaded by a few people on his course to join them and had booked his ticket. Thirty pounds had covered the journeys to and from London, a night at the hotel and entrance to a club. The relatively quiet night out that he was used to in Oxford had been replaced by a crowded experience with loud music and a variety of drinks that Will had never heard of. Somehow, he had met a girl in that club and she had accompanied him back to his hotel. She was named Christina. The next morning she had gone home fairly early, when she'd awoken she seemed quite embarrassed and it hadn't taken her long to make her excuses and leave. They had texted each other for a few days afterwards but the spark that alcohol had kindly given them both had gone and it hadn't taken either of them long to lose interest. Will would never forget Christina but had no intention of meeting her again. For a few days his one night stand had bothered him but he had come to realise that it was one of those things that happened and shouldn't be dwelled upon in too much detail.

Will looked at Lucy and they danced together and the memories of Christina ran through his head. For a few moments he considered why these all-but-forgotten thoughts would haunt him but he almost immediately knew why. He hoped that Lucy would be different and somehow he knew that she would be. Christina had been very attractive and for the weeks after the event his housemates had constantly stated that she was 'way out of his league'. At first Will had been proud of what he'd done that night but as time passed he realised that he had just been another student to have virtually anonymous sex on a night out. He resented that and soon realised that he wasn't the right person for that kind of life. He wanted commitment, a relationship but university had never given him such an opportunity, nor had the couple of years since. However, Will was in the Isle Club, dancing with Lucy and for a brief moment, he imagined the two of them being together for some time.

The music changed and a song that Will wasn't familiar with began to play, his thought moved back to reality. He and Lucy were dancing together but he felt an awkwardness that wouldn't leave him. Lucy was beautiful and Will knew that the alcohol he had consumed that evening had given him a level of confidence that he hadn't felt before. Despite this, Will couldn't bring himself to make any kind of move. He thought back to what Harry and the others had said to him before he had left:

'Just be confident Will,' Harry had told him, 'if she's invited you out then she probably likes you. Just stay calm and who knows what might happen?' Royce had butted in at that point:

'She wants to shag you mate, go for it!' Harry, Jason and Royce didn't know about Will's experiences in London and, from the latter two particularly, many jokes were made about him being a virgin. He wanted to set the record straight but knew that only more picking would be the result.

They had danced for a while. Lucy had clearly wanted to avoid Sofia and Karl and it was clear that they had wanted to be alone from the moment that they had started kissing. Will stopped dancing very suddenly as the music ceased. He was pushed back as everybody on the dance floor moved and made a gap in the middle. A voice announced that DJ Freedom was about to start his set in a way that Will found to be cheesy. The entire club seemed to erupt in a state of over excitement and for a few minutes nothing could be heard but screams, cheers and one brunette girl that was near Will shouting that she loved the DJ. He walked towards a platform that took him to the DJ booth and his set began properly. Will knew most of the songs that he played, mostly because he stuck to the charts and they were something that Will tried not to stay in touch with.

As the night progressed and they drank more, Lucy seemed more nervous and on edge. Will continually asked if she was alright but she'd insist that all was fine. Lucy bought another round of drinks and Will was really starting to feel their effects by this stage. He didn't care, as for the first time he could remember, he was enjoying his time in a nightclub

Will had spotted Harry, Royce and Jason standing by a bar. His immediate reaction was to grab Lucy's hand and drag her further into the dancing crowd. She went with him and smiled as she started to dance again. After a few minutes she placed her hand on Will's shoulder,

'Are you having a good night?' Will nodded and they continued to dance. Suddenly, Lucy stopped and held her head in her hands.

Will was worried and didn't know if placing his hand on her shoulder was the right thing to do or not. In the end, he decided to. 'What's wrong?' He asked and for a moment, Lucy didn't respond. 'We can leave of you want to?' Lucy shook her head.
'No it's fine. You're having a good time, I don't want to go.' Will shook his head.
'I'm only here because of you! If you're not enjoying it...?' Lucy hesitated for a moment then nodded. 'Come on then, we'll go.'

They pushed through the hundreds of people that were occupying the dance floor and made their way towards the door. As he was about to leave, Will looked back and saw that Harry was giving him the thumbs up. He blushed and briefly waved at his brother before leaving the club. Harry turned back to Jason and Royce and directed their attention away from Will and Lucy. Will gave an appreciative nod to his brother before he walked into the foyer and then out of the door.

When they'd left the club, Lucy had grabbed Will's hand and walked quickly with him. They went to the end of the strip and into an area that was less populated. They found a bench in the darkness that was sheltered by some trees. They both took a seat, Lucy was breathing heavily by this time and took a moment to compose herself.
'I'm sorry,' she looked Will straight in the eye, 'I just needed to get out of there.' Will smiled at Lucy and assured her that everything was ok. She took a deep breath and seemed to hesitate before she talked again. 'I suffer from a form of depression. I just have mood swings. Sometimes I'm the happiest person in the world and others I just, I just can't stand anything. I guess I just had a bit of an attack in the club. I thought I'd be ok. I'm sorry Will, I didn't want to tell you. I wanted to seem normal.' Lucy had paused before her last word and Will hesitated for a moment, before placing an arm around her shoulders. She snuggled up to him, placing one of her arms across his chest.
'I still think you're wonderful.' Will didn't know where he'd found the courage to speak from but he was glad he'd said it. Lucy smiled at him and suddenly leaned in close. They kissed. Will didn't know for how long, it felt amazing, better than anything else ever had. They both withdrew at the same time and smiled at each other. Lucy was smiling, brighter than Will had ever seen before.

'That was nice.' Lucy couldn't stop grinning. With an unprecedented level of confidence, Will placed his arm around her again and the kiss resumed.

For a few moments they just sat on the bench and held hands. The music from the strip boomed loudly in the background and prevented any silence that there may have been. All of a sudden the moment was broken by Professor Loch running past them urgently and down to the nearest Security staff.
'Call the authorities immediately!' Loch was panting after his run, the bouncer seemed less than interested but after he said something else that Will was unable to hear, the bouncer joined Loch. As they ran past, Will stood up.
'Professor, I have the emergency number!' Loch stopped running for a moment and looked at Will.
'Come with me then William, but brace yourself.' Will ran with the Professor and the bouncer, Lucy joined them.

Will was on his phone, trying to contact the emergency department as he ran into the town square. It seemed eerie in the darkness, the only lighting was coming from the fountain that he had been pushed into earlier that day. He saw a tall silhouette of a figure standing beside it. As he moved closer he realised that this was the figure of Amerigo. The bouncer ran to Amerigo and spoke to him for a moment, Will couldn't hear what was said but knew that something was very wrong. Will and Lucy reached the fountain and stood next to the Professor. They looked down to the ground and saw what the Bouncer was inspecting. Lying a short distance from the fountain was a blonde woman. The bouncer shook his head after checking her pulse. She was dead.

Part Two - The Sin

Eleven

Half four in the morning those bastards had called him and now six hours later he was on a boat, speeding towards the island. Inspector John Kirshner had been on holiday with his wife, so far it had been going fine and he was having an uncharacteristically relaxed week but that just couldn't last. Corzones Island was mostly populated by people who spoke English and therefore it had been very quickly decided that an English speaking inspector was needed to head up the case.

During his briefing, Kirshner had been told very little, just that the deceased was a woman in her mid-twenties and that she had an unmistakable stab wound through her chest. The scene of the crime had been cleared quickly, so that all would seem normal when a bunch of inebriated holidaymakers evacuated the nightclubs. Kirshner had been assured that plenty of photos had been taken and that the island's head of Security, a man named Luther Powell, had made a detailed report of what had been at the scene. As Kirshner's car had picked him up to take him to the sea port, the body hadn't been identified but it was hoped that by the time he arrived there would have been developments.

The weather was scorching hot but Kirshner had decided that he'd better look the part, he removed a slightly crumpled-looking suit from his luggage and put it on, making an unenthusiastic attempt to neaten it out in the process. He'd said goodbye to his wife, who was almost as unhappy with the situation as he was and left. Outside his hotel he had waited for far longer than he had expected to and decided that he'd treat himself to a cigarette until the car arrived. Considering both the island's authorities and his station back in Britain had insisted that it was urgent and that he left immediately, the car was annoyingly fifteen minutes late. By this stage the first suggestions of sunlight began to appear in the sky and a few birds had started to sing.

The drive to the ferry port had been dull as the driver had spoken little English, therefore conversation was out of the question almost straight away. Kirshner attempted to read for all of two minutes before he felt sick, he never read well in cars anyway and the lack of light made him have to strain his eyes harder than he was willing to. Besides all of that, he was tired, grumpy and his mind was already on the case, considering the information he had been given so far. Who the hell on that island would want to stab anybody and why? He knew that he had a few days of hard work ahead of him as well as countless angry phone calls from his wife who he knew wouldn't have followed his advice of going back to sleep and would instead be sitting in a chair with coffee, muttering under her breath about how her holiday had been ruined. She'd begged Kirshner not to go, to tell his superiors that he was on holiday but the truth was that a holiday in the sun just wasn't what he'd wanted and that this kind of distraction was more welcome than he'd choose to admit.

Kirshner had just turned forty-six and looked every minute of his age. He was fairly tall and athletic, he always made sure that his days started and ended with a run. He'd been an officer for years and worked hard, making his way through the ranks until two years before when he finally made inspector. There'd been a big party to celebrate his promotion and that was the final day that his job had been rewarding. Suddenly he had a team underneath him that looked to him for guidance and advice that he wasn't particularly good at giving. Nevertheless Kirshner knew his job and would always do his absolute best at it. It wasn't something he wished to admit but the idea of cracking a murder case again appealed to his natural thirst for adventure. As he sat in the car to the ferry port, he amused himself by thinking that this was just like one of those police show specials when they'd go abroad for an episode or two to solve a crime. Naturally the Inspector always won, regardless of the backdrop to the case.

He'd left his hotel at about six in the morning and by half eight he was ready to board the ferry to Corzones Island. The only problem was that there wasn't a ferry and instead he was greeted by a small man named Sergeant Churenzo who had come from the island to meet him. Churenzo led him to a small dinghy that was moored just around the corner from where the ferried docked.
'No ferries for another two hours I'm afraid, we'll have to go on this. Forty five minutes and you'll be on Corzones Island

Inspector...?' Churenzo allowed the last word to linger, making it clear that it was a question.

'Kirshner,' he replied, 'Inspector John Kirshner.' Churenzo nodded. 'Inspector Kirshner, right. If you'd like to climb down to the boat?' Churenzo beckoned to Kirshner to go first and he did so, hesitantly. Kirshner wasn't very good with boats and had spent the majority of the car journey mentally bracing himself for the ferry. At being presented with the dinghy he was horrified, his only consolation was the fact that it was surrounded by handles in which he'd be placing a great deal of grip and trust.

His nerves were not in any way eased by the life jacket that Churenzo handed to him once he was on board. It didn't fit very well over his suit and looked like it was a little past its best. The boat itself however seemed to be new and hardly used, this was confirmed by Churenzo who told him that it was only used in emergencies. It moved quickly but bounced around a lot, meaning that Kirshner's hands were firmly attached to the boat in an unbreakable grip. A lot of spray flew up, soaking Kirshner and almost certainly destroying his pinstripe suit.

He also realised that, as in the car, conversation was out of the question as Churenzo had to give all of his focus to piloting the boat and navigating it over the surprisingly choppy sea. After what seemed like an eternity, Kirshner was finally able to see the island in the distance. His first thought was that it seemed to be very green and after a short while, he was even able to make out individual palm trees. Once he had seen the island it seemed to approach quickly and Kirshner couldn't help but feel that all seemed calm and relaxed. Despite the choppiness of the ocean, the island was free of wind and as he observed the coastline, he didn't see anybody.

'Ten in the morning is early on Corzones, nobody is awake yet.' If what Kirshner had heard about the previous night's events was true, he found this to be unlikely. Apparently the body had been seen by quite a few people and despite its early removal, the island's authorities had struggled to keep it secret. Word had got out and a minor state of panic had erupted before Security staff had assured that everything was under control and sent everybody home. Their attitude towards events once they had woken up remained to be seen.

Finally the small dinghy arrived in the docks and Kirshner was met by Powell. He was smaller than Kirshner had expected and fitted awkwardly into his chief's uniform. His hair was very short and he carried an air of ex-military about him. Kirshner struggled to identify his age but eventually decided to settle for a guess of early-thirties.

'Do you have any luggage that needs taking?' Powell asked, holding out his hand expectantly.

'I was told that it would be sent along later.' Kirshner hoped that it didn't take too long to arrive, his suit was soaking and the sun hadn't quite risen far enough to dry him out sufficiently. Powell assured him that he would receive it as soon as it was on the island but Kirshner knew that it wouldn't arrive until at least the first ferry did, which still had an hour to go if what Churenzo had said was accurate.

Powell led Kirshner to a vehicle that looked like a quad bike with the roof of a golf buggy added to it.

'We find that these buggies are the easiest way to navigate the island, once we're at HQ I shall arrange to have one given to you.' Kirshner nodded, knowing that he'd enjoy travelling on a buggy almost as little as he did his journey on the dinghy. In the end it wasn't as bad as he'd expected and the journey to Security HQ was short. It was a large, hexagonal building with a dark blue motif, a similar colour to the uniforms worn by the Security Officers. It was tucked mostly into the foliage of the jungle but there was a clear path going all the way around it, accompanied by a road. The buggy sped past the front entrance that was for the public and around the back.

There were buggy spaces around the side and an entrance that was more secure. As the buggy pulled into its allotted space, a young Security Officer ran out to them with his hands full. He reached Kirshner just as he'd finished dismounting the vehicle.

'Inspector Kirshner?' Kirshner nodded. 'I have your Security pass here and the written reports for you to study. If you'll come inside we've made a space available for you with all of the facilities that you should need. If there's anything missing then just ask me. My name's Harper by the way, I should have told you that at the start. Sorry.' Kirshner nodded, smiled and assured the young officer that all was fine.

Powell offered to show him to his desk and they entered the building together. As they walked through the open plan office, Powell began to relate some more information: the victim's name was Zoë Parker and she was twenty-four. She had drugs in her system when she'd died as well as something else, possibly a poison that had been administered by the murder weapon. Further tests were being conducted to try and confirm the last part.

Eventually Kirshner and Powell reached a small room at the opposite end of the office from the entrance. It was an interview room that had been hurriedly adapted for purpose but it seemed to suit. There was a phone, a computer and a pile of documents that included instructions and a phone book of the island. Somebody had hung a cork board on the wall and a few images related to the case. In the corner of the board was a map of the island with the locations of Zoë's apartment and where she'd been found already labelled. Another label was close to the site of her body being found, on looking carefully, Kirshner saw that this was a nightclub that Zoë had been in up until about an hour or two before her body had been discovered.

Kirshner spoke to Powell for quite a while, gaining the answers to a few minor questions and getting to grips with the case. One piece of information that had come forward was that Zoë had been seen with one of the local DJs quite a bit before her death and they concluded that speaking to him would be a good place to start. They were both set to leave when Harper arrived and announced that a witness had arrived at the station of his own accord and wished to speak to 'someone in charge'. Kirshner decided that he wanted to speak to this man and told Powell to talk to the DJ without him, they agreed to meet afterwards and share whatever information they had gained.

As he made his way to the interview room containing the witness, Kirshner hoped that this case could be solved quickly. His short time on Corzones Island had made him appreciate the holiday that he was having beforehand all the more, despite its apparent shortfalls. Boredom had become the preferable option. He needed to phone his wife but from the moment he'd first climbed on to the dinghy there hadn't been a good time and this still wasn't it unfortunately. She wouldn't be happy but he had to see this witness who had apparently claimed that they 'didn't have much time'. Kirshner hoped that it wouldn't prove to be a waste of his.

He entered the interview room and was greeted by a tall, thin man who was wearing a suit, far more expensive that Kirshner's own. He had a pencil moustache which he occasionally stroked with his tongue, probably unconsciously. It seemed to be very greasy due to overuse of product, as did the rest of his jet-black hair.
'Argyll,' he said as Kirshner entered, holding out his hand for Kirshner to shake, 'Argyll Devonshire. I'm the part-owner and manager of the Isle club, as I'm sure you're aware the biggest night hotspot on the island.' Kirshner nodded and introduced himself in return. He offered a seat to Argyll, who accepted.
'This is a very grim business, officer. I certainly hope that what I have to tell you will help.'
'Bear with me a moment, Mister Devonshire.' Kirshner took a moment to make the interview tape work, it was far more technical in comparison to the simple device that he was used to at home. Eventually he found a button marked 'record' and pressed it.
'Please continue.' Argyll considered for a moment and sighed a deep breath.
'It isn't easy for me to say this I'm afraid, Detective Kirshner but I think I have a good idea of how and why the killing occurred. Young Zoë, I didn't know her well but she'd been fraternising with my top DJ for some time and I believe that he was quite infatuated with her. It's a weakness that many on this island display, they fall in love with those that they shouldn't.' Kirshner listened and decided to let Argyll tell the story in his own words as opposed to interfering and pushing him to the point. 'Last night she had arrived at the club with this DJ and they shared a number of drinks together in the VIP lounge. Normally we don't let people like her in there but I find it important to keep my people happy, you understand?' Kirshner nodded. 'They both seemed uneasy, like there had previously been a problem. Eventually, a small argument erupted between the two of them, the conclusion of which was her walking out. He chased after her and was gone for quite some time. I was worried that he'd vanished before the start of his set and just before I considered finding a replacement, he reappeared. He was stressed but distant, like there was something that he was trying to block from his mind. He went on and performed as well as he would any evening. After his set he chose to stay behind, saying that he wouldn't be seeing Zoë again that night. Normally they

dash off together but this was the second night in a row that she had left early. His behaviour was suspicious to say the least.' Kirshner gave Argyll a moment, just to confirm that he had finished speaking before asking his question.

'And this DJ's name?' He already knew from Powell's report what the answer would be. 'DJ Freedom. His real name is Franko Young. He's British, from Newcastle I think.'

Kirshner attempted to gain more information that would be useful from Argyll but he didn't really have anything else. The case stood however that unless Franko Young, AKA DJ Freedom had an alibi for the time that he wasn't in the club, this case may already be solved. Kirshner was glad, he'd barely been on the island for an hour and it seemed that already things could be wrapped up. Of course there would be mopping up to do and a confession from Young himself would help a great deal. He decided that he would go and join Powell to see the suspect DJ for himself. He said goodbye to Argyll, escorting him out of the main entrance before going to find Harper.

Kirshner had been given his own buggy to get around the island on but chose to have Harper show him the way instead. He didn't know his way around yet and needed to get there quickly, just to make sure that Powell didn't inadvertently say anything that may compromise the case. Ideally he'd be there to see Franko's reaction first hand when Powell broke the news of the death to him. Argyll had assured him that, if he was innocent, it was incredibly unlikely that Franko would have heard about the murder yet as he'd gone straight home once he'd finished at the club and had a habit of sleeping in until lunch time.

Harper drove the buggy at a speed to where Franko was staying. Kirshner had to admit that from outside, the block of apartments seemed to be quite grand and from a certain angle even looked luxurious. Once he'd actually set foot inside however his opinion changed drastically. The corridor looked used and untidy. The floors were stained and in some places the walls were even graffitied. Harper had walked with Kirshner to the door of the apartment but the Inspector decided to send him back to wait in the buggy, he'd probably find himself overruling Powell at this point and knew that it was best not to allow the young officer to see this happening. Harper left, seemingly unconcerned at being sent away but Kirshner knew that he must really feel otherwise. With a sigh, Kirshner knocked on the door.

It was answered by Powell who was immediately surprised to see the Inspector in front of him.
'Inspector Kirshner,' Powell spoke with a whisper so that the occupant of the apartment wouldn't hear him, 'I didn't expect to see you here. I've just broken the news and he hasn't taken it very well.' Kirshner grumbled that he needed to see Franko himself and almost pushed past Powell who still seemed confused.

The inside of the apartment was a state. On one wall was a kitchenette with a pile of unwashed dishes and empty takeaway packets lying unceremoniously on the work top. A young man, assumed to be Franko by Kirshner, was sitting on the bed, his head in his hands and his feet resting in the centre of a pile of empty beer cans.
'Detective Inspector Kirshner,' he said, flashing his identity card to the man, who looked up briefly, 'I'm afraid I need you to come with us back to the statio... back to headquarters.' Franko looked up again, a confused look on his face.
'Why's that? I don't know anything.' Kirshner saw that this wasn't going to be easy and sighed again.
'You're a suspect in a murder case and we need to ask you some questions in a more formal environment.' Powell stepped forward to argue, a reflex that came naturally to him after years in charge of Security.
'I don't think that's necessary Inspector...' Kirshner didn't want to but Powell had left him in the situation that he had been dreading.
'I am in charge of this investigation Security Chief Powell and I shall make decisions like this. Mister Young here is our primary suspect and I want him taking in.' Powell hesitantly nodded in agreement.
'I didn't kill her! She was amazing and we argued but I didn't kill her!' Franko wasn't going to calm down and Kirshner had to order Powell to place him in handcuffs before leading him out of the apartment.

Franko left the room first, closely followed by Powell who looked back at Kirshner and shook his head. In the last half an hour this had gone from being a simple case with a cooperative team to a disaster. Kirshner had angered his closest ally, failed to see

Franko's reaction first hand and driven the suspect to state of hysteria. Kirshner knew there and then that his time on Corzones Island was going to last much longer than he'd hoped. As he locked the door to Franko's apartment the one thing that he was trying to avoid flew through Kirshner's head: doubt. Perhaps they didn't have the right man after all but so far, DJ Freedom was all that they had to work with.

Twelve

'Did you see the body?' The bouncer had his hands placed on Lucy's shoulders.

'No.' she lied. She'd seen before Will had, or so it seemed. He'd seen it and tried to avert her eyes but it was too late. The dead woman looked cold, all of the life had vanished from her skin and it remained like it shouldn't quite be there. Lucy also saw the pool of blood that surrounded the body, it looked black in the darkness. The bouncer, who Lucy had later learned was named Tony, produced a small torch and checked the pulse. It was only as she stared away they Lucy noticed Will's hand, clasped tightly around her own. Will was on his phone, trying to contact island Security, eventually there was an answer.

'Professor!' Loch turned to Will and took the phone, beginning to speak into it.

'Security? Yes, there's a body in the town centre... I didn't witness anything no, I had just met a friend when we discovered it.

The Professor's phone conversation continued, Security promised to send people immediately and asked him to remain on the phone. Amerigo walked over to Lucy and Will, shaking his head. He walked over to the fountain and dipped his hands in the water for a moment to wash away the blood.

'I'm sorry that you two had to see that.' He said.

'I didn't see anything.' Lucy hoped that if she said it enough then she'd start to believe it herself.

'Do you know what happened?' Will asked, breathing heavily. Amerigo shook his head.

'I don't know. I was going to meet the Professor as he left the club for a few quiet drinks when I came across her, exactly as she is now.'

Loch walked over to the group.

'Security needs everybody to stay here.' He said, trying to sound calm. It had become too much for Lucy, she could feel her heart starting to beat faster.

'I can't,' she started to walk away, 'not with that here.'

'Lucy, wait!' The Professor sounded a little more serious now, like he was giving an order. Lucy didn't obey and her walk turned into a run, Will was by her side.

'I'll go with them, we'll just be around the corner.' Tony ran and caught the other two.

They quickly walked around a corner and found themselves back on the strip. Lucy dashed to the nearest bench and sat down.
'Just keep calm,' she told herself as Will joined her, 'it'll be ok.' She felt her breathing become heavier still and waited a few seconds for the panic to come. But it never did. Will had placed his arm around her and suddenly, Lucy felt safe.
'You'll be ok.' He whispered to her in a calming voice and somehow, she did feel happier.
'You're sure you didn't see it?' Tony asked his question again Lucy gave a shake of the head as a reply.
'I did,' said Will, sounding grim, 'it was horrible. I can't understand why somebody would do that to another person.' Tony sighed.
'I used to think the same. I was in the army and I just became used to it. Still, I haven't seen anything like that for a long time.'

In the distance they heard sirens.
'That'll be Security.' Tony stood and began to walk back to the town centre.
'Just give us a moment.' Tony nodded at Will's request but made them both promise to not be too long.
'It's best to talk to Security now and get it out of the way.' He said, before vanishing around the corner and leaving Lucy in Will's arms.

There was a silence for at least a minute but Lucy didn't mind. She'd returned Will's hug and placed her arm around him as soon as Tony had rounded the corner. For a few moments, they sat still, holding each other. If the body hadn't intruded on their evening, Lucy knew that she'd be so happy at this stage. Any hope of that seemed to be a distant thought, no more than a product of her imagination. It was a terrible night but at least she had Will sitting next to her.

She decided to break the silence.
'I'm sorry.' She didn't exactly know why that was what she had chosen to go with straight away but knew it had to be said. Will sounded confused when he replied:
'For what? You didn't put the body there.' Lucy shook her head.
'I didn't mean that. I meant the kiss. We're both drunk and I...'

79

'It doesn't matter,' Will interrupted, 'it really doesn't. I enjoyed it.' Lucy felt herself smile, unable to stop. She looked at Will to see that he had the exact same smile on his face.' Will's smile suddenly faded and he sighed. 'We should go back to the town centre.' Lucy nodded and released Will from the hug. Together they walked back around the corner.

The Security team consisted of four buggies, each carrying two officers. They were led by a man named Powell, who was the Security Chief for the whole island. Much to Lucy's relief the body had been covered by a plastic sheet.

'We need to get it moved quickly,' Lucy heard Powell say, 'if it's not gone by the time the clubs empty then this whole thing will become a lot more difficult for all of us.' Powell then began to pay attention to his witnesses. 'I'm afraid we'll need to take all of you to HQ, we won't take too long I promise and then we'll make sure that you're all dropped at your accommodation.' Lucy didn't want to but knew that really she had no choice in the matter. She climbed after Will on to the back of a buggy that was then driven to Security HQ. By the time that they arrived, the music of the clubs had started to fade and the sound of crowds dispersing could be heard.

Lucy was taken to an interview room where she sat alone for a few minutes, Will having been ushered into the room next door. Lucy struggled but somehow managed to remain calm as she waited. Powell eventually entered and took a seat opposite her. He pressed record on a device at the edge of the table and assured Lucy that everything was ok, he just needed to know exactly what happened. She told him. She told him about the Professor dashing along the strip, telling somebody to call Security. She told him about running to the town centre with the Professor. She told him about Will, who shielded her view from the body. It didn't take Powell long to work out that all Lucy could really tell him wasn't anything particularly helpful. He said that she may be called back for clarifications at some point but in the mean time she was allowed to go.

She left the interview room to see Will sitting on a sofa, already free from his interview and waiting for her. Powell joined them. 'If you wait here, I shall find somebody to take you back to your accommodation.' He handed them a card each, telling them to phone him if they needed to for whatever reason. Again, Lucy and Will found themselves alone together.

'Was your interview ok?' Will asked with a sound of concern in his voice. Lucy nodded and assured him that everything was fine.

'Will, come back to mine please?' Will looked surprised.

'Are you sure?'

'Yes. I don't want to be alone tonight. If that's ok with you?' Will gave that comforting smile again.

'Of course then, I will. I'd only have to put up with a hundred drunk questions from my brother and his friends if I went back to mine anyway.'

So it was agreed and when an officer came to take them home, they asked him to drop them both at Lucy's. This reduced his journey and allowed him to get to bed earlier so he quickly agreed. They left the Security building as the first signs of daylight began to appear over the horizon. They boarded the buggy and for every moment of the journey that passed, the light seemed stronger. There were even signs of the sun itself poking out as they arrived at Lucy's apartment, not that they stayed outdoors to admire it. They were both tired and it had been an immensely difficult night. Lucy couldn't get the image of the girl, lying on the ground and covered in blood, out of her head but Will's presence made it easier to cope with.

'I'll stay on the sofa then?' Asked Will, as they entered the apartment. It was as she'd left it which indicated that for the second night in a row, Sofia hadn't made it back. Lucy wasn't surprised. 'No. There's room on my bed for us both, if we squeeze.' She smiled at Will, who again looked surprised. 'That's if that's ok with you?' Will nodded and assured her that it was fine. Lucy stayed fully clothed as she climbed into her bed and Will stayed the same. She snuggled up to him and he saw it as a sign to put his arm around her. Lucy found herself smiling again, smiling and comfortable.

Neither of them spoke for a few minutes until Lucy found herself saying something unexpected.

'I saw it you know. I told them that I didn't but I did.' Will took a moment to reply.

'I thought you had. I couldn't be sure and I hoped that you hadn't but I knew that really...'

81

'It was horrible. To see death like that, to see somebody who had recently had their life taken away from them.'

'I know,' said Will, 'archaeology means that I spend a lot of time around death but ancient death. Nothing that close, that real.' The conversation ended there and Lucy rolled herself on to her side so that she was closer to Will.

'Goodnight Will.' She whispered, almost silent.

'Goodnight Lucy. Sleep well, I promise everything will be alright.' His reply made her smile again. Somehow, against all odds, Lucy was able to sleep and drifted off very quickly in his arms.

Thirteen

Amerigo had seen the body just as Professor Loch had arrived.
'You're here, good.' The Professor spoke quickly and quietly, as if
he'd had a lot to cover in a short time. Amerigo cut him short
straight away.
'Not now Professor. Get in touch with Security.' Loch looked
confused for a moment until his eyes rested on the same place as
Amerigo's.
'Bloody hell!' he exclaimed, Amerigo had never heard him swear
before. 'Stay here, I shall find somebody.' The Professor ran back
the way he came, towards the strip. Amerigo stood alone and
silent, looking around carefully. He had a strange feeling, as if
someone was watching him. A scan of the immediate area proved
this feeling to be incorrect.

It only took Loch about a minute to return and he was
accompanied by Will, Lucy and one of the bouncers. Amerigo had
no idea how he'd found the two youngsters or why he'd brought
them with him. The attention of the group was divided between
investigating the body, calling Security and making sure that the
two younger members were alright. It didn't take long for Lucy to
dash around the corner, followed by Will. Tony, the bouncer had
followed to make sure that they stayed nearby which left Amerigo
alone with the Professor.
'Now what the hell is happening?' The Professor seemed angrier
and less calm than he normally did, there was even a hint of
accusation in his voice.
'Nothing, this is exactly how I found her!' Amerigo's reply was
immediate and contained its own bit of anger, was the Professor
accusing him? Loch sighed and shook his head.
'You were the first here, if they knew that then naturally they'd
point the finger at you.' Amerigo nodded in grim agreement. 'I
believe you my friend, I believe that you didn't do this. You tell the
stories but I know you're not part of whatever is going to happen
on this island. I'll give you an alibi, say that we were together when
we found the body.'
'Will that work?'
'Not if they don't investigate us too closely, I should be able to
prevent that. But I need one thing in return.' Amerigo's suspicions

were confirmed. 'I need you to help me uncover and stop whatever is going on.'

'Your trip here isn't about archaeology then, Professor?'

'It is as much as it was last time. I'm here to find out exactly what did happen before this island was colonised and why the order are becoming more prominent now. It's all over the Internet if you know where to look. A summons, "come to Corzones Island, the time is right."'

'You think that they were responsible for this?' Amerigo nodded towards the girl.

'You *don't?*' Amerigo nodded sternly and sighed.

'It will be them. I've been warned that something is coming.'

'Then we shall talk about it tomorrow, the less we know before our interview the better. When asked, say that you met me on the strip.' Sirens began to sound in the distance and with every passing moment they grew louder. Loch suddenly fell silent and he knew that the conversation was at an end, for now.

So Amerigo had been correct, Professor Loch was an archaeologist, a damn good one with an impressive reputation but very few people knew of his extra-curricular activities, just as very few knew about Svoros. Amerigo had suspected his involvement with The Order of Velza for some time and recent signs and requests had confirmed these suspicions. They had supposedly stopped operating about twenty years ago but there had always been talk around the island, whispers that something would one day bring them back together. Amerigo had known Svoros since about that time and for most of it, there had been no suggestion that he was anymore than a native of the island, who had chosen to open a café at the time Giorgio Corzones had bought the island and planned to develop it.

Amerigo thought back to his recent feelings about living on the island and somehow he knew and indeed had known all along, that he was never really going to go anywhere. He looked at the dead girl on the floor and as much as he knew that she should make him want to leave and never return, the adventurous side that he had possessed ever since he was a boy had made him want to stay. There had never been a suggestion before this that the brotherhood would do something so sinister but the fact that Loch was here to investigate them and what Svoros had said proved beyond all doubt that this was just the start of something far more dangerous.

The words rung still in Amerigo's ears: 'Something big is coming my friend, if you aren't with us then please don't be here when it arrives.' Was it just a warning, or was it more of a threat maybe? For a brief moment Amerigo started to consider what he was feeling to be fear but he was quickly distracted by the arrival of the Security Officers.

They were taken to Security HQ and quickly separated from each other. Will and Lucy left on the first buggy, the Professor on the second, Tony on the third and finally Amerigo on the fourth. Upon arriving at HQ he didn't see any of the others and was quickly escorted to an interview room. The Security Officers had been polite but he hadn't received any of the sympathetic treatment that it seemed Will and Lucy would do as they left. He stared at the clock which was hanging on the wall and watched the minutes tick away.

Eventually an officer calmly entered the room, Amerigo knew him as Powell, head of Security on the island. Powell smiled and Amerigo returned the gesture as he sat down. Powell was a reasonable man and good at his job, which made Amerigo feel uneasy about slightly adjusting the truth. The Professor needed his help though and he wouldn't be able to serve that purpose if he was a murder suspect.
'Sorry about the delay Amerigo, wanted to get those two out of the way as quickly as I could. They're on their way home now.'
Amerigo told Powell that he was glad, that they should never have seen it. All he could assume was that the Professor panicked and brought them to the scene without thinking but such a lapse of judgment wasn't characteristic of Loch.

Amerigo went through the sequence of events and told Powell how he and the Professor had been due to meet and did do at the end of the strip, before walking to the town centre and discovering the body together. Professor Loch had run for help while Amerigo had stayed with the corpse. He told the rest of the story exactly how it had happened until Security had arrived. Powell simply nodded and listened intently, making the odd note on a small pad despite the fact that the whole thing was being taped.

Once Amerigo had finished his story, Powell considered for a moment and his eyes flicked over his notes.

'Tell me about Julius Loch, I believe you've met before?' Amerigo exhaled and considered his answer, he had to be careful about what he said.

'The Professor came to the island just before its development started. He was sent to look at the ruins and evaluate the archaeological significance of this place.' Powell nodded.

'Is that the only time you've met before?'

'Met? Yes. Although we stayed in contact. He was interested in how some places were being preserved, such as the temple around my bar.' Powell nodded and concluded that he had no further questions. Amerigo was free to go but would probably have to return for a follow-up at some point.

As Amerigo sat silently on the back of a buggy being driven by a Security Officer, he couldn't help but shake the feeling that Powell didn't quite believe what he'd said. He'd only lied once, in exactly the way that the Professor had told him to. But then again, he'd seriously hung back on telling the truth about Loch. What he couldn't tell Powell was that the world was a far greater and more mysterious place than he would ever believe and that, while being a leading archaeologist, Professor Loch was also what was known as a 'Super', a Supernatural Investigator. His job was a secret he shared with very few people. The only reason that Amerigo knew the truth was that on his last visit to the island, as well as surveying the temple, the Professor was on the trail of a man wanting to steal an ancient artefact from the island. Somewhere, hidden away and apparently untapped by all apart from this one man, was a treasure trove of what Loch had described as 'objects of evil', pieces of ancient technology that were designed to corrupt the world in ways beyond comprehension. Amerigo had inadvertently helped to corner the individual in question and learned of the Professor's true motives then. The fugitive, whose name Amerigo had never learned, threw himself into the ocean and took the secret of this treasure trove with him to his watery grave.

Amerigo arrived back at his house, one of the few actual houses left on the island and waved goodbye to the officer who had delivered him there. He fumbled in the darkness for his keys and opened the door. He walked straight to the drinks cabinet and produced a bottle of local rum, pouring a more than generous measure into a glass and sinking it down straight away. He wondered what had happened to the Professor, whether he'd been

86

interviewed before or after he had and whether he'd been allowed to leave as easily.

Sitting in his armchair, Amerigo had two final thoughts before he drifted off to sleep. The first was for the welfare of Will and Lucy, he hoped that the evening's events hadn't traumatised them too much. The second thought was that because of the Professor's arrival after Svoros' warning, there was virtually no chance that the poor girl's murder was motivated by anything that was right and good on Earth. It appeared that the order of Velza had returned and that the time for their supposed arising had come.

Fourteen

Will awoke with his arm still around Lucy, the effects of the alcohol and his streak of self-confidence had vanished. He considered numerous ways of moving his arm without waking Lucy up but decided that they probably wouldn't work. He had no idea what time it was and the back of his throat was dry, a taste of the previous night's cocktails still lingered in his mouth. More than anything in the world, he wished for a glass of water or perhaps an orange juice. Looking around, he saw that his phone was on the floor and just possibly within reaching distance, at least that would tell him the time. If he was lucky then maybe he could get home before Harry, Royce and Jason awoke and could therefore avoid a tirade of awkward questions regarding his whereabouts and just exactly what had happened to him and Lucy. Of course the answer wasn't a happy one and he would have to tell the group about finding the body, a series of events that he didn't hurriedly wish to recount.

Will stretched out his arm in attempt to reach his phone but he was just millimetres away from reaching it when he slipped and jerked suddenly. Within a couple of seconds Lucy, who had been sleeping soundly with a light smile on her face, began to stir. Will decided to admit defeat and removed his arm, picking up his phone in the process. It was almost lunch time and he had slept in far later than he'd originally thought.

'Good morning,' came Lucy's calm voice in his right ear, 'did you sleep alright?' Will rolled over to face Lucy. Her hair looked slightly messy but otherwise she looked just as wonderful as she had the previous night.

'Very well, considering.' A dark look came over Lucy's face for a brief moment, as if events of the previous night had only just returned to her. She very quickly smiled and sat up.

'Coffee?' She asked while stretching her arms. Will yawned and nodded, stretching himself. Lucy stood up, climbed over Will and off the bed and walked out of the small room.

Will went to join her but quickly realised that he wasn't wearing his shirt, he must have removed it in a moment of near-consciousness. A quick scan of the floor resulted in him finding it near to the door. He picked it up, put it on and quickly did up the buttons. He walked through to the main room. Lucy was standing by the kitchenette, two mugs in her hands and the kettle boiling. She placed the mugs on the almost-clean work top and started to rummage in the cupboard for coffee filters.

'Don't think we have much milk left, might have to have it sort of dark.'

'That's fine.' Will smiled and seated himself on the sofa.

The coffee was made and they quickly drank it together while discussing possible plans for the day. Will suggested the pool, the beach or perhaps that nice café again for a spot of lunch. Lucy thought for a moment before suggesting that they returned to the Temple Bar. Will offered to make a picnic before they went if that was the case, he could stop off at the supermarket on the way back to his apartment and get what was necessary. Lucy seemed to like the idea so once coffee had been drunk and they'd agreed to meet at twelve, Will started the walk back to his apartment.

He had ninety minutes to get back to Lucy but the time he had to get back to his apartment was considerably shorter. Harry and the others wouldn't be in bed for that much longer and if they awoke to find that Will wasn't there then he would simply never hear the end of it. The journey to get food was more important though and the supermarket always seemed to take a long time to navigate, even if you knew exactly what you needed to buy. Will's list was short: freshly baked bread, butter, various kinds of meats, cheese and some salad.

Corzones Island's supermarket had regular deliveries from the mainland and was always well-stocked. It was also surprisingly large, probably bigger than it needed to be and it always seemed to be busy. They were open for twenty four hours every day and catered to as many drunken people wishing for a snack after a heavy night in a club as it did sober people after one of their daytime meals. When Will arrived it was probably in the quietest state it would be all day, most people still hadn't surfaced after the previous night and weren't yet aware of the horror that occurred in the town centre. Will forced the thought from his head, deciding that he didn't want to even think about the events of the previous night, at least not the ones that occurred in the town centre.

Will's first destination in the supermarket was the fruit and vegetable aisle and he found himself trying to find the best quality lettuce that he could. As he rummaged through, his instinct told him that he wasn't quite alone. He looked around and saw a tall, bald man in large wire-framed glasses, whose attire seemed to be an attempt to fit in with the general fashion of the island but failed miserably. He was in his thirties, maybe forties and spoke with a clear English accent, hiding all trace of which region he came from.

'Sorry if I startled you sir,' Will considered the strange man for a moment and saw a pile of pristine leaflets in his right hand. He knew exactly what this was about, 'may I have a moment of your time to discuss your experiences on the island and perhaps offer you a new perspective?' Will sighed, God never had a place in his life and that certainly wasn't going to change on Corzones Island.

'I'm sorry, this isn't a good time.' Will turned away and hoped that this would end the conversation but the same instinct that had originally alerted him to the man, told him that he was still standing there. The man took a moment to gather himself before continuing.

'My name is Father Merco, tell me young man, are you aware of the ungodly things that happen on this island?' Will shook his head, he was usually polite but this man was really starting to annoy him.

'That's what this island's for, it isn't going to change so why bother?' Father Merco didn't have an immediate response and after a moment he thanked Will for his time anyway before dashing away.

Will chose a lettuce for his sandwiches and turned to head to the next aisle when the worst thing he could possibly have imagined happened. He found himself facing Jason and Royce. He sighed as they walked up to him.

'Here he is,' said Royce, loudly, 'and just where did you spend your night? Harry was worried about you.'

'I was alright.' Will could feel himself going red, these two had reached their own conclusion about what had happened and Will knew that whatever he said, nothing was going to change that.

'I'm sure you were. Jason managed to calm Harry down, he pointed out that the bird you were with in the club probably wouldn't try to eat you afterwards.' The annoyance that Will had felt when Merco was speaking to him hadn't abated and with every word uttered by Royce, it grew. He knew that he had to keep calm.

'It wasn't like that.' The denial sounded pathetic even to him, and he knew that it was true. From Jason and Royce's perspective, Will had left the club with a girl and hadn't returned that night. On Corzones Island, that only really did merit one logical conclusion. Will's pleas of innocence fell on deaf ears and he decided that he didn't want to tell them exactly what had happened the previous evening just yet. He could only relive the events of finding the body once and would much rather that Harry was around when he did so.

Royce and Jason stayed with Will for the entire time that he was at the supermarket and for the walk home. Topics discussed included how lucky Will was to 'get some' when they hadn't, details of what he and Lucy had 'done' (questions were asked in far more detail than necessary) and if Will would be alright with one of the others 'trying it on' with her that night. The last point annoyed Will further and he ended up snapping at them to leave her alone. After that questions turned more in the direction of 'do you love her or what?'

Mercifully the walk to the apartment came to an end and Will managed to get some time alone while in the shower. A few more comments came through the bathroom door but Will chose to ignore them. He emerged from the shower and dried himself off before brushing his teeth and getting dressed. He'd chosen a different pair of shorts and a nice shirt that Harry had given him on his previous birthday, it was tie-dyed red and had cost more than Will would usually consider spending on a single piece of clothing.

Will emerged from the sanctuary of the bathroom to a few more sniping comments from Royce. However he was quickly silenced by Harry, who had emerged from his long sleep and decided to battle through his hangover. His eyes were only half open and he held a large, strong cup of coffee in his hand. He saw Will and grinned, Jason and Royce had clearly spoken to him already. 'Good morning little brother,' he suddenly seemed a little more awake, 'I hear we had a good night last night?'

'Whatever those two told you, it isn't true.' Will spoke firmly and hoped that his brother would shut his friends up.

'So you didn't stay out all night, only just getting back?' Will had no response, that part *was* true despite being out of context. 'That's what I thought.' Harry grinned again and quickly reassured Will that he had only been joking. Apparently Jason had already told Harry of Will's protests.

After some more joking, the matter was finally settled as a serious atmosphere came over the room and Will related the tale of the previous night's events. Even Royce appeared to look a little awkward, regretting the jokes he'd made and at one point he even said something that almost sounded like an apology. Will accepted and thanked him. Not long afterwards, Jason and Royce suddenly left, claiming that they'd forgotten something while at the supermarket but Will knew that this was of Harry's design to get them out of the way while he spoke properly to Will.

They both sat out on the balcony and talked across the table, which was still covered in empty bottles and cigarette ends from the previous night. Harry had a bottle of water cradled on his arms, he occasionally took a sip as they talked.
'Are you sure you're alright now?' Will nodded, not entirely sure if that was a truthful answer. 'What have you got planned today? Are you seeing Lucy?'
'Yes. That's why I was at the supermarket, I'm making us a picnic. We're going back up to the dig I told you about yesterday.' Harry laughed.
'Archaeology? That's work to you! You're supposed to be on holiday.'
'I know but I enjoy it. It was Lucy's idea anyway.' Harry grinned.
'Are you sure there isn't anything happening between you two?'
Will started to protest again but then calmed, realising that he could talk to Harry properly and it wouldn't be shared with the other two.
'Well, we kissed after the club. A bit.'
'You made a move? I'm proud of you Will. It just shows that anything at all can happen on this island.' Will shook his head. Really Lucy had kissed him, he had just gone along with it but he was glad that he had.

The conversation with Harry lasted for a while longer, until Will saw the time and realised that he would have to hurry if he was to keep his appointment with Lucy. He dashed inside the apartment and to the kitchenette, making the sandwiches as neatly but as quickly as possible. Harry decided that he would return to bed for an hour or so and vanished into his room along with his bottle of water. Will looked at the time and saw that he only had fifteen minutes to get to the town centre. The sandwiches were thrown into a bag and he dashed out of the door, shouting goodbye to Harry but receiving no reply as he left.

At almost midday, the island had started to awaken properly. People were making their way towards the various attractions that they had chosen to fill their day with: pools, beaches, the theme park, cafés and some were even going to bars for an early start. It took Will a moment to realise that Lucy's decision to return to the temple effectively meant that they would be spending their whole day in a bar. He didn't care but suspected that Amerigo or the Professor's generosity would result in him drinking far earlier than he would do normally. Nevertheless, he pushed on and eventually arrived at the town centre.

The scene was very different to how it had been when Will had sped away on the back of a Security buggy. Part of the reason that he and Lucy had chosen to meet there was that they felt that seeing it in a normal state would give them a kind of closure. As Will looked around the square, he felt the complete opposite. He immediately identified the exact spot that the body had been lying in. Now it was just a normal part of the town centre and plenty of people were passing by, they probably knew that a body had been found but they'd never know that they were walking over and around the place that it had been. The Security Officers had said that they wanted to clear everything up as quickly as possible and they had done. Not even twelve hours had passed but to Corzones Island it was already a memory, an echo of the past that doubtlessly the management would wish to forget entirely. For the first time, Will realised that the girl must have been killed for a reason and that somebody had killed her. Somewhere on the same island was a murderer. Where had they gone once they'd killed the girl? Back to where they were staying? Or were they still around, watching events unfold from the darkness. Had they seen him and Lucy together? The thought made him shiver. The one thing that Will was certain of was that now he'd met Lucy, there was no chance that he was going to let what had happened ruin his holiday. If he had a problem with it, he'd talk to the Security

Officer who had told him to phone, or better yet still, Professor Loch, who seemed to have an answer for everything. After that there was Harry, who was the most caring and understanding person in the world when his friends weren't around.

Will didn't notice Lucy arrive, he was too lost in his own thoughts and concerns. She tapped him on the shoulder and made him jump as he suddenly returned to the present. Yet again she looked wonderful, wearing a summery dress that still seemed to be practical enough for spending the afternoon at an archaeology site, she also wore a large straw hat. Will hugged her briefly before they decided to begin the journey into the jungle and up the hill to find the temple. Will hoped that the events of the previous night wouldn't affect the day and as he and Lucy walked together, Will felt calm for the first time since he had awoken.

Fifteen

Waking up next to Will had been a perfect start to the day for Lucy. She was certain that they'd hugged all night and it comforted her in just the way that she had needed. She hoped that it had the same effect on him. Being out of bed for only seconds, Lucy had realised that Sofia still hadn't made it home and wondered if she'd see her friend at all that day. Plans with Will were immediately made and after he'd drunk a coffee (Lucy had had her customary tea but had made a note of Will's choice the previous day) he'd left, promising to make lunch. Lucy wanted to return to the dig, not just because she had enjoyed it there yesterday but also because she felt that being around the Professor and Amerigo, as well as Will of course, would make her feel better. Security had suggested that if she wanted to leave the island at any time before her departure date because of what had happened then it was an option and she wouldn't be charged, she just had to notify them. Will was staying and that was enough to convince Lucy that she wasn't going anywhere.

She had toasted some bread for her breakfast and had eaten it with a generous spread of butter and another cup of tea. Sofia had returned and looked slightly worse for wear. Apparently she hadn't had much sleep as Karl snored quite loudly. Lucy didn't care, she was glad that Sofia hadn't come back last night as she didn't want her friend to reach any wrong conclusions about her and Will. Sofia decided she was going for a nap and Lucy went for her shower.

She stood in the bathroom on her own after she had showered and looked into the mirror as she brushed her hair. It was only at that point that Lucy remembered she and Will had kissed. The thought made her smile for a moment before she considered how quickly Will had left after his coffee. Did he regret it or was he embarrassed? Did he even remember it? They'd both been drinking all afternoon so amnesia was a possibility. It was probably just another drunken kiss. But then again, he had agreed to meet her again and even sounded like he wanted to. And he'd stayed with her all night just to make sure that she was alright after what they'd seen. Maybe Will was different. Maybe...

'No, you're being silly.' Lucy's reflection silenced her thoughts and she continued to ready herself for the day.

She left her apartment and immediately put on her sunglasses as there wasn't a single cloud in the sky. She'd decided to apply sun cream before leaving and was glad that she had done, the sun's rays battered down on her and the heat immediately felt intense. She'd packed a bottle of water into her bag and knew straight away that she'd drink it all very quickly. Dehydration was something that people were often warned about on Corzones Island but took very little notice of until it was too late and the majority of people admitted to the medical centre were usually suffering for just that reason. There were even posters about it up around the island as well as 'free water' stations. It was perhaps a losing battle though as most of the island's population were far more interested in drinking alcohol than water. Lucy had felt very thirsty for a great deal of the previous day and knew that after the heavy nights' drinking she was at risk.

When she arrived in the town centre, she saw that Will was already there and noticed the place he was staring at, it was where the body had been. She walked up to him and tapped him on the shoulder, he jumped quite violently but immediately calmed when he saw who it was. It had been nearly exactly a day since the two of them had met at the fountain but it seemed to have been so much longer ago, already Will felt like an old and reliable friend, if not more than that. They quickly agreed to move, deciding that they didn't want to stay in the town centre for any longer. They walked up the hill, past all of the shops that they had looked in the previous afternoon.

After entering the jungle and finally, some shade, Lucy decided to remove the bottle of water from her bag and have a drink. She offered to share with Will who was relieved, having forgotten to bring drinks to go with their picnic. It wasn't long before the two of them were entirely alone, accompanied only by the quiet thud of music in the distance. Lucy had become more used to it now but still noticed it on occasion. From up here all of the different sounds and songs faded into one, single consistent drum beat that had no end.

They eventually decided to stop for food in a small clearing, just off the jungle path. The floor was dry but a layer of grass made it comfortable to sit on. Will produced the sandwiches and they started to eat. A lot of effort had gone into them and Lucy had to admire how much dedication Will put into something as simple as lunch. He'd also brought a bag of crisps and an orange each. They ate slowly and talked, not about anything special and certainly not about anything that had happened the previous night. They talked about home and their families, the lives that they had left for two weeks on the island. Will spent most of his days dating and cataloguing various artefacts in a quiet lab somewhere. Lucy would normally have expected somebody to find that job boring but not Will, the enthusiasm in his voice when he told her about it was unparalleled.

The food was all eaten and the contents of the bottle of water sunk to well below a quarter. They decided that it was time to continue their walk up the hill and to the Temple Bar. It wasn't too far away now and they knew that the Professor must be there by that point. They recommenced their walk, sweating quite a bit in the heat. As they were almost at the bar somebody dashed past them, clearly in a great hurry. Lucy only caught a glimpse as he rushed off down the path but she could have sworn that it was Karl. She dismissed this however, Karl was probably with Sofia by now and they'd no doubt found somewhere to continually kiss for every hour that the day would permit them.

They eventually reached the bar. Amerigo and Professor Loch were talking quietly about something they didn't wish anybody else to hear, as made apparent by Amerigo clearing his throat and the Professor quickly looking around to see who had joined them. 'Good afternoon you two!' He smiled politely at them both, 'I trust that you managed to sleep well?' Lucy nodded, as did Will who started to go red as Lucy looked at him. Did he regret staying with her? All they had done was hugged through the night. 'Good,' said the Professor, interrupting Lucy's thoughts, 'I have a few things for you to do, if you'd be interested in helping around the site today? I'd like to start excavating by one of the walls, just a small trench you understand?'

The Professor continued to brief them both for the day while Amerigo watched from behind the bar, he wasn't as cheery as he had been the previous day and at one point when Lucy met his eyes, all she saw was concern. Will enthusiastically grabbed a trowel out of one of the Professor's bags and began to dig while Lucy stood by, wearing gloves so she could bag up and label anything of interest that he found. They began by an ornate piece of wall that was located about thirty yards away from the bar. Patterns that had been mostly worn away by the centuries stood on the golden stone, Lucy admired them.

Before long, Steve had arrived with another case of the Professor's, presumably containing more equipment. Loch thanked him and took the case, opening it with a key that he produced from his pocket. He quickly rummaged inside and produced one thing, a small device with a purple light on it. Steve walked over to Will and Lucy and began to help with the digging, asking them about their night. Will began to reel off the events of the body to Steve, Lucy decided not to listen, concluding that hearing the story again wouldn't help her banish it from her mind. She looked over at the Professor who was holding the device that he had removed from his case. He held it close to him and pressed a button before waiting. Long seconds passed before the device bleeped and Loch quickly pocketed it and returned to Amerigo, who had been tapping away at his laptop behind the bar. The Professor whispered something to him which made him seem even more concerned, before walking over to Lucy, Will and Steve with a smile.

'How are you managing?' Loch asked as he inspected the trench that was beginning to form in the ground. Will was sweating and in need of a break so he stood up and walked to the bar, ordering a glass of water. Lucy joined him and ordered the same and within a flash, Amerigo had filled them two glasses of mineral water and garnished them with a lemon. He offered ice, which they both gratefully accepted. They sat at a table and drank their water as Will slowly regained his breath. Lucy told Will in a hushed voice what she'd seen the Professor do with the device and he said that he had no idea what the piece of equipment could have been but pointed out that a lot of what Loch had seemed to be 'pretty advanced stuff' and that some of it seemed to be at a prototype stage. Lucy nodded in agreement but couldn't help feel that it was something else, that the Professor was perhaps not all that he seemed.

Sixteen

The interview room was too warm and despite asking multiple times, Powell had promised Kirshner that the air conditioning was working perfectly. He gave up in the end and decided to focus his attention on the more important matter of Franko, who had literally been left to sweat it out for some time now. Kirshner sat opposite Franko and next to Powell, who had assured him that he would remain silent throughout the course of the interview. Powell was obviously a good man and just as good at his job but this was Kirshner's case and only he could wrap it up as quickly as he wanted to. Powell had learned that protests were useless but remained professional and helpful, Kirshner admired him for that and had to admit that if he were in the Chief's position then he may have lost his temper.

Franko was still stunned at the news of Zoë's death and continuously protested his innocence. The more he did so, the more Kirshner believed and even felt sorry for him. His time cooking in the interview room hadn't improved his already terrible odour: a mixture of sweat, sleep and alcohol. As Kirshner and Powell had sat down he had started to tremble, his hands shaking. Kirshner was sitting eye-to-eye with the DJ and saw that he had been crying in the time that he had been left alone.
'Mister Young, this interview is being recorded. You are here in regards to the murder of Zoë Parker...'
'It wasn't me!' Kirshner chose to ignore the protest and continue.
'...who died last night. Where were you immediately before you started your set, Mister Young?' Franko took a moment to consider his answer.
'I... I was walking. Zoë and I had argued earlier on and I needed to clear my head.' This wasn't going to be simple, unless he had an alibi.
'Were you with anybody?' The answer was of course, a 'No'.
'I needed to be alone. You know what Inspector, I've met a lot of girls on this island and they all want a piece of me, the "legendary" DJ Freedom. Zoë was different, she cared about me, not my job, not my credit card but me, as a person. Franko Young. When we argued, I hated it and I stormed off. Later on she came to the club to find me, she was upset about what had happened and wanted to talk but I'd drunk too much by then so she left. I went after her a

moment later and couldn't find her so I just walked to sober up. I at least wanted to be in a good state when I saw her again.'
'And were you?' Asked Kirshner.
'I never saw her again,' Franko was struggling not to cry, that at least was clear, 'and now I never will.' He buried his head in his hands, occasionally emitting a sob. This was enough to convince Kirshner to look for a second suspect but unfortunately not enough to allow him to release Franko just yet.

'You've changed your mind, haven't you?' Kirshner hated coffee machine chat but could tell that Powell needed to hear it straight away.
'Yes. I don't think he did it. I'm not releasing him until we have to though.' Powell nodded.
'I really didn't want you to bring him in.'
'I could tell. And perhaps you were right Powell.' This was painfully awkward, Kirshner took a moment, 'I'm sorry.' Powell nodded in an understanding manner.
'This will be easier if we work together. I've been a soldier and a police officer in the past so I know what I'm doing here. I'm not just a jumped-up bouncer.'
'Yeah, you're right.' Kirshner said, 'What now then?' Powell thought for a moment.
'What about the people that found the body?'
'A scientist and a couple of kids wasn't it?'
'That's right. Well, an archaeologist and a local originally, the others arrived after.' Kirshner considered for a moment, he'd read the reports of their interviews and it all seemed to be fine. Their stories added up and they'd all been entirely cooperative. Where is the logic in committing a murder and then calling it in?

Kirshner drank his coffee while sitting on one of the sofas in the open plan office. It was much busier than it had been when he had first arrived and everybody seemed to be doing something. He listened and heard some of the callouts that they were receiving. It was nothing surprising, a bit of vandalism here, a drunken fight there and so on. From a Security perspective, the island was already in what at home would be referred to as 'Saturday night mode'. It was however only the mid-afternoon and Kirshner was sure that things would only get worse as the day progressed. He knew that he'd never be able to work on the island full time and suddenly found a new level of respect for Powell, who he was now

100

willing to treat as an equal, a partner. There was no fast route out of this case and off the island. Meera would have to wait, continue to play the unhappy and abandoned wife while lying in the sun, reading her book and relaxing. He'd managed to phone her and although she complained, she seemed to be absolutely fine. She'd fallen asleep again not long after Kirshner had left and stayed in bed until about ten. He promised her that he would return soon but wasn't just going to abandon the case.

He'd been so certain that Franko was the killer, when he had been speaking to Argyll it had made so much sense: The DJ had fallen out with his girlfriend, squeeze, whatever she was and killed her. His interview with Franko had seriously diminished his certainty and then he noticed that other things just didn't add up. Where would Franko have got a poisoned blade from and why would he have used that? Surely it wouldn't have been a planned murder if it was just a couple's dispute, more of a sudden reaction that had gone wrong. Franko had made the one mistake that Kirshner had learned you shouldn't make on the island. He'd fallen in love. Whether he knew it or not was a different story but what he'd seen in the interview room wasn't shock or general upset, he was grieving.

He found Powell and decided to buy him an apologetic lunch, the Chief accepted and offered to show him some of the best places to go. Kirshner didn't realise until after he had made the offer that he didn't have any idea where they would go or even what currency was used on the island. Luckily, it turned out to be what he had on the mainland and he was able to carry out the gesture.

Powell drove the buggy and they headed towards the town centre to choose a café. Kirshner was thankful that he was finally able to relax, sleep may not yet be an option but something to eat would be much appreciated. He had managed to find five minutes to eat a chocolate bar out of the vending machine in HQ but that was all he'd had since waking up. He wondered if the cuisine of Corzones Island would be as varied and enjoyable as it had been on the mainland but he quickly learned that it wouldn't be. Around the town centre he saw various fast food eateries as well as places advertising 'full English all-day breakfasts'. Reaching the conclusion that he wouldn't be having paella for lunch, Kirshner settled on a local café that Powell had recommended, Café Solar.

The café was run by a harmless looking local who must have been in his sixties. Kirshner had to admit that he made a very good breakfast. Sausages, bacon, mushrooms, tomato, hash browns, egg and beans filled the plate, threatening to overflow. Powell slowly poked away at his but Inspector Kirshner decided to discard his manners to satisfy his hunger and shovelled the food into his mouth, hardly giving himself time to breathe in the process. As he started to slow, Powell started a conversation with him, not about the murder or even his work, just about life. Kirshner's had been fairly simple: he'd wanted to be in the Police from when he was very young and every day of his life led up to the one that he finally joined. He'd worked hard and made his way up through the ranks and, while very proud of what he had achieved, there was still something missing for some reason.

Powell's life had been far more interesting. He'd served in the army but resigned after about seven years, when his girlfriend had found out that she was expecting a baby. He'd lived in a state of blissful engagement until he'd discovered that the child wasn't his. He'd left his office job and found his way into the Metropolitan Police. That wasn't for him however, it didn't excite him like the army had but he stuck at it. Eventually he saw that Corzones was looking for people to join its own Security force and so he signed up. He'd been made the chief within two years and had worked hard almost constantly in that position from there onwards.

As the two lawmen ate, a man with a bald head entered carrying a pile of leaflets. He walked over to the owner of the café and loudly introduced himself as Father Merco. His mission was to clean up the island of Corzones. Powell made a joke about him being here for the same reason as they were but Kirshner was too preoccupied with the strange man. Why was he on Corzones Island? Surely he didn't believe that he was really going to make a difference? There weren't enough of these people in a sober state for him to get through to. Nevertheless, after his speech Father Merco went from table to table and distributed his leaflets. The owner of the café looked on, a stern expression on his face. Father Merco wasn't able to engage anybody properly in conversation and with a regretful shake of the head, he left.

They finished their lunch and Kirshner settled the bill, as he had promised. They both made their way back to Security HQ, stopping so that Kirshner could buy a newspaper on the way. He needed to have some connection with the real world and this appeared to be his best option. They arrived back at HQ and Powell went to check how other things were developing around the island that day. Kirshner again found himself sitting on the sofa, attempting to read his newspaper but finding that his mind was far too preoccupied with the case that he had been thrown into.

As time passed, Kirshner realised that he would have to let Franko go. He ordered that a close watch be kept on the DJ, just in case he was smarter and a better actor than he'd been given credit for. He watched from the sofa as Franko was led out and gave an encouraging nod as their eyes met. Doubtless Franko would be posed a hundred questions from Argyll upon his release but that wasn't Kirshner's problem. The truth was that his problems were becoming more and more apparent with every passing minute. He had an unsolved murder and only a few thin pieces of evidence to go on at best. He looked at the board with all of the case's information stuck on to it and his eyes moved over to the pictures of the Professor and Amerigo.

Seventeen

Karl had awoken next to Sofia again and smiled. That was two nights together now and he had enjoyed them both immensely. Taking her to Lovers' Cove had been a stroke of genius on his part and she had melted into his arms. He couldn't imagine being with anybody else for the rest of his holiday. Looking over Sofia's shoulder, he could see that she was awake and looked incredibly tired. She groaned.

'I drank too much last night.' She rolled over and looked at him and he had to admit that since Lovers' Cove she had fallen from grace. She still looked beautiful and Karl didn't want to be separated from her at all but her makeup barely hid the signs of tiredness, hangover and heat exhaustion. Karl climbed out of bed, pulled on a pair of trousers and walked to the fridge, producing a bottle of water. He opened the lid and passed it to Sofia, who was struggling to sit up in his bed. She thanked him in a croaky voice and drank deeply.

He walked into the bathroom and locked the door behind him. As he did so, he felt his phone begin to vibrate in his trouser pocket. He knew that the call would be important and answered it straight away. It changed everything, this was no longer a holiday for him and he had a clear list of things to do. The first of which was to send Sofia away, he would rejoin her later. She wasn't impressed but still kissed him before she left. Her breath was terrible but then he imagined that his own wouldn't be much better.

After a quick shower, Karl dressed himself in mostly green clothes, they might help to hide him when he needed them to. He sat down and had a large breakfast, consisting of toast and cereal, with a glass of orange juice. He then returned to the bathroom and brushed his teeth and styled his hair, with the customary precision. After studying a detailed map of the island, he left his apartment with the exact knowledge of where he had to go.

He arrived in the town centre at first and witnessed the furore of something involving a dead body. Rumours had apparently being going around that a girl had been found there. Everything started to make sense, that was the reason he had been called and given the instructions. He felt sorry for the girl that had been killed but there was no sign of her now, Security must have hurried to move her body during the night because rumours were all that he heard as he listened to various conversations. Nobody knew of any actual sightings of a body and none of the stories he was hearing added up. Karl snapped back to what he had to do, he didn't have time to stand around the town centre listening to idle gossip.

He headed up the hill from the town centre, past the shops and into the jungle. It wasn't long before Karl was all alone, accompanied only by the occasional birdsong and the ever-increasing thumping of music. He knew that he had a considerable walk ahead of him and chose a speedy pace, ducking off the path on the odd occasion that he heard anybody else approaching. He thought it best that nobody saw him in the jungle, not if he didn't want to raise suspicion. At one point he heard a buggy approaching and quickly jumped behind a bush, he looked out to see the buggy pass, containing a rep along with his target, Professor Loch.

This sighting had confirmed to Karl that the information he had been given over the phone was correct. He continued his walk up the hill, ducking out of the way again about fifteen minutes later as the same buggy came down the hill, this time with no Professor in the passenger seat. This was a good thing, it meant that there were fewer people at the location to spot him.

Eventually, Karl made it to the Temple Bar, the sound of calypso music and dazzling coloured lights that were hung around trees confirmed this. He found a large piece of ruin to hide himself behind and peered around it. The Professor and another man, who looked local and was standing behind the bar, were talking to each other.
'I said exactly what we planned.' The local man's voice was loud, despite his attempts to quieten it.
'Good,' said the Professor cautiously, 'now what do you know about this cult?' The barman breathed deeply before responding.
'A man named Svoros, he is involved with them. He came to me yesterday evening and told me that I should leave the island if I didn't wish to join him.' The Professor looked around thoughtfully and Karl quickly ducked back behind the rock but he knew that he had been too late. The Professor must have seen him, there was no doubt about it. Karl decided to not risk being caught and ran into the nearest clump of bushes. He kept running, knowing that he had

105

to get what he had heard back to the town. Somehow his running downhill and through bushes led him to the path. He ran past two people who were walking in the opposite direction, he didn't have time to see who they were. 'I've heard enough,' he thought to himself. He had confirmed what he had been told to.

As he neared the bottom of the hill, Karl's phone vibrated in his trouser pocket again. He answered it.
'There is a man of God on this island. His name is Father Merco and I don't think he'd approve of the Professor, I want you to find him and make sure that he doesn't. He's bald and around the town centre.' The phone went dead and Karl promptly headed towards his destination, working out what he would say. He knew why the Professor was on the island and decided that it would make wonderful ammunition in turning Father Merco against Professor Loch, this was an ingenious idea on the leader's part and would probably provide the distraction that was needed.

Karl was in the town centre, he looked around carefully, trying to find this Father Merco. His search didn't last long as he saw somebody that couldn't be anybody else walking out of a café, looking like they didn't quite fit in and holding a clump of leaflets in his hand. On the walk down the hill, Karl had chosen his plan of attack and now it was time to put it into action. He clumsily dashed over to Merco.
'Father,' he said, allowing a slight hint of desperation to sink into his voice, 'please Father, I need to talk to you.'

Merco was instantly suckered in, pleased that not only was somebody wishing to talk to him but also that they had sought him out. They walked together to a quieter area in silence and found a bench.
'What is it that concerns you, my son?'
'On this island Father, there is an unquestionable evil. A man who wishes to disturb the devil himself.' Karl continued to talk in much the same vein for a few minutes, telling stories of the Professor's attempts to unearth pure evil and use the power for himself. Merco had been softened up and now it was time to deliver the final blow. 'Father, are you aware of who the Supers are?' A look of horror flashed in Merco's eyes, he knew exactly what Karl meant, as was expected. The various churches had a habit of following Supers wherever they went, condemning everything that they did. Karl

106

had studied the Supers, he knew what they were like and how they operated and he knew that they wouldn't understand what was going to be achieved on Corzones Island.

The result was exactly what Karl had hoped for, Father Merco was going to go to the temple ruins to speak to Professor Loch about the errors of his ways. He'd had only one question:
'How do you know of the Supers?' Karl had been prepared for this question with an answer that wasn't too far away from the truth. 'My brother,' he replied, 'vanished a few years ago while away in Ireland. These Supernatural Investigators were involved, I believe that they chose not to save him so that they could add to their evil knowledge.' Father Merco nodded and muttered that he was sorry. He took his leave, apologetically insisting that he needed to see the Professor as soon as possible.

Karl took a moment to sit on the bench and smile to himself, he'd done good work and now he decided that he could devote a moment to pleasure. He texted Sofia, promising her just as much of a wonderful time the next time that they met. He even suggested that they returned to the cave in Lovers' Cove for more of what had happened last time. Karl had liked it and he knew that Sofia had too. The free stay on the island and being able to avenge his brother should be payment enough but Sofia was another benefit.

Sofia took a few minutes to text back, her unhappiness had been forgotten and she was very much looking forward to seeing him again. Karl had to allow a smile before standing and walking towards the place his instructions had been coming from. He needed to speak to Svoros face to face. He walked into the busy town centre and looked around, all of these people were ignorant of what would soon be happening, of the significant part that the island would be playing in the future of the world and how they would all benefit. In a few weeks, maybe even days time, they would all know not only the legend of the Velza but also the truth behind it.

Karl arrived at his destination: Café Solar. He entered to see the busy café and Svoros, its owner, standing behind the counter. Svoros gave a half smile at the sight of Karl.

'I saw that you were busy and thought that you may need some help in the back room?' Svoros nodded and they both walked through the curtained doorway and into the back.

'It is done?' asked Svoros.

'Exactly as you instructed. Father Merco is on his way to talk to the Professor as we speak. The knowledge that he was a Super came as no real surprise to him.' Svoros smiled.

'And what did you learn from your trip up there?'

'Amerigo told him about you, as you suspected. That was all I heard before they saw me.'

'They saw you?' Svoros sounded angry and even a bit sinister.

'For less than a second. They couldn't have identified me.' Svoros sighed.

'You had better hope so Karl. You've done good work today, go back to that girl. Remember that you will be needed again soon.' Karl nodded and left. 'Thank you very much.' Svoros shouted after Karl, cheerily as he walked through the café. Keeping up appearances of course, nobody could know what was going to happen yet.

He walked slowly to Sofia's apartment, enjoying the heat of the sun and the atmosphere of the island. It was hardly noticeable that anything had happened the previous night and people were happy. Every moment of happiness, every sound of joy meant more to Karl than anybody could comprehend. The island was the world's hub of positivity and nobody like Professor Loch or Father Merco could be allowed to ruin that. Great things would happen very soon.

Karl arrived at Sofia's apartment, she was alone as Lucy had gone to meet that strange-looking Will again. Idly making conversation, Karl asked Sofia where they had gone.

'They've gone to see that Professor again,' she answered, to Karl's horror, 'Will used to be one of his students so they're helping him at the temple.' No! This couldn't be true! Karl knew from that moment onwards that Sofia wasn't pleasure anymore, she was business. As soon as Svoros found out, and he would, he'd want Karl to get as close to Sofia as possible and then close to Lucy and Will. Fate had dealt him a cruel hand but he was too far into the game to fold now. He smiled as he and Sofia began their walk towards Lovers' Cove. At least he could enjoy this afternoon.

Eighteen

The first thing that all reps spotted on the notice board in the morning was that there had been a body found in the town centre. There was no doubt that it was a murder but the powers that be wanted it to be kept as quiet as possible. If anybody asked then Steve wasn't allowed to say anything but 'an incident was being investigated'. It wasn't even a convincing denial but Steve's hangover was too strong for him to really care about island politics. Luckily customer relations weren't part of his job today as he was soon to rejoin the Professor at the Temple Bar for another day of archaeological interest. Steve had to admit that under Professor Loch's guidance, he was beginning to learn the trade.

He hadn't known anything about the murder when he was out the previous night. The Professor had left the club in a real hurry, as if he'd had somewhere to be. Steve hadn't really paid attention to this as the evening was completely dominated by Sarah who had drunk as much as he had. They had kissed a few times and continued to do so for the rest of the night, getting more and more passionate as time progressed. Before they knew it, half-six in the morning had arrived and DJ Freedom had ended his set. They left the club with their arms linked, the other reps who had survived until the end were gossiping loudly about how they had ended up together. Steve didn't care, he was enjoying this night more than any other he'd spent on Corzones. He and Sarah had both ended up at his hotel room with more to drink.

The next morning a headache was the first thing that Steve had registered, the second was the various bits of discarded clothing that scattered the floor. He looked to his left and saw that Sarah was still asleep. The next thing to gain his attention was his watch, he picked it up and looked it to see that it was nearly one in the afternoon. Without waking Sarah he climbed out of bed and slipped on his discarded pair of boxers before slowly dragging himself to the bathroom. He was far too warm so he splashed some cold water on to his face, it had the secondary effect of waking him up properly. He looked at his own reflection in the mirror and gave it a knowing smile, it returned the gesture instantly.

He jumped slightly when the door opened. He looked around to see Sarah wearing his dressing gown.

'Morning you. I trust we had a good night?' Steve nodded, while loading his toothbrush with toothpaste. 'I'd love to stay for a bit longer but I'm supposed to induct people into block D in a couple of hours.' Steve feigned disappointment that she had to leave but the truth was that he wanted to be alone so that he could prepare himself for the day. 'Perhaps we should do the same later? I'm only on duty for an hour so as soon as you're done perhaps we could find each other?' Steve was struggling to believe what he was hearing, surely this was just a one-off thing? That's how Corzones Island worked. Still, Steve agreed to meet as soon as Professor Loch didn't need him anymore. Sarah wrote her phone number on to the back of an information leaflet, got dressed and left, leaving Steve with a peck on the cheek as she walked out of the door.

As soon as Sarah had left, Steve showered quickly, dressed and phoned the Professor's bungalow. It turned out that he was still there and hadn't yet started his day properly either, so Steve promised to pick him up on a buggy as soon as he had checked in at Rep HQ and picked one up. Reps all stayed in the same hotel block which was located very close to the HQ building so Steve only had a short walk. The heat didn't help his dehydration whatsoever but he didn't care. When he arrived at HQ he would have a glass of water before heading to the beach bungalows. He intended to work as little as possible that day and was sure that the Professor wouldn't object. He couldn't imagine a man of even the Professor's constitution wanting to do a full day's work at these temperatures after a late night out.

It was when he arrived at HQ that he began to feel that something was wrong. Firstly, he was asked if he knew anything about the murder by a fairly new rep who was exiting the building as he entered it. Secondly, he was asked if the Professor had told him anything yet today and when he explained that he hadn't yet seen the Professor, he was met with disappointment. He then walked into the break room, which contained the notice board. In the middle of it, in large red letters was the sign that explained everything:

ALL REPS PLEASE PAY ATTENTION

*Last night at approximately 3:30 a body was found
in the town centre area. An investigation is
underway and our Security team is cooperating with
the Police.*

*We have no reason to believe that there will be
any other related incidents. If you are asked at all
by anybody staying on the island, you MUST NOT
discuss the issue with them in detail. Tell them that
there was an incident and that it is being investigated.*

Any further questions should be directed to Karen

Steve read and re-read the note. The time was almost exactly the
point that Professor Loch had left the club and the fact that he had
been asked about the Professor by other reps confirmed to him that
somehow, the archaeologist was involved. Steve knew that there
would be an explanation and decided to seek it from Loch himself.
He saw Karen in the next room, a conversation with her would be
best avoided so he left quickly through the exit that led to the
buggy parking area. He jumped on a buggy and sped away towards
the bungalows, his head full of questions that he hoped the
Professor would have some answers to. He passed Sarah on his
journey and waved at her as she was heading to HQ to check in for
her induction shift.

He arrived at the Professor's bungalow and knocked on the door,
considering what would be the most tactful way of asking what
had happened. He considered for a moment that it could simply be
a rumour, or that he had come to the wrong conclusion but
somehow Steve knew that Professor Loch would have in some way
been involved. He wasn't the killer or he wouldn't have been free.
Perhaps he'd seen or heard something?

The door was answered quickly by the Professor, who today was
wearing a beige blazer and red trousers.
'Good morn... afternoon Steve,' The Professor seemed calm, 'I have
two more cases that need taking up to the site and unfortunately
one of them is too large to travel with a passenger as well. Could
you perhaps take me up there and then return for the second case?'
Steve assured the Professor that he didn't have any problem with

111

that, assisting an archaeological dig was far more enjoyable than working as a normal rep.

It was on the journey up the hill that Steve finally asked Loch about the previous night and this murder.
'Rumours have started again? They seem to follow me everywhere. I left the club just after I had said goodbye to you. I'd promised to meet Amerigo for a drink in a smaller bar once he had finished at his own. I met him on the edge of the strip and we walked together to the town centre to see if anywhere was still open there. As we were walking through, we found the body on the ground. It was a girl and she had been stabbed. I went to find help and found that disagreeable doorman from earlier in the evening, unfortunately I also found William and Lucy. For a moment, my judgement lapsed and I told them to come with us and call Security.' So Will and Lucy had seen it too, Steve felt sorry for them. It can't have been a pleasant experience. The Professor continued: 'Security arrived soon after and we all went to the station and were questioned. After that they let us go and I returned to my bungalow.'

The Professor dismissed any further questions, saying that he didn't want to discuss the issue anymore and not long after, they arrived at the Temple Bar. Naturally it was completely empty apart from Amerigo, who was wiping down the tables as they arrived. The sound of the buggy pulling to a halt made him look up. 'Professor! And Steve. Good afternoon to you both.' Steve nodded and the Professor responded with a 'Good afternoon'.

Amerigo and Loch began to talk so Steve went back to his buggy and unloaded the smaller case that they had brought with them. It was incredibly heavy but he managed to get it to a table and place it down. He then walked up to the Professor and asked if he should go and get the other one. Loch nodded and passed the bungalow keys to Steve while saying nothing but a muttered 'Thank you'. Steve walked back to his buggy, noticing that Amerigo and Professor Loch began to speak very quietly to each other. This was the stage where Steve first began to feel that something wasn't right, a slight feeling of suspicion began to come over him but he chose to ignore it.

The journey down the hill felt long to Steve, with so many thoughts running through his head. Amerigo and the Professor obviously had a secret to keep but surely it couldn't be murder? They were both so kind and despite looking, talking and acting like they had no place on the island, they fitted in almost perfectly. Loch had only been there for a day but Steve felt that he was now part of the place and that great discoveries were to be made.

He arrived back at the bungalow, unlocked the door and opened it slowly. He saw the case immediately, it was the same design as the others but considerably larger. It hadn't arrived with the Professor and apparently he had taken delivery of it earlier in the morning. Steve's thoughts quickly drifted to the murder again. The Professor had been vague with him and instinct told Steve that there was far more to the whole thing. Allowing the temptation of curiosity to get the better of him, Steve chose to have a quick look around the bungalow. He didn't do anything too intrusive and was careful to leave no evidence that anything had been moved. An almost five minute search provided nothing but a few archaeological papers and the usual paperwork that is left in each apartment, maps, points of interest and so on. Steve elected to turn his attention to the large case that he was to transport up the hill. He could see why the Professor had sent him back for it, the buggy would only just accommodate its sheer size. Again, curiosity began to control Steve and he attempted to open it and see what was inside. There didn't appear to be a lock so it should have been simple to open but for some reason, the latch just wouldn't move. In the end he had no choice but to give up but another question formed in Steve's mind: What kind of archaeological equipment was so secret that it had to be locked away with such complexity? Steve admitted defeat and loaded the case on to the back of his buggy.

The drive back up to the site seemed even slower and contained even more questions than the outbound journey. Steve's thoughts began to taunt him, morphing into possible situations of the Professor and Amerigo committing an unspeakable murder in the darkness. But why? What would be their motivation?

By the time he returned to the bar, Will and Lucy had arrived and were hard at work by a large piece of ruin. Will was digging and seemed to be tired out by the work while Lucy was collecting unearthed shards that may prove to be of some interest. Steve dragged the case off the buggy and into the bar. Despite being larger it felt considerably lighter than the previous one and more fragile. He carefully placed it down next to the table that contained the other. The Professor left his conversation with Amerigo and shouted out a word of thanks. Steve acknowledged him and decided to go and help Will dig for a while.

Will had been grateful for the help and after a while he and Lucy decided to take a break, getting themselves drinks of water and relaxing at a table that was covered by shade. Will didn't look like he was up to much and Steve had to admit that he was impressed by how much he had dug. The trench was probably made more out of love of his profession than actual strength.

Steve's digging continued for some time and every time he looked at Professor Loch, he had been locked in a hushed conversation with Amerigo, apart from at one point when he had rummaged in the larger case and produced a small device that he seemed to inspect on the odd occasion. Eventually, Will and Lucy returned to the trench and began to sort through what Steve had unearthed. The Professor walked over and looked a few minutes later, checking that everything was alright. Will confirmed that he would be happy to dig for a while yet so Professor Loch turned to Steve and told him that if he wanted to finish early he could do. The Professor smiled and with a twinkle in his eye, knowingly told him to catch up on some sleep.

Steve left the site, promising that he would do despite not having any intention of resting. By that time, Sarah would have finished her shift and as soon as he was away from the dig, Steve called her. She answered her phone almost instantly.
'It took you a long time to call, I was starting to think you weren't interested.' The conversation remained light hearted throughout and they decided to get dinner together in one of the island's nicer restaurants. Nowhere was very expensive on the island as they simply wouldn't receive any business but there were a couple of places that did nice food and Steve knew them all well. He and Sarah were to meet on the beach at five and get cocktails from 'The Shack', a small wooden bar located in one of the quieter areas. The food there was good but Sarah said that she'd prefer something in the town and then maybe even another journey to the Temple Bar after that. Steve was happy to go with whatever she wanted, he was in a very good mood and enjoying his time on the island at last.

He returned to his apartment and had his second shower of the day. The digging had made him sweaty and he probably still stank from the previous night anyway. He was very thirsty despite the fact he had drunk water regularly all day. He pulled a large bottle out of the fridge and poured himself a pint, downing it in one and refilling the glass immediately. The second glass lasted slightly longer, accompanying him through the entire process of preparing himself for a night out. He finished the glass just before he cleaned his teeth. His clothes carefully selected and his hair styled, he was ready to leave for the beach.

The beach was a fair walk from his apartment so Steve set off with a good twenty minutes to make the journey. Most of the island's attractions were located in one area and all within a short walking distance from the town centre. The only places that required more of a walk were the luxury bungalows, in which the Professor was staying, the theme park that had been built further around the island and of course Amerigo's bar. One area of the island was off limits to all and contained the private residence of Giorgio Corzones, a vast mansion with its own private beach, swimming pool and helipad. Steve had never seen this part of the island as it was entirely isolated and there had never been any need for him to go near there. Some of his friends who worked for Security had been there a couple of times when people had tried to break in but otherwise it was the most unexplored part of the island since its development.

As Steve walked, he found that yet again he was haunted by the thoughts that he wanted so desperately to remove from his head. The Professor had been uncharacteristically cagey about the events of the night before. He'd left the club quite suddenly it had seemed and with Amerigo was keeping something secret. He thought he'd seen suspicion in Lucy's eyes also and when she and Will had taken a break, she hadn't stopped looking at Professor Loch the whole time. She had been there but hadn't seen the whole thing, the Professor had asked her and Will to join him. Could that have been part of his plan? Had he somehow been involved with the murder and brought them along as sympathetic witnesses. Will's faith in his old lecturer certainly hadn't come into question but it was quite possible that he was blinded by awe and his previous association with Loch.

These thoughts and many similar stayed with Steve until he reached the beach. Sarah arrived a moment later, wearing a sparkly dress and a flower in her hair. Steve complimented her on it and she revealed that she had found it on her walk home after induction duty and decided that it would fit her look. They went to the bar and had cocktails. She bought them and assured Steve that it was her treat as a way of saying thanks for a wonderful night before. As time pressed on, they decided to have a second drink each before moving into the town.

'This one is on me.' Steve insisted and Sarah asked why. 'For the wonderful night that we're going to have this evening.' She smiled and blushed in a not-so-subtle way.

Their conversations continued but Steve found himself being distracted by his thoughts again. Sarah noticed that something was amiss and asked him what was wrong. Steve hesitated at first, realising that he hadn't yet aired his suspicions out loud. He told her everything, that the Professor had found the body, that he had been secretive and everything else that had happened throughout the day. As he said what was on his mind, Steve felt it becoming more real and he convinced himself further. Sarah listened carefully to his every word and when he had finished, she bit her lip nervously. Steve could tell that she was anxious that he wouldn't like her reply.

'This isn't easy to say but nothing like this has ever happened on Corzones Island before. You said yourself that the Professor is strange and I agree with you. When we were walking from his bungalow to the strip he seemed to be fine but he did disappear a lot when we were in the club and he left very suddenly.' Steve sighed.

'It doesn't make any sense though, why would he do something like that?'

'I don't know,' replied Sarah, 'why would anybody willingly end the life of another human being? You've spent more time with him than anybody else since he arrived on the island and if you're suspicious then you should tell Security. Apparently they've brought an inspector in from England, talk to him just to set your mind at rest if nothing else.' Steve nodded, Sarah was right and he wouldn't be able to rest until he had a definitive answer. 'I'll come with you if you'd like?' Steve nodded and Sarah took his hand. 'We'll go now and then hopefully you'll be in a better mood for dinner.'

They walked together to Security HQ. It wasn't far away but it seemed to take an eternity to reach it. Steve didn't know if he was doing the right thing or not but Sarah was right, he had to be sure and Security had interviewed the Professor already. If they were certain that everything was ok then it would at least set his mind at rest. What if the Professor was innocent though and he was simply moving this inspector's suspicion away from the real killer? Throughout the walk Steve was completely silent, he looked at the ground as he got further and further into the maze that his thoughts had created. At one point Sarah gave him an encouraging squeeze of the hand and smiled at him.

'Thanks for coming with me.' He sounded pathetic and he knew it but he couldn't turn back now, not after he had spoken his thoughts out loud and Sarah had agreed with him.

They walked into the entrance of Security HQ and asked the young receptionist if they could speak to whoever was in charge of the murder case. He asked for the reason and before Steve could reply, Sarah insisted it was something important that they couldn't disclose. Steve was glad of her support, he'd never have done this if he was alone and his thoughts would have turned to fears. The reception officer dashed off into the back and an agonising wait began. Sarah led Steve over to a chair and they sat down next to each other. She assured him that everything would be ok and repeated that this was the right thing to do. Steve really started to doubt that though and was ready to turn around and leave when the Inspector walked out of the back and introduced himself.

'Detective Inspector Kirshner. I believe that there is something that you wish to speak to me about?'

Nineteen

Kirshner had read the various reports over and over again as well as listening to the interview tapes. The kids knew nothing, that was obvious but there was something about the Professor and Amerigo that didn't seem quite right, something in their voices that only years of interviewing suspects could teach you to hear. There was an uncertainty when Amerigo spoke, nothing that could be used as evidence but Kirshner's instinct told him that he must have lied and thought about it as he did so. He decided to keep quiet about it for now, Powell was investigating other things and didn't need lectures about gut feeling to distract him.

Franko had been released and returned to his apartment, not knowing that Harper was keeping track of him every step of the way with orders to follow him everywhere, even into the nightclub if he had to. The young officer had seemed quite enthusiastic about this until he was reminded that on-duty Security Officers were not permitted to drink under any circumstances whatsoever. Kirshner had assured him that he didn't need to maintain his cover of an everyday nightclub visitor in that much detail. There had been two reports in from the young officer so far, one in which Franko had arrived back at his apartment and a second when he had gone to the supermarket. Kirshner had to admit that Harper's dedication to his task was impressive and he'd even managed to list every item bought by the DJ. There wasn't anything incriminating about sandwich fillers and a magazine however so Kirshner had simply told Harper to carry on. He would be replaced for a short time to change into clothing more appropriate for his stint in the club that evening. A conversation with Argyll had resulted in Harper being given an all-access pass. He probably wouldn't need it but it didn't hurt to take these kinds of precautions as he had learned many times in the past.

Kirshner was entirely void of leads and the tail on Franko only seemed to go further towards proving his innocence. He decided that one more read of the reports might produce something but fifteen minutes later he was in exactly the same place that he had been beforehand. Zoë hadn't really associated with anybody else since arriving on the island with a group of friends. The friends had told the officer sent to inform them of what had happened that she had met Franko on one of their first nights on the island and they hadn't really seen her since then. Another dead end.

Kirshner decided that he would take a break and went outside to where the buggies were parked. He lit what he realised was his first cigarette on the island and enjoyed the quiet moment to himself. A tiny moment of contemplation made him realise however that it was far from quiet. The sound of music was already unbearably loud, thumping away in the background. There were buggies coming and going, called out to small incidents that probably weren't of any real significance, vandalism didn't interest him in the slightest. His cigarette did however and he savoured every moment of it, knowing that it would probably be late into the night before he would have another.

He was just taking his last drag when the reception officer burst through the door and looked in the opposite direction before turning and seeing him.
'There you are sir. There's somebody at the front desk who wants to speak to whoever is in charge of the murder investigation.'
'Why exactly?' asked Kirshner, hoping that it wasn't just another curious or paranoid kid on holiday, worrying about their own safety. Apparently seven or eight had appeared over the course of the day and Powell had dealt with one of them who had managed to reach a state of minor hysteria.
'He just said he wanted to speak to whoever was in charge. He seemed pretty shaken up.' Kirshner sighed, this was probably another false alarm and waste of time but he decided that he was probably best off speaking to this person. Everybody else had been calm when they arrived and upset when they left without gossip so maybe this person really did have something. Either way, Kirshner wanted to do something related to the case that may be productive as his continuous report reading seemed to be aimless.
'Alright then, I'll speak to him.' Kirshner followed the reception officer through the large open-plan workspace and through to reception.

A boy and a girl were sitting in the chairs, she was holding his hand and apparently trying to comfort him. Perhaps this one really did have something to contribute, something *was* disturbing him.
'Detective Inspector Kirshner,' he said in his professional voice, 'I believe that there is something that you wish to speak to me

about?' They both nodded and Kirshner led them to an interview room. They introduced themselves as Steve Leason and Sarah Coogan and they were both reps on the island. Kirshner began to hope they might actually have something to contribute, surely reps wouldn't be chasing rumours like everybody else? The girl remained silent and as Steve's story progressed it became clear that she had only come along for moral support.

Kirshner realised very quickly that this was something important and before Steve could get into the full flow of his story, he decided to summon Powell to the interview room. Kirshner left them for just one minute while he found the Security Chief but when he returned, things had changed. Steve seemed to have clammed up and wasn't speaking as openly as he was before. Kirshner knew that he had to alter the situation quickly. Steve wasn't nervous and it was guilt that he was feeling. He'd already mentioned the Professor, he had been assigned to assist him while he was carrying out an archaeological study of the island and had spent the day with the academic. Not always a good thing but the fact that he was at HQ now meant that throughout the day his suspicions had grown. Kirshner was grateful that Sarah was there too, she was encouraging Steve to speak and after a few moments he did so, much to Kirshner's great relief.

The gist of the conversation was simple. Steve had been with the Professor in the Isle Club the night before when he had left suddenly. The next morning he heard that there was a murder and the Professor was being mysterious about the whole thing. The time that the Professor left the club tallied quite well with the time that the murder would have taken place. Steve still wasn't giving him enough to act on though, just adding to the suspicions that he had already. He pushed Steve further, trying to get something, anything that could have been of use. The Professor and Amerigo had been talking to each other in hushed voices all afternoon but that still wasn't enough. Even the fact that the Professor had locked cases full of mysterious objects wasn't enough to work with.

Kirshner and Powell left the interview room, giving Steve a few minutes more to think about anything else. Kirshner was close now, he knew that there must be something to incriminate the Professor, he just needed one thing to go on. He talked to Powell who remained not fully convinced.

'We could bring him in? He was there and he has locked cases of God knows what.' Powell considered for a moment.

'I've been on this island for a long time now Inspector and while here I've heard rumours, legends about cults working on the island and some great unsolved mystery. The knife was interestingly shaped and dipped in poison, sounds like a ritualistic killing doesn't it?' Kirshner nodded, he could see what Powell was getting at.

'We've got enough to search his equipment.' Powell nodded in agreement. 'Then let's go and assure those reps that everything is under control. After that, I want you to assemble a team to go up to that temple and search both Loch and Amerigo. If there is one thing in any of those cases that doesn't add up then I want them both brought back here.' Powell agreed.

They went back to the interview room, Steve seemed to be even more tense now but Sarah continued to have her calming effect on him. Kirshner explained that everything Steve had said had been very helpful and had advanced the investigation. It was true, Kirshner and Powell may not have any solid evidence but they did have a reason to start looking for some. He decided to show Steve and Sarah out of the building himself, giving them the customary speech telling them to come back if anything else occurred to them. Sarah promised that they would but by this stage Steve had completely clammed up, feeling guilty about what he'd said. It would take him a while but. Kirshner knew that Steve would see that he had done the right thing eventually.

Walking into the open-plan workspace, he saw that Powell had assembled quite a large group of Security Officers. He'd made it more of an operation than Kirshner had planned but he could see why. Island Security had to seem to be pro-active when it came to dealing with this crime. The Professor and Amerigo were now prime suspects in the case. There was also a safety element, the temple was located in quite an isolated part of the island and it would be very easy for the suspects to disappear as soon as the officers arrived. They were waiting for Kirshner to brief them. He stepped up to the centre of the office, took a deep breath and spoke:

'These men are suspected of murder. As far as we are aware, they are now both in one place. We are going to strike, we are going to bring them into custody and when they are, this entire crisis will be over! Let's get going.' A simple speech but Kirshner knew that the Security force wasn't in the mood for speeches, this murder was their darkest day and they were as eager as he was to end the crisis as soon as possible.

Kirshner walked out of the back of the building to where the buggies were parked and saw that two Jeeps had been acquired. They sat in the middle of the parking area and had the Corzones island logo printed along their side. Powell directed him to the front Jeep, the vehicle that would be leading the convoy. He climbed into the passenger seat. Powell drove.
'How certain are you that it's them?' Powell asked. Kirshner smiled.
'As certain as you are, or you wouldn't have put this much of a force together.' Powell smiled, making Kirshner feel far more comfortable about the situation. He'd already made one incorrect call that day and didn't want to make a second, the fact that Powell was backing him up this time was a huge encouragement.

Compared to the buggies the Jeep was an incredibly comfortable ride but unfortunately it only just fitted on to the narrow path that led into the jungle and up the hill. There were a few occasions in which Kirshner was certain that they would hit a tree that leaned over but Powell was an expert driver, having obviously made the journey on a number of occasions in the same vehicle. Neither of them spoke while in the Jeep, the situation was too tense and Kirshner was running through what he knew about the Professor in his head, making sure that there was nothing that would easily make the case against him fall apart. There had to be something in the bungalow, Steve had said that he didn't recognise some of the pieces of equipment and that they certainly didn't look like anything archaeological. The Professor must be involved in something supernatural. He *had* to be.

As they reached the end of their journey, Kirshner noticed bits of rock, crumbled walls and the trees beginning to thin. He would have solved the case in less than a day of being on the island and perhaps stopped a number of other murders happening. After all if this murder was related to the legends on the island and the professor really was part of some cult, it was hardly likely that one murder would suffice. Kirshner braced himself, he knew that in a couple of minutes he'd be confronting his suspects and nothing could go wrong.

'This is it, the Temple Bar.' Powell sounded just as anxious as Kirshner when he spoke. The Jeep pulled up and they were both ready to make their big arrest.

Twenty

The morning had been simple. Amerigo had left his bed and made the journey up to his bar, ready to open it for another day and to forget the events of the night before. He did a few final bits of cleaning before opening everything up. It was almost lunch time and he didn't expect to see anybody until much later, he found that standing in the sun and listening to some music improved his mood. The Professor would arrive at some point and maybe Amerigo would finally be able to get some answers. So far the Professor had been secretive but their time together had been short and any explanations that he may get were likely to be longer than they had been before Security had arrived.

The truth was that Amerigo had a feeling now, a very particular and haunting feeling that he knew immediately to be fear. Dark days were coming for the island and if Svoros was now as involved as he suspected they were in a great deal of trouble. Amerigo took a seat in front of the bar and stared into the jungle, the response that he received was a light breeze and the sound of the music from across the island.

The jungle was familiar but that was the only thing that hadn't changed. At one time the locals lived in what was little more than a small fishing village. They lived there because they wanted to and apart from a small ferry that made the daily trip to the mainland, they were entirely isolated. That was the way that they had wanted to be. Amerigo came to the island when he was much younger. A relative who he barely knew had lived on the island and died in her nineties, Amerigo's branch of the family tree were her closest living relatives and she had left her house to them. They had all ventured out: Amerigo, his sister and mother and they spent the most relaxing week together, isolated in the sun. They had returned to the mainland after a week and life had continued as normal for quite some time.

Something about normal life didn't work for Amerigo, he had a good job, plenty of money and a very nice house right by the coast. His mother aged almost overnight however and died not long after. Amerigo and his sister owned more houses than necessary so they decided to settle for one each. His sister, Donica, had chosen to keep their mother's house. It was the largest and most expensive and Amerigo didn't want it. There was only one place that had ever made such an impact on his life and that was the house on the island.

With his sister's blessing, he moved to it soon after but made regular visits back home, to his sister who had fallen in love and was to be married and to his mother's grave, the calmest place off the island and a location he could never stay away from for very long. His mother's death was the thing that had given him what he wanted more than anything else, the house. He would never have moved away while she was alive but he had finally been able to leave without feeling unbearable guilt.

From the moment he had first seen the island, growing larger and larger as they crossed the ocean, Amerigo knew that he had found paradise and not long after he started to live on it, he found that he fitted into paradise very well. The small island community lived happily together, made up of just fewer than two thousand people. It was a fairly old community but there were enough youngsters for a small school. Amerigo had opened a small pub on the island, in very much the style he had seen when he had visited England in his youth. It was a success and very popular amongst the locals. Its continuing success was what led to him being asked to run the Temple Bar in which he now sat.

As landlord of such an anachronistic yet successful pub, Amerigo learned all of the island's legends and myths from the locals straight away and they had interested him. The community had only existed since the end of the Second World War but they had taken care to document everything about the island's possible history, pulling together an impressive library that was run by a toothless old man who never seemed to talk but always smiled. It was his death that seemed to start the process of the island's development. Soon after his library had been bought by a 'party interested in the history of the island'. His family who lived on the mainland had virtually forgotten about their old relative and had given that the go-ahead, probably surprised to come into such a considerable amount of money seemingly out of nowhere. It was soon after that the sponsored expeditions began, academics from all over the world came to the island, to look around and to write. Some people even came just for a holiday. The island's popularity increased and at the same time so did the profits of all local businesses. Amerigo found his pub became very overrun in a short amount of time. Some people became unhappy and left the island, arguing that if their home had become like a city then the city should become their home. The opportunities there were more attractive and nearly all of them knew somebody there already.

For a short time, Amerigo had been blinded by the success of his once-modest business. It was in his pub that he first met Giorgio Corzones, not his real name of course but he used it for business purposes in an attempt to appear more exotic. Amerigo had never heard his real name and never expected to. On that night in the pub, he never imagined for a moment that this stranger would be any more than another visitor to the island, seeking somewhere different to experience the sun. A few weeks later, Amerigo recognised the man's face on the front of the local newsletter with a large caption announcing that he was the future of the island plastered underneath it.

Svoros had been the person to object the most at first and he had been given a private meeting with Mister Corzones to settle any problems. Whatever happened in that meeting Amerigo didn't know about, but Svoros was suddenly convinced and was the first local in agreement to start a business on the new converted island. For the first time ever, paradise was unfamiliar to Amerigo but he decided that he would follow his friend's example and add his support. If paradise was adapting to the twenty first century then so should he.

It was around that point that the Professor first visited the island. He had wandered into Amerigo's pub on one of its final few nights of existence. He had ordered a drink and began to talk about his work as an archaeologist. Amerigo was immediately able to tell that there was something different about this man, something strange and unexplainable. After a few days of extensive conversation and the two of them developing into good friends, the incident on the cliff edge happened and Amerigo learned of Professor Loch's true line of employment. Amerigo had seen a man die, something he had never experienced before but knew he had to keep it a secret. The Professor explained to him and assured him that all would be covered up by his superiors and if the story about 'dark objects' ever got out then it could be a disaster. Power crazed individuals would flock to the island and try to unearth such secrets. The picture that Loch had painted was clear: paradise would be shrouded in the most unbearable blackness.

Amerigo had attended the official event to mark the changing of the island's name. He was now a resident on Corzones Island and on one day when he joined the Professor at his work by the temple, he discovered the place that he wished his future bar to be. The Professor had left soon after and the island rapidly changed into what it eventually became: a holiday paradise full of hellish ways. Amerigo enjoyed it and it made him feel young again, owning a 'hidden gem' of a bar and relating the legends of the island to anybody who happened by.

Amerigo soon found that people became more interested in the legends, including many of the original islanders who had stayed behind but none more so than Svoros, who began to talk often about 'the untapped power of secrets'. People were starting to believe the legends that Amerigo had heard and told others almost every day since he had come to live on the island. He and Svoros grew far apart, maintaining their friendship in name only. It was because of this that Amerigo was now able to believe that something had happened to his old friend and that something else was going on around the island. He had sensed for a while that something wasn't right, the reason he had started looking at returning to the mainland.

Over the years Amerigo's visits had become less and less frequent but he still stayed in contact with his sister and as soon as he had said to her that he was considering leaving the island, she had approved of the idea. Donica's children had grown into adults without ever really knowing their uncle and certainly never visiting that strange little island that he lived on. They were now too old to enjoy a holiday on Corzones and had families of their own.

Amerigo journeyed through his thoughts, fears and memories for about an hour when the sound of an approaching buggy interrupted him. He was still staring into the jungle and feeling the cool breeze. It was the Professor and Steve arriving for the start of their day's work. The Professor quickly sent Steve to pick something else up from his bungalow and within a moment of the buggy departing, Loch smiled at Amerigo.

'You seem to be alright.'

'I have seen death before Professor, as well you know.' The Professor looked into the distance, a contemplative look on his face. He raised his eyebrow and sighed, never removing his vision from the jungle.

'I suppose you have, I'm sorry old friend. I find that I tend to affect other people's lives in a negative way. I did it to you six years ago and I did the same this morning. Poor Will and Lucy.'

'You weren't thinking when you brought them to the town centre, were you?' Another sigh from the Professor, this one even more full of regret than the last.

'Perhaps a momentary lapse of judgement,' his voice deepened, 'or perhaps I really am accustomed to death that much. I see it so often Amerigo.'

The Professor's frustrated sighing continued for some time, revealing a negative side to him that Amerigo hadn't previously been aware of. Professor Loch had only ever wanted to help people, to save them from what they couldn't understand but it seemed that he failed just as much as he was successful. Suddenly the fear returned for Amerigo upon realising that the Professor was so fallible, he'd always seen his friend as the person that was able to deal with these things. Amerigo then realised that Loch was deliberately showing this side of his character, this was an act of trust, not pessimism.

A serious conversation started between the two of them regarding their handling of the Security interviews.

'I said exactly what we planned.' Amerigo tried to speak quietly.

'Good,' said the Professor cautiously, 'now what do you know about this cult?' Amerigo took a deep breath, considering for a moment. This was it, Amerigo was about to speak his worst fears out loud.

'A man named Svoros, he is involved with them. He came to me yesterday evening and told me that I should leave the island if I didn't wish to join him.' The Professor was about to reply when something caught his eye. He looked around quickly, Amerigo looking in the same direction. They both saw the same thing disappear into the jungle.

'Who was that?' The Professor spoke urgently.

'I don't know, he's not from the island. He must have been a kid that got lost.'

'Then why didn't he ask for directions Amerigo? He was eavesdropping.' Amerigo didn't want it to be true but knew that the Professor must have been right, there was no other possibility. He had just heard Amerigo tell the Professor about Svoros and in all likelihood, it was Svoros who he'd be reporting what he'd heard to. The Professor must have been reaching the same conclusion. 'Whoever is in charge of this operation must have supporters all over the island.'

'You mean that Svoros has followers?' It sounded ridiculous as Amerigo spoke the words but as a second had passed Amerigo came to realise that he was probably right. 'The Order of Velza', it was in the name. They were an order, a cult, a group of people gathering together to share their beliefs and ideas. Perhaps even for something more. Either way, Professor Loch gave a stern nod.

Will and Lucy had arrived before their conversation could continue further and began to help with the work again. It wasn't long before they weren't just helping and instead they were doing all of the work. The Professor walked to the bar and leaned on it, speaking to Amerigo in a hushed voice.

'The case that I've sent Steve for, it contains a piece of equipment that could give us some answers.'

'Answers, Professor?'

'Yes. Answers as to just how much of a danger Svoros and his friends could be. By sundown we shall know if there is any truth in those persistent legends.'

'How so?'

'All supernatural phenomena gives off a kind of energy, something that can't normally be detected.'

'But your equipment can pick it up?' The Professor nodded as Steve arrived on the buggy, bringing the case with him.

He dumped the cases on the table with the others, went to Will and Lucy and began to help dig what was now an impressively sized trench. The Professor edged over to the largest case and opened it, producing a small machine with a purple light emanating from the top of it. The Professor pressed a few buttons and it began to make a quiet whirring sound. He walked back to the bar with the device and placed it down next to him.

'We'll know soon.'

'And what if there is a real danger?'

129

'If there is then we need to do everything we can to stop whatever power, whatever secret this island contains from being unearthed.' The device didn't provide any immediate answers but Professor Loch assured him that it would do, it would just take a few hours.

He dismissed Steve, stating that there was nothing else that he could do that day. By this stage Will and Lucy had decided to take a break and had ordered glasses of water. They sat together at a table towards the opposite end of the bar, talking quietly between themselves. Amerigo smiled, they seemed happy together. The Professor continued to look at his device, concerned. He had explained quietly that it was scanning the whole island, bit by bit to find anything that gave off this mysterious energy signature.

The bar remained quiet, the only predominant noise was the continuous calypso music. People never seemed to notice its sound but Amerigo liked it because it was entirely at odds with what people were used to on the island. It was different. Occasionally the Professor would tap his fingers along to it on the bar and whistle, apparently recognising some of the songs. The quietness was suddenly shattered when a bald man burst into the bar. He was shouting but his voice clearly wasn't accustomed to doing so. 'You! You are the super, aren't you?' The Professor looked shocked that he had been identified. He span around, alert as if he was expecting some kind of attack. Luckily the only weapons that the bald man had were words.
'How do you know who I am?'
'Know who you are? There are many on this island who know of your evil, one of them has come to me and warned me. You interfere with evil that no mortal soul should ever consider getting close to.' The Professor suddenly calmed, Amerigo imagined that this was a situation that he was used to.
'Allow me to guess,' the Professor didn't sound antagonistic in any way, he was ready to have a discussion with this man, 'you are a representative of a church?' The bald man took a deep breath.
'I am Father Merco. I've come to this island to make a difference.'
'So have I.' the Professor sounded confrontational again. 'Father Merco, I respect your view, I really do but believe me I am not the real evil here.' Merco and the Professor continued to argue for some time. Will and Lucy dashed over and stood next to Amerigo, Lucy looked uncertain of who to support but Will looked at Loch

with interest. Eventually, Merco left, but promised that he would return and that he would be watching the Professor closely.

The Professor turned and walked to the bar, leaning on it and staring into the jungle with a blank expression on his face. Will and Lucy both looked at each other, unsure whether asking for the explanation that they so obviously wanted was the right thing to do. It was the Professor who spoke first, his tone was grim and he didn't move his eyes as he spoke.
'I'm sorry Will, Lucy. I'm sorry that you've been dragged into this.'
Will listened to the Professor's every word with keen interest but Lucy openly wore a look of suspicion on her face. Amerigo remained silent, knowing exactly what the Professor would say to them as he had heard the same speech six years before. 'I should have just carried on being an archaeology lecturer, that was simple. I am a Supernatural Investigator, 'Super' for short. I'm here to investigate events on the island. There's an unsolved mystery here as well as a build-up of other events.' Will shook his head, trying to understand what he was being told.
'Other events?' He asked. The Professor nodded.
'Supernatural rituals and...'
'Devil worship?' Interrupted Will, a sound of excitement on his voice. The Professor paused for a moment before turning his head from the jungle to the people he was speaking to.
'Not quite William. Supernatural happenings, they're an energy. A source of power that we can't really comprehend. If the legend of the Velza is true then the original inhabitants of this island were wiped out by a power that they had no hope of understanding, the same with the expeditions that came here.' Lucy was still visibly unconvinced.

The Professor's explanation was cut short. The temperature was dropping and the sun was starting to distance itself. The reflections of the trees extended and all sunglasses were removed. The Professor continued his explanation to Will and Lucy, telling them the full story of his first visit to the island, his suspicions of Svoros and the true events of the night before. He stopped, silent as the sound of a buggy approaching could be heard. It was Steve. He jumped off his buggy and ran into the bar.
'Professor, I'm so sorry I've made an enormous mistake!' Loch ran to Steve and placed his hands on the reps shoulders.

'What's happened, what's wrong?' Steve took a deep breath, he seemed to be close to tears.

'The Security forces, they're coming here to arrest you. They think that you killed that girl. I'm so sorry, I went to them and told them that you seemed suspicious.'

Amerigo stepped forward, he knew what had to happen now.

'You have to go! Into the jungle.' Steve turned to Amerigo.

'You too. They suspect you both.' The Professor shook his head.

'No! Steve, why would you... No, it isn't your fault. I spent too much time trying to keep my secrets. Will, Lucy, can you please tell Steve what I have told you?' Will nodded and after a short moment of hesitation, so did Lucy.

'I'm sorry Professor.' Steve shook his head and hid his face in his hands.

'Don't worry Steve. I still trust you. Lucy and Will are going to explain the truth to you. I'm going to need your help, can I rely on you?' Steve took a deep breath and nodded. The Professor tapped his shoulder and thanked him. The sound of sirens suddenly became apparent in the distance. Amerigo had run around the bar and grabbed his laptop.

'We have to go now Professor. I know this jungle better than any of Security, we'll be alright.' the Professor nodded.

'Can I rely on you three to keep Security busy for us?' Will, Lucy and Steve all nodded. Steve insisted that he was sorry again but the Professor assured him that everything was alright.

Amerigo ran, faster than he ever had done before. He led the Professor into the jungle and within moments the bar had vanished behind them, replaced only by trees and other foliage. Even the calypso music had vanished, replaced by silence that was only occasionally interrupted by the few birds that circled the treetops and the sound of sirens in the distance. Wildlife on Corzones was a rare sight, it always had been. Perhaps the legends kept them away. Amerigo and the Professor continued to run, the sound of the sirens suddenly disappeared and he knew straight away that the Security forces had reached his bar. They were on the run now, suspected of murder and there was very little to prove their innocence.

Amerigo looked at the Professor and noticed that he had grabbed the device for detecting supernatural energy before they had left. It began to make a sound.

'It's finished its scan.' The Professor stopped running and stared at the device, Amerigo quickly did the same. It made a quiet pulsing bleep as it readied its report. 'It's quite simple Amerigo,' said the Professor, 'a green light means that Svoros is worshipping a fiction. A red light...'

'A red light means that this island is in a lot of trouble, right?'

'A red light means that not only is this island in trouble but so is the entire world. You've always said that this island has secrets Amerigo and now we're about to find out how true that is.' The wait seemed to last an infinite amount of time but Amerigo knew that it was really only a few short seconds. The purple light flickered for a moment before eventually turning red.

'What do we do now?' Amerigo asked.

'Amerigo, we run.'

Part Three - The Run

Twenty-One

A lot had changed and things were much clearer to Steve now. He'd told Inspector Kirshner about the Professor and immediately regretted what he'd done. He ran over things in his head again in a matter of seconds and came to the conclusion that the Professor must be innocent. Despite all of his suspicions he knew somehow that he had been wrong. He'd left Sarah alone just outside the Security building and jumped on to the nearest buggy, speeding towards the Temple Bar as quickly as he could. He had to warn the Professor and Amerigo, they were good people and he had been wrong about them. Upon revealing his suspicions to the Inspector, they had started to feel wrong and even Sarah's encouraging words failed to change his mind back.

As he sped up the hill he expected to be overtaken by the Security forces, they had better vehicles than him but he was determined to give the Professor a chance. Somehow he made it up to the bar before anybody else, but only just. He didn't have time to speak to the Professor properly but he was promised that Will and Lucy would explain everything to him. There was something else, something he didn't know and his mistake became clearer to him with every passing second. The sirens could be heard so Amerigo urged the Professor to leave immediately and they both ran into the jungle, disappearing instantly.

Steve expected Will and Lucy to be angry with him but they both started to explain the situation, getting as much information in as possible before the Security forces arrived. He decided to hide himself and then to 'arrive' at the scene just after the Security forces, it was probably best that they didn't know he'd given the Professor a warning. As the sirens were almost on top of them, Steve jumped over a wall and hid himself before making his way back to his buggy, luckily it was parked a little bit down the hill as he'd jumped out and run to the bar in desperation towards the end of the journey.

When he walked back up to the bar he heard an irritated Kirshner speaking to Will and Lucy.

'Are you sure that you don't have any idea where they went?' Kirshner didn't sound as calm and comforting as he had earlier on, he now sounded frustrated, angry even. Something told Steve that his approaching the bar again might not be a good idea but he was determined to see what had happened to the Professor and Amerigo. He couldn't just walk away now. He strolled into the bar casually, looking as confused as he possibly could upon seeing all of the Security Officers. Kirshner was towering over Will and Lucy who were sitting in the same chairs that they had been when he had left them a few minutes previously. A Security Officer stopped him as he was about to walk in but Kirshner turned around and saw him.

'What're you doing here?'

'I wanted to make sure that Will and Lucy are alright. Did you get them?' Powell stepped forward.

'The Professor and Amerigo have evaded us,' Kirshner rolled his eyes, he'd have preferred Powell to not reveal details about the case. He was obviously trying to keep things 'by the book' but on Corzones Island, things were different, 'They won't be at large for long though, we'll find them. Don't worry.' He didn't say anything to the contrary but Steve was far from worried. He knew that the Professor and Amerigo would get away and just how important it was that they did so.

Lucy explained things to Steve that he would have found impossible just a few days before but somehow, because the Professor was involved, he believed it all immediately. He believed that Professor Loch was really some supernatural secret agent and that he was investigating strange goings on around the island. Steve had even heard rumours of an occult group at work, although he'd laughed all of these off previously. What if it was true though, what if there was far more to the island than he or anybody else had ever imagined. Steve knew that this was the truth, if the Professor was to lie, he wouldn't attempt to insult their intelligence with such an incomprehensible excuse.

Kirshner turned his attention back to Will and Lucy.

'What are you two doing here anyway?' It was Will who answered. 'Having a drink.' Kirshner didn't look convinced, his reply was instant.

'So coincidentally you two are the only people at the scene of the Professor and Amerigo running away as we arrive. You, the only other people who were there with that body apart from the bouncer?' Will and Lucy nodded.

'We didn't realise that the Professor and Amerigo were suspects. We were helping with some of the archaeological work.' Will showed the palms of his hands as he spoke, they were covered in dirt and showed plainly that he had been digging all afternoon. 'Believe me, we haven't done anything. Those two just ran as soon as they heard the sirens...' Will cut himself off suddenly, he knew he had made a mistake.

'So they've only just run?' Will nodded, defeated. Kirshner turned to Powell, a glint in his eye that suggested he might just be starting to enjoy the situation. 'Security Chief Powell, would I be correct in assuming that this island has a canine tracking unit?' Powell confirmed with a nod. 'Excellent. Get them brought up here immediately. I'm sure that they won't struggle to find our two fugitives.

Powell instantly produced his phone and ordered that the dogs be brought up as quickly as possible. The voice on the other end confirmed that they'd be up soon. It was a ten minute drive and that was when travelling at non-emergency speeds. The Professor and Amerigo had a very short time to make their escape. Kirshner seemed to lose interest in Will and Lucy as he made his plans. One of the officers brought him a large and detailed map of the island, which he placed over a table and began to inspect. After a moment he looked around and saw Steve again, standing there quietly.

'Oh, you can go. But stay contactable, we might need you.' Steve promised that he would. He walked out of the bar and towards his buggy when Kirshner's voice sounded again. 'Can you do me a favour?' Steve turned around and nodded, Kirshner pointed at Will and Lucy.

'These two, can you take them down the hill. I don't need them anymore and this place is closed. The owner appears to be missing.' Steve nodded and beckoned his two passengers towards the buggy. They didn't hesitate and without a word joined him. 'I want to speak to you two again!' Kirshner's voice followed them down the hill as they left but they didn't reply.

The journey down to the town centre was made in silence, all three of them were too relieved to have got away themselves to speak,

136

nervousness about the Professor and Amerigo didn't even need to enter the equation. Towards the bottom of the hill, as they were about to exit the jungle a jeep sped past with four or five dogs in the back. They'd be up to the bar within five minutes and on the hunt within a few seconds. Steve had not to worry about it, he was certain that the Professor and Amerigo would escape. They had to, even if only half of what he had been told was true.

He left Will and Lucy in the town centre at their own request and continued on to HQ where he left the buggy. He had to find Sarah. It was only at this point that he realised that he'd simply abandoned her. He hoped that she hadn't made other plans. It had only been half an hour, maybe forty-five minutes. She had to be contactable. He checked his phone and saw that she had tried to call him a few times but given up half an hour ago. He had some considerable excuses to make up that evening. He dialled her number and pressed his phone to his ear. It began to ring and he prayed that she'd answer. A few rings passed and with every one Steve began to feel slightly more miserable. Just as he was about to give up, there was an answer.
'What the hell were you doing?' Steve couldn't tell her the truth, not that he'd just aided the escape of two murder suspects.
'Sorry, I wanted to check that everything went alright. I was scared and...' He heard Sarah exhale on the other end of the phone and couldn't immediately tell if it was a good sign or not. Steve decided to talk again before she could. 'Where are you?' There was a moment's silence before the reply came.
'I'm in my apartment. Just about to get a shower as it happens. I thought I'd hear from you again so I decided to get ready beforehand.' Things suddenly looked very good.
'I'll give you time to get ready and come up then.' There was a pause and Sarah gave a little giggle.
'I was hoping you'd arrive before I had the shower.'

A few hours passed before Steve and Sarah headed out for the night. Their first choice was to go to Sinners, one of the larger clubs on the island but it looked like it had already passed its peak and most people were now heading towards the Isle Club. Steve and Sarah discussed their options before deciding that another evening in the gentle care of DJ Freedom wouldn't be too bad. They walked over to the entrance and saw Tony at the door, looking slightly more tired than he usually did, probably because

137

of his late night being interviewed by Security. Upon seeing Steve and Sarah, he beckoned them forward and allowed them to enter without queuing.

The Isle Club was its usual loud self. DJ Freedom wouldn't be on for at least an hour yet so they decided to join the queue. The bar was so busy that it was possible that Freedom may actually have started by the time they were served. Luckily however they managed to get to the bar quickly and ordered a double round to avoid going back for some time. They were two of the lucky few people who were able to get a booth, managing to take it for themselves as a group of three guys moved over and on to the dance floor. After a minute or two, Steve placed his arm around Sarah, unsure of how she would react but he found himself relaxing when she shuffled closer to him and placed her head lightly on to his shoulder.

The drinks continued to flow and cocktails were soon replaced by shots. Steve dived into the queue for the bar while it was at its quietest, the moment that DJ Freedom emerged from the doors and made his way across the dance floor to the DJ booth. He got to the front of the queue instantly but found that the bar staff were just as distracted as the crowd was. Steve finally managed to get the attention of one girl and a few minutes later he had rejoined Sarah at the table with a tray full of drinks, most of them a bright colour. They drank them very quickly and Steve began to feel drunk, Sarah was obviously the same.
'I'm having a really, really, really, great night." Sarah looked straight into Steve's eyes as she spoke and he stared back.
'Yeah, me too. Just what I needed. Thanks.' He smiled, not averting his gaze. Sarah looked down for a second, deep in thought.
'I still don't get what happened earlier.'
'I just had to see what happened.' Steve found deceiving Sarah much harder than he had with Kirshner earlier on.
'You're such a bad liar Steve.' Before he could reply she leaned in and kissed him, placing her hand on the side of his face and stroking his stubble. It lasted for a minute, maybe two. Steve wasn't sure. 'But I don't care.'

Twenty-Two

Will and Lucy jumped off the buggy in the town centre and thanked Steve. They were both relieved, if not amazed that they had somehow managed to get away from the bar. Will was still processing everything that he had learned over the last hour or so and couldn't quite believe half of it. The Professor had spoken quickly and given them a lot of information in a very short space of time. Will had a thousand questions that he wanted to put to his old lecturer and didn't even have chance to ask one of them. The one he wished he had asked most of all was 'where are you going?' The Professor and Amerigo knew what was going on and nobody else did. The only thing they could really do was lie low, as Amerigo had hurriedly suggested before running into the trees.

'People will know won't they? That we helped the Professor and Amerigo?' Lucy seemed worried but Will had been thinking the exact same thing. This murder had been pinned on them and the real culprits were out there facing no suspicion at all. It seemed that they also had a rather sinister agenda. Will wondered if Professor Loch really knew what he was apologising for. 'Bringing them into this' didn't seem to even start to cover it. Will looked at Lucy who was visibly shaken, she bit her lip as she always seemed to do when she was nervous.
'We'll be alright. The Professor and Amerigo both said that they would look after us.' Will knew his answer was feeble but he felt like he had to somehow convince both himself and Lucy that everything would be fine. Lucy was about as convinced as he was. Will decided that getting something to eat would take their minds off things.
'Where do you want to eat? I'm paying.' Lucy looked around and pondered for a moment.
'You choose, I don't know where. And I really don't expect you to pay for me.' Will didn't know what to say, or even where to choose.
'Let's walk a little and think about it.' Lucy nodded and they began to walk.

They passed many places to eat and examined the menus as they went by but nothing seemed to appeal to either of them. Eventually they found a restaurant that was located quite far away from the town centre, it specialised in fish. Will ordered sea bass while Lucy decided that she was going to try something new; squid. They also ordered a bottle of wine which arrived quickly.

'You really aren't paying for both of us Will, this is an expensive place.' Will shrugged and assured her that it didn't matter. He hadn't exactly come to the island empty handed and had nothing else to spend his money on. It was his idea to go to a restaurant again so he would pay. That wasn't an issue to be settled until the bill arrived however and in comparison to other issues raised throughout the day, it was almost completely insignificant.

Their starters arrived, both of them had gone with crusty bread and a local fish pâté which had a phenomenal smell. After taking a single bite, Will concluded that it was even nicer than he'd guessed it would be. Lucy seemed to be enjoying herself too. She seemed happier now, like the worries from the town centre earlier on had evaporated.

'Are you alright?' The question seemed to come from Lucy out of nowhere and Will wasn't entirely sure how to respond. Was he alright? Right there, in the restaurant he was more than alright. He was happy and he wouldn't want to be with anybody else in the world. The events of the last day and that afternoon's revelations continued to whisper away in the back of his head however and no matter how hard he tried to ignore it, the voice never faded away completely.

'More than alright.' It was a terrible answer and far from the truth, he was hoping that he'd perhaps have said something more interesting. Nevertheless Lucy smiled.

'Good. So am I. We'll look after each other Will. Who knows when we'll next see the Professor or Amerigo but as long as we have got each other then we'll be alright.' Again Will found himself considering a hundred different replies but none of them seemed to be quite right. Instead he nodded and took a generous gulp from his glass of wine.

They finished their starter and not long after the main course arrived. Will immediately regretted his decision as Lucy's squid looked incredibly good. They remained mostly silent as they ate, tired from the afternoon's work. It was only at this stage that Will realised that his clothes must be filthy and that there were even still a few specks of dirt over his hands. He didn't care though. Lucy hadn't commented on it so she obviously didn't mind and the food was so good that he wanted to focus entirely on that. His concerns for the Professor still resurfaced on occasion, but he ignored them. He knew that the Professor and Amerigo would be able to look after themselves. He looked out of the restaurant's large arched windows and saw that it had gone dark despite the fact that he hadn't even noticed the light begin to fade. That would help the Professor though, if he was still at large. There was no natural light in the jungle and Amerigo knew every inch of it from the various explorations that he'd made over the years. This also helped Will to settle a bit and he began to enjoy his food more.

Lucy requested a taste of the sea sass, Will accepted on the condition that he could have a bit of the squid. Both meals were exquisite. Will hadn't eaten much of his fish as the other parts of the meal were equally as nice. Perfectly cooked new potatoes and grilled asparagus with some other roast vegetables covered in just a slither of melted cheese. Back at home this would have been an incredibly expensive meal and even on Corzones it wasn't cheap compared to the other places that he had eaten. Lucy was also enjoying her food, savouring every bite she took of the squid and saving the tentacles until last. She was unsure about them but Will assured her that from past experience they were completely edible and in his opinion, the best bit. When she finally built up the courage to sample them, she agreed.

When asked if they wanted dessert they both took a moment to consider. The meal had been very filling but Lucy reasoned that she probably could manage just a little ice cream and Will agreed that he would have the same. Their ice cream was served in a glass bowl with a wafer stuck into one of the scoops. It also arrived with two shots.
'Our compliments,' said the waiter as he placed the drinks down, 'I hope that you enjoyed your meal.' Will and Lucy both nodded, saying 'yes' through a mouthful of ice cream. They took the shots together, clinking the glasses and splashing the tiniest bit of liquid over the edge before downing them. It had a nice flavour, like marzipan but with another fruity flavour. They slowly finished their ice creams and by the time that he had finished, most of Will's was liquefied.

They chose to walk after their meal. They had decided earlier on that they wouldn't be going to a club again, one night had been enough and they were both tired from the night before and the afternoon's work that they had done. The beach was inviting and deserted when they had arrived. All of the people drinking there before making the journey to a club had left and nobody had quite got to the stage of requiring a drunk walk to end their night just yet. As a result Will and Lucy were alone with the sound of the waves and the surrounding darkness. They sat down in the sand next to each other and enjoyed the peace. Unfortunately complete silence couldn't be achieved as the music from the various clubs could be heard clearly. The section of beach that they were on wasn't far from the strip and the sound had no trouble travelling towards them.

'That was a lovely meal, thank you.' Will had won the small argument and in the end had paid for the full meal, promising Lucy that it really was his pleasure. 'You really don't have to keep looking after me you know?' Will was unsure of how to answer, was that really how Lucy saw their friendship?
'I'm not here because I'm looking after you. I want to spend time with you Lucy.' Again the music prevented total silence but this was the closest that their evening was going to get. Lucy seemed surprised by the answer, caught off guard and struggling to find a reply.
'Really?'
'Really. Yes.' Even through the darkness, Will saw Lucy smile.
'I like spending time with you too Will. Thank you.'

Their time on the beach continued and Will was the most relaxed he'd felt all day. There was no murder, no mystery, no hatred of the island and no expectations to live up to. There was just him and Lucy. She lay down in the sand but Will remained sitting upright.
'I love the feeling of sand in my hair,' said Lucy, 'it takes days to get it right again after but I don't care.' Will stared towards the sea, into the blackness.
'I wonder if they're out there.' Lucy sat up and looked with him.
'Who?' She asked.
'The Professor and Amerigo. They could have jumped on a boat and gone.' Lucy considered this for a moment.
'They won't have done. I had my doubts about the Professor earlier on Will but no, now he's told the truth it all makes sense.' Will nodded, Lucy was right. The Professor and Amerigo would stay on the island and do whatever they had to. The only thing that worried

him was the knowledge that at some point he and Lucy would have to help and that could place them in all kinds of danger.

They decided to end their time on the beach and walked slowly together to Lucy's apartment. Will asked Lucy if she didn't mind going back to hers again, as it was a better option than them both returning to his.
'Sofia won't be home all night so don't worry. You don't have to come back with me if you don't want to though?' Again, Will wasn't sure what the correct reply would be.
'I can go back to mine if you want, leave you alone?' Lucy immediately shook her head.
'No, I'd like you to stay Will but only if you want to.' Will smiled, he couldn't help it.
'Of course I want to.'

The conversation quickly changed and soon they were back at Lucy's apartment. They walked in together, quietly just in case Sofia had returned but it was immediately apparent that they were alone.
'Do you want a drink?' Lucy walked over to the fridge, opened it and began to inspect what it contained. 'Only got beer left though.'
'Beer is fine.' Lucy handed Will a bottle and took one for herself. She pulled an opener out of a large handbag that was propped up next to a chair. She opened Will's bottle and then her own.
'Come on, let's go out on the balcony.'

Lucy's apartment was three floors up and the balcony offered an impressive light show in the darkness of the night. Will looked out for a moment and enjoyed the sight until he was joined by Lucy who had replaced the bottle opener in her bag.
'If I don't put it back then I'll lose it. Go on, sit down.' Will sat himself down on one of the plastic chairs, looking out into the decorated darkness. Lucy sat next to him and shuffled her chair closer. 'Beer isn't up to much but it's something.'
'Yeah.' It went silent and Will had no idea how to break it. In front of them was a twisted firework display as spotlights reached into the sky, moving around and covering the air while the constant sound of music doubled for the explosions. Will had many things he wanted to say to Lucy and thought that this might be the time. He allowed the silence to endure however.

Lucy broke the silence in the end. The question was forced but it served its purpose.

'So why did you become an archaeologist?'

'It's what I wanted to do, what I've always wanted to do so I just did it.' Lucy smiled.

'That's good,' she said, 'it's not very often that people get to do what they want to.'

'I suppose you're right. What about you?'

'My job? A clothes shop is probably the best place to work if you want to become a designer. That's all. Not exactly what I want to do but close enough.'

'You enjoy it though?'

'Yeah. Not as much as you enjoy archaeology though,' Will didn't quite understand what she meant, 'you're doing exactly what you wanted to do. I'm trying to find my way with mine.'

'Something will come about,' said Will encouragingly, 'I was lucky that I just found what I wanted to do straight away as I left uni.' Lucy nodded.

'You're right. I won't give up, ever. One day I'll design something famous.'

'I'm sure you will, I *know* that you will.'

'Is there anything else you'd like to do?' Will considered his answer for a moment.

'A lot. Archaeology is the only thing I've ever wanted and actually achieved really.' Will realised that he was beginning to sound miserable. 'It just means I have more to do though.'

There was another brief silence and again it was Lucy who interrupted it. She suddenly sounded nervous, as if she was finding whatever it was difficult to say.

'Will?' Will turned to look at her?

'You... You know that kiss yesterday night...?' Will had been dreading this. She was unhappy, of course she was. She regretted it.

'Don't worry.' Will spoke without considering his response.

'What do you mean?' Lucy seemed confused.

'Don't worry. I understand. You didn't mean to, it just happened and we'd both drank a bit and you were just trying to...' Will found himself suddenly quietened as Lucy placed a finger over his lips. She shook her head.

'Not quite.' She spoke quietly and removed her finger. She was shaking quite visibly but she leaned closer to Will and planted a kiss on his lips. Their heads moved apart but their eye contact never ceased.

'Why did you do that?'

'Because I wanted to. Because you're a wonderful guy Will.' Will felt himself going red, he hoped that the darkness would hide it. 'You're wonderful too,' he tried so hard to find a good reply but that was the best that he could manage, 'I just never thought that you'd...' Lucy shushed Will and he fell silent immediately. 'Stop worrying about that and kiss me again.' He did.

Twenty-Three

Darkness had never closed in so slowly but it was bound to come soon, it needed to. Dogs were barking in the near distance and there was no way that they could safely leave the jungle and move to some water to lose the trail until pitch blackness had taken over. The Professor seemed to be fine but Amerigo could feel the breath starting to leave his body and tiredness kicking in, threatening to take him over completely.

'This is madness!' He immediately regretted shouting, if a Security Officer was close enough to hear it then he'd have just given away their position.

'I agree,' said the Professor, 'I should have seen this coming.'

Amerigo didn't want to fall out with Loch but had to say his piece. 'You're right. There was no need to stay as secretive as you have done. You keep too many secrets from those that can help you Professor.' Amerigo expected an argument but didn't receive one. The opposite almost, Loch seemed to take on board what he had said. The dogs barked again, louder this time and much closer. 'It appears that we are being hunted like animals.'

'Don't worry Amerigo, at least we have one thing on our side?' Amerigo admired the Professor's enduring positivity. He decided to humour his friend.

'And what is that?'

'We are innocent.'

While the Professor spoke the truth, Amerigo's spirits weren't lifted. The sun was setting and with every passing second the sounds of the dogs faded further into the distance and their chances of a clean escape increased. The jungle was huge and at times difficult to negotiate while running, the Professor tripped over at one point but they kept moving. Amerigo knew the area well, having explored its every inch while walking during the old days, when the island had been quiet. He knew that they were close to a small river that ran from the highest point of the island right down into the sea, they could lose the dogs there but after that where would they go? Did the Professor really have a plan?

They continued on through the jungle until the night had completely closed in around them. After the Professor tripped again and Amerigo himself almost fell to the ground, they decided to walk.

'The river isn't far, we can travel further up the hill alone that...'

'No.' For the first time Amerigo detected tiredness in the Professors voice.

'No what?'

'We don't go uphill Amerigo, we go down.'

'Down? Are you mad? Down the hill is densely populated, we won't even last five minutes.'

'We need to get to my bungalow, there's some equipment hidden there that is essential if we are going to combat whatever is really going on here.' Amerigo couldn't believe his ears, Security would have the Professor's bungalow under watch if not guarded by now. Going there was an almost certain recipe for their arrest.

Nevertheless the Professor insisted and once they had found the river, they began to head downhill.

The loud sounds of music across the island became more apparent as they went closer and closer to the town. Amerigo concluded that they had travelled far enough in the water to have lost any scent and decided to walk on dry land again. Despite the ambient heat, walking in wet shoes was very uncomfortable and cold. They decided to sit down for a moment, allowing their feet a short time to dry the best that they could.

'So this equipment, what is it?'

'Emergency supplies. All Supers are issued with them, just in case.'

'In case of what?'

'Well, in case prevention doesn't work and some kind of real danger is unleashed.'

'Real danger as in some kind of devil figure?' The Professor looked stern.

'Possibly Amerigo. In my experience it can be far worse than that. Devil figures are usually just symbols of hatred personified. It's when they can fight back that you have to worry.'

'And you think that whatever is here can fight back?'

'If people are trying this hard to unearth something it can only ever be for one reason: power. If there is some kind of force or being on this island then you can be certain that it will be the key to some kind of Earth-dominating power.'

'Granting three wishes, that kind of thing?' Amerigo smiled as he spoke, making light of the situation was all he had left now that understanding was beginning to depart.

'The sort of people that commit such a brutal murder aren't the ones you'd want even one wish granted to, are they?'

They started to walk again, heading away from the river and deeper into the jungle, using its cover to cross to the part of the island in which the Professor's bungalow was located. They only nearly encountered other people on one occasion. A group had decided to have their pre-drinks in a clearing not too far from the town centre and were laughing and joking around a light emanating from a phone. They were easily avoided, making so much noise themselves that it masked any that the Professor and Amerigo would make. The Professor held a finger to his lip to signal to Amerigo to keep quiet as they passed, not that he needed telling at all. They passed by and continued into the jungle and towards the bungalows.

All sign of Security had disappeared some time ago but Amerigo remained cautious. He knew Powell quite well and knew that the Chief would never give up. From the little he'd seen of Kirshner he very much assumed that he would be the same. With one last look behind his shoulder, Amerigo emerged from the jungle and on to the unlit beach, the moonlight being the only guide. The Professor followed closely behind.
'Your bungalow is about three hundred metres that way.' Amerigo pointed along the beach to where the lights of the expensive accommodation could be seen through some palm trees.
'If I recall correctly then there was a large rock not too far from where I was staying. Do you think we could make it there without being seen?' Amerigo nodded.
'We shall have a good view of anybody who may be guarding from there.'
'That was exactly my plan, old friend.'

Amerigo and the Professor ran through the sand and into the clump of palm trees. They both stopped and looked towards the bungalows, the Professor's was clearly in view. Amerigo pointed towards a rock that was about half way between themselves and their target, Loch nodded and they broke from the cover of the trees and darted towards the rock.
'It seems clear.' said Amerigo, peeking out from behind his cover, 'No wait.'

A Security Officer emerged from behind the building, he was patrolling it in a circle.

'Only one then, Amerigo. He wouldn't be covering the whole perimeter if there was somebody else around the back.'

'What do we do? Sneak past while he is around the other side?' The Professor shook his head.

'Unfortunately Amerigo we must temporarily part ways.' Amerigo had seen this coming.

'I play the scapegoat?'

'Not quite. Distract him, get him away from here and lose him while I get inside. If you do a good job of losing him then we shall be able to meet in there.' Amerigo had more running to do so he began to prepare himself.

'What if I don't lose him?'

'You will Amerigo. You know this island better than any of those guards.' Amerigo was grateful for the Professor's confidence but wasn't entirely convinced by the plan.

After waiting for a moment and wishing the Professor luck, Amerigo broke from his cover and ran across the beach.

'Hey you, this area is off limits!' The guard was yet to recognise him and Amerigo had to quickly change that if he was going to be followed.

'I need to get something from inside that building.' A look of recognition came across the guards' face as he finally identified Amerigo through the darkness.

'Stay where you are,' there was a slight hint of fear in the guard's voice, 'we can resolve this easily and peacefully right now.' The poor guard thought that he was confronting a murderer alone and in the dead of night. Amerigo suddenly ran in the opposite direction and towards a patch of jungle. The guard hesitated for a moment but followed, suddenly finding his sense of bravery.

Amerigo hid at the first opportunity behind a bush. The guard ran into the jungle and slowed, producing a torch from his pocket and shining it around.

'I know you're here somewhere. Please just come quietly, you can't hide forever.' The beam of light from the torch shone all around and almost exposed Amerigo, who was holding his breath as he crouched to ensure that he was utterly silent. He knew what he was going to have to do and wished that there was another way but running again wasn't an option, the guard was much younger and fitter than Amerigo was and with such a little head start he would surely be tackled and caught within a moment. There was no choice for Amerigo, he would have to render the guard unconscious.

The guard moved around, constantly shining his torch around and looking desperately into the darkness. His breathing grew heavier as the fear and desperation began to kick in again. Slowly he moved in Amerigo's direction, jumping slightly as he rustled a small shrub underfoot. The distraction was just enough to give Amerigo the break that he needed. He lunged out of his hiding place and towards the guard, striking a hard and sudden blow to the back of his head. The guard collapsed and Amerigo regretfully stood over his handiwork. He couldn't leave the guard here, it would take an incredibly long time for him to be discovered and there was no way of knowing just how much damage had been done. Amerigo picked up the unconscious guard and began to carry his body back towards the bungalows on the beach.

He left the body behind the same rock that he and the Professor had hidden just a few minutes before. There was a light on in the bungalow now and the door was open, it seemed that Amerigo's distraction had been successful. He made his way to the door and stuck his head inside to see Professor Loch standing over another case. This one was smaller than the ones that he had taken to the temple but seemed to be packed tightly with various bits of unidentifiable equipment. Loch produced something that looked like a gun, Amerigo stared at it in horror.
'You can't use that thing? What if we're caught with it?' The Professor looked confused for a moment but his expression quickly changed to one of amusement.
'It's not what you think it is. This thing wouldn't do any harm, not to humans anyway.' The Professor placed it into a beige rucksack with a few other strange-looking objects. 'What happened to that guard?' Amerigo felt his regret yet again.
'He's having a little lie down. He'll be alright I think. It may be wise to send the Security forces some kind of signal as we leave, just so that we know for sure that he will be found.' The Professor nodded.

A few minutes passed, they consisted of the Professor carefully selecting equipment and placing it in his bag while Amerigo looked nervously out of the open door, making sure that nobody detected them in any way.

'We should take some food too. Can you go to the kitchen and grab whatever you can find? I went to the shop this morning and there should be some things we can take with us.' Amerigo nodded and went to the kitchen. The cupboards contained some snackable foods as well as some bottles of water. He quickly placed them all into a bag and carried it through to the main room, where Loch was still selecting equipment. He held a rectangular device in his hand with a small screen in the centre and a few buttons underneath. 'Brain pattern scanner. It tells you if somebody is being controlled or not.' Amerigo nodded.

'Does it happen often? Possession?' The Professor nodded.

'Far more often than you'd like to think.' Amerigo placed the bag of food next to the Professor. 'There's another rucksack on the table over there, would you mind?' Amerigo walked to the table and picked up the rucksack. He placed the bag of food inside it and zipped it up.

'That should be enough to last us a few days Professor, what then?'

'Amerigo, in a few days this will be all over and we shall go back to having the usual unlimited supply of food. Well, either that or we'll have no need for any food whatsoever but let's try and not think about that maybe?' The Professor smiled but Amerigo failed to see the funny side. This wasn't a time for joking and Loch still hadn't told him everything about what was going on. Information seemed to be coming over in tiny little pieces. Amerigo trusted the Professor but his making light of the situation, probably through familiarity more than anything else was frustrating.

Amerigo returned to his post at the door, looking outside for any sign of life that there may be. He immediately noticed some lights in the distance that were slowly moving along the beach and closer to them.

'Professor,' Loch continued to ready his bag and didn't respond, 'Professor!' He looked up at Amerigo.

'What is it?'

'I think we are about to have some company.' Loch stood and walked to the door.

'They must have tried to contact the guard. It's only one set of lights, one buggy.'

'I think it might be time for us to leave though.' The Professor grabbed the two rucksacks and passed the one full of food to Amerigo.

'I agree, let's go. Switch the light off.' Amerigo flicked the light switch while the Professor made a very quick scan of the room to check that he hadn't left anything behind.

Sirens from the Security buggy could be heard now and the lights were alarmingly close. Amerigo ran out of the bungalow, followed closely by the Professor who slammed the door shut behind him. Amerigo pointed to the patch of jungle that he had previously tackled the guard in and they both ran for it, vanishing into the trees moments before the vehicle arrived. Amerigo looked back to see that the unconscious guard had been found, at least he was now safe. One of the guards was reaching for his phone as Amerigo lost sight of him through the trees.

'Where do we go now then?' Despite his reservations about the way the professor was treating the situation, Amerigo knew that the Professor would be one step ahead of everybody else.

'Last time I was here and we faced that unfortunate fellow who was after one of the star binders, there was a cave. I suspected that this cave was where he had found the object but when I looked at it I couldn't find any evidence of anything there at all. I want another look at it, I have a funny feeling that I missed something last time.' More mystery but Amerigo didn't bother to ask for a full explanation. Surely what had happened with that man wasn't linked to this in any way but if the Professor wanted to investigate it then there must be a reason. Unsure whether he'd even make it to this cave, Amerigo chose to continue following his old friend, hoping somehow that they could clear their names along the way.

Twenty-Four

Inspector Kirshner was awoken by Powell. He had fallen asleep in one of the blue armchairs that were scattered around Security HQ, despite only intending to sit down for five minutes and drink his coffee. He looked to the floor and saw that the cup was almost still full but a quick dip of his finger into the drink told him that he had been asleep for some time, it was cold.

'How long have I been here?' He sounded much grumpier than he had intended to but that was probably just an instinctive reaction to being woken up.

'Just over an hour. There haven't been any developments and you haven't slept for over a day, I thought it might be best to leave you.' Powell also looked tired, having probably had less sleep than Kirshner over the last couple of days but he seemed to be able to continue. He did have youth on his side though, something that Kirshner had learned to stop relying on many years beforehand.

Kirshner had been in a bad mood ever since he had been awoken the previous day but this had been amplified greatly by the Professor and Amerigo managing to slip away. It was however, the final bit of proof that he had needed: they had to be guilty or otherwise why would they have run as soon as they had got wind of Security heading towards the bar? Kirshner chose not to dwell on it however and after questioning Will and Lucy, who he was certain had something to hide, he decided to return to HQ and coordinate the search for his fugitives from there.

Things hadn't got any better from that point though; the dogs hadn't taken long to lose their scent and that aspect of the search was called off, search parties in the jungle had produced no evidence and of course there had been no sighting of them at all. Powell had quickly informed him that Amerigo knew the island well after living there for so long and that the Professor's survey had been incredibly comprehensive on his previous visit and he knew a great deal more than most others did. Kirshner had done a search online for the Professor's report of his study six years previously but found it to be mostly unreadable, full of historical jargon and a system of dating that meant nothing to Kirshner. The Professor had found about fifty 'sites of interest' and most of them were scattered around the jungle.

Kirshner's other lead didn't seem to have developed at all either. Although he was now fully convinced that Franko had nothing whatsoever to do with the murder, he had insisted that Harper stayed on the DJ's tail. There had been some signs of good luck as the room next to Franko had been vacated that afternoon by the couple who were staying there. They had probably got wind of Franko's arrest and put two-and-two together, reaching the conclusion that they would be more comfortable in some alternative accommodation. With a little help from Powell, Harper had managed to secure the room for himself and had started a more reliable system of surveillance. The only reports he had received were that Franko had spent most of his free time crying before readying himself for his night of work. Harper had heard a phone conversation that involved Franko saying that he wasn't really up to working that night but after a few minutes he concluded that he would still play his set. Kirshner was amused by the fact that it was probably Argyll, the man who had tried to turn Franko in, that was demanding he work that evening regardless. He would ask Powell to watch that man closely, he clearly had some kind of agenda.

As it went dark the search parties checked back into HQ. Kirshner had wished that they would continue but none of them knew the jungle well enough to keep searching it in the dark. Powell had made arrangements for a thermal satellite scan, just in case they were still hiding in that area and had lit a fire that may have showed up. There wasn't any such luck however, although scans would continue through the night. Kirshner had asked for a guard to be placed at the bungalow in which the Professor was staying as well as Amerigo's house although he doubted that they'd be stupid enough to go to either of those places. This was proved wrong about an hour later when an unconscious guard had returned with two others who said it was clear that somebody had been in the house. A short time later the unconscious man had awoken and told the medical officer that it had been Amerigo who had knocked him out.

The most interesting development had been that his request for information on the Professor had been granted but what had come through seemed to be very vague, as if even his records had something to hide. After some more investigation had produced negligible results, Kirshner decided to share his thoughts with Powell.

'I've never come across anything like that before, government agent?' Powell smiled thinking that he had just made a joke but it was something that Kirshner was really considering. An uneasy feeling came over him and foolishly for the first time he was only just beginning to consider what the motive may be for the killing. If the Professor had done it then it wouldn't just be a random act. Had his fascination with the legends of the island led him to start to test some of them? A ritual killing maybe! But that still didn't explain why his records were so vague.

His case had progressed no further but at least Kirshner had found some different literature to stare at. He'd read the reports and information regarding the case so much that a book about the various legends of the island provided a welcome change. As he flicked through the various legends he found that they made about as much sense to him as Professor Loch's studies had. It didn't take him long to realise that he needed somebody to explain the legends to him personally. Kirshner asked Powell for a list of people who had lived on the island before it had been developed. The Chief appeared to be curious as to why Kirshner had made this request but he granted it quickly. The list arrived and Kirshner was surprised at just how small it was. The development of the island had left very few members of its original community. Almost everybody on the list owned a business of some kind on the island.

Kirshner looked at the list again and didn't really know where to start to so he asked Powell who was most likely to know about the legends. Powell looked at the list and considered carefully. 'The person you really need to ask is Amerigo, he was famous for telling stories in that bar of his.' This interested Kirshner further, surely it couldn't be a coincidence that the man currently on the run with the Professor was the island's authority on the legends. 'Him, that's who you want,' Powell pointed to one of the names, 'he's lived on this island all of his life and apparently knows a thing or two about the legends. Thinking about it I did see a book on the islands 'history' while we were having lunch in his café yesterday.'

Daylight had finally taken full control of the island and the few people that hadn't overdone it the previous night were beginning to emerge. The café had just opened when Kirshner and Powell

155

arrived and yet again they ordered a full English breakfast. It didn't take long to arrive, the owner placed it down on the table.

'Would you like to take a seat?' The owner checked over his shoulder to make sure that he had no other customers, he didn't, so he sat down.

'Can I help you officer?' He spoke with a thick native accent but pronounced his words perfectly and clearly.

'You are Svoros yes?' The man calmly nodded. 'I am Inspector Kirshner and I'm sure you already know my colleague, Security Chief Powell?' The man nodded again and gave Powell a familiar nod. 'We need some information from you.'

'You're investigating the murder aren't you? I can assure you that I know nothing about that.' Kirshner shook his head.

'We're not here to ask you about the murder, well not really anyway. I'm interested in the legends of this island and I've been told that you are the best person to ask.' Svoros considered for a moment and then smiled knowingly.

'So you haven't caught Amerigo yet then? He's the real authority on this island.' Kirshner nodded.

'Very shrewd, no we haven't found him but we have search teams out in the jungle.'

'You won't catch him that way. Amerigo knows the jungle, he had a passion for walking through it from the day he moved here. He has a passion for the whole island, as have I. It's the reason that we are amongst the few who have stayed.'

'Would his passion stretch as far as testing the legends?' Svoros considered the question, seemingly torn between his sense of right and wrong and his loyalty to his friend.

'Testing them by murder you mean?' Svoros shook his head, 'No, I don't think so. I've seen Amerigo tell the stories, there is a fire in his eyes but that is his sense of adventure, his curiosity with the unknown. Not a murderous instinct. I don't think Amerigo even believes those stories.' Kirshner took a big bite out of a piece of hash brown and took a moment to search for his next question.

'Do the legends involve murder at all, as a ritual perhaps?' Svoros looked uncertain.

'Possibly. At least one version of them may do.' He waved his finger at them, 'I know, let me check.' Svoros walked behind the counter and reached up to a bookshelf that was behind it. As Powell had correctly observed the previous day, there was a large book upon it entitled 'The Possible Histories of Velza Island'.

Svoros returned to his seat with the book and blew a layer of dust off its cover, it clearly hadn't been read for some time.

'Velza Island was what it was called before the development, I assume?' Svoros nodded.

'Giorgio Corzones paid to have the name changed. I disagreed with that at first.'

'And you're alright with it now?' It was a pointless question but Kirshner knew that he had to keep the conversation going if he was going to get any real information out of the old man.'

'This island is constantly changing, I would be a fool to not change with it.' Svoros flicked through the book and stopped at a certain page, 'Ah, here we are.' Kirshner took another bite of his breakfast while looking curiously over at the book. Its pages were browned with age and the font was almost unreadable. Nevertheless Svoros had no problem deciphering it

'This page talks of 'blood locks', a method of hiding secrets with only blood being able to reveal the truth.' Kirshner turned to Powell.

'Was the girl missing any blood?'

'Apart from what was spread over the ground you mean?' Kirshner flicked his eyes towards Svoros to remind Powell of his presence. A sudden air of professionalism suddenly came over the Security Chief. 'I can check.' Powell excused himself and produced his phone, leaving the café to make his call.

Svoros continued to flick through the book in silence for a short moment before looking up at Kirshner.

'You think there isn't something quite right about that Professor, don't you?' Kirshner diverted his attention from the remains of his breakfast to the old man.

'What do you mean by that?' Svoros gave a half smile.

'Something you can't quite put your finger on? I felt the same the first time he visited this island. I avoided him as best I could. He was meddling with things that should be left well alone.' Kirshner suddenly felt uneasy.

'What do you mean?' Svoros leaned in, his eyes wide and his voice stern.

'Inspector Kirshner, a bit of archaeology can never really do any harm but some things may have been confined to history for a reason. This book is a work of fiction, there isn't any denying that but where did the fiction come from? Every legend has to start somewhere and that of the Velza has more provable historical fact than most.' Kirshner almost sighed with disappointment, Svoros wasn't going to impart any kind of valuable insight and was just another local who had been captivated by the legends in his youth. 'Do you really think there's any danger though, in what the legends suggest?'

'What do you mean by "danger" Inspector? One person has already died and you think that may just be because of some words that have been passed down. Nobody knows where the legends came from really. It certainly wasn't from my father and his companions who settled on this island, nor was it from the infamous explorer Willow, whose expedition vanished. I'm sure you've read that this island wasn't discovered until much later than the rest of the world? Almost like it wasn't there. I'm sure you also know that the prevailing theory is that this island had an indigenous population that kept its existence a secret. Do you really think that's possible Inspector?' Kirshner shook his head. 'Something kept this island hidden from the rest of humanity for a long time and the great mystery is how and why? What if Inspector, what if some kind of power was existent here but completely dormant and what if somebody was trying to disturb it?'

Powell suddenly entered the café again, his phone conversation having ended. Svoros sat back in his chair and relaxed. Powell retook his seat and quickly finished his breakfast. Little more was said before they left the café but as Kirshner was about to leave through the door, Svoros shouted after him.

'I hope I have been able to help, Inspector.' Kirshner nodded and politely thanked the old man.

The journey back to HQ was made in almost complete silence, Kirshner took a moment to consider what had been said to him. Svoros perhaps didn't believe the legends completely but his questioning of them had been unnerving, historical accounts didn't entirely make sense and now somebody who was on the island to unearth the past was suspected of murder. The Professor's lack of background still remained a disturbing mystery as did what Svoros had said about the island harbouring some kind of power. It was all supernatural nonsense of course but perhaps the legend did come from somewhere. After some considerable thought, Kirshner decided that keeping his investigation within the realms of reality was probably his best move. He'd learned nothing more about the Professor but had found his possible motive for the murder.

Kirshner returned to his book about the island's legends, unlike Svoros' it had been printed fairly recently and now that he had been familiarised with the background, it seemed to be more readable. Everything that Svoros had told him about the legends seemed to be confirmed by the book, particularly the part about a blood sacrifice to reveal the island's true secret. The one thing that the book never mentioned however was just what that secret could be. In some ways, Kirshner found that the book seemed to be encouraging people to discover what the secret was for themselves, perhaps that was what had caused the Professor and Amerigo to commit the murder? Svoros had said that Amerigo didn't believe the legends, at least not to the point that he would commit murder to explore them but after being influenced by the Professor, who knows what could happen?

Kirshner was more convinced than before that it was the Professor behind the killing, perhaps with Amerigo being involved too. Svoros had known Amerigo for a long time and his speaking in defence of the bar owner's character had convinced Kirshner that he may have been manipulated into the situation that he now found himself. Murder was murder though and Kirshner had to get to the bottom of it. This was no longer the simple case he expected to solve within a day but a complex series of events that may have been influenced by a legend dating back further than anybody could really understand. Kirshner had to know now not only for certain who had committed the murder but also why and whether it was possible for a similar murder to be committed in the future for the same reasons. As long as a legend existed then there would always be somebody wishing to test it.

Kirshner continued to read through the book but the words seemed to blur before his eyes and become unreadable. He passed over words without registering them properly in his mind and suddenly the text failed to make any sense at all. His eyes were heavy and just as Powell entered his makeshift office, he yawned uncontrollably.
'You're too tired, I shouldn't have woken you up before.' Kirshner shook his head.
'Nonsense, I shouldn't have been asleep earlier.' Powell shook his head.

'Nothing is happening, the search parties have no idea what to do and we have nothing else to investigate. Harper tells me that DJ freedom had a very boring night, staggered straight back to his apartment as soon as he had finished apparently. Go and get some sleep, I promise that somebody will phone you the instant that there is a breakthrough.' Kirshner was ready to argue again but another yawn forced itself from his mouth. He nodded and agreed that he did need to rest. 'We've had an apartment ready for you since before you first arrived, perhaps you should go and unpack?' Kirshner nodded, admitting to both himself and Powell that for the first time he realised that he would be spending some time on the island.

With the last of his energy he dragged his case into his apartment and placed it on to the first spot of empty floor space that he could find. He walked into the bedroom and saw, to his great relief, that the bed was ready to sleep on. Back on the mainland he had been greeted with a pile of sheets for him to arrange by himself. He removed his shoes and lay down on the bed. For the first time in thirty hours, comfortable sleep came over him and his mind was free from thoughts about the murder of Zoë Parker.

Twenty Five

The sand was so hot that Sofia's feet burned as she walked across the beach of Lovers' Cove. She held on to Karl's hand tightly, not wanting to let it go. She pulled Karl towards the sea, deciding that the water would be the best way to cool her feet. They paddled for a little while but the water never went above their knees, it was calm and there were no waves at all. Eventually they moved back on to the beach and lay down on the sand, they found a spot that was sheltered by a rock so the heat was just about bearable.

Sofia looked straight into Karl's eyes as she lay next to him and smiled. She knew that she would spend the rest of the holiday with him, it was just too perfect to do otherwise. He cared about her and that was more than any guy she'd met recently had done. She had enjoyed their time together and ever since Lucy had found Will, she hadn't needed to feel guilty about leaving her friend. They were supposed to spend some time together this holiday and they probably would do at some point but they had come to Corzones Island to enjoy themselves and it had simply turned out that other people were who they'd rather spend their time with. Sofia knew that it wouldn't affect their friendship and she was sure that Lucy would feel the same. After all, it would only last the length of the holiday.

As evening drew closer and sun was just starting to go in, the sand quickly cooled and Sofia's feet were thankful. It had been late afternoon before she and Karl had met up and they had decided to spend as much time as they could on the hidden beach. Sofia had taken a dress to Karl's apartment and left it there before they'd walked into the jungle and climbed down the rocks on to the beach. Her plan was to shower and change at Karl's so that they could go out together that evening.

The sun started to set and Sofia's afternoon on the beach with Karl came to an end. They walked together back to Karl's apartment. As they did so, Karl stopped suddenly by a notice board. Such information points were common around the island and since she had arrived, Sofia had paid little attention to them. While she was on the island she didn't care about local news but for some reason, this board had managed to command Karl's attention.

'What is it?' She asked, holding on to his hand just in case something was wrong.

'That man, I know him.' Karl pointed to a piece of A4 paper that had the images of two men printed on to it. Karl pointed to the man on the left, he was in his mid-forties and had dark hair, his face held on to a quizzical expression 'I know that man!' Sofia squeezed Karl's hand. She recognised the man in the picture somehow but couldn't quite place him. A caption below the image read:

Wanted for questioning in regards to
the recent murder. If anybody sees
these men then please contact Security
immediately.

Sofia desperately tried to place the man in the image, she had seen him somewhere and recently.

'He is known as Professor Loch,' said Karl, 'he meddles with things that aren't right.' Upon hearing the name, things suddenly started to make sense to Sofia. That was the man that Lucy and her friend had been spending so much time with. Suddenly a feeling of worry came over Sofia, perhaps her friend was in danger. Sofia tried to call Lucy but there was no answer and her panic began to increase. Karl was still shaken up too but he managed to reassure Sofia. 'That poster says that the Professor is on the run along with that other man, no mention is made of your friend. She will be fine, I promise.' Sofia knew that Karl was right but sent Lucy a text asking her to promise that she was alright. She received a reply soon after, telling her that Lucy was in a restaurant with Will and was perfectly okay. Despite this her worries didn't leave her.

When they arrived at the apartment Sofia had her shower. She emerged from the bathroom about forty five minutes later, wearing her best dress and sporting a new hairstyle. In front of her she saw a table with a candle lit in the middle and two plates neatly laid out. Karl was standing in the kitchenette over the single stove, a large pan was bubbling away. He looked over his shoulder and saw the enormous smile that was on her face.

'Surprise. I hope you like it.' Sofia placed a hand over her open mouth.

'It's wonderful,' she said, 'really wonderful. Nobody has ever done anything like this for me before.' That was a lie, Sofia had seen her fair share of romantic gestures but it was the only thing she could think to say that would make Karl realise how much she appreciated it.

The meal was delicious, Karl had simply made pasta but the thought and dedication that had gone into it did impress Sofia. He had a bottle of Chardonnay in the fridge, ready to accompany the meal. It was drunk almost as quickly as the food was consumed. Sofia enjoyed every sip of it, being spoiled in such a way was always nice and she was very fond of the person doing the spoiling on this occasion.

After the meal they spent little time in deciding what they were going to do, their evening would be spent with so many other people in The Isle Club, drinking too much and dancing but the fact that they were together made it so good. Very few people entered the Isle Club and then left together a few hours later but she and Karl had done once already and would do for a second time this evening. Nothing seemed wrong, Karl wanted to spend time with her as much as she did with him so after their meal and bottle of wine, they left Karl's apartment and headed out.

The streets of Corzones Island were busy, full of people who were all heading to the strip. As they walked by, Sofia noticed that some people were already too drunk and were leaning against walls and buildings. Some were feeling lazy and ordered taxis to take them, despite the fact that the walk only took five minutes. At this time of night the island was multicoloured, the streets were illuminated by colourful fairy lights while the sky was entirely covered by the revolving patterns of various spotlights emanating from the strip. Sofia could hear the music loud and clear, even from this distance. Various songs from different clubs battled for control of the attention of anybody that was outside, encouraging them to go to wherever was loudest and sounded the best. As always on Corzones island though, one place managed to dominate the others. Sinners was in a close second, their 'heaven & hell' inspired house music ringing through the narrow streets and across the vast areas of grass but the clear winner was The Isle.

Despite its length, their time in the queue seemed to be short. They kissed a few times as they waited but nobody else seemed to notice. Everybody was too preoccupied with that fact that in such a short amount of time they would be experiencing what was often

163

cited to be one of the greatest club experiences on the planet. The lights of the strip seemed almost overpowering, every club was competing to be the most noticeable and the brightest, hoping that they could appeal to the consciousness of anybody who had been affected by the island.

They got into the club and went straight to the bar. Karl bought them both drinks and they went to dance. Sofia danced happily for a few minutes, not allowing the fact that a few splashes of her drink went over the edge of the glass and fell on to the floor to bother her, she was having such a good time that she didn't mind. Karl had placed his arms around her and they moved closer together, their bodies pressing into each other.

Time didn't seem to pass at all but very soon afterwards DJ Freedom made his usual entrance and marched across the dance floor into the DJ Booth. Sofia saw his face as he passed through a spotlight, just for a split second. He looked tired and upset but she thought no more of it as she turned her attention back to Karl. As Freedom started his set, they kissed again before continuing to dance as the time slipped away.

A few drinks and hours later, Karl and Sofia were still dancing. Sofia was starting to tire now and Karl appeared to be distracted, no longer constantly smiling as he had been on the beach that afternoon. He carried on but Sofia could see that with every passing second he wanted to be there even less.
'What's wrong?' She spoke into his ear and moved back to observe his reaction, he forced a smile and continued to dance but Sofia was worried now and far from enjoying herself. She took Karl's hand and gestured towards the door. He nodded and grasped her hand tightly.

They left the club, still hand-in-hand and walked towards the nearest bench. The strip was quiet now as most people had settled on the club in which they would be spending the night. A few couples who had decided to leave early merrily walked past them as they sat and a bouncer leant against the wall of The Isle Club, smoking. Even when sitting down, Sofia kept her hand firmly in Karl's.
'What's up?' Sofia tried extra hard to sound sincere but the amount she'd had to drink made it very difficult. Karl looked at her, his

164

face had gone very pale and anger was present in his eyes just as much as sadness was.

'He's here Sofia, that man. That Professor Loch.' Karl let out a deep sigh, he almost appeared to be crying.

'I know that you don't agree with what he does but why does that upset you so much?'

'It isn't that Sofia. I have met him before, just once. It was the night my brother died.' Sofa was shocked, she didn't know about this at all but suddenly felt another rush of fear for Lucy. A moment passed in silence and Sofia realised that she had to say something. 'I'm so sorry, I didn't know. What happened?' Karl's breathing became stuttered, he was struggling not to cry and every second that passed made him fail slightly more.

'He was near to my home town, doing some research or something. One night my brother and I walked past where the Professor had been working on our way home. There was a light coming from some nearby trees and Ralf went to look, telling me to stay by the road. I had drunk too much. I heard a shout, it was in an English accent, "You shouldn't be here!" he said. There was a loud crash and the next thing I knew, my brother was running towards me. There was another bang and I saw Ralf fall to the ground. There was a flash of light, so blinding that I had to close my eyes and when I reopened them my brother had gone. The Professor tried to speak to me but I ran. When I reported it to the police they told me that the Professor had already left on his return to England. Ralf wasn't pronounced dead, just missing because there was no body but I know what I saw and I know that the Professor shot my brother. He deals with things that are wrong, that shouldn't exist.'

Sofia was entirely speechless, what could she possibly say? She didn't believe that something other-worldly was going on but there was no doubt that the Professor was dangerous. Sofia walked slowly with Karl back to his apartment, saying the most comforting things she could think of. His story was less than believable but she could tell from his emotional state that something had indeed happened that night. Her first priority was to get him home safely and calm him down. In the morning she would return to her own apartment and warn Lucy of how dangerous this Professor must be. If he was on the run now then Lucy wouldn't be with him. Her priority was Karl, his upset was like nothing Sofia had seen before. His apparent memories of the night his brother had vanished haunted him.

165

The night was long and Sofia got little sleep, too many thoughts occupied her head and Karl's snoring didn't help either. She managed to drift off eventually but the sun awoke her as it shined in through a crack in the curtains. Karl was already out of bed and seemed much calmer by then. He vowed that he would find out what the Professor was doing on the island but promised Sofia that he would rest a little longer while she returned to her apartment to see Lucy. As she left he gave a smile and kissed her on the lips. She smiled back.

On returning to her apartment Sofia found that Lucy was in the shower. A few minutes passed and Lucy emerged looking surprised.

'I wasn't expecting to see you yet.' She said. Sofia tried to force a smile but she was too tired to be convincing.

'Karl wanted to be alone for a bit. He's been upset all night and I've been trying to calm him down.' Lucy immediately looked concerned which relieved Sofia slightly as it meant that her friend may actually listen to what she had to say.

'What's wrong?' Asked Lucy.

'He knows that Professor you've been spending time with. He's a bad man Lucy!' Lucy sighed.

'Not you too Sofia. Professor Loch is innocent.' Lucy moved closer to her friend and spoke in a hushed voice.

'Listen, the Professor is on the run at the minute but he's fighting for good. Me and Will are helping him.' Sofia backed away from her friend, unable to believe what she was hearing.

'You're helping a criminal? That is mad!'

'Listen Sofia, something strange, something that isn't right is happening on this island and the Professor is here to investigate it, maybe even stop it.' Sofia was getting angry now, had Lucy managed to lose herself in some pathetic fantasy?

'So you're telling me that Karl is a liar? He is upset, I've been with him all night, trying to make him feel better. The Professor killed his brother Lucy! Somehow they let him get away and now he's on this island and on the run for another murder!' Lucy shook her head.

'That's nonsense.' Sofia was furious now. How could somebody she called her best friend be so stupid and ignorant about something so obvious?

'If you are hiding anything Lucy...'

'Well I'm not! I don't know where he is or anything. If Karl is involved with what's happening on this island then you should stay away from him!' Sofia laughed, she couldn't help it. She'd suspected this all along but Lucy seemed to now be confirming her thoughts.

'I get it now Lucy, you're jealous aren't you?' Lucy laughed straight back at her.

'Jealous? Jealous of the fact that you've pulled some wanker who will move on as soon as someone else looks at him?' Sofia wanted to slap her but thought better of it. Lucy dashed into her room and locked the door.

Sofia sat at the table alone for a few minutes, unsure of what to do or say next. She wanted to calm down but couldn't, not when she knew that soon Lucy would emerge from that door and possibly even put herself in danger. She was associating with a murderer. Sofia didn't know what to do. She didn't want to stay away from Karl for too long, he may have tried to appear happy as she'd left but it was more than clear that he wasn't.

Lucy emerged from her room with her bag in her hand.

'I'm going out. I hope you'll stop being so stupid by the time I get back later.' Sofia didn't know what to say and she only had a few brief seconds to give a response. Lucy stormed over to the door and opened it.

'I'm not the stupid one, bitch!' What a pathetic response! Sofia hated herself for saying it straight away but by then Lucy had slammed the door behind her and vanished. Sofia breathed deeply, trying to hold back tears. She didn't manage. She cried harder than she could remember doing so before. Everything had gone wrong. Karl was unhappy and she had fallen out with Lucy on what was supposed to be their dream holiday. She didn't know what to do but as the minutes went by, one thing became clear to her. Lucy was helping the Professor, she'd even admitted it and as a result she was placing herself in far more danger than Sofia had originally thought.

She made a decision that she struggled with for a few minutes but knew that she somehow had to act. Shaking, she walked over to the room's phone and picked it up. Beneath the handset were a series of numbers, she dialled the number '7' which passed her on to the

Security department. The line was silent for a moment before a voice came from the end.

'Island Security, how can I help?' Sofia took a deep breath, she was doing the right thing.

'I'm worried about my friend. She's involved with that Professor person on the posters and I think she's in a lot of danger.'

Twenty Six

Will arrived back at his apartment and this time he had managed to get in before Harry, Jason or Royce had awakened. There was a larger pile than usual of empty bottles left lying around and on the table he noticed a small bag with traces of a white powder inside it, he decided that it was best not to ask questions. Will opened the fridge and produced a carton of orange juice but on looking for a glass to pour it into he found that there weren't any left in the cupboard. Before his morning drink, he would have to do some washing up. He went to the sink and began to fill it with hot water and splashed some washing up liquid into it. The green substance that produced few bubbles and had been part of the 'complimentary package' that was left in a feeble-looking basket on the table when they had arrived. Will washed a few of the glasses and a bowl for him to eat some cereal out of afterwards, despite his uncertainty as to whether they'd have any milk or not.

Will was happy to see that Harry was the first to get up. He hadn't seen his brother since their conversation the previous morning and amongst other things wanted to let him know that he was alright. Harry seemed to be distant but was glad to see Will. He assured him that his hangover had been caused by only drink and that he'd left the others with everything else. The subject quickly changed. 'Another all nighter? This place really has changed you Will.' Harry gave a cheeky grin which increased in size once Will began his protests yet again that nothing had happened. Harry took one of the washed glasses from the side of the sink and filled it with water, drinking it in one gulp. He refilled the glass and pointed towards the balcony. 'Shall we go out there?' Will nodded, the sun was already quite intense and he would enjoy breakfast while sitting in it.

The balcony was in just as bad a state as the apartment. A pile of glasses and bottles lay on the table. Will produced his sunglasses from his pocket and took a seat looking out towards the sun 'Somebody had a heavy night then?' Will smiled, he was much calmer than when he had spoken to his brother the previous morning.

'Yeah, little bit. We had a few girls from upstairs over for drinks. It was fun.' Will felt that he was sitting on something and reached down. His hand rose holding a discarded bikini top.
'So I can see.' Will discarded the top on the ground next to him.
For once Harry looked slightly embarrassed, a reaction that Will knew he wouldn't be showing if anybody else were around. Harry quickly changed the subject.
'So you and this Lucy girl? That's two nights you didn't make it back Will.'
'It really isn't anything, we just kissed a bit, that's all.' Harry smiled and raised an eyebrow.
'A second kiss? This is getting serious.'
'No it isn't,' Will protested quickly but then thought about what he and Lucy had said to each other, 'well I don't think it is. We sort of hugged all night.' Harry smiled but didn't comment.

They remained on the balcony for the best part of an hour before they were interrupted. Harry had asked Will if he wanted to bring Lucy to the apartment, something that Will didn't want to do at the moment but he wasn't going to tell his brother that. They both heard the door open and looked into the apartment to see Royce entering, wearing his clothes from the previous night and a huge smug grin on his face.
'Alright bitches.' Harry tutted and informed Will that he hadn't been looking forward to this moment. Royce had ended up with a girl not long after arriving at Sinners and they had left together soon after that, not to be seen again until now. Royce described how his night had progressed in unnecessarily graphic detail and even mimed some parts of what he was saying.

Will switched off and didn't really listen to what his temporary flatmate was saying. Instead he thought about Lucy and what they were going to do that day. They had agreed to meet in the town centre again and decide exactly what to do then, but they were unsure what that would actually be as going up to the Temple Bar again wasn't an option. It had been closed and more likely than not it would still be swarming with Security Officers. Will felt like he couldn't simply just sit around but at the same time there was nothing that they could do to help the Professor and Amerigo, all they could do was wait to hear something. Will was unsure as to how they would actually make contact, they couldn't be out in the open, as soon as they showed themselves they would be arrested.

170

The more Will thought about it, the more useless he felt. He had been told that he, along with everybody else on the island was in great danger but he had no idea how to start doing anything about it.

He talked a little longer with Harry and Royce before retiring to the bathroom for a much needed shower, he hadn't changed or washed properly since his afternoon of excavating at the temple and he felt as unpleasant as he must have appeared. Whatever the day was to bring, he wanted to face it in the most hygienic way possible.

After readying himself Will left the apartment and began his walk to the town centre. He was running a few minutes late but knew that Lucy wouldn't mind. It was another sunny day but this time there were some clouds starting to manifest in the otherwise perfectly blue sky. Will wanted a more relaxing day than he'd had previously but knew that was unlikely. He wouldn't be able to rest properly after everything that had happened, just as he hadn't slept very well the previous night. Both he and Lucy had remained awake until very late, a combination of their worries and the constant thudding of music in the distance. There had been quite a bit more kissing too as well as sitting together on the sofa with their arms around each other. Will had enjoyed it and from her reactions it seemed that Lucy had done too. He'd also appreciated a night of not going out and drinking too much, it was a nice change.

Will arrived at the town centre to find that despite his lateness, he had got there before Lucy. He took a seat close to the fountain and waited. On a nearby notice board Will saw the images of the Professor and Amerigo with a list of their supposed crimes underneath. It was hard to believe that anybody could believe the two men were guilty of what they were accused. In their pictures they both looked so harmless, Will knew that wasn't true but not in the same way that the rest of the island suspected.

Time passed and still Lucy hadn't arrived, Will decided to send her a text to let her know that he was waiting. Five more minutes passed and there had been no reply. Will started to worry. What if somebody had got to her, the person that the Professor and Amerigo had warned them about maybe? Will looked over and saw Café Solar, that's where he worked or so Amerigo had said.

171

What if the man in the café had seen Lucy arrive and grabbed her before Will had made it there? It was quiet enough, not many people had yet appeared from their apartments. That was ridiculous though. Suddenly another thought entered Will's head and this one was more unpleasant than he would care to admit. What if Lucy had stood him up? What if she had thought about everything that had happened and decided that she didn't want anything to do with him? She would normally have texted back straight away, she always seemed to when they were together and she received a message from Sofia. Will realised that he was being paranoid but the more that time passed, unpleasant and unhappy thoughts haunted him further.

'William.' The voice came from behind Will and made him instantly turn around, he was ready to defend himself from a potential attacker. He recognised the man who had said his name though, it was Powell the Security Chief who had interviewed him after the body had been found. Will knew that this could only be about one thing and he had to be very careful about what he said. 'I've told you and that Inspector everything that I know already.' Powell sighed.
'We need to talk properly Will. I don't think you have told me everything,' Powell seemed less caring than he had previously, his eyes carried a serious look, 'we have been told that you and Lucy withheld information and even helped the Professor escape.'
'I've not withheld anything!' Will had to stand his ground, the Professor and Amerigo were depending on him. Powell sighed and cast his eyes to the ground for a moment. When they were levelled with Will's again he seemed to be even more serious, even stern.
'I was hoping that we wouldn't have to do this. Lucy was uncooperative too.' Lucy's absence was suddenly explained, the Security people had got to her.
'There's nothing that I can do.'
'I'm sorry Will but we both know that's a lie. I'm afraid I'm going to have to arrest you.'

Will was speechless and remained so for the entire journey to Security HQ. Powell escorted him to a street just a short distance from the town centre in which a buggy was parked. He pointed to the back seat and Will climbed on. Powell took the driving seat and just for a second, Will could see a look of unhappiness upon his face. He wanted to tell the truth but he'd never be believed and may put the Professor, not to mention Lucy and himself, into further danger. He hoped that Lucy was alright and had remained as silent as he had. She wouldn't say anything. She was possibly the most loyal person that Will had ever met and she probably wouldn't even be feeling the slight sting of temptation that he was now.

They arrived at HQ and Powell drove the buggy around the back, parking it right by the rear door. Inspector Kirshner was standing alone just next to the entrance, smoking a cigarette. Upon seeing Powell and Will, he threw it on to the ground and extinguished it with a firm stamp of his foot.

'Come on.' Powell now sounded completely void of the compassion that he had showed two nights ago. Just as he was told Will stepped off of the buggy. Powell gestured to the door with a nod of his head and Will began to walk. Kirshner remained still but followed Will with his tired eyes for every footstep that he took. It was only a short distance from the buggy to the door but it seemed to take Will an eternity to make the journey. It was only as he walked through the door that he realised that Powell was standing immediately behind him, walking at exactly the same speed.

After a walk along a narrow corridor, Will arrived at a huge open-plan office space. Most of the computers were occupied by various officers, some typing up reports and some monitoring images from Security cameras. It was an impressive setup and Will quickly realised that it was possible to see many locations across the island, however, the jungle seemed to be a blind spot along with Amerigo's bar. Perhaps its reputation as a quiet destination that was ignored by most visitors to the island wasn't such a bad thing at all. Had it been wired into the Security system the forces would not only be aware of just how close they were to catching the Professor and Amerigo but they would also have evidence of Will, Lucy and Steve assisting their escape. The fact that no such evidence existed strengthened Will's resolve not to provide any.

There was no sign of Lucy at all although Will knew that she must be in the building somewhere. One of the interview rooms had its door closed and a blind was covering its small window, Will figured that she must be there. Powell pointed to another room two doors down from that one and Will walked in its direction. He had no idea what his rights were, Corzones Island had brought in a

British inspector to assist with the murder but it was notorious for governing itself, especially in the case of law. Giorgio Corzones must have had friends in all of the right places as his procurement of the island included the ability to govern it in any way he saw fit was unprecedented. During his reading about the island before the holiday, Will had discovered that a team of 'top lawyers and politicians' and been involved in the law-making process of the island. For appearances sake they had ruled drugs to be illegal but it was no secret that the Security staff would turn a blind eye in the majority of cases. That was one of the island's big points of appeal to many of its visitors. Some people referred to it as 'the place in which the future will begin' and that made Will feel uncomfortable. He didn't like the idea of businesses being able to buy entire masses of land, no matter how small and forgotten they were beforehand. At least this owner was better than most, he was happy for the island to be studied, as Professor Loch's presence had proved.

Will entered the interview room, followed by Powell and Kirshner. It was the exact same room that he had been brought into after the murder. He was directed to the seat that he had occupied previously and sat down. He somehow had to persuade Powell and Kirshner that he wasn't involved with what was going on. What could it have been that suggested to them that he did know something? It wouldn't have been Lucy, it can't have been. But then again, Powell did know exactly where to find him. Was that just the excellent Security system that the island had or was it because Lucy had told them where to go?

Kirshner and Powell said nothing of Lucy as they interviewed him, they were far more interested in what had actually happened the previous day at the Temple Bar. They wanted to know what the Professor had said to them before he had left and why he had lied to them at the time. They seemed to emphasise repeatedly that he was not a murder suspect and they hadn't brought him in to ask about that. At one point Powell even asked him what kind of effect seeing the body of a murder victim had on him. Will remained defiant throughout, saying anything he could that might persuade them that their hunt for the Professor was a step in the wrong direction. The one thing he didn't mention was the involvement of Svoros, the café owner. He had no evidence and it would almost certainly be dismissed as lies provided by the Professor anyway.

174

After the interview, Will was returned to the open plan office and smiled as he saw Lucy, who was sitting on a blue sofa close to one of the large windows. Powell directed Will to take a seat in the same place. Lucy smiled upon seeing him. Her eyes were bloodshot, she had clearly been crying. What had Powell and Kirshner asked her? Was it the same set of questions or had they played on the fact that she had depression? They will surely have done a check on them both and seen it from her records. All Will knew was that whatever had been said had upset her, which made him angrier than he had felt since his arrival on Corzones.

Powell and Kirshner left them alone, saying that they would have to wait. Will's first instinct was to put his arm around Lucy, he did so without really realising. She smiled again but it seemed forced, like she didn't really want to. Will was confident that it wasn't him, but the interview, that was causing such an uncertain reaction. 'Are you alright? What did they say?' Lucy sniffled before she responded, Will hoped that it didn't involve the interviewing methods of Powell and Kirshner.
'It was Sofia. I'm so sorry Will. It was my fault.' This didn't give Will any answers at all. He'd never properly met Sofia apart from in the Isle Club but Lucy had spent a considerable amount of time telling him about her best friend and holiday companion.
'What do you mean?' he asked, 'I told her about what was happening, I hoped that I could trust her but she flipped. She seems to think that Karl has history with the Professor and that makes him guilty. I don't understand. Sofia told Security though. It was my fault, I shouldn't have trusted her.' Will sighed and looked to the ground, desperately trying to find a way to comfort Lucy. Trusting anybody with what was going on was a mistake but Lucy wasn't a person who trusted easily. This could be a severe blow to her confidence. Will still had his arm on Lucy, he shuffled slightly closer to her and quietly whispered to her that it was alright and that she didn't need to worry.

They didn't say much to each other as they waited. Will had a suspicion that they had been placed on the blue sofa together for a reason. It was possible that they were being listened to. Powell and Kirshner had vanished from sight almost immediately and all other Security Officers seemed to be entirely ignoring the fact that they were there. Will whispered his suspicions to Lucy and she simply replied by nodding. Perhaps the paranoia that he had demonstrated in the town centre was getting the better of him but it was just possible that his theory was correct. He hoped he was wrong.

Eventually Powell returned to the room and walked straight over to them. He looked tired and frustrated but as he spoke to them he tried to return to his calm demeanour that he had demonstrated on the night of the murder. He took a seat next to them and sighed. 'I'm going to ask you both a question now. I want you to reply honestly, very honestly. I'm starting to think that it's possible that the Professor and Amerigo are innocent. I'm not certain and they're still my prime suspects but if you have anything to say then I'm willing to listen.' Lucy looked straight at Will, she was scared. Had Powell discovered something else? Neither of them spoke so Powell tried again: 'Is there anything about the Professor or Amerigo that you can tell us? Perhaps not to incriminate them but to tell us why they are doing what they are? They heard us coming and ran, surely you don't believe that's the action of an innocent person?' Again Lucy looked worried, she wouldn't say anything. Will however decided that he would. After much consideration he realised that he would receive one of two reactions. Either he would be ridiculed by Powell or he would be believed. His story, the truth, was so ludicrous that he expected he would be laughed at but telling the truth was the only way that he and Lucy would ever be released.
'I need you to promise me that you'll believe what I say.' Powell looked sceptical and considered for a moment before nodding. Will took a deep breath and considered his answer. Lucy grabbed hold of his hand and squeezed it, she didn't want him to say what he was about to.
'The Professor investigates the supernatural, that's why he came to the island. He didn't commit that murder but he thinks he knows why it happened.' Powell looked very unsure, his expression instantly told Will that he hadn't been believed. Powell sighed again and looked at the floor, shaking his head.
'I want to let you go,' he said, 'but you have to help us.'
'I'm trying to!' Will tried to make his protest sound as genuine as possible but it was clear that he was thought to be not telling the truth.
'Please stop lying.' Powell stood up and walked away without another word. Lucy looked straight into his eyes, making no secret of her disapproval.

There seemed to be a change after a few minutes though, Powell returned with Kirshner and asked Will to repeat himself. Will wasn't sure why but he did so, it was the truth after all. Without a word both Powell and Kirshner walked away. More time passed and Powell returned again.

'Can you provide proof of what you said?' Will was surprised, there was nothing he could do to prove anything but it seemed that Powell was finally willing to listen. Will shook his head, he wasn't sure what he could do but he knew that the proof must exist.

'Have you searched his accommodation?' It was Lucy who spoke and Will had to admit that her suggestion was a good one.

'We have,' said Powell, 'and we didn't find anything that could relate to the case at all. Just a load of archaeological equipment.' Will had an idea.

'Are you sure it was all archaeological?' Powell considered for a moment.

'We didn't identify it all but we assumed that the Professor had access to equipment that wasn't yet on the market.' An opportunity!

'I'm an archaeologist too. Less qualified than the Professor but I can tell you if something isn't what it's meant to be.' Powell considered this,

'Wait here.' He dashed off. Of course, Will and Lucy wouldn't have gone anywhere, they couldn't have done as they would have certainly have been stopped before they could leave. They were under arrest after all.

Powell returned after about half an hour. The afternoon was getting late now and Will realised that he had been in Security HQ for quite a few hours.

'If I took you to the Professor's bungalow and showed you his equipment, could you prove what you have said?' He could, he knew he could but would doing so place him into more danger? He couldn't trust anybody apart from Lucy but this was an opportunity to prove the Professor's innocence. At least he hoped it was. Will looked to Lucy who gave a tentative but encouraging nod. Will turned back to Powell.

'Alright then, I'll try.'

Kirshner was conspicuous by his absence when they travelled to the bungalow. Will had got the impression that the murder was his case and that he would be along for every step of the journey.

Surely his admitting that the Professor was involved with some strange activity was considered to be some kind of a breakthrough. Nevertheless it was Powell and two other Security Officers who accompanied them to the bungalow. Will found himself on the back of a buggy again while Lucy was on another. Powell drove one to himself and stayed slightly behind, perhaps he was concerned that either Lucy or Will would jump off and wanted to be in a position to grab them easily if they did so.

They arrived at the bungalow and Powell produced a set of keys, after a few moments of fumbling and trying to find the right one, he opened the door. Inside the bungalow they found an organised mess. It was clear that it had been thoroughly searched but Will noticed something else, some cases that resembled the ones that the Professor had taken to the dig were open. Those cases had appeared to be very complicated to open and Will had suspected that they were somehow linked to Professor Loch's fingerprint. He must have been there. Will couldn't be certain but he knew the Professor and knew that he wouldn't have left the cases open unless the situation demanded it.

'The Professor's accommodation. Find something you don't recognise if you can, Will.' This was it. Will had never disbelieved what the Professor had told him but he knew that he would find some kind of evidence here if it was true. Lucy remained by the door, she said nothing but watched intently as Will walked over to the cases and began to rummage through them. At first there seemed to be nothing that he didn't recognise, some of it was quite advanced but it still related to what he understood to be archaeological. He'd almost given up when he spotted a gap in the side of the case. He picked at it and found the base pulled away to reveal a hidden section. The equipment in there didn't seem to be so archaeological and looked like something from a science fiction film. It was all the same horrible plastic white and contained flashing lights, mostly green and purple. Will didn't understand any of the equipment, he produced one piece that was shaped slightly like a gun, a gap in the case showed that one piece of equipment that was just like it had been removed.

Powell and the other two Security Guards seemed to panic slightly when Will lifted the gun-like object and even Lucy looked alarmed.

'Be careful with that!' Powell's voice sounded insecure but he made no action to stop Will picking up the object. Despite looking weapon-like it had no firing mechanism. 'What is it?' Powell looked at Will expecting a perfectly simple answer. The truth was that Will had no idea but it certainly didn't appear to be anything that he would link with archaeology. More than anything else, Will felt relieved. Perhaps he hadn't admitted it, even to himself, but he had subconsciously started to question what the Professor had told him the previous day. This device was proof that the Professor at least had access to something that was unexplained and Will was happy to make the logical leap that everything else he had been told was the truth.

He showed the gun-like device to Powell and assured him that he didn't know what it was but it had no archaeological significance. Powell sighed again, like he always seemed to when he was uncertain but he nodded.
'Very well then, the Professor has more to him than meets the eye. We had better return to HQ.'

They left the bungalow, Powell locked it up safely again before returning to the buggies. The journey back was the same as it had been on the way. Will and Lucy were on separate buggies and unable to speak. Will wished that he could say something to her. She had been unhappy at his telling Powell the truth and hadn't said a word to him since. Will just hoped that what he had done was for the best. He hadn't said anything to help Security find the Professor or even anything that would incriminate him further. It even seemed that Powell was starting to believe Will was telling the truth. He could only hope that this was the case.

They returned to Security HQ and were directed back to the blue sofa that they had been sitting in earlier. Powell quickly disappeared and left them alone. Will didn't care if he was being listened to now, he had to speak to Lucy.
'Well?' It was a simple thing to say but Lucy seemed to understand. She also appeared to throw caution to the wind in regards to what she said.
'That was risky Will but you did the right thing.' Will was relieved, he had been worried the whole time that Lucy had somehow felt that he had betrayed not only the Professor's trust but hers too.
'I had to tell them. They'd have kept us here if I hadn't.'

179

'They're keeping us here anyway.' She was right, Powell hadn't made any suggestion at all they would be allowed to leave but he had acted as if he had started to believe what Will had said. He remained hopeful.

Lucy had really been affected by the fact that Sofia had spoken to Security. That much was clear. He wasn't sure how she knew her friend had been the one to say something and he didn't dare ask, it would probably lead to more tears and the last thing Will wanted was for Lucy to be more upset. They did speak occasionally while they were sitting together but that didn't make the time pass any more quickly. They were on the sofa for a long time and apart from one offer of a drink from Powell, they remained alone.

Lucy seemed to be more comfortable now, the signs of her crying had vanished and she and Will talked a little more. There was one question that Will had been wanting to ask Lucy ever since their kiss the previous night. Will knew that the majority of 'romances' on Corzones Island came to an abrupt end once the holiday was over and he had feared all along that he and Lucy would follow that pattern. They were alone together and Will had to ask.
'I was wondering Lucy, when we're back home would you like to meet up? Like properly I mean.' Lucy remained silent for a moment, just enough time for Will to feel another stab of paranoia. But then she smiled. It was that wonderful smile that he had seen when they'd kissed.
'Of course I would.' Will found himself smiling too, He and Lucy were under arrest and embroiled in something far more sinister and strange than either of them could ever really comprehend but somehow they had both managed to make each other happy despite the circumstances. Lucy gave Will a kiss on the cheek and for a short moment he was able to forget the troubles that Corzones Island had brought upon him.

Twenty-Seven

Sofia left his apartment and Karl slept for a little longer. He had been foolish the previous night, allowing the sight of the Professor to affect him in such a way. Telling Sofia the story of what had happened had been a huge mistake but every word he had said was the truth. His brother had vanished that night and he was certain that the Professor had somehow murdered him and disposed of the body. That archaeological site must have contained all kinds of scientific equipment, including what was needed to make a loud bang and a flash.

To Svoros, Karl had to show that he had entirely got over the events of that night and that his participation in what was happening in the island was entirely free of emotion but the truth was that Karl had joined the brotherhood for revenge. After his brother had died Karl had tried to convince the German Police that the Professor was responsible but he wasn't believed. After that he had begun to find out as much as he could about him and that was how he had discovered Corzones Island. He had travelled there to try and find out what the purpose of the Professor's visit had been and it was then he had met Svoros.

One morning he had walked into the café looking particularly unhappy. On that visit he hadn't spent a night at any of the clubs or socialised, he had spent his entire time looking at the various archaeological sites on the island and trying to discover if some kind of inexplicable murder had taken place there. He hadn't found anything at all and nobody that he had spoken to even remembered the Professor

Karl had been fed up and while at the café he had asked Svoros just on the off-chance that he could somehow help. Svoros told Karl about the Professor's visit in detail and even shared with him the fact that somebody had supposedly died that time too. Karl no longer had any doubt that Loch was a killer. He had done it on the island as well as in Germany. From that day Karl promised that he would somehow get revenge on the Professor, even if that meant acting outside the law.

Svoros had told Karl many things. He had explained where the legends of Corzones Island had come from and what they really meant. There was a power on the island, a power that could be harnessed and used to create a better world where men like the Professor didn't have such influence. Svoros had taught Karl the truth, the Professor was a Super, a member of a secret organisation that were dedicated to stopping all supernatural activity. They were no less superstitious fools than anybody who followed a religion, choosing to fear power as opposed to using it for the betterment of mankind. Karl had joined the dots and reached the conclusion that the Professor had been meddling with a source of this power on the night that he killed Ralf. The murder of somebody innocent to purely satisfy his selfish need to keep things as they were.

Karl arrived at the café as soon as he could that morning and walked in to find it empty apart from Father Merco who was imploring Svoros to help him. Svoros had made his opinion of this man clear previously, he was a meddling fool whose views were prettier than those of even the Professor. Karl's meeting with him the day before had all been part of Svoros' plan. Merco was telling Svoros about his journey to the Temple Bar and how the Professor had dismissed him. The truth was that by telling Merco about the Professor's true identity, Karl had been gaining his confidence. Merco knew exactly who Svoros was. The old man had told Karl that Merco had been to the island before for his own series of investigations and fate had revealed Svoros' fascination with the legends and the discoveries he had made. Merco had apparently returned frequently since then and Svoros had always said that he'd have a part to play.

Their conversation was quite heated and Karl had entered towards its conclusion. The gist seemed to be that while Merco distrusted Svoros, the Professor was more of a priority. Svoros seemed to be agreeing with everything that Merco said, especially that the Professor had to be found as quickly as possible. Upon seeing Karl enter, Svoros invited Merco to speak quietly in the back, a trick that had been used to gain the confidence of a few people on Karl's numerous visits. Merco walked through the curtain after Svoros and out of sight. Karl walked towards the café door and locked it, just in case. After a few moments Svoros emerged from behind the curtain.

'We won't be hearing from Father Merco for some time. Perhaps you'd like to help me move him to the cellar and secure him?' Karl nodded, walking behind the counter and through the curtain. Merco was unconscious in a chair, a jar and a cloth lay next to him. Chloroform had often been a favourite of Svoros' methods of silencing people.

Merco was heavy and Karl struggled to drag him down the steps towards the cellar, Svoros only provided minimal help. They placed the unconscious man on a large wooden chair and bound him to it with some ropes. Svoros was very careful to cover the Father's mouth, the last thing they needed was for him to make a noise that could be heard from the café. Svoros returned upstairs while Karl stacked some boxes between the stairs and Merco to shield him from view, just in case anybody was to wander down.

Once his job was complete, Karl returned upstairs to see that Svoros was now occupied by a group of customers but upon his return to the kitchen, they both had a chance to speak.
'Is he secure?' Karl nodded. 'Good. I need you to pay a visit to our friend Argyll. His little stunt of providing the Inspector with mis-information about that DJ of his could have cost us dearly. Make sure he knows that he either does as he's told or incriminating evidence of what he did may just start to emerge.' Karl looked confused but Svoros was quickly able to elaborate. 'It was Argyll who killed the girl for us. He's very loyal when his own interests are involved.'

Karl left the café and began to walk towards the Isle Club. It was a short distance away but the journey gave him enough time to contemplate what he had just heard. He'd never doubted that Svoros was somehow involved with the murder but was surprised to learn that it was Argyll who had done the deed. Argyll had been part of the order for a long time but it couldn't be made clearer that the only person he was really loyal to was himself. Svoros had always said that one day Argyll would go too far but it appeared that this time he'd been allowed another reprieve. The girl had been murdered to incriminate the Professor but Argyll had used it as an opportunity to get DJ Freedom out of his way. This had failed and thankfully it was the Professor that was now being hunted by the island's Security forces.

Karl arrived at the Isle club and ducked into an alleyway at its side. The narrow passage encircled the entire building and contained the staff entrance. Karl walked straight through it and into a long corridor that was dimly lit. He knew exactly where he was going, he had carried messages to and from Argyll before. He walked into the large office at the end of the corridor, its door was maroon and a pattern was carved in to it.

Argyll was sitting at his desk, dressed in a suit as usual. He looked up at Karl as he entered and sighed.
'Shut the door,' he said, 'I need to keep a low profile.'
'I'm sure you do Argyll. The Security forces are aware of you now and they'll be watching your movements. Svoros wants you to remember that evidence of what you did *does* exist and if you don't follow the plan again it may come out.' Argyll tutted.
'Threats Karl? Is that all you can bring?'
'Svoros is advancing things, we need to be ready in the next few days. He wants to see you at midnight.'

Argyll grumbled about having a club to run but Karl knew that he wouldn't disobey Svoros, especially when he was on such shaky ground. Karl left and phoned Svoros, informing him of Argyll's response. Karl was hoping that he would be allowed some time to himself now so that he could go and meet Sofia, however Svoros had another job for Karl to do and this one involved him getting his hands dirty.
'With Argyll in line we are able to begin now, properly. The Professor is as good as out of the way and now we need to remove his friends.' Karl received his orders and took a moment to allow them to sink in. From what he had to do now there was no going back. He fully believed that Svoros was right though and knew that he must do as instructed.

Karl walked along the strip and into the town centre again, he crossed it and continued in the opposite direction, towards the majority of the island's accommodation. What was in his pocket suddenly started to feel very heavy. Svoros had told him to take it everywhere a few days previously but he never imagined that he would be using it so soon. He received a text telling him exactly what apartment to go to as he approached the right block. He climbed the stairs to the third story and walked along the corridor until he found the right room. He knocked on the door and waited for a reply.

The door was answered by a man wearing only his boxers.
'What is it?' The man asked.
'Steve?' The man looked at Karl, surprised that he knew his name.
'What is it? Who are you?' Karl breathed in deeply before producing what was in his pocket. Without a second thought he lunged forward and sent the knife deep into Steve's flesh. With a look of pure shock on his face, Steve fell back. Karl barged into his room and looked over towards the bed. Lying in it with the covers up to her neck was a familiar face, Sarah.
'Svoros sent me. It's time.' Sarah smiled.
'Good,' she said before climbing out of bed and dressing herself. Karl looked down on to the floor next to him. Steve was lying in a slowly-forming pool of blood. Sarah finished dressing herself and looked down at her former lover.
'I'm sorry,' she said plainly, 'you were so sweet.' Sarah left the apartment and with a slight glance over his shoulder, Karl did the same. He shut the door behind him as he went.

Karl returned to the café while Sarah went back to her own apartment. She'd expressed some concern about forensics but Svoros had assured Karl over the phone that any such evidence wouldn't matter. By the time Security had found Steve and any possible evidence it would be too late. Velza would already have been revealed to the world. Svoros was happy when Karl told him what he'd done, it was exactly what the old man had instructed. Any friend of the Professor's was a threat to their plan and had to be stopped.

Svoros had done some thinking since he had sent Karl to see Argyll beforehand. He had heard that Security had picked up two other people who were linked with Professor Loch and suspected that they may be able to partially convince them of his innocence. Svoros vanished into the cellar for a moment and returned with a leather bag.
'You must be very careful with this. Place it close to Security HQ and it should solve a few of our problems.' Karl knew exactly what was in the bag and knew that there was no choice. Svoros had trusted him with what had happened over the last hour and he couldn't betray that trust. He left the café with the bag in his hand.

He walked across the town centre and was about to head in the direction of Security HQ when he saw Sofia. She called his name and waved, her timing couldn't be any worse at all. Karl waved at her.

'Oh my god I'm so happy you're here. I needed a walk. Lucy is a bitch, she's helping that Professor and doesn't believe how bad he is, even after I told her what you said.' Karl knew that this was a problem, what if Lucy had linked him with what was going on? 'You need to ignore her Sofia.' She nodded.

'I did do. What are we going to do today? Can we go to that beach again? I love it there, with you.' Karl wanted to say yes more than anything else. After what he'd done he just wanted to unwind, to get away from it all even if it was only for the shortest time. As he was considering his answer, Karl's eyes drifted towards Café Solar, Svoros was standing in the window, just watching him. Svoros couldn't know about Sofia, especially considering she was supposed to be on the island with Lucy. For her own safety and the success of his own job, he had no choice.

'I'm sorry Sofia,' his voice was deep, fighting against every word that he said because he didn't want to have to say it, 'I think we need to be separate.' Sofia's eyes widened with upset, she didn't understand but there was no way in which Karl could explain it to her. He couldn't see her again, that would put her in danger and even though it was only supposed to be a bit of fun, he cared about her enough not to put her in that position.

'No Karl, please. I love our time together.' Her lip was trembling and Karl could see the tears beginning to form in her eyes, this was harder than he had expected it to be.

'I'm sorry Sofia, for your own good just stay away from me.' Karl turned and walked away. He didn't look back but that didn't block the sound of her sobs. He felt a lump in his own throat, he didn't want to leave her, to end what had happened between them on this holiday but he had no choice. He was on the island to avenge his brother and obeying Svoros was the only way that he would ever be able to do that.

Karl's thoughts of Sofia lingered in his mind, the sound of her sobbing followed him as he entered the jungle and walked towards Security HQ. He had to focus though, so many people were relying on him. So many people that had been waiting for so long were now on the island and ready for the day that they had been preparing for, ever since the island began to be developed. What Karl was about to do wouldn't only remove the Professor's other friends from the equation but it would also render the Security force entirely useless.

Karl approached Security HQ calmly. Quite a few officers were coming and going from the building but to them Karl looked just like another tourist. He carried the leather bag over his shoulder and walked right up to the building, staring up at its impressiveness. It was a glistening blue and large windows surrounded it entirely. Karl walked around the side and found a rubbish bin that was close to a large panel of glass, it was the perfect place. Through the window he saw two people sitting on a blue sofa, one of them was Lucy and he couldn't tell from behind but the other must have been Will. He dropped the bag into the bin and walked away. Nobody had even noticed that he was there.

Twenty-Eight

Amerigo stared out towards the glistening blue mass of water. He couldn't quite believe that the Professor had brought him to there of all places. It was one of the most famous parts of the island but nobody was willing to admit it. This part of the island was always occupied by couples, thinking that they had found some kind of secret getaway that was theirs and nobody else's. The truth was that Amerigo had known about Lovers' Cove since one of his first days on the island, so many years ago. He had met a local girl called Talia who had taken him there almost immediately. They shared a kiss together but by the time Amerigo had moved to the island properly she had been long gone. At first he was disappointed, a part of him had hoped that she would have been part of his life on the island but it wasn't to be.

He and the Professor had spent their night in the jungle, close to one of the rivers that flowed through it. They had taken turns to stay awake and watch the darkness for any other signs of humanity while the other slept the best they could on the hard ground. They had eaten peaches from a tin, one of the many snacks that the Professor had in the bungalow when Amerigo was packing the bags. The Professor seemed to have no trouble sleeping when it was his turn to but Amerigo had been kept awake by the sound of running water and the fear that Security would surround them at any moment. Corzones Island was his home and he knew that it was in extreme danger of being torn apart by Svoros and his followers.
'Something big is coming my friend,' Svoros' words repeated themselves in his mind, 'if you aren't with us then please don't be here when it arrives.' What was Svoros trying to do? The Professor really thought that he was trying to harness some kind of unimaginable power, "something that we aren't intended to comprehend". Amerigo was struggling to grasp the situation, what this power may actually be didn't enter the equation at all.

Lovers' Cove was fortunately empty when he and the Professor arrived, it was before lunch time so this was understandable. The Professor opened his rucksack as soon as they arrived on the beach and started to root through it, eventually finding what he was looking for. It was a circular device that was mostly filled by a radar-like screen. He examined it for a moment and began to walk in various directions as he tried to follow it. Amerigo just looked straight out to sea. It was a sight he was used to but this time it made him feel trapped and imprisoned on the island. There was no way he could leave and if the Professor was right then it could very soon be consumed by an incomprehensible evil.

The Professor stopped staring at his device and instead diverted his attention to the ocean. He seemed to sniff the air and even stuck his tongue out at one point to get a taste of it.
'Julius, this isn't a good place to be,' the Professor seemed to ignore Amerigo though and continued to stare blankly into the distance, 'Professor! This is too open, come on.' He blinked and turned to Amerigo, a sincere expression covered his face.
'There's something here Amerigo, something not right,' the Professor raised his eyebrows, 'something wrong.' Amerigo had to laugh.
'This is Lovers' Cove, Professor. A lot goes wrong here but it's never usually worse than an unplanned pregnancy.' The Professor didn't appreciate the joke and instead narrowed his eyes, returning his gaze to the sea.
'No Amerigo, something worse than that. I felt it the last time I was here. Come on, we need to go into the cave.' Leaving his bag for Amerigo to carry, the Professor walked towards the cave that was virtually hidden in the cliff face.

Inside everything seemed dry, it was completely sealed from water and the tide never travelled that far up the beach. Loch produced a torch from his bag and shone it deeper into the tunnel. It turned off to the left and continued much further than the torch would reveal.
'Have you ever been to the end of the tunnel?' Amerigo nodded.
'Yes. It opens into a small chamber that's a little wider than this, there isn't anything significant there though.' The Professor smiled and pointed the torch down the passageway again.
'I can almost guarantee that there is Amerigo, it's just that you and anybody else that has ventured here have missed it.' Amerigo wasn't sure how he should reply so he decided not to. Normally he would have ridiculed what was said but this was Professor Loch and if he suspected that there was something else in this cave then chances were very high that something else would be found. However he didn't know where or how they would find something. Every inch of this cave had been explored by every child on the

island before its development and since then it had seen countless couples who were hiding away in secret.

Time passed, an hour or something in that region, and the Professor hadn't moved away from the wall of the cave's entrance. He shined the torch on to little spots and examined them for a few moments before moving on to another apparently random section of rock. Amerigo quickly grew bored and sat down, leaning against a rock and looked out of the cave's mouth. Yet again his view consisted entirely of sand and sea. After a short amount of time he heard voices and another quick peek out of the cave showed him that a couple were walking along the beach, hand-in-hand. 'Professor.' Loch didn't respond, 'Professor! I think we are about to have company.' The Professor showed an almost childlike disappointment at being pulled away from his work but he agreed to move deeper into the cave. There were many gaps and corners that they would be able to hide behind should the couple intend to explore the deepest part of the passage.

As he moved further into the cave Amerigo looked over his shoulder and saw the couple entering it as he moved around a corner. He and Professor Loch were plunged entirely into darkness until the torch was reactivated.
'I don't think they're moving any further than the entrance,' Amerigo whispered and looked along the tunnel again, 'it seems that we are safe.' The Professor looked thoughtful and stared further into the darkness.
'This chamber at the end, show me.' Amerigo agreed and taking the torch began to lead the way.

It took a short time to arrive at the chamber, five minutes at the most and the Professor had returned to his state of curious excitement. He took the torch from Amerigo and shined it all around the room. All Amerigo saw was the rock walls that surrounded them on all sides but the Professor still insisted that this room was full of secrets.
'What do you see Amerigo?'
'Rock,' Amerigo replied, 'and sand on the ground.' The Professor shook his head.
'This room is arched, there's some slight wear and tear but what you have is a perfectly arched ceiling. It was manmade.' The

Professor ran to the end wall and rubbed it slightly with his fingers before putting his ear right up to it.

'This was sealed a very long time ago.'

'Sealed?' Amerigo was asking questions again, like an overly enthusiastic student. The Professor was more than happy to adopt the role of teacher.

'Yes Amerigo, sealed. Now if only I can find the correct point.'

The Professor spent the next half hour exploring every inch of the far wall, examining the ceiling and brushing away some of the sand to see if it covered anything. He didn't produce any immediate results but persevered in his search. Suddenly in the torchlight Amerigo could see his eyes widen.

'Amerigo, pass me a knife!' Amerigo rummaged through the bag until he found a penknife, he passed it to Loch.

'No pain and all that...' The Professor used the knife to cut deeply into his own hand. As blood started to pour out of the wound, Loch pressed his hand against a certain part of the wall and waited for a moment. Nothing happened. The wait continued and was eventually broken by a cold rush of air that seemed to be coming through the wall. Amerigo edged closer to it.

'What's happening Professor?' Loch didn't respond, he stood still, staring at the rock wall before him.

'It's working.' The rock wall started to glow and slowly it became brighter and brighter until it hurt Amerigo's eyes. He had no choice but to squeeze them together to protect them.

After a minute Amerigo tentatively opened his eyes again slightly to see that the light had faded. He opened them fully to see that the wall had also vanished and the Professor was examining the newly opened doorway.

'Blood lock. They killed the girl, took a sample of her blood but had no idea where to place it. It's so simple, a normal lock where blood works as the key. We've found this place before Svoros has.' Amerigo smiled for a brief moment but then remembered the situation.

'Does that mean that we have just released an unstoppable force?' The Professor shook his head.

'No, we've found the entrance to where it may be located though.' Some blood dripped from the Professor's hand. 'I believe that there's a bandage in the bag Amerigo, could you please find it for me?'

Amerigo found the bandage and helped the Professor apply it. They then walked through the newly formed doorway together and shone the torch into the darkness. The arched corridor seemed to continue for a while and they followed it slowly. Loch noticed that the walls started to contain images and symbols. He inspected them for a moment before realising that he wasn't able to translate them and that they should move on and return when they had gained more information.

Their walk continued and eventually they arrived in a large room that the torch wasn't able to illuminate fully. By now Amerigo was able to see what the Professor had meant before, the cave had indeed been a manmade corridor and this room looked far too impressive to be of natural design. From what he was able to see, Amerigo concluded that the room was spherical and probably stretched across about fifty metres. The Professor directed the light from his torch to the middle and they both saw a stone table located in the exact centre. He gestured that they towards it and Amerigo nodded in agreement. They edged towards the table, the torchlight constantly moving location and revealing further impressive aspects of the room.

The table in the centre was covered in sand and dust but bits of something that appeared to be paper stuck out. The Professor carefully extracted one of the bits of paper from under a small rock. He shone the torch on to it and examined it for a moment. 'Can you see what it says?' asked Amerigo. The Professor sighed. 'No. It contains the same symbols as were on the wall, it must be an alphabet of some kind but I don't know how to crack it.' The Professor brushed some of the dust and sand from the table and it became apparent that it was covered in other bits of paper. Amerigo transferred his attention to the walls and they seemed to be covered in small cubbyholes, some of which had more bits of parchment jammed into them. 'Amerigo,' said the Professor, 'I think we've found a library.'

As they examined the area it became clearer to Amerigo that the Professor must be right. After some searching and carefully inspecting everything that was on the table, Loch found a piece of paper that was larger than the rest. He shone the torch on to it which revealed a whole host of symbols spread across the page.

'Eureka.' The Professor was quiet, breathing his words more than speaking them. 'Amerigo, do you know what this is?' Amerigo took a long look at the paper, hoping to find something intelligent to say. All he saw were incomprehensible symbols, they looked simply like squiggles and didn't correspond to anything that he had ever seen before. One of the symbols suddenly stood out though, it seemed to be like the Greek letter Omega.

'That's Omega.' The Professor nodded.

'It's the alphabet, the Rosetta Stone for whatever we have down here, apparently a rudimentary form of Greek.

'Greek? But we're nowhere near Greece.' The Professor nodded in agreement again and searched hard for an answer.

'Perhaps we aren't now but...' The Professor quickly gathered a few of the pieces of parchment and laid them out across the table, making sure he didn't cover the large one. His eyes quickly began to move between the alphabet and the other pieces of paper. He mumbled odd phrases to himself: "unimaginable power...", "consumed by the ocean..." And it was a few minutes before he returned his attention to Amerigo.

'Amerigo I don't believe it.' He seemed to be breathless with excitement, 'I never thought that it really... Well. Amerigo it does all make sense. I noticed it as soon as we entered the cave, there was no water and then the stone barrier that the blood lock removed, all to protect whatever was down here. We're in a survival system.' It made no sense to Amerigo but he continued to listen, knowing that some kind of explanation would soon emerge. 'This one over here,' the Professor pointed to one of the bits of parchment, 'this one is more recent than the others, the paper isn't even nearly as old. There are thousands of year's difference. It speaks of finding a way to the surface and an imprisonment of...'

'An imprisonment of what?'

'I don't know, it doesn't say. Why couldn't they say?' The. Professor stepped back from the table, and shone the torch around the library once more. 'Amerigo, you have helped me achieve an archaeologists dream. Corzones Island is Atlantis!'

'Atlantis? As in the lost city?'

'Almost, certainly what the legend is based on. It all makes sense.'

The Professor excitedly raised his hands into the air, not noticing that his bandage had come slightly loose. A small droplet of blood flew from the wound and fell on to the stone table. In the distance a deep rumbling could be heard. The Professor and Amerigo stared into the darkness.

Twenty-Nine

'But there's more than that. There has to be. You just looked the other way and when you turned around you noticed that they had simply run away?' Inspector Kirshner had tried the same line of enquiry over and over again but Will wasn't providing any answers. He was being too vague to be telling the truth but no matter how many times he was pushed, stubbornly he refused to provide a satisfactory response. Lucy had been equally unhelpful when she had been spoken to before, the only information that she was willing to provide was the fact that Will would be in the town centre. She had only told them that because they wouldn't let her phone him and she didn't want to leave him waiting alone.

Two people he couldn't charge with anything, his only evidence was the girl who'd come forward and since her initial accusation she had seemed to have fallen silent. Powell had sent an officer to her apartment but she hadn't told him anything and reportedly she had done little but cry. Suddenly she had run out of the apartment and lost the officer. She had been found about half an hour later in the town centre, crying even more than she had been earlier. The fact that a girl had been sitting in tears on her own yet ignored by anybody who walked past told Kirshner a lot about the mentality of those on the island and also explained why hysteria over the murder had been minimal.

Kirshner watched on a feed as Powell talked to Will and Lucy who were sitting awkwardly on the blue sofa in the corner of the office. Neither of them wanted to say much but Will did eventually speak. Apparently the Professor had some kind of second job, something that had to be kept secret. Kirshner thought it to be nonsense until Will mentioned that he was some kind of "supernatural investigator". Kirshner started to listen very intently and watched the feed very closely, Will seemed to be telling the truth, or at least he thought he was.

Powell returned to Kirshner and asked his opinion on what Will had said. Kirshner agreed that the best thing to do was search the Professor's bungalow with Will and see if anything could be found to support their claims. Powell took Will and Lucy to the bungalow with a couple of other officers but Kirshner elected to remain at HQ. He returned to his various notes about the island's strange history and its numerous legends. If the Professor was there to investigate supernatural occurrences then surely he wouldn't be trying to fuel them? And Amerigo, he had known the Professor before, had something else happened then? Is that why he had placed his trust in Loch so suddenly? For the second time on Corzones Island, Kirshner was beginning to doubt something of which he had previously been certain. Were Will and Lucy covering for the Professor because they knew that he had been set up?

Powell returned with the two youngsters and dashed immediately to Kirshner's office.
'I'm going to get it checked but I think we've found exactly what they said we would, strange equipment designed for no archaeological purpose.' Kirshner sighed, his case was crumbling around him yet again. The phone rang and he answered it, the voice on the end asked for Powell. He passed the phone to the Security chief who answered. After a few short seconds his face suddenly fell and a look of horror began to manifest itself in his eyes. Kirshner knew immediately that this was more bad news.

The phone call ended and Powell looked mortified.
'What is it?' Kirshner couldn't stand the tension of waiting.
'Victor Corzones, son of Giorgio is about half an hour's helicopter flight from landing at the private residence. We are both to be there by the time he arrives.' Another pointless distraction but Kirshner knew from his long career that it wasn't wise to argue with his paymaster.
'We can't inform him that we have practically no evidence and seriously doubt the guilt of our main suspect.' Powell nodded in agreement,
'We have a fifteen minute buggy ride to find something to tell him.'

Their journey on the buggy was silent and unproductive. Neither of them knew what to say to Victor when he arrived or how they would even summarise the situation. They couldn't tell him what they had learned about the Professor but at the same time they were both now far from certain that he was guilty. All they had was the fact that they'd ruled out Franko Young (and even taken Harper off his watch) and that the Professor was barely a suspect.

There were links to the supernatural but would they be able to word that without sounding completely insane?

The private residence of Giorgio Corzones was very impressive. It was one of the largest houses that Kirshner had ever seen and its grounds were even more extravagant. It was completely surrounded by a gold fence and guards were scattered around its perimeter. One part of the vast lawn was a helipad and three more officers stood around that. Powell parked the buggy on the driveway and they both dismounted and walked to the helipad. Kirshner could see behind the house now. Amongst some trees was a path that led down to a private beach. Through some of the leaves he could see the sea, glistening a perfect and undisturbed blue.

An elderly man in a suit exited from the main door of the house and slowly walked towards the helipad.
'That's Parsons, personal butler to the Corzones family when any of them are in residence on the island. Don't say anything in front of him that you don't want Victor to hear.' Knowing exactly what Powell meant, Kirshner nodded. He was about to reply when his phone rang, it was the worse time possible. He answered the phone and was told by a voice on the end that the equipment was unidentifiable but after calling "a contact" they had verified that it was very specialist indeed. Kirshner hated it when analysts talked in cliché, but it seemed to be a habit that they couldn't avoid. It now appeared that either the Professor was on the same side or that they had a specialist in an unknown subject who had gone rogue. Either way it left Kirshner in the dark and with nothing to tell Victor Corzones when he arrived.
'That was HQ.' he told Powell, being careful to reveal nothing to the butler, 'They've verified that equipment is what we suspected.' Powell gave a serious but knowing look and a small nod. Meeting Victor on his arrival was a dangerous waste of time, they needed to focus on searching for the Professor, it was perhaps even more important now that he may be an ally.

The sound of the light breeze and birdsong was suddenly interrupted by the sound of an engine and rotating blades. A few moments later the helicopter appeared over the trees and headed for a perfect landing on the helipad. Everybody shielded themselves from the breeze. The chopper landed but Kirshner couldn't see anything due to the black tinted windows. The door opened before the blades had fully stopped moving and a young man with long red hair jumped out. He was wearing an expensive white suit and had a scowl on his face.

Introductions were given by Powell.
'Mister Corzones, this is Inspector Kirshner. He's the man who has been brought in to investigate what has happened.' Kirshner couldn't help but notice that Powell avoided at all costs using the word 'murder', this was probably for the best. Victor offered his hand which Kirshner shook in the most professional manner he possibly could. He found it hard to respect the authority of this man straight away, partly because any respect he was due had been bought by his father but also because he was no older than the average person visiting the island for a dose of alcohol, drugs and sex.

'My father really isn't impressed with you two.' Authority didn't suit Victor and Kirshner found himself wanting to argue with the young man but he held his tongue. 'The idea was that you were to find the party responsible for the murder and sweep the whole case under the carpet within a couple of days. However, he has been told that you have a huge manhunt in action across the island and nobody in custody at all. Can you offer an explanation gentlemen?' Kirshner knew that Powell would reply but in case he was asked personally he decided to have a few words ready. The wind increased and suddenly Kirshner, Powell and everybody else standing by the now-silent helicopter covered their ears.

Thirty

It was a deep rumbling, at first coming from the bowels of the darkness. Across from the path that Amerigo and the Professor had entered the library was another arched exit and there was no doubting that the growing sound was emanating from there. Amerigo was still reeling slightly from the testing of his sight by the light that had been made by the wall as it faded but the sound that began to grow made the light seem insignificant. It was a scream. A deep scream plagued by hatred and pain that had wanted to escape for so long. It pierced through the darkness and exploded into the library, consuming even the slightest trace of anything else. Even the Professor had covered his ears to block out the unbearable sound.

**

The curtains weren't open and only a few thin lines of sunlight were allowed to break into the room, illuminating the pool of red. For some time now, an hour or maybe two, the only sound that Steve could hear was his own heavy breathing and even that was quietened by the sheer pain that he felt. He couldn't move despite trying so hard, it just hurt so much. All he could do was focus on staying conscious and hope that when the time came and he heard somebody walking past, he could make enough noise to be noticed. He still had the knife embedded into his stomach which managed to stem the bleeding but he knew it was only a matter of time.

The darkness began to close in and Steve sensed that his breathing had become more laboured and desperate. His eyes were heavier than he ever imagined they could be and every part of his being was telling him to simply close them and allow the pain to end. Things started to become blurred and before he knew it he had succumbed to the blackness. This was it.

And then he heard the scream, it was louder and clearer than anything that his ears had ever registered before. Its sheer force gave him the energy to throw open his eyes again in alarm. He didn't know what it was but the sound seemed to travel past him and over the rest of the island. He couldn't even begin to fathom what it could have been, what kind of force could produce such a

199

striking sound but he knew one thing. He knew that the Professor must somehow be involved. Loch hadn't given up and now Steve had to increase his efforts to do the same.

**

The sound rushed past Karl as he walked away from Security HQ. Svoros had told him that one day he might hear this sound but it was only upon hearing it that he realised he never actually believed it. The scream could only mean one thing and that was that the first steps to unlocking whatever secret power Corzones Island held had begun. Could this be Svoros? Had the old man finally found the place that he had been looking for? Or could it be somebody else? Was this a sign that all was over, had it been the Professor who had found Velza? All Karl knew for sure was that this sound made him regret nothing and that, as he had been told, many great things were about to occur.

**

Sofia had an ice cream. It was rather pathetic, but being bought the dairy product by the Security Officer who had been told to look after her had stopped her crying. He seemed nice and after a few occasions where she had called him 'Officer Harper', he had insisted that he use his first name, Talfryn. They chatted very little but she had learned that he came from Wales and had been working on the island for nearly three years. Their conversation was meaningless but it helped her take her mind away from what had happened with Karl and her argument with Lucy. She had been stupid to lose her temper with her best friend in such a way.

Many people were in the town centre and they all seemed to be going about their own business until they were distracted by a rumbling in the distance, it sounded like thunder at the height of the storm but it was a more constant sound and it slowly grew louder and louder until it was unmistakably a scream. It seemed to be a man's voice. Sofia looked around the town centre but quickly realised that it was nobody close to her, it was too loud and everybody seemed to be surprised, even scared by it. Sofia felt scared too and threw her hands over hear ears as the intensity of the scream increased. It wasn't natural, wasn't right and as far as she could tell it enveloped the entire island. Harper was doing the same as he stood next to her, covering his ears and wearing an expression fearful discomfort. Sofia looked to her feet, she didn't know when it had happened but she had dropped her ice cream in the commotion.

**

Powell was about to reply to Victor when the rumbling began and seconds later it was an all-consuming scream. Kirshner couldn't tell where it came from but it seemed to travel, heading towards them in one direction and departing in the other. Victor backed away and covered his ears, falling to his knees and looking up, he looked more childlike than he had beforehand when trying to establish his position of authority. Kirshner looked to his side and saw that Powell's reaction was no different. As the scream increased in volume he found that his own hands were clasped over his ears, desperately trying not to allow any of it in. It wasn't just the volume that was so uncomfortable, the sound itself was dark, horrible and unnerving. It wasn't right it was... Kirshner gasped as he thought of the right word... Evil.

**

Lucy hugged Will and Will held her tightly in return. They were scared enough already but the scream was too much. It was loud, intense and seemingly uncontrollable. Around the Security office everybody looked confused or scared. There was no way of comprehending what this sound could possibly be. Will tried to tell Lucy that everything would be ok but he couldn't even hear his own words due to the volume of the sound. Will looked around to try and find its source but it was coming from all directions and was completely untraceable. It was everywhere.

**

The one person who smiled upon hearing the scream was Svoros, he was sitting behind the counter in his café, looking at a book containing an ancient drawing of a round, flat rock. He knew the island perfectly, every tiny inch of it but he had never been able to find that rock. The scream told him that somebody had and that they had discovered its secret. It had to be the Professor. Svoros wasn't worried by this however, Professor Loch had simply unlocked a door that he and his followers were now able to enter. Soon the power of Corzones Island would be his to control.

**

The scream lasted for a minute, maybe a few seconds more before it faded away to a slight rumbling, just as it had started. The whole island heard it, everybody was touched by the sheer anger, fear and hatred that it expressed but nobody could quite explain what it was. After it had faded into the ocean, there was a perfect silence, nobody knew what to say or could even comprehend what they had heard. Through the jungle, in the town centre, at the ruins of the temple, across the apartment blocks, along the strip and over the beaches there was a perfect kind of nothingness. All music had ceased in the clubs and bars and the whirring of the buggies had stopped. Nobody wanted to move, to make a sound or to continue. Everybody was breathless. The only sound that anybody was able to make out was the ringing in their own ears and even that faded away after very little time. The island was consumed by an enduring silence that nobody wanted to break.

There was one sound though. A sound that couldn't be identified before amongst the thudding of the music, the inane chatter of anybody nearby and the constant buzzing of buggies that were either coming or going. From a litter bin just to the side of Security HQ's entrance was a bleeping. Nobody noticed it, not even the two people who were closest to it, Will and Lucy. They were shielded from the sound by a thick pane of glass. It rhythmically pulsed in a way that could make anybody insane after the right amount of time. When the scream had entirely faded away and silence ruled supreme, the bleeping began to grow faster and louder, building up to reach an almighty constant. And then it stopped. For one second there was real silence. And then there was the loud sound of a tremendous explosive blast. The ground shook and there were flames all around.

Part Four - The Wounds

Thirty-One

For the second time in a minute Will found that his ears were ringing but this time it was much worse. He hadn't been ready, there was no warning, no build-up. There was only the bang. Will went through a detailed thought process of not being able to hear before he realised that his vision had also become incredibly limited. There was smoke, lots of smoke. He dared not breathe, surely that was the wrong thing to do. He rubbed his eyes and the smoke started to clear a little, at least he could see. Things still didn't look normal though, there was something wrong. He wasn't upright, he was lying down. Everything looked sideways. Everything *was* sideways but Will took a moment to understand why. He'd been thrown to the ground, but by what?

He panicked as he couldn't see Lucy, despite the fact that just a few seconds before they had been sitting right next to each other. Had she left? Had the blast been her leaving? No, that was silly. She must still be nearby. The office was a large room and there was no way that she could have exited so quickly. It wasn't the office anymore though, bits of it stood, remnants and echoes but it wasn't the office. It was a mess, a disaster zone. A bomb! It had to be a bomb. With a surge of absolute horror, Will realised that he had been at the centre of an explosion.

He was alive, that was something but his main concern was Lucy and she was nowhere to be seen. He couldn't be sure that his sight had fully stabilised yet though, things did seem quite blurred. Perhaps she was right next to him, perhaps they were still even hugging. No, he could feel. He noticed that he could feel a great deal of pain. Perhaps the damage from the blast had been much worse than he'd originally thought. He wiggled all of his fingers and toes and felt a slight relief that all of his limbs were still at least intact. He couldn't feel any other weight, bits of the roof seemed to have fallen around him but none of them had landed on him. He tried to stand and nearly managed to but it wasn't quite an option just yet.

He tried talking next, his voice wasn't very clear and at first he didn't quite recognise it as his own but he definitely heard a sound, his ears were clearing, progress! He tried rolling on to his back and with great difficulty, he managed to. He tried the voice again, managing to form a coherent word this time.

'Lucy,' he yelled, 'Lucy where are you?' No response. Nothing at all. He rolled over back on to his side and reached out, seeing if he could feel his friend close by but there was only rubble.

He'd been holding his breath and only realised how long it had been when his body forced him to breathe, he took a gulp of air but found that it contained a great deal of dust and ash. He coughed uncontrollably for a moment but managed to stop when he pulled his shirt up over his mouth and nose, managing to provide himself with a barely-effective shield. He shouted Lucy's name again and tried reaching out but he still didn't find anything.

Looking around, Will could see other people now and they were moving about. Some seemed to be running away while others were clearing bits of rubble and revealing bodies, a lot of them didn't move. Suddenly he felt a hand grab his shoulder from behind and looked around to see a Security Officer. The Officer pulled Will to his feet and supported him for a moment until he was able to stand by himself. Sound was starting to return now, firstly it was the sound of alarms that struck Will but then he registered a great number of screams too. The Security Officer grabbed Will by the shoulders and looked straight into his eyes, spoke but Will wasn't able to make out what was been said to him at first. The Officer moved his head closer to Will's and spoke with more volume.

'Will, I need you to help me!' The Officer pointed to the remains of the sofa that he had been sitting on just a few moments before, a lifeless hand was reaching out from underneath it. Lucy.

Will dashed to the sofa and with the help of the Security Officer he was able to move it. A large piece of ceiling fell close by as they lifted Lucy up. Together they carried her towards an opening that had once been a wall. There was a rumble and more roof started to fall.

'The whole building is coming down!' The Officer's statement was immediately backed up by more falling rubble, this time worryingly close. Not letting go of Lucy, Will and the Officer increased their pace and somehow managed to make it outside before the entire roof caved in. They emerged from the resulting dust cloud and walked over to a grassy area that was a safe distance away.

Around them were other people, some only suffering from a few cuts and bruises but some bore more unpleasant injuries. Will looked to the Security Officer who had carried Lucy out. His left arm was in a funny position and clearly broken, which explained why he had asked Will for help. Will then looked down and saw Lucy, she was breathing but unconscious, Will breathed a sigh of relief but his worry returned a moment later when he considered what the extent of her injuries may be. She didn't look too bad, she had fewer cuts than he did and nothing looked as if it had been broken. The sofa had probably protected her from the worst of the blast but her unconsciousness could well have been from a bash on the head.

Sirens rang in the distance and slowly grew louder. Eventually Will saw some medical buggies turn the corner and come to a halt by the remains of Security HQ. An army of medical personnel ran from the buggies and headed to the various parties of injured. A small dark-haired woman in her thirties ran towards Will and began to look at him.
'Forget me, I'm fine! Look at her!' Will pointed to Lucy and the woman nodded and knelt down next to her. The nurse's examination of Lucy was brief and she rattled off an explanation of what was wrong but Will couldn't quite hear her, his ears hadn't fully recovered and the surrounding mayhem proved to be too much. The nurse yelled over to one of the drivers who brought his buggy straight over.
'She needs to get to medical, now!' The driver picked up Lucy and placed her on the back of the buggy. Without even waiting to be invited, Will jumped on the back and with a nod, the driver sped away. Will looked back to see that the nurse had redirected her attention to the Officer who had found Lucy and was looking at his arm.

It didn't take them long to arrive at the medical centre but when they were there it seemed to be an eternity before anybody paid them attention. They were busy and there were more people injured than actual staff. Looking over his shoulder, Will could see the enormous plume of smoke over the trees that was still billowing from the remains of Security HQ. He hadn't taken note of how extensive the damage was but judging from his experience inside there couldn't have been much of it left standing. His attention was drawn, yet again, back to Lucy who had received no attention since arriving at the medical building. She was still unconscious and lying on the back of the buggy. For the first time, Will noticed a cut above her eyebrow, a thin trickle of blood had run down it and dried next to her eye. His instant reaction was to brush it away but he decided that it was best to avoid the wound.

A porter eventually rushed out of the main entrance with a trolley and ran over to Lucy. The driver helped him to move Lucy on to the trolley before he dashed into the building. Will followed through the doors and inside but it wasn't long before a young nurse stopped him. He tried to argue but it was too late, Lucy was rushed around a corner and out of his sight. Realising that he wouldn't be allowed anywhere near her for some time, Will walked back to the reception area and sunk into a chair. He looked down and saw that his shorts were ripped quite badly and that his exposed legs were covered in dust and a few grazes. No doubt one of the medical staff would pay him attention soon but for now their priorities lay with the more severely injured. Will thought back to the Officer who had requested his help in removing Lucy, he had saved her life and Will would never be able to truly express how grateful he was. He hoped that the Officer would be alright and began to regret the fact that he hadn't got the Security man's name.

Time passed and the day turned into night. Hundreds of people had entered and exited the hospital with a series of injuries, all different levels of seriousness. There had been no sign of Lucy though and no reports of her progress. Just what was wrong and how serious was it? With every moment that went by Will found himself feeling more anxious but surely if there had been bad news then he would have been told about it? The wait became painful, he had to know!

He stood up, feeling a slight pain in his leg that hadn't been there before, and walked through the doors into the corridor. It was empty and he didn't hesitate to walk along it. Turning the corner that he had last seen Lucy whisked around, he was greeted with another corridor, identical to the one that he had been on. Its walls were a ghostly white and its floor a sickly green. It was lined with doors leading off into small rooms, a small sign in the window of each one giving the name of its patient. Will read them all carefully but saw no mention of Lucy so he rounded another corner and was greeted by the same sight yet again.

Will was certain that somebody would appear and remove him from the building, taking him even further away from Lucy but his determination to find her was too strong, he couldn't stop now. He had to know that she was alright. Another corridor and another set of signs, none of them bearing Lucy's name. The next corridor that he found himself upon was exactly the same again but the first door on his left had 'Lucy Gough' written upon it. Will hesitated for a moment, what if it was bad or if somebody was already in there. He heard footsteps from around the corner and knew that they would reach him in a few short moments and that would be that, he wouldn't be able to find out about Lucy for a long time. With a deep breath Will threw open Lucy's door and entered the room.

The room was shrouded in complete blackness at first but after a few blinks Will was able to make out his surroundings. It was quite small and mostly filled by a large bed. A window was open, allowing a cool breeze and the usual sound of music through. Even after an enormous explosion, Corzones Island would continue to party as if nothing at all had happened. As Will closed the door quietly behind him there was some movement from the bed.
'Who's there?' The voice was unmistakably Lucy's.
'It's me.'
'Will?' Will dashed forward to the bed and saw Lucy staring up at him through the darkness, she smiled.
'I'm so glad you're here.'
'I've been waiting in reception. Are you alright Lucy?'
'Just a bump on the head. No lasting damage apparently.' Will felt an overwhelming sense of relief and hugged her. She let out a gasp of pain and Will backed away quickly.
'I'm sorry.' Lucy smiled again.
'Don't worry Will, I'd like that hug.' Will went to hug her again, carefully this time.

Their embrace lasted for a minute or so before Will stood upright again. Lucy sighed.

'I should be out of here by morning, you should go.' Will shook his head.

'No,' Will sat down in a chair next to her, 'if you're here all night then I am too.' He heard Lucy laugh.

'Please Will, don't have an uncomfortable night just because of me. I bet you haven't told your brother that you're alright! He'll be worried.' Lucy was right, Will hadn't even thought to contact Harry and tell him what had happened. The explosion would probably have even been on the news, his family might be worried about him. The same went for Lucy, everything was so hectic that it was incredibly unlikely that any family would have been contacted.

Will took Lucy's mum's phone number from her and produced his phone from his pocket, the screen was cracked but it was still useable. Lucy told him what to say and asked to speak herself after explanations had been done. The important point for Will was to assure Lucy's mum that everything was ok. He dialled the number into his phone and pressed the call button. It rang a few times before there was an answer.

'Yes, hello. Who is this?' The voice on the end sounded panicked, Lucy's mum must have heard about what had happened.

'Hello, Mrs Gough? My name is William, I'm a friend of Lucy's.' Will was quickly interrupted.

'Where is Lucy? Is she alright. I saw about the explosion on the news and... Oh my God, why are you calling? Something is wrong, isn't it?'

'No,' Will spoke as quickly as she had, 'Lucy's fine. She just asked me to explain to you what happened before she speaks to you herself.'

'My daughter is there? Please, put her on now!'

'I will in a moment, I promise. There was an explosion Mrs Gough, both Lucy and I were caught in it and she was injured.'

'Oh my God!' Will had said the wrong thing. He quickly needed to rectify the situation.

'She's received medical treatment and she's alright now. I'm going to put you on.' Will heard an "Oh yes, please!" as he moved the phone away from his own ear and passed it to Lucy.

She spoke to her mother for about ten minutes, the conversation consisted of Lucy assuring her mother that everything was absolutely fine and that in a few short hours she would be out of the medical centre. After the conversation ended, Will took back his phone and contacted his own family to pass on the message that he was alright. Apparently Harry had already called home to find out if Will had been in contact. After speaking to his mother, Will phoned Harry and explained most of the day's events, he decided that for now the truth about the Professor was probably best left out of the conversation.

Will and Lucy were then alone together again with less to worry about. There was a point where a nurse peeked through the door to make sure that Lucy was ok but Will wasn't seen. As the night went on and Will managed to calm himself down a bit more, he began to wonder why a bomb was planted at Security HQ, surely whoever had framed the Professor would want Security to be working at maximum efficiency, so why attack them in such a way? Will didn't want to think about it, right now he and Lucy were both safe and as selfish as it sounded, that was all that mattered to him.

Thirty-Two

Even the Professor had been scared by the scream, he appeared to be horrified. Moments before he seemed to be the happiest man on the planet having just discovered what he deemed to be the holy grail of finds: Atlantis. Now he was staring into the dark passage with a look of sheer horror in his eyes. He'd known what that sound was, that much was clear. Amerigo dared not ask anything or even say a word, would making a sound cause the scream to be heard again or was something coming along the corridor? Were these the final few seconds of his life, spent in a cave watching the man he genuinely believed to be above fear virtually cowering in a corner?

Much to Amerigo's relief, Loch eventually stood up straight, blinked and replaced his expression with a smile.
'Interesting,' said the Professor who was still not removing the corridor from his vision, 'That would explain what all of the fuss is about then.' Amerigo decided that this was the best stage to put his questions forward.
'What on earth was that?'
'A scream,' said the Professor calmly, 'didn't you hear?' Amerigo nodded.
'Yes, I heard. The whole island will have heard that!'
'That was the scream of a very ancient force that is, and hopefully will remain, trapped below this island. It's all in these documents,' the Professor pointed towards the bits of parchment on the stone table, 'the people of this island lived happily in a prosperous society until they were invaded by a force known as "the Velza", you see Amerigo, Velza wasn't the people, but the thing that destroyed them. A demon if you really want to simplify it.'
Amerigo still didn't understand and the Professor could tell, so he continued. 'The people of the island sought to destroy this demon and somehow managed to sink it into the ocean, moving to underground survival chambers. This newer account here, it tells of the island rising, roughly around the time of Willow's exploration. The natives lured the weakened demon below ground and sealed it here. They mustn't have adapted well to living on the surface after all of that time though.' Amerigo shook his head.
'You have always dismissed the stories of this island as crazy but you're able to believe that?' Professor Loch nodded casually.

'Yes. Whatever drew Velza here in the first place must have given the natives some of its powers, for want of a better word. It makes sense Amerigo, it really does.' Amerigo was less than convinced but he trusted the Professor's judgment. If that was the working theory then so be it.

The Professor seemed to return to his more panicky state.
'Oh dear.'
'What is it Professor?'
'Well Amerigo, you were right. The whole island will have heard that, including Svoros and his followers. And now they know that what they're aiming for exists and is very accessible. That scream was a cry for help, a plea for release to be heard by anybody stupid enough to do so.'
'And that's exactly what they are.' The Professor considered for a moment.
'We need to hand ourselves in Amerigo.' This was surprising, surely freedom was the one thing that they needed now even more than they had before. 'We'll find Steve and talk to him, perhaps he can put me in contact with an officer who's willing to listen?'
'What if they don't listen?'
'It's a risk that we have to take Amerigo. By disturbing whatever is down here, we have put into motion whatever plans Svoros has. Do you think he'll rest now that he knows the secret of the island has been uncovered? Now that he has definitive proof that his ambitions are achievable? A lot is going to happen Amerigo and it will happen in no time at all now. There was evil in that scream, pure uncontrollable evil that will grant Svoros nothing. He and his followers are simply a means to an end for this Velza.'

As they walked through the cave and back to the beach neither of them uttered a word. Amerigo spent his time contemplating what the Professor had said and just how right or wrong he could be. The scream had shaken him, of that there was no denying but otherwise he seemed to have his wits about him completely. Perhaps finding Steve was the best thing to do. Amerigo wasn't certain as to whether this would allow them to 'hand themselves in quietly' though as the Security forces would surely know of the link between Steve and the Professor and if they had any sense at all they would be watching his apartment. The last thing they needed was a big scene made out of their arrest. Amerigo felt that Loch didn't seem concerned, his silence was usually a sign that all

211

was well as he had nothing to boast about and no subject to be an expert on.

It was dark on the beach and the couple who had driven Amerigo and the Professor deeper into the cave had long gone. The sound of the waves crashing on to the shore line was drowned out by the continuing monotonous thump of dance music to which Amerigo had become so familiar over the last few years. It was too dark to see the ocean but Amerigo knew roughly where it would be at this time of the evening and that staying as far up the beach as possible was wise if he didn't wish to get wet feet.

'A torch perhaps, Amerigo?' The Professor phrased this as a question but Amerigo knew full well that it was an instruction. Amerigo was still holding the torch that had been deactivated as they reached the cave's entrance, Amerigo had thought to turn it off just in case anybody had remained at Lovers' Cove into the night. It was a rare occurrence as most of the people who spent their days there were eager to go to a club but sometimes the odd couple who preferred being alone together would stay there under the cover of darkness.

In silence the Professor and Amerigo climbed the rocks and moved into the jungle. The torch went out now, just in case some of the Security forces were out searching for them. The moon's light provided adequate guidance over the vines and roots that surrounded them and luckily neither of them even nearly tripped up. The jungle covered them well and they didn't detect any sign of other people but Amerigo knew that to get to Steve's apartment they would have to step out into some very public places and that created a danger of them being found before they could even make it to the young rep. The Professor was adamant that they had to try, Amerigo questioned whether revealing themselves was a good idea but the Professor insisted that they couldn't act alone anymore and that outside help was essential.

The situation must have become more serious than Amerigo really understood. The Professor did this kind of thing all the time and Amerigo had assumed that the speech in the cave had been the Professor's usual reliance on exaggerating but even now he still seemed afraid and repeatedly insistent that things had moved beyond his capabilities. Surely contacting his fellow Supers would be the logical thing to do but he seemed to be completely ignoring that as an option. Amerigo knew that the Professor wouldn't tell him why but couldn't help think that a bit of transparency wouldn't do any harm in the current situation.

Loch still seemed to be excited about discovering what he thought to be Atlantis and Amerigo had to admit that if it was true then he was also very excited, he was one of the two people who had been there. Unfortunately he was on the run and had greater priorities to concern himself with. From the moment that the Professor had walked into the Temple Bar things weren't going to be normal but he never expected it to be quite like this. Amerigo had initially hoped that this time the Professor's visit would remain death-free.

Thinking of his bar, Amerigo realised how much he was missing it. The Temple gave him a relaxed lifestyle to which he had become accustomed. He had met many interesting people throughout his time there, some of them just wanted to get drunk but others came with a story to tell and that was what Amerigo loved. He'd met people from all over the world who had done some amazing things but none of them had been quite as impressive as the Professor, none of them had opened his eyes to a different reality that was perfectly real but hidden from plain view. Maybe he'd never return to the Temple, if he was unable to prove his innocence then those days were truly over. Amerigo didn't understand why that concerned him so much, only a couple of days previously he had been seriously entertaining the idea of leaving the island for good but now it felt more like home than ever before.

Once out of the jungle, Amerigo and the Professor had to work hard to avoid the crowds. It did seem to be quieter than usual somehow and there was talk of an explosion. The Professor seemed to be itching to find out more but he knew better than to break cover for the sake of island gossip. He was certain that Svoros would be behind it but it made no difference currently.

They managed to get to Steve's apartment block unseen and started to climb the stairs when voices could be heard coming in the opposite direction. Amerigo pointed to a pillar that they could hide behind and they did so until the voices had passed and their accompanying footsteps had vanished downwards into the distance.

Before he knocked on the door, the Professor took a good look around to make sure that they weren't being observed. All seemed to be alright. It was a quiet knock, one that would attract any attention from inside the room but nothing from the surrounding area. There was no reply so the Professor knocked again, slightly louder this time. Nothing.

'He might not be here Professor, perhaps he has gone to a club or to that lady friend of his.' Loch knocked again without replying. After a moment he reached into his pocket and produced a paper clip.

'We shall have to wait for him to return then. I'm sure it will give us an opportunity to sleep for a short while. Steve won't mind.' It was a good idea and Amerigo had to admit and on top of everything else, nothing seemed wrong with a spot of innocent breaking and entering.

Amerigo couldn't tell that something was wrong at first, it all seemed to be quiet and calm but after entering the room fully he registered an unpleasant smell that made him feel uncomfortable. It was probably just down to the poor state that Steve kept his room in but as he continued to walk a sense of foreboding grew. 'Something isn't right.' The Professor hummed in agreement. Suddenly there was a noise from across the room, a weak groan. 'Lights Amerigo!' The barman reached for the light switch and flicked it. The room suddenly illuminated and the source of the groan was revealed. Steve was lying on the floor, his face a deathly shade of white and a large pool of dark, thick blood surrounded him.

'Amerigo,' the Professor fell to his knees next to Steve and examined his pulse, 'Get on the phone. It's time that we came out of hiding.'

Thirty-Three

His father had given him very simple instructions: give one hell of a bollocking to the people in charge of Security. Victor wasn't particularly keen to do this as he'd got on well with Powell the few times that they'd previously met, but this new Inspector that had arrived sounded like he was due a shouting at. As he stepped from his helicopter he saw the Inspector, Victor very much began to look forward to reprimanding him. The opportunity never arrived however, as he was about to speak the scream came. It was unbearably loud and for a moment Victor thought that it wasn't going to end. It did but it had shaken everybody in sight, inducing a state of panic and confusion, even stone-faced Kirshner looked stunned by what had happened.

Everybody began to regain their composure when there was a sudden loud rumble in the distance. Nobody knew what it was at first, one of the Guards suggested that it was an aftershock of the scream. Phones rang and quickly the Guard's theory was disproved. Powell looked shocked, even more so than he had at the scream.
'That was HQ,' he said, 'there's been an explosion. They don't know how many are dead or injured but the building is collapsing as we speak. I'm sorry Mister Corzones but we have to get back there. Remain here where it's safe.' Kirshner looked equally as distressed by the news and with a polite nod he ran after Powell and they jumped into a buggy.

Victor was left alone with a few Guards and Parsons, the housekeeper.
'Sir, we should move into the house.' Without waiting for an agreement, Parsons moved towards Victor's luggage and picked it up. Seeing that the elderly man was struggling to carry everything, Victor took hold of one of the larger cases and carried it himself. Parsons protested, insisting that he could manage but Victor waved away his concerns. He had known Parsons for a long time and he was a good man. He had always taken the utmost care and pride in his work. Victor had been well looked after by the man, far better than he ever had by his father.

They arrived in the entrance hall of the mansion and Victor found that he was tired from carrying just the one bag, he couldn't even begin to imagine how exhausted Parsons was. Luckily for them both, Victor's room was nearby. He had chosen a room at the top of the nearest staircase to the entrance upon first moving into the house. His reasoning being that it was the shortest stagger on his way back from the clubs, a decision that had served him well on many an occasion. In a drunken state it could take a fair few minutes to reach the other end of the house and the noise that he'd make would almost certainly wake the rest of its occupants.

Upon reaching his room, Victor decided that he needed a few moments to himself so he decided to dismiss Parsons and put a hold on unpacking his cases. He lay down on top of the bed and stared blankly into the ceiling. A death, an explosion and no real explanation as to why it was all happening. How on Earth could all of this be justified, what was it achieving? His father had sent him to deal with it but he had no idea what to do, even the Security forces seemed completely unable to help and despite Victor's immediate dislike of Kirshner it was clear that he was the best man for the job, even if his appointment was only due to the fact that he was the only British detective in the area. His nationality had been something his father had characteristically insisted upon.

Victor didn't lie still for very long, his worries and his eagerness to experience the island for the first time in almost a year overwrote any chance of rest or reflection. It was beginning to go dark and that meant that the island was about to party. He knew it wasn't necessarily the right thing to do but explosion or not Corzones Island would continue to party on. It seemed to be a deep-rooted instinct in everybody on the island: drink on regardless. One thing that his room possessed that probably no other on the island did was a drink's cabinet. It contained a very nice but expensive bottle of whiskey that he enjoyed starting his night with. The bottle was more full than he remembered but that was no bad thing, plenty of it would be consumed that evening.

A couple of drinks went down very easily and a third was about to as there was a knock at the door. Victor sighed and placed the glass on a table before walking over to the door and opening it. Parsons was standing on the other side with a Security Officer.

'This is Hammond, he has been assigned to ensure your safety.' It was clear that Parsons knew Victor would be unhappy with this but there was no point arguing. 'It's a direct order from your father.' Victor sighed.

'Very well. Hello Hammond.' The officer nodded. He was tall and muscular, the typical bodyguard. He wore a tight-fitting black polo shirt, of which the short sleeves revealed a series of tattoos. Victor had met and dealt with many men like this and in all cases their presence had proved to be entirely unnecessary. Victor was used to everything, from kidnap and murder threats to people throwing eggs at him in the street. Unfortunately Giorgio Corzones had proved to be an unpopular figure amongst some parties and his son had felt their wrath.

Hammond was the ultimate professional, though Victor didn't want him around he'd had far less subtle bodyguards in the past and he also made an excellent driver. Victor enjoyed a few more glasses of whiskey before changing into his designer shirt and shorts and leaving for the clubs. Hammond drove him down there in the Rolls Royce, it took a while to start as it hadn't been used since Victor was last on the island but he always enjoyed a ride in it. Victor had spent a moment trying to decide where to go but he knew that there was really only one choice, The Isle Club. He'd heard great things about DJ Freedom's sets and had decided that it was time to witness one for himself.

The conversation with Hammond on the way to the club was limited but as Victor had guessed from his tattoos, he was ex-military and had worked for some top celebrities before coming to the island and serving its unique 'VIP Programme'. He often found himself dealing with some of the same people as he had in the past. That night though he was with Victor who had requested that he be given as much space allowed. Hammond seemed to understand, stating that unless it was necessary he would be virtually invisible. Victor appreciated that and promised that he'd be rewarded if he provided such a service. His father was willing to pay good money for somebody to protect him constantly and Hammond may well prove himself to be the right person.

The Isle Club hadn't changed a bit. A new pattern on the walls and a new shot behind the bar perhaps, otherwise it was exactly as Victor remembered. It was relatively quiet but the night was still

217

young and the explosion, whatever it had been, would have been enough to put some people off. Nevertheless as time went on people started to flood in. Hammond stayed true to his word and retreated to a corner, occasionally striking up conversation with some other Security staff. Quite often when he was shadowed by a bodyguard, Victor felt that he was under a watchful eye and that he had no real privacy on a night out. He knew that this was indeed the case with Hammond, to do otherwise would be unprofessional but at least he gave the impression that he wasn't watching constantly.

There were many girls in the club, Victor would end up taking one of them home, he knew that. As soon as a girl found out his identity then generally she would not take her interests elsewhere. Victor found it too easy sometimes but he didn't care. When he was in a club he was just another visitor to the island. True he had to be careful and enjoyed far fewer drugs than others did but there was always the risk of the media being around. He had received many a speech from his father about maintaining the family image and keeping the business alive. It was expected of him, a responsibility that he'd never asked for or even wanted. The island should be his to enjoy, just like it was for everybody else and despite the responsibilities his father had given him, Victor was going to enjoy that evening.

He spoke to one girl named Lauren and despite his identity she wasn't interested. Victor had to admit that he was impressed to find somebody on the island with principals. He moved on, like he always did. His name brought him a good night but it never seemed to bring attachment. Moving on was all that Victor could do, everybody wanted his money or his name but nobody wanted him it seemed.

The majority of people on the island were mostly happy, or at least under the impression that they were but Victor knew that the positivity of the island was just a phantom emotion, created by hype and a collective delusion by all that were there. It was rare that somebody was visibly unhappy but in the Isle Club that night, sitting alone was a girl who looked like she was having anything but a good time. She held a pint of beer in her hand and stared into it as if she was expecting some kind of revelation. Victor didn't struggle to guess what had happened to her.

In his reluctant role of island boss, Victor decided to go and talk to the girl and ask her what was wrong. At first she was distant, giving a simple 'yes or no' as answers but after a couple of minutes she looked up and saw Victor properly and gave a faint smile. After that the conversation was much more a dual effort. Victor had guessed most of it already; she'd come to the island, met a guy, thought she'd instantly fallen in love and then she had suddenly been abandoned.

She was called Sofia and she spoke of the man in question with both admiration and contempt in her voice. Her drink had gone from being something to stare at to entirely consumed within a matter of minutes and Victor found himself offering to get her another. She was reluctant to accept but when he revealed that he didn't actually have to pay she took him up on his offer.

Victor hadn't revealed his identity to her yet, he wasn't trying to impress her or get her back to his house, this was just a simple act of kindness. It was rare that Victor had the chance to do something like this, just to be somebody's friend. Maybe he was gaining from somebody else's poor fortune but it wasn't hurting her, quite the opposite in fact as she seemed to be happy. Victor didn't have any friends on the island, just staff that followed his every instruction and people on holiday, with no interest in him until they knew who he was or what he was worth. Sofia just saw him as good company.

It continued for an hour or two, the talking, drinking and smiling. The conversation stopped being meaningful after a very short time and quickly descended into nonsense with the aid of more alcohol. DJ Freedom arrived, making an entrance that Victor understood to be identical every day. He asked Sofia if she wanted to dance but she seemed to be affected by another wave of unhappiness. It was at that point that she revealed the other thing that was worrying her. She had fallen out with her best friend the morning before and hadn't heard from her at all since the explosion. Victor assured her that it was very unlikely that her friend would have been involved but she didn't sound convinced. It was like she was still holding something back, her concern for her friend seemed to be just far more than a fallout. Victor offered to find out what had happened, simply implying that he had 'friends on the island' who would be able to trace her. Sofia surprisingly refused, stating that if something bad had happened she wasn't ready to hear it yet. She'd had enough upset for one day and Victor understood. Sofia went to the toilets and Victor discretely asked Hammond to find out what he could about the girl. Sofia had told him that her friend's name was Lucy Gough, that should be enough for Security to do a check on her.

Victor went to the bar and ordered an expensive bottle of Champagne with two glasses. It was ready in a bucket of ice on the table for when Sofia returned.
'Why have you bought this?' She asked in her thick Spanish accent.
'Why not?' replied Victor, 'I like to drink Champagne but it's incredibly dreary to drink it alone. I hope you like it?' Sofia took a small sip from her glass and nodded to Victor in approval.
'It's lovely. Thank you.'

They both found themselves on the dance floor, it was Sofia's decision after she had concluded that she was happier and had reached the "slightly tipsy" stage. Victor was also beginning to feel the effects of the drink and the bottle of Champagne was draining away at an alarming rate. Sofia was still not telling him something but he didn't pry too much, after all he was withholding information about himself from her. She made another trip to the ladies and Hammond took the opportunity to inform Victor that Sofia's friend had suffered an injury in the explosion but she was fully stable and would be out of the medical centre the next morning. At least there was some good news. Victor decided not to tell Sofia just yet though as that was what she'd wished and did seem to be considerably cheerier anyway. She rejoined him and they returned to their booth, both quite surprised that it hadn't been taken by anybody else.

The kiss was sudden and unexpected but Victor was as responsible for it as Sofia was. They just locked together. Victor hesitated, knowing that Sofia was upset but she assured him that she was thinking clearly. There was a moment of silence, it wasn't awkward but clearly they both required the time to gather their thoughts. The conversation continued over another bottle of Champagne and more kisses followed.

Victor still hadn't told Sofia who he really was, she was interested in him without knowing that and it was a novelty that made him happy. It didn't take long for the truth to come out however. As they were drinking Argyll, the owner of the club, walked up to them.

'Mister Corzones, I had no idea that you were here this evening,' he acknowledged Sofia for a brief moment, not really paying her that much attention, 'Naturally if you and your lady friend would like a booth in the VIP area then that can be arranged.' Victor looked to Sofia for an answer but she gave a subtle shake of the head. Victor refused Argyll's offer. 'Very well. Naturally you can just come upstairs if you change your minds.' With a smile and a handshake, Argyll disappeared through the doors and back to his private area.

'Are you sure you don't want to see VIP? There are usually a few famous people in there.' Sofia just looked at Victor.

'He called you "Mister Corzones"?' Victor nodded. 'Do you own this island?' Sofia was visibly gobsmacked, Victor smiled and shook his head.

'I don't. My father does. But as you can see it does get me a few favours.' Sofia smiled, grinning from ear to ear.

'I'm so sorry, I had no idea.' Victor smiled.

'That's fine, don't worry. We're both having a good night after all, why let the family business get in the way?'

Victor was relieved that Sofia didn't act any differently after that. Their night continued in the same way that it was progressing beforehand. They both drank and laughed a lot but every now and again Victor could see that look of upset and worry in her eyes. He decided to not push the issue further and that he would save the news about Lucy until the following morning. DJ Freedom finished playing and people began to leave the club. Victor expected to see Argyll again but didn't complain when there was no sign of the owner. He'd never liked Argyll. He always seemed to be a bit sleazy and was only ever interested in himself. The whole act of greeting Victor and offering him a booth in VIP was simply so that a good report of the club would be delivered to his father.

'So, you live in that big house that people keep talking about?' Victor smiled.

'That's right.'

'Can I see it?' Victor nodded. They were outside the club now and Hammond was nearby, probably expecting Victor to say goodbye to Sofia. He seemed to be quite surprised when they both walked

221

towards him but he remained just as polite and professional in Sofia's presence.

They got back to the house and Parsons was standing by the door, having being alerted by Hammond of their return some moments before. After Victor and Sofia had exited the car, Hammond drove it around the house towards the garage. Parsons asked if anything was required to which Victor replied with an assurance that everything was fine and that he should return to bed. He did so and left Victor alone with Sofia. They both went into the kitchen to find that Parsons had laid out a spread of meats, cheeses and bread. 'It isn't exactly a kebab but I hope you like it.' Sofia nodded and followed Victor's lead as he took a plate and began to fill it. He was very hungry having not eaten properly before leaving to go to the club. He offered Sofia a drink and even considered opening a bottle of wine but she assured him that all she wanted was a glass of water, he elected to have the same. He would probably have a lot of work to do and a lot to worry about the next day and he'd drunk more than enough already for one evening.

They finished eating and sat themselves on a sofa in the next room, Sofia snuggled up to Victor.
'Thank you,' she said, 'Thank you for cheering me up and for all of this.' She kissed him again and before either of them knew what was going on, they were walking up towards Victor's room. They entered the room as quietly as possible, even though Parsons and Hammond slept at the other end of the house and would both probably be fast asleep. They kissed again when the door was closed. When the embrace ended they parted and Victor could see that the look of upset had returned to Sofia's deep blue eyes. She must have been aware of it too as she quickly tried to hide it and kiss him again. He shook his head and sat down on the edge of his bed, inviting her to join him. With a faint smile she did.
'I know you asked me not to but I did find out about your friend.' Sofia looked horrified for a second before giving a faint nod.
'Is she alright?' Her voice trembled, as if she was still unsure about hearing the news.
'She's injured but will recover by morning. You were right, she was in that explosion.' Sofia jumped up.
'I need to see her!'
'She'll be fast asleep by now Sofia. I'll take you to her in the morning.' Sofia smiled and nodded and for the first time since

Victor had met her, seemed to relax. She sat back down on the bed and smiled at him, then put her arms around him and hugged him incredibly tightly, squeezing the breath out of him in the process. 'Thank you.'

'You can sleep here if you want, I can get a spare room made up for you and...'

'Can we hug? I don't want to be alone tonight.' Victor nodded and a few minutes later they were under the covers of the double bed, holding each other tightly. It was only then that Victor realised that not only had he made Sofia feel happier but she had done the same for him. He'd spent so much time worrying about what was happening on the island and the role that his father had given him. Perhaps there was hope for Corzones Island and the people that chose to go there yet.

The next morning Victor awoke to the news that his father had decided to come to the island and deal with matters himself after all. He treated Sofia to a nice breakfast before taking her back to her apartment. He then continued on to the remains of Security HQ, now just a smouldering mess. Perhaps it was the news of this disaster that had caused his father to travel to the island himself, it wouldn't be compassion that had influenced his journey though, it would be the desperate urge to protect his own interests.

Thirty-Four

If they found out about any of this at home then not only would his career be over but he would be a laughing stock. Kirshner had heard that Corzones Island changed people but he was now going against his every instinct. The lights were dimmed to the point where they may as well not have been switched on and apart from the four of them, nobody was within a mile's radius. He'd taken some convincing that this was the best place to meet but Powell was adamant that secrecy was the only way.

Kirshner had been surprised when the Professor had made contact offering to hand himself in but the attack on his friend had obviously changed things. It was very quickly clear however, that it wasn't just the attack that had altered events, the Professor and Amerigo had discovered something. Upon finding Steve, they'd called for a medical vehicle but then asked to be put into contact with the Head of Security. Kirshner had been with Powell at the time of the call, they were searching the remains of Security HQ after the fire-fighters had cleared out. The loss of life was much smaller than initially feared but the explosion had claimed its fair share of victims. Powell was speechless for a good few minutes before simply stating that he would bring whoever was responsible to their knees. Kirshner admired his passion but couldn't help but notice that he was now very emotionally involved and his ability to think straight had been compromised.

The call came through, it was the Professor begging Powell to do everything within his power to get a medical vehicle to Steve's apartment as quickly as possible and in return the Professor would hand himself in. Powell didn't hesitate to send a medical team to the location straight away but by the time that they arrived Loch and Amerigo had vanished. Powell was furious and within a few minutes had managed to convince himself that the Professor was behind not only the murder (despite previous doubts) but also responsible for the explosion. Kirshner was less convinced and managed to calm Powell down before the next phone call came.

Professor Loch was willing to go ahead with his promise, he and Amerigo would give themselves up on the condition that it happened at a secret meeting of their choice. Both Kirshner and

Powell were hesitant but they allowed their curiosity to affect their decision and an agreement was made to meet at Amerigo's bar, just the four of them, at three o'clock in the morning. The Professor's final words were used to assure them that not only was he innocent of the murder and planning the explosion, but that he also had information that could help them.

'Do you believe him?' Powell's tone made his standpoint clear, he did. Kirshner had to consider for a moment. As far as he was aware the Professor and Amerigo were acting alone bar some help from Steve, Will and Lucy. At the time of the explosion it had been established that Steve had already been stabbed and Will was in the building with Lucy. They didn't have anybody else working with them. The Professor had also stated that he knew about the origins of the scream which occurred just moments before the explosion happened. Along with all of the other evidence, this did convince Kirshner that it was worth at least listening to the fugitives to see if they could begin to make sense of the situation.

The Professor and Amerigo were late to the bar but only by a few minutes. They didn't have the advantage of a buggy to ensure that they were there on time and Kirshner understood that it must have been a difficult hill to climb. Their lateness was probably also to ensure that Powell and Kirshner were alone, a quick check would have only taken a couple of minutes and would certainly have occurred to two people who had been on the run on a relatively small island for over a day. Kirshner had to admire the fact that they had managed to evade everybody for so long and was surprised when they revealed how much information they had managed to gather.

The Professor stayed noticeably quiet but Amerigo poured himself a drink and began to reel off information.
'They have been asking me to join them for some time now, I don't know who else is involved but I know they are lead by Svoros, the owner of Café Solar.' The man that had served them breakfast the previous day and given them so much information, Kirshner struggled to believe it but he had promised to listen and that was what he intended to do. Amerigo continued, 'Until recently I thought they were nothing more than an eccentric cult, all robes and chanting in Latin but recently there has been talk of an event, a

force that they wish to harness. It's always been linked to the legend of the Velza but I have never fully understood how.'

Kirshner's scepticism was beginning to kick in again but Powell seemed to be listening intently, even declaring at one point that he had heard similar whispers. Amerigo stopped mid-speech and walked behind the bar to pour himself a large glass of rum. He threw a couple of ice cubes into it and began to drink. Kirshner wasn't sure why he didn't stop the man, technically Amerigo was under arrest but his curiosity allowed the barman to continue.

'Svoros killed the girl because he knew that the Professor and I were due to meet and they wanted him out of the way.'
'So you're claiming that you were set up?' Powell was immersed in the story and was believing every word of it.
'That is right. Svoros came to me as soon as the Professor arrived, he said that something was coming and even told me to leave the island.' Amerigo took a large gulp of his drink as Kirshner decided it was time to speak himself.
'And what about the kids, why did they get involved?'
'We never wanted them to.'
'One of them has been stabbed!' The Professor stepped forward, speaking for the first time since they'd met.
'Steve was stabbed because he helped us. What do you think that explosion was for?'
'To weaken the Security forces?' Powell's offering made sense but the Professor immediately had an alternative answer and Kirshner had to admit that it fitted.
'That might have been their secondary objective but that explosion was intended to kill Will and Lucy because they had helped us also. Since we went on the run we have had no contact with them and they were still targeted. How are they?' It was only at that moment that Kirshner realised that the Professor and Amerigo would have no idea what had happened to their friends.
'They're both alright. Will was mostly uninjured and Lucy had to be taken to the medical centre, she will be alright though.' A look of relief had crossed the Professor's face. From the moment he had heard that Will and Lucy were in the explosion he must have assumed the worst.
'I suggest that you place a guard on them. The fact that an attempt has been made on Steve's life suggests that the same will happen to them.

'What next?' Amerigo seemed glum, as if he was still expecting to be arrested, a thought that still tempted Kirshner.

'We need to remain hidden, nobody can know we have contacted you.'

'And why is that Professor?'

'Inspector, it is very likely that if Svoros has a following across the island, there is somebody inside the Security force. If that is the case then you may be placed in danger too, it seems that anybody we've spoken to is a target for this cult.' The Professor made perfect sense and managed to make Kirshner feel uncomfortable. Could he really be in any danger? It did seem as though this cult wouldn't stop at anything to protect their own interests.

Plans and agreements were made. The Professor and Amerigo would be allowed to stay hidden but given every resource they required, Kirshner would stay with them for as much time as he could. He made it exceptionally clear to them that they were still suspects but if they were able to prove that this force of evil was at work on the island then they would be allowed to go free. Kirshner wasn't able to explain the screaming sound himself but the Professor was able to give the closest thing to an idea as to why it happened. What Kirshner wasn't able to believe was that Corzones Island was the lost city of Atlantis risen again, he liked to think that he had an enquiring mind but this was one claim too far. However, the Professor seemed determined and insisted that he would be able to prove it eventually.

Powell went away and made a phone call, arranging for a Security Guard, Paisley, to be stationed outside Lucy's room. Upon his arrival he found that Will had stayed with Lucy and was asleep in a chair next to her bed. Normally he would have been made to wait in reception but after all that the two youngsters had been through, Powell gave special permission for him to remain. It would be easier to guard and protect them both in the same place after all. In the morning Powell would go to the medical centre before Lucy was discharged and make sure that their story matched up with the Professor and Amerigo's. He was certain that it would but needed to be sure.

He left to return to the remains of HQ to try and piece the Security forces back together. A temporary replacement had already been set up in the reps' headquarters. Kirshner remained with Loch and Amerigo who decided that they would start by showing him the hidden cave that they had discovered. Kirshner only realised that this would involve a long walk as the sound of Powell's buggy disappeared into the jungle.

The walk was indeed long and tiring and by the time they had reached their destination, the first strips of sunlight had begun to illuminate the trees. Another day had started and Kirshner was still on Corzones Island and now involved with far more than he'd ever expected to be. If the Professor and Amerigo were right then this was no longer just a murder but an entire conspiracy that he had to crack.

Full daylight was almost in place when they climbed down the rocks and on to the beach. It was a hidden cove with no other means of access. The sand was clear and showed no footprints or evidence that anybody had ever been there, it had all been washed away by the ocean. For a moment Kirshner's instinctive lack of trust began to rise again, he was with two murder suspects in a very isolated place. For some reason though he knew that he had to trust them. They'd had plenty of opportunity to do him some harm and he felt that they really did have something to show him. According to the Professor they were going to see proof that this island was once the legendary city of Atlantis. Corzones Island being the same place didn't make any sense. Corzones was filled with its own legends, everybody knew that but none of them related to what the Professor claimed to have discovered.

Kirshner followed Loch and Amerigo into a cave and was passed a torch as they walked away from all signs of the sunrise. It didn't take long at all for the torch to be essential.
'Now look at the walls Inspector, they aren't natural. They were carved into that archway shape that you see. At this point here, Amerigo and I found a wall, sealed by a blood lock.'
'What is a blood lock?' It was Amerigo who answered as the Professor excitedly trotted off in front, examining the wall.
'The Professor had to cut open his hand and spill his blood on to the stone. It just faded away. Ancient magic he called it.'
'And do you believe in magic, Amerigo?'
'Inspector, after the few days that I have had I find that there is very little that I'm not willing to believe.'

The tunnel continued for quite some time before it opened into a large circular room.

'A library Inspector!' The Professor seemed to be right, the chamber did resemble a primitive library. Kirshner's eyes were quickly drawn to the large round stone table in the centre of the room. Loch beckoned him towards it. 'Here it is, this parchment here is your proof. It tells the entire story of some kind of super being sinking the island, all of this is a survival system but the problem that they had was that whatever sunk them was down here too, locked away and just waiting. Eventually it found the power to raise the island again and the natives escape from underground, knowing what they must do. They'd passed down the same bit of information for millennia. They escaped and imprisoned whatever that creature was down here.'

'What happened to the natives?'

'Wiped out I'm afraid Inspector. Every nation in the world was looking to expand at the time this island rose and it was discovered very quickly by an explorer named Willow and plenty of others like him. They weren't used to life on the surface and they died out, taking their secrets with them.'

'But that means the creature is still down here.' The Professor nodded, a serious look suddenly removing the sense of boyhood excitement that had consumed him before.

'That scream, that's what you heard. A creature of immense power that has been trapped in the darkness for so long. It can smell changing events, it knows that people are worshipping it and it's building itself up for the great escape. It will even know that we are here now.' This made Kirshner feel incredibly nervous.

'Are we safe? I mean if that thing knows we're here...' The Professor nodded and waved his hand, indicating that Kirshner should remain calm.

'The Atlantans were clever Inspector, they'll have used more than one blood lock to imprison this creature.'

'What else is there?'

'I don't know.' Amerigo had remained silent up until this point but he now decided to intervene.

'Svoros will. Svoros will know what secrets bind this monster.'

Kirshner accepted it all, he had no choice. This was absolutely insane but he had heard that scream, its anger and its intensity could only have emanated from something that had been trapped for thousands of years. Despite the Professor's continued assurances that they were in no immediate danger, Kirshner didn't feel comfortable and wanted to feel nothing but fresh air and sunlight.

They emerged on to the beach, at first the sunlight dazzled Kirshner but his eyes quickly readjusted to the brightness.
'Can I use your phone please, Inspector?' Kirshner nodded and passed his phone to the Professor. 'I'm calling in other Supers.'
'Who?' Asked Kirshner. The Professor sighed.
'Amerigo, explain to him.' Loch walked along the beach making a very hushed phone call while Kirshner listened to Amerigo's explanation of who the Professor was, what he did and how they'd originally met. There seemed to be one common link between the Professor's visits to the island: death. Perhaps it followed the man everywhere he went, a fact that Kirshner was all too ready to judge before he realised that his line of work was exactly the same.

Hours passed and the three of them sat and waited on the beach, mostly in silence. Occasionally a question would form in Kirshner's mind and the Professor would try his best to answer it, usually creating another three questions in the process. They couldn't move as the team of Supers would be arriving by boat and were using Kirshner's phone to identify their arrival location. This was the only place on the island that was hidden enough and their arrival had to be of the utmost secrecy. The Professor did offer to remain there with the phone if Kirshner wanted to leave but the Inspector didn't want to let either he or Amerigo out of his sight in case they were to vanish again.

A young couple did attempt to climb down on to the beach but Kirshner flashed his Inspector's badge and claimed that the area was off limits due to an ongoing investigation. They grumbled and left, seemingly taking no notice of what was going on despite the events that had occurred over the previous few days. Kirshner lay flat on the sand and stared into the cloudless sky and against his every instinct, allowed sleep to close in.

He awoke some time later, the Professor and Amerigo were still there, sitting next to each other swapping stories and legends. It was Amerigo who noticed that Kirshner had woken up.

'Inspector,' he spoke loudly as if warning the Professor that his story had to end, whatever they had been talking about it was private, 'how are you? Did you sleep well?' Kirshner nodded.
'How long was I asleep?' Amerigo shrugged.
'We didn't really count. Four hours, maybe five. It is after lunch time now.' Kirshner jumped to his feet and produced his phone from his pocket. There were many missed calls from Powell, the Security Chief must have been worried about him after not hearing anything. It had been about seven hours since he'd left Kirshner with two suspected murderers after all. He decided to phone Powell and assure him that everything was ok.

The Inspector listened carefully as Powell spoke, things had gone from bad to worse. He ended the call and ran to the Professor and Amerigo.
'Listen, it's about your friends...' The Professor silenced Kirshner and pointed out to the sea. A boat was speeding towards them.
'This will be it!' The Professor waved at the incoming boat which grew larger and larger as it approached the shore.

Kirshner was the first to notice but Amerigo wasn't far behind.
'Professor, how many boats are coming?'
'Just the one, why?' Amerigo pointed slightly to the left of the boat that was now near the shore, there was a second in the distance. And a third.
'Over there. More of them.' The Professor used his hand to shield his eyes from the sun.
'You're right. There shouldn't be.' Kirshner could see the first boat clearly now, it contained five men, all with shaved heads and numerous tattoos.
'They don't look like Supernatural Investigators.' Kirshner's eyes widened as he saw one of the men produce a gun. 'They're armed.' Loch shook his head.
'This isn't right, into the cave!' They began to run towards the cave but were stopped by a series of gunshots. The sand around their feet leapt up at them as the bullets hit it.

The first boat reached the shore and the five men jumped off, all drawing guns as they did so. They ran towards Kirshner, Loch and Amerigo who all raised their arms.
'I apologise but I've always wanted to say this.' Kirshner and Amerigo gave each other a confused look.

'What?' asked the barman. The Professor smiled and turned. 'Gentlemen, we surrender. Take us to your leader.' Kirshner noticed that Amerigo gave a subtle laugh.

Thirty-Five

Will tried to remember exactly what had happened. It had all been so quick and his mind was racing in a million different directions. He was still crying. Maybe he'd stopped at some point but he didn't really know. He didn't even remember how he'd got back to his apartment but here he was. Harry was with him, that was a small consolation. He'd told his brother everything since. Before it had been his and Lucy's secret but now there was no Lucy and a great deal that Will couldn't simply keep to himself.

It had still been dark but only just. Will had been discovered in Lucy's room in the medical centre about half an hour before. He'd been told that he was allowed to stay as it was the safest place for both of them and that a guard had been placed outside. Apparently the explosion had been targeted at them because of their association with the Professor, a thought that had crossed Will's mind previously. He didn't know how Security knew all of this but could only assume that they had caught up with the Professor. He'd tried to contact Steve but had received no answer. Upon being questioned about the rep, the guard on their room had chosen to remain quiet, saying that he couldn't tell them at present. Something had gone terribly wrong but Will didn't know what, all he knew was that he and Lucy were safe and under watch. They simply sat there in silence, lost for words in each other's company for the first time in a few days. They held hands to reassure each other that everything would be alright.

Lucy spoke eventually.
'You didn't have to stay Will, now it looks like you're stuck.' Will smiled.
'I'm stuck with you though, it could be a lot worse.' Lucy laughed.
'Just how long have you been waiting for me?'
'Ever since the explosion,' Will looked at his watch, 'nearly twelve hours ago.' Lucy shook her head.
'Go and get some proper sleep. I'm not going anywhere, am I?'
'I'm staying. I got you out of that burning building and I'm staying to make sure that you're ok.' Lucy shook her head.
'You really are my knight in shining armour, aren't you?' Will smiled.
'I suppose I am.' He leant in and planted a kiss on her cheek.

'When we get away from this island, what should we do first?'
'What do you mean?' Will looked confused.
'Our first proper date Will, where should it be?'
'I'll let you choose. I'd only end up taking you to a museum or something.' Lucy laughed, it was a nice laugh though. The conversation ended but they continued to smile at each other with no noise to interrupt for quite some time.

The beautiful silence was broken by the sound of a buggy speeding nearby, Will assumed that it must be more people being brought in and took no notice as the buggy drew ever closer. After a second there was a thud against the door, Will separated his hand from Lucy's and edged towards it. He took a hold of the handle and began to slowly turn it. It ripped out of his hand as somebody on the other side turned it with great force and threw the door open, causing Will to stumble backwards.

It took Will a few seconds to realise who was standing in the doorway but eventually managed to identify Karl. Behind him was the guard, unconscious and lying on the floor. Karl brought his right hand from behind his back to reveal that he was holding a gun. Will took a breath ready to shout but Karl warned him not to.
'Silence, absolute silence from both of you.' Will backed away from Karl and towards Lucy. The sound of the buggy was incredibly close now and with a brief glance over his shoulder, Will saw that it was directly outside the window.
'You two are going to climb out of the window and on to that buggy, do you understand?' Will nodded, focusing on the gun in Karl's hand. Karl pointed at Lucy. 'You first.'
'She's injured and barely conscious.'
'Then help her. Get her out of the window.' Will was about to protest but Karl made a gesture with his gun.
'Do it Will, there's no point in you getting hurt.'
'You're much more clever than Sofia gave you credit for.' Will saw the look of worry cross Lucy's face.
'Where is Sofia? What have you done with her?' Karl smiled.
'She is fine. I have left her alone. Now do as you are told, or I might have to find her again. This is the last time I'll tell you Will, help her!' Will nodded and walked over to Lucy, helping her to her feet. She was clearly in pain but nodded at Will to indicate that he was doing the right thing. 'Hurry up!' Karl was beginning to grow impatient but Lucy wasn't able to move any faster.

Luckily the window was quite large and easy to climb out of, it would have been near impossible if Lucy had to climb any higher. The medical staff had instructed her to sleep through the whole night and not to move under any circumstances and now she was climbing out of a window at gunpoint. The buggy was parked right up against the window and driven by a girl with long blonde hair that she had tied up. Like Karl she was dressed entirely in black and was holding a gun. Lucy climbed into the buggy.

'Buckle yourself in.' The girl spoke sharply and waved her gun as she did so, Lucy did as she was told and fastened herself in. The girl then produced a pair of handcuffs and used them to attach Lucy to the buggy.

Will turned back around to Karl who gestured with his gun. 'Now you, climb into the buggy.' Will took a deep breath and was about to do as he was told when there was a loud bang. Everything seemed to slow down. Will looked out of the window at Lucy who had a look of sheer terror on her face, his gaze moved to the girl in the driving seat of the buggy, she also looked shocked. Will turned around to see Karl falling to the ground, he had dropped his gun. Another look at the girl in the buggy told him that she was about to shoot in his direction so he leapt out of the way and towards Karl's gun, which he somehow managed to grab. It was at that point Will looked up and saw where the bang had come from. The guard in the doorway had regained consciousness and shot Karl, who was lying on the floor in pain but alive. Will stood and ran to the window to see the lights from the buggy disappear into the distance.

'Lucy!' He shouted as loud as he could but received no reply and the lights slowly faded away.

Two hours, maybe three had passed, Will wasn't completely sure. He was waiting, just waiting and doing nothing to find Lucy. Nobody had any idea where she had been taken and Karl had fallen into unconsciousness after being shot. He couldn't tell them anything and even when he was awake it couldn't be certain that he would. Powell had come to the medical centre to speak to him, the guards had been dismissed and the door closed, what Powell had to tell Will was entirely private.

'We're alone now Will, we can speak properly.' Will assumed that he was about to be interrogated again about the Professor, a horrible tactic to use against him. Powell just smiled however and assured Will that Lucy would be found as soon as Karl awakened. Will wasn't so sure but what Powell had to say next did comfort him to some extent. 'I've spoken to Loch and Amerigo, they're fine. They're working with Inspector Kirshner as we speak to both prove their own innocence and find out exactly what is going on here.' Will was happy to hear that the Professor and Amerigo were helping the Security forces but it still didn't help with finding Lucy. Will even found himself getting frustrated when Powell told him that they couldn't raid Svoros' café as any suspicions they had about him had to remain absolutely secret for the time being. That was the place that Lucy was most likely to be so they should move on it immediately. Surely her presence there would be enough evidence? Powell reasoned however that it wasn't likely that they'd take her there as Svoros would be working hard to ensure that no suspicion fell at his door.

Will was also informed that Steve was in a bad way. He had been stabbed but had made it to the medical centre with a chance of being saved. Will asked if he could see the rep but he was in surgery and nobody was allowed near. He'd had a few guards placed on him, in case there was another attempt on his life. Will was scared, with the other two down he would be their only remaining target and they seemingly weren't going to let anything get in their way.

Will left the medical centre with an escort and went back to his own apartment. Powell promised to join him as soon as possible and insisted that his brother, Royce and Jason remained inside until he did. Will was unsure about staying there, surely it would be one of the first places that Svoros' people searched. Powell promised him that he'd be safe and upon his arrival at the apartment, Will did feel slightly more confident. At least ten officers were scattered around, including one on the balcony.

Harry had already been told of the situation and dashed over to Will and gave him a rare hug as soon as he entered through the door. Out of the corner of his eye, Will saw Royce and Jason in the doorways of their rooms, listening carefully.

'Shit Will we've been worried about you.' Harry seemed very emotional, the macho facade he usually maintained around his friends had vanished entirely.

'I told you that I was alright when I called.'

'You were in a fucking explosion! And then nearly kidnapped, I mean what the hell? What is it that these people have against you?'

Will gestured towards his room, remembering Powell's advice not to discuss anything to do with the Professor in front of anybody he didn't trust completely. This conversation would have to be between just him and Harry, knowing less would probably keep the others safer anyway.

Will walked into his own room followed by his brother, who sat down on the bed. Will closed the door and chose not to seat himself, he leaned back against the wall instead.

'There is a cult on this island, Harry. I don't know what they want but it's bad and Professor Loch is here to stop them. They killed that girl the other night to frame him and it worked, it's only now that the Security Officers have started to accept his innocence and work with him.'

Will talked for a long time, telling Harry about everything from the Professor's real line of work to Lucy's kidnapping. His brother simply listened and muttered the odd 'Bloody hell' as Will described the explosion. Upon explaining how he rescued Lucy from the collapsing building, Will was referred to as a hero for the second time that day. He couldn't feel any further from heroic though and as his story continued and time passed, Will couldn't help but feel useless and desperate for some news about Lucy, anything at all.

Once he had completed his account of the previous four days to Harry, Will asked for some time alone. He and Harry had agreed how much (or little) it was alright to tell Royce and Jason. Harry left the room to do so.

He must have slept, probably not for long and he didn't remember dreaming but consciousness had lost him. He awoke to a fresh dose of fear, not so much for his own safety but for Lucy's. There was a knock at his door and when Powell entered he felt an inkling of hope, he must have some news! The news wasn't what Will was hoping for however, Lucy hadn't been found. Karl had woken up and after some "persuasion" had said that Lucy had been taken to Corzones mansion. Will didn't understand why the place hadn't been checked instantly. Karl's interrogation was to continue but in the meantime a raid on Corzones mansion and its grounds was out of the question.

Powell left Will alone again but this time he didn't lie down, instead he changed out of his dirty, dusty and ripped clothes into something fresh. He knew what he had to do, even though he didn't like the idea. He left his room and pleaded with Powell to reconsider, suggesting that he just investigated the mansion subtly instead of mounting a full raid.

'I can't Will. What if Karl had been instructed to send us there as a signal to Svoros that we were on to him? The Professor insisted that we did nothing until he was ready and I'm sorry but that's what we're going to have to do. There's more at stake here than finding Lucy. They took her with them. They could simply have killed you both in the medical centre but they took her and they wanted to take you. Don't you understand, they must have had a reason for that. They need her alive.'

'They didn't need her alive when they planted a bomb right next to her!' Powell nodded in agreement with Will's protest.

'Things must have changed since then.' Will hoped that the Chief was correct.

The only problem for Will was that he couldn't simply leave it like that, he couldn't accept that Lucy would be alright in the hands of her kidnappers, they'd already killed indiscriminately and if it somehow turned out that Lucy wasn't any use to them... Will shook the thought from his head and went into the bathroom, locking the door behind him. Harry and Powell were both being incredibly supportive but they weren't doing anything and that's what needed to happen. Perhaps it really was time for Will to play the hero.

The bathroom window was small but Will managed to squeeze through it without making any noise and thankfully he wasn't in the sight of any of the guards. He held himself close to the wall and peeked around a corner, there was somebody outside the front door of his apartment and he was never going to get past them. He had to act quickly, it would only be a few minutes before Powell and Harry became suspicious and he had to be as far away as possible by that point. He looked in the opposite direction and saw an emergency ladder that led down to the ground and thankfully it was tucked out of general sight. He ran for the ladder and climbed down it as quickly as he could, trying his best not to remember that he was slightly scared of heights.

Once he'd reached the bottom of the ladder it got harder. The building was almost completely surrounded by Security and they were checking the room keys of anybody coming and going. He ran for some nearby bushes, praying that nobody would look in his direction. He made it into the bushes without any alert being raised so assumed that he was safe. Nearby he could see a large brick wall in which some bins were surrounded. He could climb over the wall and out of his apartment complex. It had been four minutes since he had made his escape, it wouldn't be long before his absence was noticed.

The brick wall was high but by climbing on to one of the bins, Will was able to clear it. He jumped off the wall and landed on the floor uneasily but as far as he could tell no damage had been done. He stood up again and ran away from the apartment block as quickly as he could, looking back occasionally to make sure that he wasn't being pursued. All seemed clear but he didn't take it for granted. He made it into the jungle as quickly as he could, knowing that by that stage he would require cover. It was a long walk to Corzones mansion and Will wasn't even completely sure where it was, he just knew the general direction in which to head.

In the jungle he was completely alone, the usual drone of music that could be heard blaring across the island was his only companion. There was no Professor or Amerigo, no Lucy and now he no longer even had his brother who was probably frantically worried about him. He knew that he would remain undisturbed until he reached the mansion. Powell would know that was where he was heading to and could get there much quicker. The thought of stealing a buggy had occurred to Will but he would easily have been caught and besides, his approach to the mansion had to be completely undetected, just in case Powell had been correct and his presence there would alert Svoros to the fact that Karl had spoken to them. There was also the risk that Lucy was there, somehow he would have to get her out on his own and he didn't know how she would be. When she had climbed out of the window she had been weak, still suffering from her injuries.

239

The walk through the jungle took hours, midday must have passed and still Will hadn't even seen a hint that he was near to the mansion. He had found a road however that seemed to be rarely travelled along, he could only assume that this was the best indicator he'd have as to where he was going. He stayed covered by the jungle but checked up on the road regularly to make sure that he didn't lose it.

Will wanted to stop and sit down but he couldn't. He was still suffering from some aches and pains but he had to find Lucy. He had to at least know that she was alright and if he could just prove that she was there then Powell would have to reconsider and go in to rescue her. He didn't care about any demons or what the overall plan was, Lucy just had to be safe.

Will found himself on top of a hill and after looking carefully, he walked out on to the road and looked down to see a large golden fence with a magnificent building behind it. His hunch about the road had been correct and he had successfully found the mansion. From his vantage point, Will could see that the main building was encompassed by a number of outhouses. One was surrounded with vehicles and was clearly a garage of some sort but the others, three of them he counted, could be absolutely anything.

Will's first problem was that he had to find a way in, the mansion was heavily guarded and the front gate was locked, completely removing the front quarter of the grounds as an option. He began to inspect the right side, the left being obscured from his vision by trees. He noticed that the right of the building was protected not by the fence but a thick hedge which at one point vanished into a large area of undergrowth. This was his way in, as long as he could get around to that side of the house without being seen. So far he had managed to avoid detection but most of that was simply luck. A vehicle could be heard approaching so Will dashed back into the trees and crouched down behind a bush. He peeked over the top to try and see who was in the buggy but he couldn't tell as it was moving too quickly.

Will crept through the trees and around to the side of the house. He was right about the fence ending where the bushes started but they would still be very difficult to squeeze through. He managed to find a point where part of the hedge had died and a hole could easily be made for him to climb through, the other side was just about covered by trees. As long as he wasn't inside the grounds for too long he would be able to make his escape the same way without being noticed. There didn't seem to be any guards nearby so he kicked the dead wood out of the way and began to make his way through, earning a few scratches from the surrounding thorns.

He decided to inspect the three smaller buildings first of all. The first one wasn't located too far from where he had entered the grounds so he ran straight to it. It was the smallest of the lesser buildings and was surrounded entirely by rose bushes, a gap being left only for the door. Will tried the wide blue door and found that it opened straight away. There wasn't any light on the inside due to the lack of windows but a quick fumble to the side of the door revealed a switch, Will flicked it. A bright light came on and Will saw that he was in a large shed that contained plant pots, hedge trimmers and other pieces of gardening equipment. There were definitely no signs of life however. One building down and no sign of Lucy.

Will turned off the light and left the glorified shed, carefully looking around to make sure that he wasn't observed as he exited the door. No guards were in sight, whoever had been driving towards the building must have attracted their attention completely. Will chose the next building to look inside, it was considerably larger and an aerial was attached to the roof, this one looked to be more likely. Will checked again that there was nobody to observe him and dashed towards his selected building. He stopped behind a large shrub that was just over half of the distance between the two buildings and looked around again to see that there was still no sign of any Security. Will started to get the unsettling feeling that this was all too easy, surely he should have seen at least one guard while he had been inside the grounds.

He reached the second building and found that the door was unlocked, just as the one on the first building had been. He slowly opened the door, expecting to be greeted by the thick black of yet another windowless room. His surroundings were entirely white however. The walls, floors and ceiling were all the same brightly-lit clinical white. The room was full of various bits of scientific equipment, half of which was entirely unidentifiable. One thing

241

that Will was able to identify was the figure lying unconscious on a table in the centre of the room, it was Lucy. Will dashed over to her, forgetting to close the door behind him.

'Lucy,' he checked her pulse, she was alive at least, 'Lucy wake up, please. We need to get you out of here.' Lucy remained completely unresponsive. Will noticed that she had various pieces of equipment attached to her, most notably a helmet-like device that covered her head. Will didn't dare move any of it. He'd confirmed that she was there and perhaps for now that was the best he could do. He'd have to return to Powell and tell him what he had discovered.

Will turned around quickly and heard a cracking sound accompanied by a sudden harsh stinging on his neck. He felt the area that the pain was coming from and then something cold and metallic. He could see the blurred outline of two people in the doorway.

'That's him Doctor Sorn, the one that should have been brought back with her...' The voice continued but Will was suddenly unable to comprehend the words. His vision became more and more blurred and he fell to the floor. Eventually his view turned to complete darkness and the last thing that Will could remember seeing was one of the figures approaching him.

Thirty-Six

The explosion had been magnificent and Karl could hardly believe that he had got away with it. He was safely in Café Solar with Svoros, Sarah and a few other people loyal to their cause. Svoros had promised that this was it now, the final phase and it would only be a couple of days before they had the power that they desired. Karl had never seen Svoros so happy, the scream had verified everything that he had ever believed and confirmed that his work was worth everything he had ever done.

Karl was happy too, happy that he had helped to avenge his brother in such a way that showed the world what the consequences of the Supers' actions were. Perhaps the loss of one life didn't justify others but in the pursuit of ultimate power, maybe even the power over life and death itself, some sacrifices were inevitable. Nobody could stand in their way now: the Professor and Amerigo were disgraced while Steve, Will and Lucy were dead.

'My friends. You all heard the scream, that was what we are working towards finding, that is proof that all of our dreams are coming true. That sound, was Velza himself! Our ultimate source of knowledge and power, a being older than time itself. We are close now and it is time to finalise the arrangements.' Svoros walked to the bookshelf behind the café's counter and produced a modern-looking book that was slightly larger than all of the others. He placed it down on the counter and opened it to reveal that it was hollow, inside was a much smaller book, bound in tatty leather, it looked ancient. 'The book of Velza. Nobody but I have seen it for the last fifteen years, it contains the knowledge of the people who once lived on this island. It is a guide my friends, it lists every method that has been used to imprison the one we seek. It calls him a monster, a demon but we know differently, we know that he is a being of infinite power, a being that saw the world and realised that it should be under his control. In the past, humanity wasn't ready for such a thing but now, with our help, the rest of the human race will come to accept just what a miracle of existence Velza is! You have all been loyal, all worked hard and now for the first time the majority of you are here together. Each and every one of you has played a vital part and now we have no Supernatural Investigator, no interfering children and no Security Force to stop our inevitable victory. Over the next few days we shall change the world and the entire developmental direction of our species!'

It was a good speech and its duration was almost matched by the cheers that came from the unlikely crowd. There were reps, Security Officers, people visiting the island and most noticeably residents, who had lived there for their whole lives and had seen such change. They must have been waiting for so long for these events to occur. Everybody had a reason for being there, be it a desire for knowledge or to give the world an opportunity to give back what had previously been taken. The important thing was that this group were there to make a difference, to improve life for all.

After a few drinks the café began to quieten. An agreement had been made to meet again the next day when conditions would be very different. Velza wouldn't have been released by then but another significant step would have been taken and the island would be a very different place. It made Karl happy to know that very soon he would have changed the world, all in the name of his brother. His only regret was that Ralf wasn't there to be part of it. He banished those thoughts from his head, this was not a time to focus on the upsets of his past but the great things that the near future held for him.

Karl and Sarah remained in the café, knowing that Svoros would have further instructions for them. The old man took a phone call and his mood seemed to change, the jovial look on his face quickly transforming into one of anger and even fear. He turned to Karl and Sarah as the call ended.
'They're not dead. The ones that were in the Security building, they both survived. I've been told that they are now in the medical centre.' Karl shrugged.
'So I go there and finish the job?' Svoros shook his head.
'Yes Karl, but we have also received new instructions. They are to be taken for interrogation. It has been decided that we need to track down the Professor and Amerigo. We thought that this would have happened already and the scream was almost certainly a result of their meddling. They are ahead of us and they know where Velza will be found. William and Lucy may know where they are.' Karl came to the worrying realisation that somebody had given Svoros instructions. He had always believed that Svoros was in charge of the entire operation, the knowledge that there was another

individual involved was disturbing. Who were they and what were their ambitions?

Karl remained uncertain as he and Sarah, now under the cover of darkness, hopped on to a buggy that had been acquired from the Reps HQ and made their way to the medical centre. A simple hack into the island's main database had told them in exactly which room Will and Lucy would be, now all they had to do was find it. The plan was a simple one, Karl would disable the guard and enter through the main door while Sarah would have the buggy parked outside the window, ready to make a quick escape.

Karl left the buggy around a corner from the medical centre and entered through the main entrance. It was quite late now and the majority of the staff had gone, leaving just a few night shifters who were far too busy to notice him. The computer had told him that there were quite a few Security Guards scattered around, Karl knew that they were best avoided. Luckily they proved to be no problem, he had to hide in a doorway to avoid a patrol at the end of one corridor but there was no real danger of him being discovered.

Little time passed before Karl found himself facing down the right corridor. There was just one guard and he was standing right outside the room that Will and Lucy were in. He checked his watch and saw that Sarah would be in position within less than a minute. His gaze didn't leave the watch until the second hand reached the correct place. It was time. Karl sprinted along the corridor and before the guard had any time to react, planted a powerful blow to the back of his head. The guard fell against the door, something Karl had hoped to avoid as it gave the people inside a warning that something was happening. Karl knew that they could be ready for him so elected to have his gun at the ready upon entering. He'd never fired a gun at a person before and hoped that he wouldn't start now. Svoros had given it to him with the strict instruction that it must not be used on either of his two targets under any circumstances, he was carrying it purely for 'persuasive purposes'. Karl threw the door open and braced himself for some kind of ambush but it never came. Lucy was lying in the bed and Will was standing next to her.

Karl would never remember what happened next. He was sure that Lucy was out of the window and safely in the buggy but he didn't know about Will. All he could remember was pain and darkness, both fighting to be the force that consumed him. Eventually he found himself submitting to both.

The darkness faded but the pain was still very much present. He was lying down and above him was a light, placed perfectly on the white ceiling above his head. It dazzled him at first but with a few blinks he was able to cope with it, despite it not doing anything to soothe his agonising headache.

'You're awake, finally.' Karl couldn't see who had spoken to him and the effort to move his head hurt too much. The voice hadn't been friendly or concerned but instead sounded like it was angry with him. It belonged to a man, one who was tired judging by his tone and had offered no kind of reassurance or sympathy towards him. He wasn't amongst friends, he had been caught by the enemy.

Karl attempted to reply to the voice, asking where he was or what had happened but a weak mumble was all that he could manage. A rush of agony prevented him from trying again and caused him to force his eyes shut.

Through the darkness, Karl felt a pressure around his wrists and knew that he was restrained. That was a totally unnecessary measure as he could never even mount an attempt to escape as he was too weak.

'The girl, Lucy. Where was she taken?' That was forward, Karl had expected some mock concern or at least some reassurance that he would recover before the questions started. As his sense of reason began to return to him, Karl realised that this hasty enquiry meant that they were desperate. They had no leads and Svoros' plan was still in action. Karl didn't even attempt to answer this time, he would maintain his silence.

The silence continued for some time, the owner of the voice obviously considering what his next effort would be. Karl managed to open his eyes again but his attempts to move were still unsuccessful. He remembered the loud noise and the immediate pain in his leg. He'd been shot. He couldn't remember which stage the mission had been at but the voice had already told him. He'd only asked about Lucy so it was safe to assume that Will hadn't been taken. Security's interference had happened too soon.

Hopefully the girl would be able to give Svoros the information that he required.

The silence continued for much longer than Karl had hoped and with every second the pain in his leg spread further up the side of his body. Any painkillers that he had been given must have been wearing off and he knew not to expect any more in the immediate future. So far it was nothing that he couldn't stand. Karl's thoughts drifted to how long he had been unconscious. They were still searching for Lucy and there was no evidence that anything had changed so it can't have been all that long. If he had been out for days then the plan would have gone ahead and the Security forces of the island wouldn't be in control. He was finally able to move his head ever so slightly to the left and a window came into view. The blinds were open and light was pouring in. It was daytime. He must have been unconscious for at least six hours then, probably more.

The questions were fired at him continuously. 'Why was the girl murdered?' 'Who was behind the explosion?' 'Where was Lucy taken?' The only question that really concerned him was 'How is Svoros involved?'. If they knew about Svoros then clearly the operation wasn't as safe as had been assumed. It could even mean that the Security forces had spoken to the Professor and Amerigo. Karl hoped that Lucy would inform his friends of that, perhaps she even already had done.

The questions continued, as did the hints that Karl had been completely abandoned. He had to break his silence just to request something to dampen the ever-increasing pain.
'Not until you answer some questions.' The reply was unexpected and Karl suddenly came under the realisation that he was effectively being tortured. If the pain continued then he would probably go into shock and become unstable again. There was a lot he was willing to do for the cause but dying was not part of that. He had to be there at the end, he had to see the victory that he'd worked so hard for.

The questions continued and the pain grew worse, he was in agony but did everything that he could not to show it. A lot of it he converted to anger but it wasn't the questioner that he was angry with, nor surprisingly was it the Professor. The more Karl thought about it, the more Svoros not telling him that somebody else was involved worried him. What other secrets had the old man kept? Perhaps the voice had been right, perhaps he had been abandoned. Svoros couldn't do anything to take away the pain and if the Security forces were on to him already then perhaps the plan may not succeed. The Book of Velza had been another secret. Nothing on the island had made him happy, nothing but Sofia and he had been forced to abandon her in the cruellest way. The entire plan was supposed to make him feel better, make everybody's lives better but what would the benefit be? Would Svoros and his mysterious boss really share their newly acquired power?

'Corzones mansion! She's at the mansion!' Karl regretted revealing this for a few short moments, until a nurse entered. The pain began to fade a few seconds later and Karl was yet again able to embrace sleep.

Thirty-Seven

It was large for a snowflake, the first that had fallen that year. It danced so elegantly downwards and landed on the side of Lucy's nose, instantly melting. A gloved hand delicately brushed away the resulting droplet of freezing water before returning to link arms with her again. The hand belonged to Will who was beaming, savouring yet another perfect moment. There had been hundreds of such moments like these, thousands but every single one still seemed to be unique and special.

Almost two and a half years had passed since their holiday to Corzones Island, since they had met each other in that town centre and it had felt like no time had passed at all. It had all been condensed into a few seconds but out of those seconds some of the greatest moments of Lucy's life had occurred. The world seemed to be a completely different place but no changes had occurred beyond those that were personal.

It had been a sad day when they had parted ways. All had seemed so normal around them but standing by the ferry just before its departure, saying a tearful goodbye to Will had been so unhappy for Lucy. He was to remain on the island for another day but their time together was up. They stood closely, their eyes not breaking contact. Will tentatively reached forward and stroked Lucy's fingers with his own and after a second their hands were locked together. Neither of them wanted to let go but as the final call for people boarding the ferry came over the loudspeaker, Lucy had to pull her hand separate and plant a kiss on Will's cheek. He smiled and stared deep into her eyes yet again.
'I'll see you soon.' His voice was full of hope and promise and he gave a reassuring smile.

It took almost a month for Will's promise to be fulfilled but he finally arrived in Manchester on a hot August day. Lucy was waiting for him outside the train station as he exited amongst a flurry of other commuters. Some were wearing suits and preparing to rush to a meeting while others were more relaxed and out shopping.
'You're here.' Lucy smiled and embraced Will.

'My only regret is that I couldn't get here sooner.' Will smiled and looked into Lucy's eyes, just as he had as she was about to leave Corzones Island.

They had a perfect afternoon together, it was like they'd never really been apart. Lucy had feared that Corzones Island had affected them in the same way that it had so many others, allowing them to get caught up in a manufactured hype brought on by over consumption of sun and alcohol. But no, it was real and wonderful. After some light shopping and lunch in a café that Lucy had been eager to take somebody to for a long time, the two of them caught a bus to the outskirts of the city and Lucy's flat.

It was a small place in a large building but Lucy had made it her own. It consisted of three rooms, one was a main room with a kitchenette on one side, much like the apartment back on Corzones Island had been. Two doors were close to each other on the opposite side to the entrance, one led to a bathroom and the other to a small bedroom.
'It isn't much,' said Lucy with a smile, 'but it's home.' She had rented it just after getting back from Corzones, her experiences there had made her realise that she needed the independence of living alone. She'd enjoyed it and was still close enough to home to see all of her friends and family. Even Sofia had visited upon hearing that Lucy had her own place, they'd had a night out together in town and drunk away any complications to their friendship that the holiday had created.

Will waited to be invited in, he seemed more nervous than he had while they wandered around town but that was hardly surprising, Lucy would have been the same in his position. He took a seat on the small sofa while Lucy made her way towards the kettle and filled it with water. She'd forgotten how Will liked his tea, or maybe she'd never actually known. He told her that it was with just one sugar and not too much milk, exactly the way that she took hers.

Will stayed for longer than the one night that had been planned. On the first night he had taken the sofa but after a few drinks on the second they had shared a bed and a wonderful night together. On the third night Will insisted that despite his wishes to the contrary, it had to be his last night. The conclusion of the visit was that it would have to happen again soon.

It did, just one week later. Will revealed why he'd had to leave the last time. He had started a new job, heading up an archaeological study. The Professor had ensured a good job for him after their time on the island. The more exciting news was that the study was nearby in a village named Burrowden. Will's return to Manchester wasn't just to see Lucy but also to look at houses in the area. He didn't disclose his exact wage but ensured her that it would allow him to live comfortably in the area in a house that he would be buying, not renting.

Will asked Lucy to join him on the house search and she did so. They looked around three houses but one stood out more than the others. It was Victorian and a good bus journey away from the town centre but it had a charm that Lucy felt suited Will perfectly. After looking around Will spoke to the estate agent and made an offer, the figure surprised Lucy immensely but Will was completely serious. He stated that he wouldn't be taking out a mortgage but would pay the full amount straight away. It was only at that point that Lucy realised just how good the job that Professor Loch had secured for Will must have been.

He didn't talk about the amount of money his new job had provided and Lucy decided not to ask. Instead they walked around the shops together and had another pleasant afternoon. Will then took Lucy to an expensive restaurant that evening and paid for the meal, the bill was well over a hundred pounds.

Afterwards they walked together past the closed shops, arm-in-arm.
'You've spoiled me.' Lucy had no idea how she would thank Will.
'It's fine,' he said, 'it's wonderful to see you again, especially with you being as happy as you are.' Lucy stopped walking and looked Will directly in the eye.
'I'm happy because I'm with you. This is wonderful Will, I was worried that after we left the island I'd never see you again but...' A smile from Will silenced Lucy, they both leaned towards each other and kissed.
'Come on,' said Will, 'let's find somewhere and get a drink. I do have to go home tomorrow, why don't you come with me? Meet

my family?' Lucy was speechless, she didn't know how to answer but she eventually settled for a simple and certain 'Yes'.

They spent a few days with Will's family. They were lovely and seemed to take instantly to Lucy, his mum even took her on an extensive shopping trip while Will was working. She stayed with them for a full week before returning home and to work. As he said goodbye to her at the station, Will promised Lucy that he would see her again very soon.

A few months passed and Will's visits became more and more frequent, they were spending every possible minute they could together and Lucy couldn't have been happier. They reached the big day when Will moved into his new house. He had a car full of things and his dad drove a second vehicle that was equally as packed. Harry had also joined them and assisted with the move. He seemed calmer that he had on Corzones Island, Lucy definitely preferred this version of him, the version that was away from his friends and their influences. He was happy to see Lucy again and when Will wasn't in earshot he quickly thanked her for making his brother so happy.
'He really hasn't ever been like this before.'

Harry and Paul, Will's father, left towards the end of the day as the sun was beginning to set. Nights were now drawing in earlier and there was a more than noticeable chill in the air that made Lucy shudder as she waved away Will's family. Will placed an arm around her and she snuggled up to him.
'Shall we go inside?' Lucy instantly replied affirmatively and they walked into Will's new house together.

Will emerged from the kitchen with a bottle in his hand.
'It's not as chilled as it should be but who cares, we're celebrating. Welcome to my new house Lucy.' Will opened the bottle of Champagne and poured a glass for her and then one for himself. They decided to watch a film together and interrupted their celebrations just for a moment so Will could plug in his TV. They chose from one of his many DVD's and settled down for the evening, refilling their glasses the moment that they emptied.

As time passed Lucy found herself staying with Will more than she was in her own home. It was still another six months however, before Will asked Lucy if she'd like to move in with him. For just a few moments the nervous and doubtful Will she had met a year previously began to appear again.

'I mean it makes sense, you're paying for that flat and you don't really use it that much. I'd be happy to have you here. More than happy.' Lucy agreed and a few weeks later packed the contents of her flat into boxes and the boxes into the back of Will's car. That evening an expensive bottle of Champagne was drunk yet again.

Lucy settled easily into her new home with Will. One of the rooms was converted into a design studio for her and for the first time she had the real space she needed for her work. Will spent a lot of time working but when he was at home his attention was fixed purely on Lucy. He was a fantastic cook and his film collection always seemed to provide a new gem. They were happy together and Lucy hoped that nothing would change. Her life had turned into something that she had previously not even dared to dream about.

Thirty-Eight

Will brushed the snowflake from Lucy's cheek, the cold had made her turn slightly red but she was still as beautiful as she had been on the day that they had met. Time had flown by so quickly but each individual moment lasted for a perfect eternity, Will wouldn't have it any other way. His job had proved to be interesting and enjoyable, the drive to Burrowden each day was longer than he'd have liked but he'd chosen to live closer to Manchester to be with Lucy. It had now been eighteen months since she had moved in give or take but together they were still as happy as they had been on the day they had first got together. Those early visits were so long ago but they were far from a distant memory, Will remembered how much he had enjoyed them and the feeling of unconditional happiness hadn't faded for even a moment since.

They were standing wrapped in thick coats, scarves, hats and gloves. It was early December and the traditional Christmas markets were in town. For miles there were stands, stalls and tents selling interesting cheeses and irresistible drinks. Arm-in-arm, Will and Lucy walked towards a stand that sold mulled wine. They ordered a mug each and began to warm themselves with the drink. It tasted wonderful and seconds were ordered almost immediately. They were served by a short girl in old-looking glasses who never let her smile fade, perhaps it was genuine, brought on by the warm atmosphere but Will could see an unexplainable sadness in her eyes.
'Another cup?' Will and Lucy both nodded and a few moments later they were being handed their drinks. 'Merry Christmas.' Will noticed the sadness in the girl's eyes again but the smile never left her. It almost seemed as if she wanted to tell them something but couldn't.

Will and Lucy moved on after their second drink, concluding that the night was still young and neither of them wished to have too much, not yet anyway. Will had never previously being a huge fan of nights out but since moving to Manchester and having Lucy as company he had become quite fond of some of the bars and even one or two of the clubs. They'd agreed to eat together before deciding where their night would end up. Neither of them had work the next morning so it was agreed that a late night was acceptable.

They continued to walk around the market for a while longer, looking at the various things for sale. They quickly concluded that finding a restaurant wouldn't be necessary as the food on offer at the multicultural stands was far too tempting. At one point during the discussions of what they should eat first, Lucy stopped talking and kissed Will.
'Yuck!' commented a passing child, prompting laughter from both Will and Lucy as the parents dragged their daughter away, looking slightly embarrassed. Will didn't care, it had taken him a while to get used to the idea of public displays of affection but when he considered that they were with Lucy he simply didn't care, it just felt natural.

Before finding food they decided to sample some more of the drinks, choosing a German beer this time. They took a seat amongst a series of closely-packed picnic benches and made a start on their pints. The taste was strong but Will enjoyed it, Lucy seemed less sure and drank hers at a slower pace. The benches that they were sitting on were wooden and the past few days' rain had thoroughly soaked into them, Will could feel the coldness but was luckily protected from the water by the coat that he was wearing. His attention was suddenly caught by the girl who had served him the mulled wine earlier, she walked past and looked at him with the same sad look in her eyes that she had previously. As horrible as it felt, Will chose to ignore her. There were many people in the world with a multitude of problems but he was happy, he was with Lucy and they had a life together.

They stayed in the market for some time, sampling all kinds of food and many different kinds of alcohol and as the night went on they moved from mulled wine and German beer to various kinds of liquors. They reached a point where they decided that it was time to visit their first indoor bar of the evening. They chose a wine bar and enjoyed a couple of glasses each until they had decided that it was time to venture on to a club.

A few weeks passed and Christmas came and went. Will and Lucy decided to spend Christmas day itself at home, their first one alone together. On Boxing Day they visited Lucy's family before journeying South to see Will's family the day afterwards. They made their way back to Manchester in time for new year and found themselves joined by Harry. Their house had a spare room and Harry became their guest for over a week, managing to get them tickets for a more-than-exclusive venue on New Year's Eve. Will wasn't expecting to enjoy it but he was pleasantly surprised, though he had to admit that the highlight of the evening was spending time with both his girlfriend and his brother. They rolled in the new year with expensive Champagne.

Will decided that he needed to talk to his brother about something so he took Harry to a bar, it was in fact the same bar that he and Lucy had visited after their adventures at the market. He had decided that he had enjoyed it so much that it merited a return visit and the conversation that he needed to have with Harry was a good excuse. They both arrived and ordered their drinks, Lucy was working on a job that she had received out of the blue so it was the perfect opportunity.

'This is a nice place. You come here much?' Will shrugged.
'Only once before but it seemed alright. I came with Lucy.' Harry's eyes scanned the room, taking in his surroundings. The bar itself stretched along the entire back wall, hundreds of bottles of wine and spirits were lined up along the impressively long shelves. The decor was entirely wooden and polished to the point that Harry could almost see his reflection smiling back at him. The front of the bar was made entirely of glass, providing a view of the busy, rain soaked street outside. It was rush hour and every other vehicle that passed was a bus, full of people hoping the rain would stop before they had to get off.

'You guys both seem to be good,' Harry said, 'you and Lucy I mean.' Will nodded.
'Yes, we both work hard but we're happy.' Harry nodded before picking up his glass of wine and eyeing it. He'd gone for a Chardonnay while Will had chosen a Shiraz, it wasn't cheap but he'd enjoyed it the last time. 'Actually Harry, one reason I brought you here is that I want to talk about her.' Will hadn't told anybody yet, he'd even tried not to think about it as if it were a secret to even himself. Harry looked curious and after Will remained silent for a moment of consideration he beckoned.

'Well?' Will took a deep breath, suddenly it was real. He reached into his pocket and produced a small black box. He opened it.
'It's a ring.' Harry stared at the large diamond in the ring, hypnotised by its beauty.
'I can see that Will. A bloody nice one. Are you...?' Will nodded.
'I'm going to ask her to marry me, yes.' Harry took another few seconds to register what he had seen and heard.
'When?'
'I don't know. Soon. I bought this a few months ago but decided to get Christmas out of the way. Now it's gone I don't have any excuses. I'm going to ask her.' Harry remained silent for a few seconds yet again.
'My little brother, getting engaged!' Harry said it slightly louder than intended, prompting Will to close the box and place it back into his pocket.
'Not so loud. She has to say yes first.'
'Which she will.'
'I'm not sure.'
'Don't be silly. She moved in with you as soon as you asked didn't she?'
'That was convenient though Harry. This is *marriage*.' Harry shrugged.
'I'll admit that I never expected the two of you to last, considering how and where you both met but you have done, you've proved me wrong. Now when we get back tell her that you're taking her out for dinner, go somewhere exceptionally nice and expensive and just ask her.'
'Just ask her?'
'Well what were you planning to do? Drop hints until she suggests it?' Will shook his head, he knew that Harry was right and he'd been holding on to that ring, staring at it when he was alone, for far too long.

The rain had stopped by the time Will and Harry left the bar but they still chose to get a taxi back instead of walk, Will wanted to get back as soon as possible. They paid the cab driver and walked into the house, Harry remained silent in the knowledge that Will wanted to focus. He didn't want to give Lucy any clues about what he was planning. The lights were on so she had arrived home from her job. The walk from the taxi to his front door seemed to take an eternity but Will knew that after confiding in Harry, he was ready.

They entered the house to find Lucy watching TV. She turned to them both and greeted them. Harry pointed to the stairs.

'I'll go and get ready.' He went up the stairs. He had agreed with Will that he would pretend to be meeting some friends and leave at the first opportunity. Will took a seat next to Lucy and slid his hand underneath hers.

'Shall we go out?' He looked at Lucy with a smile but made sure that his face wouldn't give anything away. Lucy shrugged.

'Where to?'

'Well Harry's out so that just leaves the two of us. I think we should find somewhere and have a very nice romantic dinner for two, don't you agree?' Lucy nodded and kissed him.

'It's been two and a half years Will, you're allowed to stop spoiling me now.'

'I was allowed to stop a long time ago Lucy, I just don't want to.'

Will decided that a small Greek restaurant was to be their destination. It was one of Lucy's favourites and Will had to admit that it was a very nice place. They took turns in the shower and got themselves ready. Will was watching a game show on TV to pass the time as Lucy finished her preparations. He was immediately distracted as Lucy walked down the stairs in a stunning red dress. He stood up and walked over to her, wrapping his arms around her.

'You look beautiful.' He didn't intend to but he spoke so quietly that it was almost a whisper. He stepped back and admired her yet again. She smiled nervously.

'I thought that this dress might be a bit too much.' Will shook his head.

'Not at all. If I could I would climb on to the roof now and shout to the world how wonderful you look.' Lucy blushed, just for a second but it was enough to make Will feel butterflies in his stomach. He knew that he couldn't stop now, Harry knew and would never forgive him if he didn't go through with what he had planned.

Will called for a taxi and then sat on the sofa with Lucy, unable to take his eyes off her. She looked amazing in that dress, it was one that she hadn't worn before. Perhaps she somehow knew that this was a special occasion but Will hoped not, he wanted this to be a complete surprise. His phone rang as confirmation that the taxi was outside and the two of them stood up. He fetched Lucy's coat and held it open for her and she put it on, planting a kiss on his cheek afterwards.

The taxi journey only took about ten minutes but to Will it felt like an eternity. On the journey he had a shocking realisation that butterflies were still active in his stomach and that he didn't feel at all hungry. He made a mental note only to choose a light meal and wondered of he'd even be able to manage that. He was nervous, more nervous than he had ever been in the past but trying so hard not to show it. So far it seemed that he was successfully doing so but he knew the worst of it was yet to come.

They had starters accompanied by a bottle of wine, a bottle that Will found himself drinking much more quickly than he had intended. Lucy wasn't too far behind him however and between them they managed to drink the entire bottle before the plates that the starters arrived on had even been taken away. Will knew that by this stage he should start to feel the effects of what he'd drunk but the nervousness and adrenaline were proving to be an effective blocker. He ordered another bottle of wine the next time the waiter came around and it arrived a few minutes later. If he was going to conquer his nerves and actually do this then he needed all the help he could find and unfortunately the only help available was red and alcoholic.

The main course came and was nothing short of divine, Will had steak in a red wine sauce while Lucy had gone for her favourite, squid. The latter was a dish Will had quickly learned to cook when he and Lucy had started seeing each other and had been a fairly regular meal since she had moved in with him. He found that they had both slowed their drinking speed and supposed that the food was mainly responsible. Lucy excused herself and left the table, leaving Will to check his pocket. He had a horrible sense of paranoia that he had somehow misplaced the box containing the ring but he hadn't, it was still there. After that it felt like a dead weight. His enthusiasm for eating completely faded and he left a good deal more of his meal than he would have liked to.

Before Lucy returned, Will caught the attention of a waitress and requested that upon his signal a bottle of Champagne, the best that they had, be brought to the table. The waitress smiled and assured Will that his wish would be granted. She looked familiar somehow, her distinctive glasses certainly rang a bell but Will couldn't think why. Behind the glasses and her smile there seemed to be something else. Will saw her eyes just for a short second and somehow was reminded of Corzones Island. So much had happened there, things that he couldn't clearly remember. A murder, Professor Loch being accused of committing it, an explosion... How had he forgotten these things? Even now the memories were hazy but he couldn't help but notice a pain in his arm, he felt it and looked at his sleeve, his white shirt was showing just a speck of red. Blood! Will didn't know how he had cut himself but when he turned back to the waitress to request a bandage she had vanished.

Lucy returned to find Will rolling up his sleeve, he was shocked to find that there wasn't a cut on his arm.
'Are you alright?' Lucy asked as she retook her seat.
'I thought I was bleeding, I must have just spilled some wine on my shirt, that's all.' Will rolled down his sleeve, noticing that the spot of blood seemed somewhat bigger than it had done before. He looked back to Lucy who was taking another sip of her wine before looking around to see that the waitress had re-emerged, seemingly from nowhere. He nodded at her, knowing that this had to be it. No more delays, no more distractions.' He stood up, prompting a look of puzzlement from Lucy. He walked around to the other side of the table and attempted to deliver a speech that he had practised so many times in his mind. He stuttered, he missed parts out and repeated himself on a few occasions. Eventually he stopped and attempted a more direct approach.
'Will you marry me?'
'Yes!' Lucy's reply was instant, she hadn't even thought about it, she'd just said yes. She grabbed hold of Will and pulled him off his knees, planting the happiest kiss he could ever have imagined on his lips. The waitress walked over with the bottle of Champagne, just as Will had asked. She poured a glass each for them as Will planted the ring on to Lucy's finger. He had forgotten to produce it from his pocket before he had asked but quickly rectified his mistake while he and Lucy had been kissing. She stared at it in astonishment.
'It's beautiful. Will this is so wonderful. I...' Lucy's ability to speak seemed to fail her for the next few moments and she settled for another kiss.

Will sat back in his seat and began to drink the Champagne, he could feel that his face was still bright red but he didn't care, this was a happy moment and more wonderful than he had ever envisioned. It suddenly all stopped. Everything froze in its place, the other people in the restaurant who were gawping at the spectacle, Lucy admiring her ring, the waiter bringing out some food were all just frozen solid. The only other movement in the room apart from Will himself was the waitress.

'Look at your arm Will.' Before questioning how she knew his name, Will looked at his arm. It was stained bright red now and unmistakably blood. He brushed his finger across it to feel that is was soaking.

'What is going on? What's happening?' The waitress shed a tear, it trickled down her face and past her still beaming smile.

'This isn't real. You're trapped here.'

'Who are you?' Another tear fell down the girl's cheek.

'I'm the voice in the back of your head. I'm one you question every time you're uncertain about your life. I'm not real either. I'm just the part of your mind that's fighting back. Right now, Lucy is seeing you frozen and somebody who was in this room is saying the exact same thing to her. You're trapped in your own dream but you've been here long enough to realise that's what it is, a dream.' Will shook his head.

'You're lying!' The girl sighed.

'No Will. Think about the last two-and-a-half years. They've happened so quickly haven't they? In fact it's only been a few hours. You're still on Corzones Island. The last real thing to happen to you... to us, was being shot by a tranquilliser. You remember right? You have to remember. You have to wake up. Whatever this is, you have to wake up.'

'Who are you? If you're telling the truth, then why are you in my subconscious?' The girl smiled.

'We met once while you were at university. My name is Stephanie, you fancied me but never said a word. You seem to have forgotten about me but your mind stored me away. I'm not important now though Will, you are. You have to wake up.'

Will could feel tears forming in his eyes. Stephanie had to be wrong but something floated through his head, a hint of a memory that proved what she had said to be true.

'You have no choice Will. You're trapped in your own dreams, both you and Lucy. This is not real!' Why couldn't it be real?

261

Couldn't he stay here in this dream. And how was Lucy here too, she hadn't been a character in a dream, she was real.

'I want to stay here,' said Will, 'I want this life.'

'You can have it! But not here. Wake up Will, wake up and make your dreams a reality.

Blackness all around and Will felt as if he was falling through it. A light appeared in the distance and Will reached towards it. It grew in size, slowly at first but then it was suddenly right in front of him. He was travelling at a phenomenal speed, at least he thought he was. He could just as easily been completely stationary with the light moving towards him. Stephanie had been right, this wasn't real. The light grew closer and closer until it hit.

Will threw his eyes open suddenly, he was lying down on a bed of some kind. He wanted to sit up but felt something holding him down, he couldn't move his legs either. He looked around to see that a series of wires emanating from various bits of metallic machinery were attached to him. There was something on his head, he could feel it, cupping him like a hat. He tried to move his hands towards it but they too were restrained.

'Absolutely useless.' The voice sounded angry. 'We shall have to resort to more direct techniques. These two can help us find the fugitive Professor, I just know it.'

Two? These two? Who was the other? Will turned his head to the right to see another bed, Lucy was lying on it, also restrained. 'A shared dream that should have given us all the answers we needed and instead we get that. Sickening. Tell Doctor Sorn that her device needs work, minds wander too easily.'

'What should we do with them now?' The second voice was less refined and free from emotion, it sounded like its owner was a long-term smoker.

'We get the information that we need and then we kill them. Svoros insists that we must trace the Professor before things can really begin.'

Part Five - The Demon

Thirty-Nine

'Out the window! Out of the bloody window! Don't you have people outside? Surely they should have spotted him.'

'We have people surrounding this building, it's only been a couple of minutes at most since he left.'

'You're supposed to be taking care of him, you're Head of Security aren't you? Why aren't you out there looking for him?'

'Harry, we will find him, I promise.' Harry wasn't convinced, too much had slipped through the fingers of the Security forces already and while they were trying to give the impression of a strong presence across the island, the truth was painfully obvious: they were short of men and entirely uncoordinated. The explosion had rocked them more than they would have been happy to admit. The entire island was in a state of anarchy but nobody had managed to realise this yet. Most people had continued as normal on their night out, a few sensible folk choosing to stay inside due to another potential bomb threat. Even many of those who had initially stayed in had eventually chosen to go out however, concluding that a bomb probably wasn't all that bad after they'd had a few drinks. Powell would disagree, he'd let slip to Harry that ten of his men were confirmed as dead with at least twice that many in a critical condition. Any injuries that occurred overnight wouldn't be taken care of for some time, the medical staff were also stretched far beyond their capabilities.

The entire apartment remained silent. Powell was waiting for some news about Will, Harry was too apprehensive to speak while Royce and Jason knew better than to say anything, they both retired to Royce's room with a bottle of beer each. Harry looked at his watch, thinking that it was too early for even those two to begin drinking but saw that it was now well after lunch time. He decided to ignore the temptation to have a drink himself. He was very stressed and very hot, the cooling effect of a beer might not have been a bad thing but he knew that he'd have no chance of enjoying it until there was some further information about his brother.

Another hour passed and absolutely nothing had happened. Harry had taken to pacing up and down the room a couple of times but he quickly realised that it didn't do any good at all. He took a seat again and tried to remain still until some information came through. It didn't take him long however, to jump up and declare that enough was enough.

'I'm going to find him.' Powell tried to calm Harry.

'If we wait I'm sure that there will...'

'Will be what?' Harry interrupted, 'We've been waiting for hours. We know exactly where he'll have gone to. Corzones mansion!' Powell sighed and looked at the ground, there was no point in arguing, he must have known that he was already beaten.

'Please just wait.' Harry shook his head.

'You're just scared because your boss is implicated, I wouldn't lead a charge on his house either. I know Will and I know how he feels about Lucy. If there is even a tiny possibility of her being there then that's where he will have headed immediately. And if she is there then it means there is something going on at that mansion without you knowing it, right?' Powell nodded, that look of defeat again crossing his face. 'And the only person who could make anything happen at that mansion without you knowing about it is Giorgio Corzones himself.' Powell nodded. Harry leaned close to Powell to whisper. 'Now, can anybody else hear us?'

The sun was extremely strong and running across the apartment complex into cover wasn't the easiest of tasks. Powell was the one who decided slipping away quietly was the best option and it made perfect sense. There was no way of knowing how many Security Officers were loyal to Powell and how many were loyal to anybody else.

'Nobody can be trusted,' Harry whispered to Powell, shocking even himself, 'You have to start accepting that this is a conspiracy of some kind. It hasn't been arranged by some kindly old café owner as Will thought it had, this could quite easily run to the top.'

'I refuse to believe that without proper evidence.' Harry could tell that Powell was holding on to his last scrap of faith for dear life. 'One of their own has already told you that Lucy was taken to the mansion, surely that's enough to make you want to seek evidence actively?' Powell had remained silent for some time, desperately searching for a response but none that satisfied him ever came. He had left the apartment through the front door with Harry and devised a plan for sneaking past the various guards who had been posted.

Powell insisted that they both turned off their phones, he wanted no trace of what they were doing and knew that the Security forces were able to track any phone on the island, it was an emergency measure in case somebody wandered off after a few too many drinks and needed to be located in a hurry. It was a facility that was apparently not used as much as one would expect but still proved to be useful on some occasions. Harry immediately turned off his phone and removed it's battery, just to be safe.

'It's a long walk to the mansion.' Powell was still attempting to dissuade Harry from continuing but they both knew that moment had passed. They decided to follow the road, it being by far the quickest route.

'Will may have stayed hidden in the jungle, it's a much longer way around. If he did that then he may not even be there yet.' Harry nodded but was certain that Will would have got there even if he had taken a longer route. Harry had neglected to tell Powell that his intention wasn't to extract Will but to help him. Will was almost certainly right and if Lucy was being kept at the mansion then she would need rescuing as discretely as possible.

The walk along the road was long and only involved hiding at the side once as a buggy containing some Security Officers went past. 'I wonder what they are going there for?' Powell seemed even more apprehensive than before after seeing the buggy. This increased even more so when a helicopter flew over. 'Oh no,' he said, 'that was Giorgio Corzones' private chopper. My phone is off, they must be trying to contact me.'

'It doesn't matter,' said Harry who was now even more determined to reach their target, 'it's just more evidence that he's involved. Will said that whatever was planned would be happening soon. What if he's arriving to oversee it?' Powell faced another internal struggle again, that much was clear.

Harry and Powell finally reached an area that overlooked the entrance to the mansion, there wasn't a chance that they were going to get in through the main gate, it was heavily guarded.

'Default Security measures for Corzones' arrival, that's what they're supposed to do if they can't get in touch with me.'

'What can we do?' asked Harry, who was hoping for a secret entrance of some description, 'Can't you blag your way in?' Powell shook his head.

'Even if I did, I wouldn't be able to take you with me and there wouldn't be any way I could have a look around on my own. Once Mister Corzones is in residence, nobody is allowed to be alone in the grounds of the mansion.' Powell looked around carefully and pointed to a small woodland area.

'Over there, we can climb a tree and over the fence, do you know how to land properly Harry?'

Powell led a very uncertain Harry over to the tree-covered area, making sure to stay hidden from any guards' view at all times.

'Even better,' Powell pointed at a gap in a hedge that wasn't covered by fence, 'We can squeeze through that.' Harry looked at the gap, it was very narrow but he was sure that he would be able to fit through it.

'I bet Will went through there.' Powell nodded in agreement.

'I suspect that you may be right.'

Powell squeezed through the gap first and ran straight behind a large tree, hiding himself from the view of a passing guard. Once the coast was clear, Harry joined him.

'What now?' Harry realised that asking such a question was a bit feeble after his brave face earlier on, the truth was that he had no idea what to do or where to start. Upon having a view of the whole grounds he had failed to make a note of the best places to look. Will would have done. Powell spent a moment looking around the tree.

'There are some out buildings scattered around. One of them is just a very big garden shed and the other is the power room, the house has its own generator.' Powell had another look. 'Of course. There's a building that nobody is allowed in, Corzones has always said that it contains a safe with some private articles.'

'A safe?' Powell nodded.

'That's right. It's a fairly large building though.'

'Large enough to keep a person in?' Powell nodded again, a grim look covering his face.

'More than big enough.'

'We'll look there first, how do we get to it?'

'With difficulty. Corzones himself is here, which means that every inch of these grounds are patrolled. We can move through it but we have to time it all perfectly.'

Powell explained the route that they would take to the out-building and gave him a rough idea of the guards' patrol cycle.
'Essentially, you have to follow me and do exactly as I say or we will both get caught without a doubt. Think you can manage that?'
Harry nodded but didn't feel entirely confident that it would work. If Will had come here it would have been before the helicopter had arrived and therefore much easier for him to creep through.

Powell pulled Harry back behind the tree as two more guards approached on their patrol.
'After these two,' Powell whispered, 'we should be able to run straight to the building without being spotted, if I've worked things out correctly.' Harry wasn't completely convinced but once the guards were gone and Powell gave the signal, he ran. Harry stayed as close to Powell as he possibly could but the Security Chief ran much faster than he did and on a couple of occasions there was a real risk of him being left too far behind.

They both rounded a corner and the building that they were aiming for was in sight. Powell stopped quickly and threw himself back behind the corner, grabbing Harry and pulling him into hiding as well.
'The door to the building opened, somebody was coming out. Stay down and stay quiet.' Powell peeked his head around the corner.
'It's Corzones.'
Harry remained silent but could hear two voices speaking in the distance.
'This is ridiculous!'
'You have to remain patient sir, one of them will reveal something useful in time.'
'Yes, but so far all we have is him obsessing over that girl.' That was Will, it had to be thought Harry. He and Lucy must have been interrogated. Powell's face told Harry that he was thinking exactly the same.

'We wait until they've gone and then we run for that building,' said Powell, 'do you understand?' Harry nodded, more determined than ever to reach the building. Corzones and the other man disappeared around a corner, heading towards the mansion.

'Now.' Powell ran, followed by Harry. The out building was only a few metres away when there was a loud bang. It was a gunshot! Powell stopped in his tracks, followed by Harry who almost ran into him.

'Do not move!' There was a few seconds of silence. 'Now turn around.' Harry and Powell did so to see two Guards, one of whom was holding the gun that had just been fired.'

'Security Chief Powell?'

'We're on an operation, please let us continue.' The guard shook his head.

'I'm afraid that won't work. There's been an arrest order put out for you and Inspector Kirshner, I believe that he has already been apprehended.' Powell shook his head.

'What the hell are you talking about?'

'We know about you and your attempts to cover up that murder, along with everything else that's going on around the island. Mister Corzones wants to speak to you personally. Now move!' Powell sighed, choosing to argue no further. He started to walk towards the mansion, Harry followed.

Forty

It had been tempting to introduce Sofia to his father but Victor
knew that taking her back to where she was staying had been the
right thing to do. After everything that had had happened over the
previous week he was sure to be unimpressed and finding that his
son had been clubbing and apparently picking up women probably
wouldn't improve things.

His father arrived during the afternoon, the sun was at its warmest
when his helicopter eventually landed. Victor had smartened up
before walking out into the grounds to meet him. As predicted,
Giorgio Corzones wasn't in the best of moods but his annoyance
wasn't directed towards Victor, instead the Security forces seemed
to receive the entirety of his vitriolic rant. The fact that Powell had
disappeared had done absolutely nothing to improve his mood,
he'd expected his head of Security to be present upon his arrival
and going dark at such a time was entirely inappropriate.
'He needs to be at the centre of it all, keeping his team together!
They've just lost a load of their colleagues.' Victor agreed with his
father's point, Powell had been off the radar for a number of hours
by then and the Security forces were starting to suffer from what
could be a terminal lack of organisation.

Giorgio's sense of impending disaster was however, dwarfed by his
stomach. He'd been travelling for a good deal of time and had been
in such a hurry that he'd neglected to eat. Luckily Parsons had
some food ready and within fifteen minutes the table was filled
with a grand selection. Giorgio immediately grabbed the leg of a
cold chicken and began to devour it.
'Sorry Victor, I'm not exactly being polite,' said Giorgio as he
wiped a bit of grease from his lips, 'I've been on the phone for the
entire journey. Seventeen people want to take us to court after their
holidays were disrupted.' Victor understood why people may wish
to take such action but it was hardly helpful at that current point in
time. Giorgio's complaints continued for the rest of the meal until
he finally asked his son how he was.
'I'm fine,' answered Victor, 'just a bit disturbed by everything that's
happening.' Giorgio nodded.

'I understand son, as soon as we manage to find this Professor Loch and his accomplices we may start to get some real answers.' Victor nodded.

'I met a girl,' he didn't know why he said it but he had to continue, 'her name is Sofia and she's staying with somebody that knows Loch.' Giorgio's eyes widened.

'Tell me more.' The tone of the conversation had suddenly reached a point of seriousness yet again. Victor explained about how he had met Sofia and what she had told him about the Professor and Lucy.

Giorgio stood and paced the room for some minutes, a habit he often demonstrated when he was thinking. Victor sat and continued to eat slowly until his father's train of thought had reached its destination.

'Victor,' there was a snappy sense of urgency in his voice, 'I need you to do something for me. It's very important and you must not say a word to anybody about it.' Victor asked what his father meant but no real explanation was forthcoming. 'I am about to write a letter. You must deliver it personally to a man named Svoros, he owns Café Solar in the town centre. This letter must reach him and nobody else.' Victor nodded so Giorgio dashed out of the room and towards his study.

A few minutes passed and when his father returned, Victor was handed an envelope sealed with wax.

'This is important Victor, the most important thing that I have ever asked you to do. Please promise me that you will give this to Svoros and not read it yourself. Reading it will only place you in danger.' Victor was confused, he'd never seen this side of his father before. Giorgio Corzones almost appeared to be scared for the first time that Victor could recall. He knew better than to ask questions and instead made all of the promises that were asked of him.

He took a buggy on his own, his father had instructed that no guard was to accompany him. The contents of this letter must have been extremely important and tempting though it was, Victor didn't even dare to consider reading its contents. Instead he drove as quickly as he could towards Svoros' café. The light was beginning to fade and he wondered if his destination would even be occupied. His father had assured him that it would be. Perhaps the café turned into a bar at the end of the day, Victor didn't know as his knowledge of any of the town centre wasn't great as he'd spent very little time there. The mansion and the strip were the only parts of the island that he was completely familiar with.

The evening was beginning as Victor reached the town centre, he immediately spotted the café just as his father had said he would. He parked up his buggy and walked towards the café's door, holding on tightly to the letter. The town centre was quieter than he had expected, there were a few people around but it wasn't nearly as busy as he had seen it in the past, although that had always been at a different time of day.

Victor looked through the window of the café, there was a light on but it was dimmed. He could see clear figures of two people inside, they were shaking hands. One of them turned to the window and noticed him so he decided that he should walk inside.

'Hello there,' he sounded more nervous than he had intended but the unanswered questions and urgency in his father's voice had made him uneasy, 'I'm sorry but is one of you named Svoros?' The older of the two men nodded.
'I am Svoros yes. You're Mister Corzones' son, aren't you?' Victor nodded.
'That's right, call me Victor.' Svoros nodded and smiled. The other man beside him remained silent. He was fairly young and shabbily dressed, wearing what seemed to be an old tatty combat uniform with holes in the trousers. His attire didn't match the climate but he showed no signs of being too hot. He had a long ginger beard and when he smiled, Victor noticed that at least two teeth were missing. This mysterious figure only served to make Victor feel more uncomfortable.

Victor handed the letter to Svoros who seemed to take some time reading it, he looked over the paper at Victor a number of times as he did so. Something didn't feel right. Svoros finished reading the letter and placed it down on a table, he turned to the man with the ginger beard and whispered something. Victor allowed his eyes to glance at the letter and managed to make out a few words: 'Do not let Victor leave.' He had no idea what the context of this was but decided that he did not want to remain where he was. What on Earth was his father involved with?

271

Both Svoros and the man with the ginger beard were facing away, communicating in the most inaudible of whispers. Victor decided to make an undetected exit, certain that he would be followed. He silently but quickly, edged towards the door and slipped out. As he looked back through the window, he could see that his exit had been noticed. 'After him!' Svoros had ordered, shouting so loudly that Victor could hear him clearly. He started to run, darting around as many corners as he possibly could. Small alleyways and side streets passed him by as he sprinted faster than he ever had before. He couldn't even begin to guess why his father wanted him to remain there but it was clear that he would be little more than a prisoner if he had done.

A million thoughts raced through his mind about what had happened on the island over the last few days and what could possibly have made his father want to imprison him with a man he had never met before. It was as he had mentioned Sofia that his father's demeanour had seemed to change, could it be her? Or was it the fact that she was friends with somebody who knew the Professor?

Victor made his way towards the jungle, it was the only chance he had of losing his pursuer who was a considerable distance behind but making up the gap in far shorter time than Victor felt comfortable with. He dashed behind a bush and scrambled into the engulfing darkness of the trees. He dashed behind cover and tried as hard as he possibly could to hide the sound of his panting. He heard the running footsteps of the bearded man come to a standstill.
'I know you're here somewhere Victor.' His voice contained an anger that Victor suspected was supposed to be hidden. 'You can come out now and you won't be harmed. In a few minutes my men will start to overrun this island and I can assure you that you'd rather be taken in by me than one of them. They can be more than enthusiastic about their work.' Victor managed to stay silent, despite the horror at what he was hearing.

He didn't move for a long time, over an hour passed and the darkness of night began to cover the island. In the near-distance he could see lights coming from the street that the bearded man had returned to after being unable to find his prey. Victor noticed very quickly that the thumping music from the nightclubs had continued uninterrupted, he therefore assumed that the threatened takeover had yet to come into effect. The more he thought about it, the more unsure he was about what it meant. Did Svoros and the bearded man really have enough people with them to take over the island entirely? Could this have been what his father had wanted to protect him from by having Svoros somehow restrain him?

More time passed and in the distance, everything seemed to be normal. People were making their way towards the strip as they would normally begin to about this time. Victor's thoughts drifted towards Sofia, she'd probably still be alone and waiting for him to call. He didn't dare use his phone and had removed its battery as soon as he realised that he could be traced that way. He decided that if there was going to be some kind of takeover then he should at least try to protect somebody and that person would be Sofia.

She had told him the previous night exactly which room that she was staying in but at that time he had drank a fair amount and a lot had happened since then. He tried as hard as he possibly could to remember what it was. He found the building without any problems but the apartment number? He was fairly certain that it had been fifty something so he made his way straight to the fiftieth floor and began to search for clues. He very quickly managed to convince himself that it was room fifty six, so he knocked on the door and waited for almost thirty seconds before it was answered by a small dark-haired man who was wearing a hurriedly-tied dressing gown. He looked less than impressed and Victor quickly saw why, just at the edge of his vision inside the room was a girl lying in bed, apparently not wearing anything.
'I'm sorry, wrong room.' Victor hurriedly walked away, not even waiting for a reply. He heard an annoyed slam of the door a short moment later.

Victor's second guess was room fifty four. He knocked on the door, hoping that his luck would prove to be somewhat better than the last time. Fortunately it was and Sofia answered the door.
'Victor!' She seemed surprised. 'I've been calling you for hours but you didn't answer.' Victor held his finger to his lips and whispered a request to enter. Sofia looked confused but nodded and Victor hurriedly entered.
'Something is wrong Sofia, very wrong.'

Victor explained everything that happened as quickly as possible and then shared some of his worries with Sofia, who it seemed that throughout the course of the day had convinced herself Lucy had probably been right about the Professor, a conclusion that Victor himself was quickly reaching. Sofia hadn't seen either Lucy nor Will at all, or even heard anything else. Victor took a deep breath, he had come to a realisation a few minutes before and decided that it was time to share it with Sofia.

'I don't think we can stay here much longer. I told my father about you and I don't think it will take too long for somebody to look here for me.' Sofia nodded.

'We shall both go then.' Sofia quickly changed into a nice dress and a wholly impractical pair of shoes. Victor looked confused, Sofia noticed.

'We hide in one of the clubs,' she explained, 'it is the last place that they will look for us after all.'

Her logic did seem to make sense so, after checking their surroundings cautiously, they left the apartment and descended to the front of the building. They both jumped suddenly as they heard a gunshot.

'I think it's started, we need to get to the strip as quickly as we can.' Sofia agreed and together they ran.

They made it to the strip without any other sounds of incident. 'They mustn't have made it here yet. If we get into a club then we can hide in the crowd. You'll be safe Victor.' He nodded.

'One thing though Sofia, if I'm found then you're not with me ok? I don't want anything to happen to you.'

'I won't leave you.' The sincerity in her voice didn't make things easier but Victor was adamant that she wouldn't be put in any danger.

'Sofia, they could use you to get to me somehow. What if you get caught and I don't?'

'Then you let them do whatever they have planned, I can take it.' Victor shook his head.

'Never. The moment they touch you, I give myself up. Do you understand?' Sofia nodded hesitantly.

They stepped out of cover and walked down the strip, their arms were linked. Victor skipped the queue and went to Tony, the doorman.

'Just two of us.' Tony nodded and ushered them in.

'Down there!' The shout was from a familiar voice, the bearded man! He was standing at the top of the road and was pointing directly at Victor. He had a few men with him now and they were holding automatic rifles. This was it, the takeover.

'Get inside and hide,' said Tony, who had worked out automatically that they were after Victor, 'I'll keep them out for as long as possible. Hide, use another exit, whatever you need to do.' Victor nodded and ran inside with Sofia. There was a gunshot followed by a series of screams. Very quickly a large group of people were following them into the club.

'They killed the bouncer!' One girl shouted loudly, Victor was horrified.

They ran into the club, Victor holding on tightly to Sofia's hand. 'They'll cover all of the exits,' he said, 'we'll have to hide in the crowd.' They pushed their way on to the dance floor and tried to vanish amongst as many people as they possibly could. After only a few seconds the music stopped and the sound of gunshots rang out. One of the mercenaries fired into the ceiling, hitting a light and causing it to violently spark. The bearded man stepped forward.

'In here somewhere is Victor Corzones! All you have to do Victor is step forward and nobody gets hurt!' Victor stayed still, holding his head low. The bearded man waited for about ten seconds for a reply that never came. That's when he grabbed the first hostage and held a gun to his head.

Forty-One

'Which one of you is Loch?' The man who spoke was more muscular than the rest of the group but had the same bald head and set of tattoos. He had a thick ginger beard and when he spoke, Kirshner could see that he was missing a couple of teeth. The whole group of men were wearing tatty combat uniforms and large black boots. They were mercenaries, Kirshner could see it straight away.

Loch stepped forward and identified himself.
'Phone. Give me the phone.' said the bearded man.
'I don't have it.' The bearded man nodded and one of the other mercenaries walked up to the Professor and punched him in the stomach, he doubled up and fell to the ground. Kirshner intervened.
'I have it! I have the phone.' The bearded man turned his attention to Kirshner and the Professor slowly made his way back to his feet.
'Give.' Kirshner handed the phone to the bearded man who took it and threw it into the sea.

The two other boats arrived, both full of identically dressed men, all armed with pistols, assault rifles and grenades. They had enough equipment to fight a small war and Kirshner feared that was their intention.
'Professor Loch, you have been causing a friend of mine quite a lot of trouble.' The Professor was still slightly hunched over and holding his stomach.
'What trouble have you been causing my friends? That's their boat.' The bearded man smiled.
'They won't be joining us.'

Kirshner, Amerigo and the Professor were pushed up against a rock and placed under armed guard, they all remained silent. Kirshner listened carefully to what was being said by the men but was only able to make out half of the conversation. The bearded man was clearly the leader and it didn't take long for Kirshner to ascertain that he was called Burns. His talking with the other men also provided some information. They were a group of mercenaries and this was just the advance party, many more were on the way. They placed a beacon in the sand and a small red light on top of it began to flash. How many more boats would it guide in? The Security forces on the island were lightly armed and after the explosion, their numbers depleted. If this was some kind of takeover then it would be quick and they'd meet next to no resistance. Kirshner prayed that their intentions weren't murderous.

They sat in silence for a few hours while the mercenaries made their preparations. Burns left quite quickly, saying that he needed to speak to Svoros. Once their leader was gone, the mercenaries seemed to be more relaxed. There certainly wasn't any opportunity for Kirshner and the others to escape but conversation became a possibility, providing it was kept in hushed tones.
'I assume that you need no further convincing of my innocence, Inspector?' Kirshner nodded, finally the Professor had been fully cleared in his eyes. The way that Burns had punched the Professor was no act or misdirection. 'Svoros will come to see us here,' the Professor continued, 'the scream will have confirmed to him that we have found something. We've led him straight to what he wants.'
'We'll still have time to do something though,' replied Kirshner, 'you've studied that library for long enough and reached no real conclusions apart from what this island is.' Amerigo shook his head.
'I am afraid Inspector that the Professor has had only a day to make his deductions while Svoros has had many, many years. The books he has read and the studies that he has done. I fear that when Svoros finds the library, he will immediately know what to do.'
There was a defeated silence, leaving the conversation of the mercenaries and the crashing of the waves as the only sounds to usher in the darkness.

The light had almost entirely faded when a buzzing could be heard coming from the direction of the ocean. It grew louder and louder, Kirshner very quickly realised that it wasn't just one object making the sound. They were boats. Probably about fifty of them. They carried an army that would allow Svoros to dominate Corzones Island completely. It appeared that he was ready to make his gesture. All along they had assumed that whatever he was scheming would happen quietly and perhaps that was even his original plan. The boats arrived at the shore and Kirshner was able to see for the first time just how many people Svoros had. They were all armed to the teeth with automatic rifles and an impressive selection of explosives.

'We have one hope,' whispered the Professor, more cautiously than their previous conversation had been, 'the team of Supers that never made it here, they were supposed to report in upon arrival. They'll realise something is wrong eventually, especially when they can't contact me either.'
'So we wait for them to send somebody else?' The Professor nodded.
'All we have to do Inspector, is buy as much time as we possibly can.' Kirshner shook his head.
'There are thousands of innocent people on this island, if a war breaks out...' The Professor beckoned silence.
'I'm well aware of that and for every death that is caused my conscience will be haunted for years to come. This is a choice that the Supers hoped we would never have to make, what is more important, a few lives or the existence of humanity itself?' Kirshner fell silent. They both knew what the answer was and they didn't like it. That is the approach the Supers would take however, the population of the entire island would be forfeited if the worst were to happen.

More time passed and the night set in fully, Lovers' Cove had turned into some kind of cut-throat bay. The mercenaries were drinking, eating and fighting but the noise always remained on a low level. Their attack would be a surprise. Kirshner took a moment to think about all of the people who would be there when it happened: Powell, Will, Lucy. Even Victor Corzones, surely he would be a target of interest. Kirshner tried as hard as he possibly could to not think about what their eventual fates may be.

Burns returned, along with Svoros who directed a particularly smug glance at the three captives. He looked as if he were about to say something for a moment but walked past without doing so. Instead he stepped up on to a rock and took a torch, shining it out over all of the mercenaries. There must have been at least three-hundred of them. Burns stood next to him with a satisfied smile on his face.
'Thank you all for coming! This is a cause that many of us have been working towards for years, some of you have even been with us throughout your entire lives. There is little I can say apart from

telling you that in the next few hours, the moment of truth will finally be upon us.' Kirshner couldn't help but roll his eyes, this was destined to be a long speech. Svoros continued, 'We are all here for our own reasons but our aim is unified, a different world! A world that is better! A world that has the power and the foresight to achieve its aims. We have often talked about the future, something that has always seemed so far away that it was little more than a dream. Tonight, dreams come true! Burns and I have discussed our next moves, the takeover of this island will be over within the next couple of hours and once we have confirmation that everything is secure, the final phase will come into action. Velza will be released! Already we have heard his scream. He knows that we are prepared for the moment and that his imprisonment is about to end! Welcome to *our* world!' Svoros stood down from the rock to a roar of applause, any need for quiet had apparently been forgotten about.

Burns was next to take to the rocky podium, he began to give instructions and break the mercenaries down into groups. Kirshner heard their plan and it was tactically foolproof. Within a few hours they would indeed have total control over the island.
'Svoros likes a show,' whispered Amerigo, 'it will be midnight when he tried to enact his plan.' Kirshner glanced at his watch. 'Just over two hours, surely they won't completely control the island by then?' Kirshner had tried his best to sound optimistic but the Professor disagreed.
'I'm very sorry Inspector, but it's completely possible. Svoros has better local knowledge than almost anybody, while I get the impression that this team of mercenaries are very professional. Security is weakened. This island will fall quickly.' Kirshner shook his head, defeated.
'I hope Powell and the other Security forces have the sense to surrender.'

The mercenaries began to scatter, heading towards the areas of the island that they were due to dominate. Kirshner was given just a brief glimmer of hope when he overheard Burns mention to a couple of others that they had to find Victor Corzones, at least he had escaped for now. No mention at all was made of Powell despite the fact that Kirshner thought that he may be a key target. Waiting until a later hour had been wise, most of the island's population would be on the strip. The clubs would be easy to storm and even easier to use to contain people within.

After talking to a lot of the mercenaries and remaining there with only a small group, Svoros made a series of phone calls, telling people to join him at Lovers' Cove. It was then that he turned his attention to the three captives. The first person to receive his attention was Amerigo.

'I wish you had taken my advice old friend. It was only a few days ago that I told you to leave the island. You wouldn't have come to any harm. Now, I can make no such promise.'

'Don't you dare call me friend!' Amerigo's response was filled with an anger that Kirshner wouldn't have assumed him capable. Svoros shook his head, his face showed a genuine look of disappointment. 'I always wanted you to be one of us Amerigo, when you see what we will form the world into, you will understand. Old friend, I'm sure that there will still be a place for you in our future.' Amerigo looked away, trying to conceal his rage.

Svoros turned his intention to Kirshner, he smiled. His demeanour turned into that of a businessman and not the friend that he had tried to be to Amerigo.

'Inspector! You did a marvellous job. You solved the case.' Kirshner ignored the attempt at mock flattery and noticed that somebody was arriving, climbing down the rocks that were the only way of accessing Lovers' Cove. Svoros looked over at the new arrival and smiled. 'You were chosen specifically because it was thought that you'd fail to cooperate with the Security forces and accept the clues that led to the Professor at face value.' Kirshner shook his head, it didn't add up.

' I was chosen by...' He fell silent as he identified the figure that was walking towards him. '...Giorgio Corzones.' He was there, in the flesh! Corzones walked over to Svoros and shook his hand.

'Is it all ready?' Corzones was not attempting to make any secret that he was involved. It all made sense really. Who else would have such influence over the island to ensure that Svoros remained hidden for so long while managing to get everything he wanted. Corzones was infamous for knowing absolutely everything that occurred across his empire. He should have been suspected sooner. His involvement also explained just how so many mercenaries were being paid. Loyalty or otherwise, they were there for the money.

After Svoros exchanged pleasantries with Corzones, his attention returned to the captives.

'You must be surprised.' Kirshner was and judging by his expression, so was Amerigo. Professor Loch smiled.

'We suspected,' he said, 'this island never made any money for the Corzones family and it isn't the sort of thing you'd expect to be a philanthropic gesture.'

'You can only be Professor Loch,' said Corzones, 'an unexpected variable but here you are. Dealt with.' The Professor remained silent, Kirshner realised that he was risking giving nothing away. He would adopt the same approach.

'Where is it?' Svoros expected his direct question to actually provide an answer as much as Kirshner did but it was always the best way to start an interrogation. Nothing about it would be simple at all but the truth was that eventually either he, Amerigo or the Professor would break. He remembered what Loch had said about playing for as much time as they could.

The interrogation lasted little more than ten minutes and to Kirshner's surprise, it was the Professor who provided the answer, pointing towards the cave. Very little violence had been used beyond the occasional punch. Svoros smiled and produced his phone. Kirshner assumed that the Professor hadn't been broken but had instead voluntarily given up the answer. He had a plan, he must have one because directing Svoros and Corzones towards what they wanted so quickly couldn't possibly be an attempt at buying time.

Svoros' phone call was brief.

'Bring him here.' Kirshner wondered who "he" was and why he was so important. Was it perhaps a priest who knew exactly how to raise whatever it was that rested under the island? The Professor looked oddly calm. Amerigo didn't look suspicious at all however, and Kirshner decided that the best course of action to take would be to follow the Professor's lead. If any of them knew what to do in this situation, it would be Professor Loch.

It was about half an hour before anything changed. Svoros and Corzones clearly had no intention of entering the cave until the person that they were waiting for had arrived. His clothes were

281

dirty and his head was covered by a black hood. Little care was taken with the man, he was almost thrown off the rocks leading down to the cove and landed very unsteadily on the sand. His hands were tied and despite his silence, Kirshner was almost certain that an arm had been broken upon his landing. Svoros simply watched with a subtle smile forming across his lips. 'Gentlemen, it is time.'

They were lead into the cave, the other captive never had his hood removed but the occasional noise from underneath also revealed that he was gagged. Kirshner couldn't even begin to speculate who this man was or why he was significant but it was clear that he had a purpose to serve. The Professor and Amerigo remained silent as they walked through the cave but Svoros was unable to hide his astonishment that the tunnels extended further than they had done before. Corzones tried to ask Loch what had happened but the Professor simply remained silent and smiled politely.

Words about 'destiny' and 'victory' were uttered on the walk through the cave, the Professor was leading the way at gunpoint, not even bothering to protest. What would be the point? It wouldn't be too hard for them to find the new passage and the library after a couple of minutes search.

When they reached the library, Svoros dashed into the centre and observed the round table.
'It's exactly as the book of Velza said.' He turned to the rest of the group. 'It's all true, this is the confirmation. If any of you doubted then this is your moment of revelation. In this chamber, tonight, we shall change the world.' Professor Loch shook his head.
'You're wrong Svoros, whatever is beneath this place was sealed away for a reason.' Svoros laughed.
'The people who sealed Velza away were primitive, they didn't understand what they had been presented with.' The Professor glared at Svoros, apparently somehow still unable to believe that his insane plan was coming together.
'Do you know Svoros? Do you really know what you're dealing with? Do you think that Velza is a demon, with big horns perhaps? Does he breathe smoke?' Svoros smiled.
'Even the great Professor Loch doesn't know what lies beneath the island. Velza is a being of unimaginable power.'

282

'A being?' questioned the Professor, 'I've encountered such *beings* before, stopped them from being released even. Whatever Velza is, it isn't a being. It's power, pure energy that cannot be controlled. Energy so overwhelming that it gained a consciousness. But it burns, Svoros, whatever it is suffers for every second of its existence. The thing that you call Velza is a natural phenomenon, a miracle of life just like humanity.'

'That's why we want to release it! It is infinitely more powerful than a mere human.'

'Maybe it is, so why do you think that you can control it?'

'I have served its cause all of my life, I will be its saviour and along with my followers we can change the world.' The Professor shook his head again.

'And why does the world need changing? Are things so bad that they have to be changed drastically by an insane ball of energy.' Svoros struck the Professor across the face.

'Blasphemy!' The Professor turned to the rest of the entourage. 'And there you have it. He worships this entity. It's like worshipping uranium. What you plan to release here is uncontrollable and could easily consume the planet. You can't negotiate with it. It simply exists and knows nothing but constant, unbearable pain.' There was no response. Svoros smiled.

'Finished Professor?' Loch looked desperate but said no more.

Forty-Two

Will stared at Giorgio Corzones. They looked directly into each other's eyes. He had a look of shock upon his face while Corzones was visibly annoyed. Lucy looked on, neither of them had realised that she was conscious yet. There was another person stood watching them, this was Doctor Fiona Sorn. She was at least fifty and had untidy grey hair. She wore a lab coat and had it buttoned up but a red blouse was just visible underneath. Lucy had first met her upon being brought to the mansion, somewhere she hadn't expected to be taken after the buggy had carried her away from the medical centre. She was taken into the outbuilding containing the lab and one question was asked of her: 'Where is Professor Loch?' She didn't know but Sorn refused to believe her.

After the question had been repeated a countless number of times, Sorn seemed to take a more sinister approach.
'We have ways of ensuring you give the answer without even knowing it.' Lucy promised that she honestly didn't know where the Professor was yet another time but her answer wasn't accepted.
'You can hide the truth from us now but your unconscious mind won't hide anything. We have developed the technology here to see into your dreams and even steer them in any direction that we wish to. If the location of Professor Loch is hiding away in there, I can assure you that we will find it.
'Please,' begged Lucy, 'I honestly don't know.' Sorn gave a sorrowful smile and produced a syringe.
'You had a chance, in fact you've had many. Having somebody read your every thought isn't a pleasant experience Lucy, I wish you hadn't made me do this.'

The needle grew closer and closer and in the blink of an eye Lucy was back at home, she'd just moved into her first flat and was decorating it in the way that her dream home would appear, albeit on a smaller scale. Something was missing from it though and as she continued to live her life and work in the new job that she'd wanted so much, she realised that Will was the missing factor.

Over a month had passed when she received the call from Will, saying that he would visit her as soon as possible. He did and from that point onwards they embarked on their relationship. They moved in together and then Will eventually proposed. A girl in the restaurant that night had told her that nothing was real and as much as she didn't want to accept it, she knew that this was the truth. The last real thing that had happened to her was the needle, closing in.

She'd woken suddenly but wasn't noticed by anybody else in the room. Both Corzones and Sorn had focused their attention completely on Will. They seemed surprised that he had managed to beat their equipment and inform himself subconsciously that it was all indeed a dream. They expressed a mix of anger and admiration. 'Only a very strong mind can get out by itself,' said Sorn who then smiled, 'or a very stupid one, a mind that lacks imagination.' She spoke with a German accent. She pressed Will with the same question that she had repeated to Lucy: 'Where is Professor Loch?' Will didn't know either and eventually Sorn gave up.

Corzones ordered that Will and Lucy be placed with 'the others.' Two Security Officers entered and marched them at gunpoint into the main building. They entered through a side door that was less impressive than the front, Lucy walked slowly, still in considerable pain after the explosion and her kidnapping from the medical centre. The guards were less-than sympathetic and told her to hurry on a couple of occasions. Will helped, supporting her at one point as she almost tripped over. Her legs were especially weak and needed resting. They hadn't said a word to each other, not since the hospital. Lucy wondered if Will had lived through the same dream that she had, was it a shared experience and if so would the feelings they had inadvertently revealed to each other affect the real future? They had spent over two years together in just a few hours.

Both were eventually pushed into a large wine cellar that looked surprisingly old, considering that the mansion had only been built about six years before when the island was developed. Bottles of expensive looking wine were stacked on racks that were so high, Lucy would only just be able to reach them. The stairs were wooden and made a loud clunking sound as they walked down them, Lucy almost slipped at one point. Once at the bottom of the steps, the guards escorted Lucy and Will around a corner to reveal that "the others" were Security Chief Powell and Harry.
'We came to rescue you.' Harry sounded fed up. Will sighed.

'It's the thought that counts.' Harry smiled, as did Powell to a lesser extent. The guards cuffed Will and Lucy to one of the large wine racks before leaving and locking the cellar door behind them.

Lucy felt weak and sat down, trying to make herself as comfortable as she possibly could while handcuffed.
'Now you two are here, we can try and escape.' Harry smiled.
'How did you know that we'd be brought here?' asked Will.
'One of the guards suggested that we wouldn't be here on our own for long, we guessed they were bringing you.'
'This is where they bring all trespassers to the mansion until Security arrives,' said Powell, 'it made sense that you'd be brought here if you weren't here already. The handcuffs aren't exactly protocol though, usually they just leave a guard.'
'Perhaps they can't spare anybody to actually guard us?' Powell nodded.
'Probably.'
'So how do we get out?' Lucy had decided that it was her turn to speak, she was uncomfortable but at least the weight had been taken from her legs for now.

The escape plan was very simple due to their circumstances. They were after all locked up with the island's head of Security and in his possession he had a key that would unlock 'almost anything on the island.' Lucy was relieved to hear that upon his capture, Powell had managed to hide the key so that it wouldn't be found when he was searched. Very few people knew about the key and the only person present in the grounds of the mansion that had any knowledge of it was Corzones himself and he was far too busy to remember something so trivial.

The key unlocked the handcuffs with little difficulty and Lucy struggled silently to her feet. She was still weak but didn't want to appear so, she knew that Will would never leave her but was determined not to slow him down. They would only have one chance at an escape and this was it. Conversation revealed that Will, Harry and Powell all entered the same way, through a gap in the fence on the east side of the grounds and if their luck held, the gap wouldn't have been found yet. Lucy wasn't convinced that it would be so easy but she unfortunately had nothing to bring to the table, she was cuffed to the back of a buggy and semi-conscious at best upon her arrival.

They slowly climbed the cellar stairs, struggling to make as little noise as possible on the steps. As they reached the top, Powell held a finger to his lips and they all listened as a muffled pair of footsteps passed the door and continued into the distance.

'The guards here are loyal to Corzones and we can only assume that he is part of Svoros' plan. That means that any authority I once had is gone. We have to warn the outside world what is happening. All communications can be monitored and I imagine that if Svoros' plan is in a latter phase, they'll have been cut off anyway. There's only one thing we can do and that is to get to the emergency station.'

'The what?' asked Harry, slightly too loudly. He was reprimanded by a sharp "shh" from the rest of the group and mouthed an apology.

'It's located in the most remote part of the island, further into the jungle in an area that hasn't been touched at all by any kind of development. It'll be lightly guarded but it contains a line that's isolated from the main communication systems. If we get to that then we can contact the mainland and tell them what's happening here. That's what I'm going to do, who's coming with me?' Will and Harry both nodded instantly, Lucy did the same with some hesitation. She might have been able to escape from the grounds of the mansion but the likelihood of her managing a long walk through the jungle was incredibly slim.

She would focus on the walk through the jungle later though, the important part was to make sure that Will escaped from the grounds and that meant that she had to do the same. Powell unlocked the cellar door with his skeleton key and opened it very slowly, peering through to make sure that nobody was nearby. They weren't so he opened the door fully and ushered the others out before closing the door behind him and locking it again to buy them what may be a precious extra few seconds.

Powell directed them through the long corridors of the mansion towards the side exit. They only had to duck into cover once as two guards walked past. Powell looked through a window and observed that the number of guards in the area had dropped, a large number of buggies had departed too.

'That should make escaping easier, right? Harry's response was a nod from Powell.

They arrived at the east exit of the building and Powell carried out the same routine of caution with the door as he had upon leaving the cellar. They were all out of the building and so far Lucy had yet to notice any real pain, she assumed that it was masked by adrenaline brought about by the escape but knew that it wouldn't last long. Powell instructed them to run towards a building that must have been at least twenty metres away, he checked that no guards were visible before giving the instruction to move. Lucy ran, alongside Will and Harry, as fast as she could. It started to hurt, sneaking around the house had been fine but running really was causing her pain.

Luckily it wasn't long before the run was over and they were joined by Powell who had moved more slowly to keep a lookout. He placed his back to the out building that they had dashed to and beckoned the others to do the same. He gestured to indicate that two guards were nearby and put a finger over his lips. Will, Harry and Lucy all nodded and remained silent. After a few short moments, the guards had passed and Powell pointed towards the gap in the fence that they would be using to exit the grounds and nodded. Harry ran first and within a few seconds was through the gap. Lucy went second and struggled to ignore the pain in her leg, her agony must have been apparent as she was joined a few seconds later by Will who took her hand and ran with her. They made it to the gap and Will waited while Lucy climbed through and then followed.

They were joined outside the fence by Powell a few moments later. 'We have to keep moving,' he said urgently, 'the further away from this place we are when they find that we've escaped, the more likely we'll remain free.' Lucy found herself nodding agreement, along with Harry and Will. She didn't feel as though she'd make it very far at all, particularly not at the speed she would need to move to keep up with them. She had to try though, upon her announcing that she could go no further, there would inevitably be an argument that was sure to slow the entire group down.

Powell directed them on to a path that would lead them to the emergency communication station and it was steep, Lucy found herself struggling even more. She was now in complete agony to the point that she was hardly able to feel her legs but she pushed on

288

further. She didn't know exactly how but she found herself on the floor. She had completely lost any sensation in her right leg apart from the searing pain. Will rushed to her assistance and slowly helped her back on to her feet. She shook her head and pushed his hands away.

'I'm sorry, I can't go any further. It hurts too much.' She sat down on the ground to emphasise her point, Will immediately knelt down next to her while Powell and Harry looked on.

'I'll stay with you,' Will whispered quietly so that the others wouldn't hear, 'don't worry.' Luck shook her head.

'You have to go.' She replied. Will turned to the other two.

'Go, I'm staying with her.'

'No Will, that communication station is more important than I am. The outside world needs to know what's happening here and who is involved.'

Shouting could be heard in the distance along with a ringing alarm.

'They know we've escaped, we have to go now Will.' Powell walked over to Will and took his arm but Will pulled free.

'I'm staying with her.' Lucy gave one last desperate shake of the head but Will completely ignored it.

'I can't stay and argue, come on Harry.' Powell ran up the path and Harry hesitated for a moment before joining him. Will and Lucy were left alone.

'They'll catch us both if you stay.' Will shook his head and helped Lucy to her feet.

'We can hide, come on let's get you off the path.' Will helped Lucy into the jungle and they both hid behind a large clump of bushes.

'They'll go straight past, I hope.' Will didn't look entirely confident but Lucy hoped that he was right.

About ten minutes passed before the sound of a buggy could be heard, Lucy didn't see the vehicle but heard it go right along the road and fade into the distance. She looked at Will who had a look of relief on his face.

'I said we'd be alright,' he whispered, 'I hope Harry and Powell will be too.'

Forty-Three

Father Merco was dead, his blood was still washing its way across the stone table in the centre of the ancient library. It had been a cold-blooded act and something that until seeing it himself, Amerigo hadn't believed his old friend capable. Svoros still held the knife, a beaming smile of wonder and accomplishment plastered across his face and a distant look in his eyes that confirmed to Amerigo that the last vestiges of his sanity had completely departed.

Merco had been the figure under the hood and according to Svoros in one of his many gloats over the previous hour, had been a prisoner for a few days. He seemed to be in good enough condition, no cuts or bruises bar the one created by the tightly tied gag over his mouth.

'We needed somebody and this man was no longer of any use to us. I had one of my people create a little tension between him and the Professor but once he'd run and hidden with you Amerigo, Father Merco was of no further use until now.' Merco's mouth was still covered but his eyes displayed his sheer terror for all to see, he'd been tricked and manipulated by Svoros like so many others. Svoros simply smiled, apparently enjoying the suffering.

'He will serve our purpose.' Svoros' voice was cold but full of excitement, the closer his plan came to being a reality the more like an excited child he seemed to appear. 'The blood of the first person to touch the seal of the prison is required, according to the book of Velza and Father Merco, you have been chosen. You shall be the one that makes the sacrifice needed to end the chaos throughout the world.' To his shame, Amerigo's first thought wasn't for Merco but instead he considered the hypocrisy of Svoros' attempts to change the world. As long as Amerigo had known him, Svoros hadn't left the island even once, to him it was the world. All he knew about what was going on elsewhere in the world was what he had seen in the news. Perhaps it was the island he wanted to change, perhaps he wanted it to be the way that it was before. If so it was with a sickening irony that the person financially backing his insane scheme was the person that had changed everything in the first place. But looking around Amerigo could see that Svoros had gained himself a large number of supporters, his methods of persuasion must have been impressive.

As Svoros spoke, Amerigo noticed the Professor become more uneasy by the minute. He remained silent, no longer trying to persuade Svoros' followers that their leader was wrong. Svoros was ignoring his other prisoners, focusing his attention entirely on his vile taunting of Father Merco, a man who was innocent of anything but attempting to share his beliefs with other people. Naturally Svoros disagreed with those beliefs and used the apparent proof of his own to torment. Amerigo wished that he could somehow block the conversation out but all eyes were on Svoros as his messiah complex flew into overdrive.

After his rants about success, power and dominion over "those who did not understand" were over, Svoros indicated to two of his followers to hold Merco over the stone table.
'Blood. That's what locks Velza away and diminishes his power. In this case, your blood Father Merco. You have the unique historical position of being the man who sacrificed his life so that humanity may be guided in the right direction.' Merco didn't speak a word, no final condemnations of what Svoros was doing nor any attempts to plead for his life.
'Hurry up.' The Professor whispered quietly, just enough so that Amerigo and Kirshner would hear him. Was he attempting to give them some kind of hope, or was it to tell them that help really was on the way. Were his looks of fear simply an act, did he really know that all would be alright? It had been hours since he'd last contacted his fellow Supers, would they interpret the lack of contact as a sign that something wasn't right. The team they'd sent never made it to the island after all. But then again, Svoros knew that and surely even now he didn't think that he was unstoppable?

Svoros slowly cut Merco's throat with a sharp dagger and allowed the blood to pour over the table. It flowed into every pattern and crack. He stepped back and watched with his disturbing smile. The two followers that were holding Merco's body stood motionless, allowing every drop of blood to flow from the wound. Everybody looked on apart from Corzones who had cast his eyes aside at the very moment Svoros' knife had made contact with Merco's flesh. His disgust at what was happening however didn't excuse the fact that he had played a large part in the events and it didn't seem to prompt any real change of heart.

A minute passed, maybe longer and absolutely nothing happened. No sounds, no shakes of the ground, no flashes of light. Svoros' face fell. He had failed, nothing at all had happened after the murder. Kirshner released an audible sigh of relief but the Professor remained still, he obviously knew something that nobody else did but there was more to it than that, a fear. It was logical that Svoros would choose another victim and obvious that Amerigo and the other two prisoners would be on top of the list of potential sacrifices. The Professor wasn't a man to worry about his own life though, not to the point that he would appear as horrified as he did. He'd wrapped his arms around himself and raised his knees, almost hiding behind them.

'It should have worked!' Svoros was furious but also starting to panic. Just a few minutes ago he was convinced that he had unlocked all the secrets he needed to rule the world and now his beliefs were being truly tested. Amerigo thought that perhaps the blood lock needed time to open but that hadn't been the case when the Professor had unlocked the way into the library.
'His blood was the first to spill on to the locking mechanism and we must surely have given enough.' Amerigo then realised that Merco had died under a severe misunderstanding on Svoros' part. His blood hadn't been the first to touch the table, it had been the Professor's when they had first entered the cave. He was still bleeding from opening the first blood lock when he touched the table. That's what had caused the scream that had consumed the island, the tiny bit of the Professor's blood that had touched the table must have weakened the blood lock but not fully shattered it. How much blood was required then? It had only been a few drops on the entrance but if this was the main lock, sealing away whatever entity Velza was, then it must be considerably more powerful. That's why the Professor had folded his arms so closely, he was hiding the fact that one of his hands was bandaged, he knew what Amerigo had just worked out already. He wasn't scared for his life, he was scared of the fact that his death, should his wound be discovered, would be what awakens this all-powerful force.

Svoros paced for a few moments, looking around the room and desperately trying to work out what had gone wrong. He looked around desperately and even inspected Merco's corpse, which by now had been unceremoniously dumped on the ground next to the table.

'Something must have gone wrong, you said you heard the scream.' Corzones seemed uneasy as he spoke, worried that he was perhaps saying the wrong thing. Perhaps even he had been shaken by Svoros' insane behaviour since he had entered the library.

Svoros stood upright and walked towards Corzones at a great speed.

'The scream! Of course Mister Corzones, you're absolutely right.' Svoros directed his attention towards Amerigo, Kirshner and Loch for the first time since they had been on the beach. 'You were here before me, weren't you?' All three remained silent, much to Svoros' irritation. 'Don't attempt to hide it. One of you is going to die but it only needs to be one of you, the one that first dropped their blood on to the table.' Silence again but a brief and subtle glimpse at the Professor told Amerigo that he was moments away from giving in. He would sacrifice himself so that his two fellow captives could live in the sick world that Svoros was planning to control. Amerigo didn't want that, he'd rather never know what the world became and as much time as possible had to be bought before the blood lock could be released. Before the Professor could give any indication that it was his blood that would release whatever Velza was, Amerigo stood.

'It was me.' Just for a very short moment, Amerigo thought that he saw Svoros' face drop. Was there possibly just a hint of regret that he was about to kill somebody he had once called a friend?

'That's very unfortunate Amerigo.' Svoros waved and the two followers that had held Merco grabbed Amerigo and pulled him over to the table. Svoros looked at Amerigo and then turned to the other two prisoners, for the first time he noticed the Professor and the way that he was sitting. A look of suspicion crossed his face.

'Amerigo, old friend.'

'We are not friends Svoros. You are about to kill me.'

'I'm sorry you feel like that. Will you show me the wound please?'

'What?' Svoros knew, he knew that Amerigo was lying and had successfully proved it. Amerigo had no cuts of any kind, not even something that he could attempt to pass off as what had first dropped blood on to the table.

'The wound that you used to break the blood lock. Blood comes from cuts but you don't appear to have any.' Svoros turned to Loch. 'You, show me your hands.' The Professor sat still but his look of fear turned quickly into defiance. Svoros walked over to the Professor and pushed him over on to his side, dragging his hands out from his sides as he did so. The bandage gave Svoros all he needed.

'It's a shame that you lied to me Amerigo. You may not consider me to be a friend any longer but I assure you that I am working to benefit you and millions of others across the world. You may have lied but I'll allow you to live.'

'Allow me to live? Allow? What the hell makes you think you have the right to choose who lives and dies? You say that you're trying to benefit the world but you have the sick psychotic attitude of a dictator who would abuse his power. You've read a few books and interpreted some legends semi-accurately. None of these things gives you the right to order the deaths of anybody. That girl you killed, the people in the explosion at the Security centre, the attempt on Steve, what have they ever done? Steve was just a rep here to enjoy himself like so many others. And Father Merco there, you enjoyed that. Nothing, not one single thing in all reality, justifies what you have done.'

'I haven't taken a single life for any other reason than necessity. That girl could have been anybody but there needed to be a death that would discredit the Professor, he could have ruined everything! As for the Security building, it contained two very dangerous people, your two young friends. The Inspector here was beginning to listen to them. The same can be said for that rep too, he was giving Loch too much assistance and our plans weren't yet ready to go ahead. If you'd have told me about this place as soon as you discovered it then so many people may have lived, including the Professor here. His interference has made it necessary for him to sacrifice his life so his blood may release what has been kept prisoner here unjustly for so long. Nobody in this world is innocent Amerigo, if they were then freeing Velza and using his awesome power for good wouldn't be necessary.'

Amerigo was sitting down in the place he had occupied before and the two followers picked up the Professor, dragging him towards the table.

'You tried,' said Kirshner, 'it was a brave thing to do.'

'I regret that it was not enough and now I am forced to watch a good friend of mine die.'

The Professor was held over the table.

'There are many people who will be glad about your death Professor Loch, many of the people on this island that believe in what I am achieving do so because of the actions of your organisation. You Supernatural Investigators have done more harm than good, you have allowed people to die to protect your pathetic status quo. How many opportunities of power and influence that can better the world have you passed by or even prevented? You represent the worst aspect of humanity, the fear of change.' The Professor defiantly shook his head.

'You don't know what you are attempting to free. The blood lock has sealed away a being that humanity can't even comprehend in a reality that is not our own. It's in a safe place, another dimension and that's where it must remain. Stop what you're doing Svoros or you will be consumed by what you think you can control. It exists on a different plane of reality, it perceives life itself on an entirely different level to us. We will simply be something it crushes underfoot before it wreaks havoc over all existence. Let it remain in its own little universe to be angry and powerful without a purpose, at least there it can do no harm.' Svoros smiled.

'You're wrong Professor. Your pathetic lies have served no purpose but to keep you alive for a few more seconds. I'm afraid that your last card has been played and nothing can save your life now.' Svoros picked up his knife and walked towards the Professor.

Forty-Four

Victor stayed hidden in the crowd for only a few seconds before he gave himself up. One innocent person had already died on his account and he wasn't going to allow anymore. The bearded man smiled as he stepped forward and released the person that he had been holding at gunpoint.

'Very sensible,' he said, 'I don't enjoy killing unless I have to.'

'And are you going to kill me?' Victor sounded as defiant as he possibly could, praying that Sofia would remain hidden. She was still back in the crowd and that was where she had to stay, unseen and out of danger. Should she be discovered, the bearded man may use her as a means of influencing Victor whenever necessary. She was a bargaining chip that must never be discovered.

'Watch him.' The bearded man pointed at another of the mercenaries who trained his gun directly on Victor.

The Mercenaries began discussing what to do next.

'We can't just leave this place now,' said the bearded man, 'We have most of the people on this island here and in our control. Keep Victor with them and keep everybody quiet. Nobody gets hurt unless it's completely necessary, understand?' The mercenaries nodded and the bearded man stepped forward.

'You all behave and you get through this alive!' The crowd remained mostly silent, a few people whimpered or made other sounds of distress. 'Now all of you sit down and remain calm.' Everybody did as they were told and sat on the cold, hard floor. It was messy and sticky due to all of the drinks that had been spilled over it.

DJ Freedom was brought through the doors from which he usually made his impressive entrance and sent to sit with the rest of the crowd. There were no cheers of joy this time, just a cold uncomfortable silence. Victor didn't understand why he was being held in such a way. How had these men arrived on the island and how was his father connected to them? What were they aiming to achieve? He decided to talk to his captors.

'You.' He was ignored by the Mercenaries but a few gasps came from the captive crowd. Clearly a more dramatic gesture was required. Victor stood up and addressed their leader directly.

'Beardy!' The man with the beard turned around and smiled.

'I'd rather you called me Burns.' He smiled as he spoke. 'Not that you have any reason to address me at all, Victor.'

'My father owns this island and furthermore it was on his instructions that you came after me.' There were more shocked gasps from the crowd, nobody had imagined that this was planned by the island's owner.

'That's correct, it's for your own safety, all of you!'

'Holding guns to people's heads and shooting Security staff is for our safety?' Victor could feel himself becoming angrier by the second; angry at the fact a good man had died, angry at the fact that his father had wished him to be held captive by these lunatics.

The conversation was interrupted by a small man with an unlikable feel about him emerging from DJ Freedom's door. He smiled and ignored the fact that at least seven guns were all pointed directly at him.

'The name is Argyll, I own this club. I assume that you were all sent by Svoros?' Burns smiled at Argyll and walked over to him to shake his hand.

'Svoros wants you to remain here with us. We now have control of every club on the strip.' Victor wasn't happy with this news, it meant that across the island there were now thousands of hostages. Argyll spotted Victor.

'He's not supposed to be here, the plan was that he'd be restrained at the café.'

'He escaped, Svoros was present so he knows about it.'

'I'd rather he wasn't here, that's all. Nothing can go wrong, he's supposed to be in protective custody, not a hostage like the rest of them.' This comment prompted more worried sounds from the crowd but they were quickly silenced by a few of the mercenaries.

Victor allowed the conversation to continue slightly further before he decided to remind Burns and Argyll that he was still standing right in front of them.

'So you're part of this sick scheme too, Argyll?'

'Your father and I share the same aims Victor.'

'And do these aims involve blowing up the Security building and murdering innocent people?' Argyll smiled in his usual slimy way.

'Nobody on this island is innocent Victor, you must know that. Admittedly I did relish the opportunity to choose the first victim, the girl Zoë.' Argyll smiled as DJ Freedom jumped to his feet.

'What the hell!' His outburst only gave Argyll another excuse to grin as a mercenary forced the DJ to sit down. Victor knew that Freedom himself had been accused of that murder and that Zoë had been close to him. Argyll had been playing his own sick game alongside whatever it was that his father and Svoros were involved in. At least his father didn't want him dead, Argyll said that he should be under "protective custody" at the café, perhaps by running he had placed himself in more danger than if he hadn't.

Victor noticed Argyll inspecting the crowd and a horrible thought suddenly came over him, Argyll had spoken to him the previous night when he had been with Sofia, would he recognise her? Even now they could still find a way to use her as a means of ensuring his cooperation. Victor was still standing and facing his captors. 'There aren't to be any more attacks. These people are innocent, no matter what you think Argyll.' The club's owner simply smiled. 'These people will be fine if they behave themselves. The world is changing tonight and this island is the centre of that change.' Argyll gave his oily smile yet again before turning to Burns. 'If you want to ensure that young Victor behaves himself, I'd pay particular attention to that girl, there.' Victor turned, he already knew that Argyll would be pointing at Sofia. She looked horrified and after everything she'd already been through he could understand why. The advertising for Corzones Island promised 'the holiday of your dreams', Sofia's experience had been far from that. There was another thing that worried Victor though, not only could she be used as leverage against him but the fact that she was friends with Lucy. It was just possible that Will, Lucy, the Professor and all of the other people Sofia had told him about were still loose somewhere on the island and there was a chance that they were the only people capable of stopping whatever was going on.

Victor knew that his father was involved with these people but the guns, the deaths and the sheer terror brought about by what was happening made him hope that it would fail. It was possible that he'd never know why his father had contributed towards all of this but the way the mercenaries were speaking told him that Svoros was the true mastermind behind it all. There was no denying that Giorgio Corzones was up to his neck in what was happening and Victor couldn't bring himself to believe that it was for a good cause. He'd always had a good relationship with his father, better

298

than most had assumed but everything that was happening on the island proved that there was a dark side.

One of the mercenaries grabbed Sofia and threw her down next to Victor, he immediately knelt down and asked if she was ok. She looked scared but nodded, even attempting a smile.
'Stay sat down please Victor, we don't mean for anybody to suffer.'
Victor sat down properly and directed an angry stare at Burns. This was insane, all of it and Victor knew that for better or worse, it was bound to end soon.

Time passed and an eerie silence was maintained throughout the room. Sofia seemed to become more worried, she hadn't heard from Lucy since the explosion and the knowledge that she'd been in the Security building at the time hadn't helped in the slightest, Victor should never have told her. They began to whisper to each other but before the conversation could progress into any detail a terrible noise began to sound. It was the scream again, just as it had been when Victor had first arrived on the island but far worse this time though and considerably louder. The entire room began to shake, Victor heard people start to scream as everybody started to panic. The mercenaries all remained calm.
'It's starting!' Burns' hard exterior seemed to have vanished and was replaced with a demeanour of pure wonder. Whatever was happening, it was obviously what Burns, Svoros and his father had intended. They had won.

Forty-Five

Will had spent most of the last two days as a prisoner of some description and was getting bored of the routine. He and Lucy had remained hidden for long into the night and no more buggies had gone past but they hadn't heard a word from Harry and Powell either. Perhaps they'd been captured again or even shot but there wasn't any sign of rescue arriving at all. It could all be over already and Will had no way of knowing. Maybe Svoros had won, the Professor and Amerigo could be dead and nobody on the island would know what was happening.

They'd talked about their experiences of being plugged into what they decided to refer to as 'The dream machine' and it had been the same. Over a few short hours they'd managed to build themselves a full life together. They'd both managed to gain work in their ideal jobs, live together and even get engaged. It had been perfect but they hadn't actually talked about the consequences of what they'd witnessed. Maybe in a few years' time it would be reality but for now a dream was all it could ever be.

It had passed eleven when Will decided that it was time for them to try to move. Lucy's leg wasn't in as much pain as it had been and she agreed that she would now be able to move, even if it was only a short distance. Will's priority was to get them as far away from the path as possible and into the lush undergrowth of the jungle. Lucy attempted to walk up the hill, in the same direction that Harry and Powell had gone but Will knew that they wouldn't really make any progress. She was just trying not to slow him down. It was true that he wouldn't leave her but the point of him staying behind was to ensure that she'd be alright, not encourage her to suffer in an attempt to catch up with the others.

Lucy had however, insisted that they continued, just in case Harry and Powell had failed. Perhaps she was right to do so, it was a possibility that the last hope for mankind rested with the two of them. Will hoped not, if his brother and a former soldier had failed then he and Lucy wouldn't stand any kind of chance. Walking in the right direction gave them both a feeling of purpose however, so that's what they decided to do.

They'd covered a fair distance and Lucy said she wasn't in any real pain but Will knew that she was suffering, just as she had all along. He wouldn't make her stop until she said so though and he suspected that she knew the same. They had to push on, had to try and make some kind of a difference. By all accounts something disastrous was about to happen and Will knew that he and Lucy couldn't just stay in one place while that was happening.

Their walk towards the emergency communication outpost was interrupted by the sound of a buggy heading their way. He grabbed hold of Lucy's hand and together they ran into the undergrowth again but they were just a fraction of a second too late. The buggy came to a halt on the road nearby. Two grizzly-looking characters climbed out.
'Just here,' said the first, 'I'm sure that I saw somebody.'
'It might be those people what escaped from the house,' the second had a deeper and more commanding voice, despite his less-than stellar grip on the English language, 'let's get them and take them to Svoros.'

Will and Lucy were close to the road but well covered and the two men had started to look a fair distance away from them, they must only have had a fleeting glimpse before stopping.
'They'll find us.' Lucy was right, they had a couple of minutes at most before they were discovered.
'Can you run Lucy?'
'Not very far, the more that I move, the worse it gets.'
'I only need you to run as far as that buggy.' Lucy smiled and nodded which gave Will the slightest glimmer of hope. If they could get to the buggy then they had a chance of getting away. It was just possible that Powell and Harry were still free and if so the distraction would probably help them.

'Alright,' said Will, 'when I say now we both run as quickly and quietly as we can. I think they've left the engine running so we just jump on and go.' Lucy nodded and Will looked around, trying to work out the opportune moment to run. He spotted it the second it arrived, both men were looking away. Will gave Lucy the thumbs-up, took her hand and together they ran straight for the buggy. They jumped on, Will was straight into the driver's seat and before the two men knew what was going on, the buggy was accelerating away.

'Hey!' It was the larger of the two men who shouted. A moment later Will heard gunshots and pressed his foot down even harder on the accelerator.

'They missed, thank goodness.'
'They weren't shooting at us Will, they fired into the air. I think they were alerting others.' Will hadn't looked back to see this but Lucy must have been right. It wouldn't be long before they were discovered, the buggies weren't exactly quiet and there must be a considerable manhunt out for them, they could expose Giorgio Corzones as a conspirator after all.

As they drove on another worrying thought surfaced in Will's mind.
'Those two weren't in Security uniforms.'
'I noticed,' said a worried Lucy, 'I think perhaps they were part of a private army?'
'Corzones can afford one.' The drive was fast and uncomfortable, Will found himself having to concentrate incredibly hard as there was no light apart from the ones on the front of the buggy and they weren't particularly strong. Anybody on the lookout would probably hear them before seeing them.

Only a few minutes passed before Lucy shouted.
'Behind us Will!' An incredibly brief glance behind showed Will that there were two buggies following them, they'd just pulled on to the road at a nearby intersection that Will hadn't even noticed as he'd passed.
'Hold on.' Lucy wrapped her arms around his waist as he pressed the accelerator down as far as it would go. He had no idea how fast he must have been travelling but his speed had become incredibly dangerous.
'Keep going Will, they don't seem to be catching up.' That was all very well but they had no idea when the road would end and what would be waiting for them there. The private army or whatever they were must have been in communication so would know exactly where he and Lucy were now.

The sound of gunshots could be heard again but a whooshing sound past Will's right ear told him that they were no longer into the air. He hoped that had been a warning shot and not a genuine attempt to hit him.

302

'We can't keep going for much longer, they'll hit us eventually.'
'We have to try!' Lucy kissed Will's cheek, giving him a temporary burst of confidence. It was short-lived however, as a line of bright lights became visible further up the road.
'Road block!' Will didn't want to take his foot of the pedal however. 'I'm going to try and ram them. Hold on as tight as you can!' Lucy's arms gripped his waist tighter than before. Will hoped that he was doing the right thing and that neither of them would come out of it too injured.

Lucy screamed as the sound of gunshots rang out again, this time from in front of them. There was a popping sound and Will suddenly found that all control of the buggy had suddenly faded. They'd hit one of the tyres. Will had no choice but to slam his foot down on to the brakes. The buggy skidded into the trees and then came to a sudden halt. He considered running for a brief moment but before he could even dismount from the buggy they were surrounded by men with guns.
'Don't move!' The one who shouted stepped forward. 'There are supposed to be four of you, where are the others?' Will smiled, Powell and Harry must still have been at large. There was still hope and perhaps the antics with the buggy had given them the time that they needed.
'I don't know,' replied Will, 'We separated hours ago. I think they were heading for the town centre.' Hopefully his lie would buy them even more time. He felt Lucy's arms, which were still around his waist, tighten to show him that she approved of his misdirection.
'Dammit,' said the leader, 'Take them to Svoros.'

Forty-Six

Kirshner had watched as Merco was murdered and Amerigo attempted to give his life to buy more time but the gesture had only worked for a few seconds. Svoros now knew that to unleash his deity, Professor Loch had to die. There wasn't anything that could be done now it seemed, Svoros and Corzones had won and no more time could be bought and even if it was, there was no sign of any help coming. He had thought that perhaps some assistance would come from the mainland after he'd failed to report in, or maybe even his wife would have raised some kind of alarm due to his lack of contact but the truth was that she was probably fast asleep after enjoying another day alone with her book next to the pool.

He'd have given everything to be back at his hotel now, no murder or conspiracy to look into and no psychotic demon worshippers to contend with. The truth of it all was though that his presence on Corzones Island had done nothing but help Svoros. Kirshner had been the one to first fall for the trick of suspecting the Professor and had spent most of his time since then on a wild-goose-chase, hindering the one man that could have really put an end to the madness.

That man was now being held over the large round table in the centre of the ancient library. Svoros was standing over him holding his knife. Like the table it was still covered in Merco's blood. Kirshner didn't imagine that hygiene was high on the priority list of a psychopath. The Inspector thought that he had seen insanity before but the truth was that throughout his entire career, he'd never met anybody who was as deranged as Svoros. He maintained that everything he was doing was for the greater good and would benefit humanity but that had been the defence of so many dictators, despots and degenerates before him.

Kirshner contemplated some kind of grand gesture but all of the speeches had been made and any attempt to run at Svoros would result in him being cut down by a hail of bullets. He held on to the thought that while there was life, there was at least some kind of hope regardless of how vague it was.

Svoros was making his speech yet again, it was almost word-for-word the same as what he had been preaching already for the last few hours, he was certainly making the most out of his "night of deliverance". The longer he continued with his ranting meant that any potential rescue was closer though. There could perhaps still be some hope. Kirshner smiled as he saw the Professor rolling his eyes, perhaps he was so bored of the speeches by this point that death actually seemed to be a desirable option.

Svoros' speech was interrupted when a group of mercenaries entered the room along with two other people. Kirshner adjusted his position so he could see who was with them, it was Will and Lucy.
'We caught these two.' It was one of the mercenaries who spoke but Kirshner couldn't quite tell which one, it didn't matter though. Options were quickly running out but Will and Lucy had proved themselves to be resourceful. The last Kirshner had heard, Lucy had been kidnapped and Will had vanished, presumably to go and look for her. That update had come from Powell who he'd heard nothing of since, perhaps the Security Chief was still at large and if so then he was the best hope that they had.

'Why did you bring them here?' Svoros seemed annoyed that he had been interrupted but this quickly changed into a smile.
'They've already escaped from the mansion, they're trouble. What do you want us to do with them?' Corzones stepped forward.
'The lovebirds, they proved to be quite the match for Doctor Sorn's experiments. We tried to gain information from their dreams and all we got was their repressed feelings for each other.' Will and Lucy both blushed. 'Let them witness our victory here and then hand them back to the good Doctor. She's already expressed her wishes to use them again.' Svoros smiled and nodded in agreement.
'Put them with the others,' he said, 'but we can't waste any more time. Velza shall now be freed.'

Will and Lucy were thrown down next to Kirshner and Amerigo. Lucy let out a gasp of pain as she hit the floor. She must have still been suffering from her injuries sustained during the explosion.
'Is this it?' Will looked over to Loch.
'I'm afraid so,' said Amerigo, 'I tried to buy more time but it's the Professor that they need to kill to unleash their...' Amerigo struggled for a word for a moment, 'demon.'

'Another murder, they're sick.' Lucy almost spat the words with disgust. It was too late for disgust now however, or hope. Svoros had positioned himself next to the Professor yet again, holding on to his knife ready to strike.

Then there was a gunshot. One of the mercenaries fell to the floor clutching a wound in his leg. Kirshner looked around along with everybody else in an attempt to see where the shot had been fired from. More shots came and a frenzy ensued. The mercenaries threw themselves about, desperate to find any cover that they possibly could. Kirshner grabbed Will and Lucy and pushed them to the floor.
'Stay down!'

From floor level his vision was even more restricted but he looked over to the entrance of the circular room and saw that people wearing combat uniforms were dashing in. Kirshner also saw that Svoros had dropped his knife and jumped into cover next to the two men that had been holding the Professor. Loch himself however, was nowhere to be seen. Kirshner assumed this to be a good thing, the Professor needed to get as far away as possible if he was the key to Velza's prison.

The gunfight was short and it was Corzones who ordered the ceasefire. Kirshner heard Svoros' voice emanate from his cover, it ordered the men to continue fighting but they stopped regardless. It appeared that their true loyalty wasn't to the man claiming to be a Christ-figure after all but to the man that would inevitably be paying them. The mercenaries dropped their weapons and raised their hands while the soldiers quickly ran around and secured the area properly, gathering the discarded guns as they went. Corzones was quickly pushed into a corner and a gun aimed squarely at his head. Svoros was pulled out of cover and also closely guarded. His face contained a bitter look of hatred. There was some disappointment in there as the reality of his defeat began to register. Kirshner nodded to Amerigo, Will and Lucy, signalling for them to stand.

When he stood, Kirshner saw that Professor Loch had taken cover at the opposite side of the round table. He also stood up and smiled. Only one of their rescuers appeared to be a woman and she stepped forward.

'Professor, you're alright. When the team we sent didn't make contact we assumed that something was wrong.' The Professor stepped forward and smiled, he shook the hand of the woman that had spoken to him.
'Keryn, thank goodness you made it.'
'We picked up an SOS from the island, it came from the emergency station.'
'Powell and Harry,' Will whispered and Lucy nodded in agreement, 'They made it.' Will exhaled as if a weight had been lifted from his mind.

The Professor and Keryn talked for a moment, it was clear that she too was a Supernatural Investigator. Loch explained in detail what had happened over the previous week. Kirshner couldn't help but notice Svoros scowling in the corner, his looks of delusion had been replaced by bitterness and hatred. Keryn stepped away from the Professor and back to her soldiers, she began to give orders for moving out.

The Professor sighed and turned to his friends.
'Are you all ok?' There was a collective nod from all but Will who pointed out Lucy's leg.
'I'll recover.' She calmly said.
'Amerigo, you nearly sacrificed yourself just to buy me some more time. I don't know what to say.' Amerigo smiled and grabbed the Professor, holding him in a tight hug. Eventually the hug ended and the Professor stepped back and began to catch his breath. There was a collective smile and a sense of relief. It was all finally over and Svoros had been stopped before he could do any significant damage. Keryn joined their group and spoke to Loch.
'There are mercenaries all over the island but we have more teams arriving. Corzones has agreed to broadcast a message for them to surrender just as soon as the teams are in place.'
'Excellent,' the Professor turned to Kirshner. 'Am I safe to assume that all charges against Amerigo and I have been dropped?' He gave a cheeky smile that Kirshner responded to in kind.
'Yes,' he said, 'you have nothing to worry about now Professor.'

After a few more minutes of relieved chat, the Professor walked over to Svoros.
'I'm sorry it couldn't end in the way that you wished it to,' he said, 'your intentions may have had elements of good but the truth is

Svoros that what is held prisoner here must remain a captive. That table operates as a portal to another level of existence, we have no real way of knowing what is there. What I can find out however, is how such a thing found its way to ancient Atlantis.' Svoros eyed the Professor silently for a moment. He then suddenly lurched forward and out of nowhere produced his knife. The Professor attempted to jump out of the way but the blade reached his arm and Svoros managed to deeply cut down it.

'Professor!' Keryn drew her gun but there was no chance of a clear shot until Svoros had pushed the Professor on to the table. Keryn opened fire on Svoros who fell to the ground, dead.

Attention turned to the Professor who pulled himself away from the table, clearly in a great deal of pain. A deep rumbling came from the centre of the stone and Loch looked at his arm. A great deal of his blood had flowed onto the table.

'Professor!' Will ran forward, closely followed by Lucy and Amerigo. Kirshner looked to Keryn who had a dark look across her face.

'Everybody train your gun on that table.' The soldiers all did as instructed.

The table began to glow a murky pink colour and the light slowly increased and decreased in a pulsing effect. The Professor stepped back and clutched his injured arm.

'It's only partially opening.' He wasn't really speaking to anybody in particular, just verbally noting it himself. Kirshner didn't know what this meant, could it somehow be stopped?

Everybody in the room clutched their ears as the furious scream emanated from somewhere in the light. A swirling effect came across the table and the light grew even brighter, changing from the faint pink to a dark and sinister crimson. The scream came to an end and was replaced by a deep unnatural rumble. The room began to shake.

'Is there any way to stop it, Professor?' It was Will who asked the question, shouting over the noise. Loch turned to him with grim look on his face and nodded.

'Goodbye Will. Get out of here.' Will shook his head, not understanding.

'What do you mean? We can't leave you here! You can't stop whatever that thing is on your own!'

'That's exactly what I'm going to do.' Keryn stepped forward.
'What do you intend to do?'
'This portal is two-way and can be sealed again with another blood lock. For it to close now my blood must be on the other side as well as this.'

The Professor pulled a test tube from one of his pockets.
'Always a useful thing to keep on you.' He smiled but it was thin and insincere. He held the tube to the wound on his arm and squeezed out blood, wincing with pain as he did so.
'You're going through there? You don't know what's on the other side!' Amerigo's eyes were wide and pleading but Kirshner knew that nobody could or would really stop the Professor.
'That portal is only partially open, it didn't get all that much blood from me but its wide enough for whatever is on the other side to force its way through. I can't allow that to happen. The only option is that it is resealed from the other side and I have to be the one that does it.' The Professor passed the test tube, now full with his blood, to Keryn. 'Once I'm through you empty that on to the base of the table, when the blood touches the stone it will be over.' He raised his voice as he finished speaking so that he could be heard over the ever-increasing sound of rumbling.

Will and Lucy were both crying and Amerigo looked as if he was also close to tears. There wasn't anything else that could be done, Kirshner knew that and so did Keryn. The other soldiers and captured mercenaries looked on. Giorgio Corzones watched from where he was being held, he appeared defeated in every way. The Professor whispered something to Keryn, Kirshner had no idea what it was but just for a brief moment she almost smiled.
'Thank you, all of you. I couldn't have stopped this on my own. Goodbye.' The Professor took a deep breath and ran at the table. He jumped on it and seemed to dissolve instantly.

'Everybody out, now!' Keryn gave the order as the room began to shake more violently. Her order was followed by all as they rushed for the exit. Will helped Lucy towards the passageway. Kirshner was one of the last few people in the room, he watched as Keryn poured the tube of blood on to the base of the table, just as the Professor had instructed.
'No!' The shout had come from Corzones who pushed away his guard and ran at Keryn. He was too late, the blood had touched the

309

table and the portal instantly began to fade. Keryn pushed the tycoon aside. The room began to shake even more violently.

'I said out!' Keryn ran for the exit, avoiding a lump of falling rock. 'The whole place is coming down!' Kirshner ran, along with the last couple of soldiers. He looked behind to see Corzones refuse Keryn's hand.

'Have it your own way!' She left him there and ran after the others. As she made it out, an exceptionally large rock fell and covered the exit.

They ran down the corridor, the earthquake was still exceptionally strong and more rocks were falling. Somehow everybody managed to make it out on to the beach safely and threw themselves to the ground as the rumbling continued, it must have affected the whole island.

Eventually it subsided and Kirshner had a chance to look up. The beach was swarming with soldiers, all wearing the same uniforms as Keryn and the men that had rescued them.

'Alright, it's time to take this island back. Tell the Mercenaries that they won't be paid, their employer is buried under tonnes of rock.'

Kirshner sat down on the sand, it really was finally over. The Professor, a man who he had hardly met, had sacrificed himself so that everybody else on the island had a chance of surviving. Less than a day before a lot of those people were hunting for him and assumed that he was a murderer. The real tragedy was that Kirshner knew already that there would be some kind of cover up. Professor Loch would be an unrecognised hero. He lay back and exhaled, hoping that his next case would be considerably simpler.

Forty-Seven

Will, Lucy and Amerigo were alone in the Temple Bar, the sun was shining and for the three of them it was the first time that their lives had been normal for almost a week. Despite all of this the mood was gloomy. Professor Loch was gone, it was a fact that hadn't properly sunk in for Amerigo until the day after the event. He'd stayed in one of the remaining hotel blocks. All rooms were let out on an emergency basis once the building had been deemed secure. The earthquake had been strong and many structures across the island had collapsed.

The Temple Bar had survived mostly undamaged, it had the advantage of having very little structure to bring down in the first place. A leg on one of the marquees had been bent but it was easily repaired and that was just as well as many people on the island ventured up to have a look. Word had quickly spread that Amerigo had somehow been involved with what had happened and people were flocking up the hill just to hear his story.

The island was slowly being evacuated, ferries were moving in and out on a constant loop and most people were leaving as quickly as they could. The number of deaths had been considerably fewer than Amerigo had expected but most people across the island had seen something unpleasant. They wanted to escape from it as quickly as possible and understandably so. The island was now safe, the mercenaries had all been placed under arrest and Svoros' co-conspirators had been arrested. A search of Café Solar had yielded extensive information about who had been involved and what their roles had been. None of the names on the list surprised Amerigo in the slightest but then after the week that he'd had, Amerigo didn't expect to be surprised ever again. The world was a much bigger and more mysterious place than he'd ever begun to imagine.

He'd been back at his bar for two days and most people had heard the stories Amerigo had to tell, as always he'd adjusted the truth. What had happened should not be another dark tale about a cursed island, the Professor would still be the hero of the tale though. History may not recognise his sacrifice but legend certainly would.

Will and Lucy didn't journey to the bar on the first day, they were busy making sure that their friends were alright and spent some time together. Amerigo didn't really know what it was that had happened to them at Corzones mansion but his instinct told him that it was something they had to come to terms with together.

When they did visit the bar, Amerigo made them the best cocktails he'd ever put together. A majestic blend of juices to create the perfect flavour and they enjoyed it greatly, toasting Professor Loch as they drank. Once the drinks were gone however, things became quiet and they each silently reflected on the events of the previous few days.

Lucy's leg was still causing her pain but a proper medical examination had resulted in her being told that as long as she took it easy there wouldn't be any lasting damage. Amerigo admired just how much she'd run despite the injury.

As the late hours of the afternoon progressed the lights around the bar began to flicker into life, some of the bulbs were out but at least electricity had returned to the island. It had been out ever since the earthquake and torches had been the main source of light. Things were starting to improve. The plan was to rebuild the island yet again and have it ready for the following summer. All ideas Amerigo had of leaving had evaporated, after seeing how damaged everything was he felt an overwhelming sense of loss and came to the realisation that it was because the island was his home, no matter how it looked or who was there. It was a place he wanted to stay and enjoy, just as so many others had done and hopefully would do again in the future.

'They'll never get back into that library, it was buried too deep and will have been completely destroyed anyway. That portal or whatever it was is lost for good.' Will had already checked the viability of an archaeological dig on the island but it was simply impossible.

They were joined in the bar by Harry as the afternoon progressed and another round of drinks started to lighten the mood.
'Jason and Royce got on to the ferry but I was told I could stay until you guys left,' he looked at Will who was sitting on a barstool next to Lucy, holding her hand. 'That's if you don't mind me being

around for a bit longer?' Will stated that of course he didn't mind and that he owed a great deal to his brother. Harry then began to tell the story of what had happened when he and Powell had made it to the emergency communication outpost.

'Powell and I got there pretty quickly but found that it was heavily guarded by those mercenaries, we couldn't find a way to get past them at all, it was only a small building with one door and there was already somebody right next to it. Powell insisted that me causing a distraction wouldn't work so all we could do was sit and wait for the opportunity. It came eventually when all of the men but one jumped on to buggies and sped off down the hill to you two,' he nodded at Will and Lucy, 'after that we easily managed to overcome the guy who was left and get inside. We managed to get in touch with Keryn who was waiting offshore with the soldiers. After that we took cover and waited for them to turn up.'

The outpost had been one of the last places that Keryn and her soldiers had arrived at and the mercenaries who had returned there after capturing Will and Lucy had already received the message that it was over. They surrendered instantly.

'It was light by then,' continued Harry, 'and we'd not broken cover at all, not even when the earthquake happened. Powell said that it was only a matter of waiting and he was right.'

The afternoon progressed and evolved into early evening. The sun began to set but Amerigo had replaced the majority of the damaged bulbs. More people began to enter the bar and order drinks, it was the only place open on the whole island but Amerigo felt that it had to stay that way, every drink he made and every smile he saw was for the Professor. Will, Lucy and Harry were mid-conversation when they suddenly fell silent. Amerigo looked to the entrance and saw why: Steve was standing there with a smile on his face. He walked slowly and the entire left side of his body was covered in bandages but he seemed upbeat. He'd just received the all-clear and was allowed to leave the medical centre.

'Luckily the Mercenaries never touched it so they took care of everybody who was injured still, including the guy that stabbed me.'

Steve explained the full story of what had happened, how Karl and Sarah had left him for dead and that the next thing he knew he was in hospital during an earthquake. Amerigo and the Professor had

313

found out about his stabbing just in time, if he'd even been a few minutes later arriving at the medical centre then chances were that he wouldn't have made it. He thanked Amerigo for saving his life and asked where the Professor was. After being brought up to date, Steve's upbeat attitude disappeared. He decided that he would accept just one cocktail, despite his doctor's orders not to drink. Another toast was made to the memory of Professor Loch and the cocktails were downed.

The bar continued to get busier, to the point that Amerigo was surprised by how many people were still on the island. The next round of drinks were made when Powell arrived. He'd just finished making his final reports with Kirshner, who had promptly left the island to return to his wife and his holiday. Powell and Harry spoke happily to each other, having become good friends throughout the night that they had remained in hiding. Powell had agreed to remain on the island in his current job. Victor Corzones, who had taken over the running of the place, had apparently been very complimentary about his handling of the situation and of the fact that he was ultimately the one who summoned help and ended the crisis.

Amerigo was disappointed to learn that his CD player had been damaged and that unfortunately he wasn't able to play anything in the background of what was proving to be a pleasant evening. It wasn't long however before somebody produced a guitar. He'd arrived on the island to write some music and had found considerably more inspiration than he had ever imagined. Music started to play and before very long people began to join in. Amerigo remembered that he had an old ukulele hidden away somewhere. He went to look through the bar's small storage hut, located a short walk away. He found the dusty old instrument and in the isolation of the jungle, tuned it up. He returned to the bar to find that it was now even busier and the few people singing along had turned into a full chorus. People were happy. Happy to be there and to be alive. Amerigo joined in with his ukulele, not knowing completely how to play every song but it didn't matter, he played the best he could and it sounded alright. He smiled, this was far removed from the usual thumping music emanating from the clubs, this was how things used to be before the island had been developed and it was fun.

Half an hour and a few text messages later, more people arrived at the bar. They were equipped with a great range of instruments and before anybody really knew what had happened, there was a band of about fifteen people, all joining in and playing along. Nearly everybody without an instrument sang. By now the sun had completely faded and the day was coming to an end. Perhaps the island would return to normality.

Lucy stopped singing and dashed over to her friend Sofia upon her arrival, apparently forgetting about the injured leg. They hugged and both apologised to each other for an argument that had apparently taken place a few days previously. Amerigo couldn't help notice the fact that the person accompanying Sofia was none other than Victor himself. He seemed as happy as somebody who had just lost their father possibly could do. Lucy and Sofia walked off together, talking about their experiences over the previous few days and Victor was left at the bar on his own.

The silence was slightly awkward so Amerigo decided to break it. 'How are you, sir?' Victor looked up at Amerigo and smiled. 'Please, don't call me sir. My father may have liked all of that but I can assure you that I am just Victor.'
'Well, "just" Victor, how are you?' Victor nodded.
'I'm coping. I still don't fully understand what went on, even though that woman Keryn told me what happened. She tried to sugar-coat it but my father was responsible for a lot, wasn't he?' Amerigo hesitated, he didn't want to tell the truth but his instinct told him that he should do. He didn't know Victor very well but had always known that he wasn't anything like his father.
'The man truly responsible for everything that happened, as I'm sure you know, was Svoros Delgado. He was a manipulative and insane man who had the enviable ability to bring almost anybody around to his way of thinking and unfortunately that was something that happened with your father.' Victor nodded. 'I suspect that once he became involved and with everything that Svoros promised him, your father didn't really have much of a choice. He backed what Svoros was planning financially, as well as his own experiments.' Victor nodded again, unhappily.
'My father always had a thing about ruling and this island was his crowning achievement. Upon buying it, he started to see himself as king of his own little empire and in the end its walls literally came crashing down around him. I shall miss him but endeavour never to

315

be like him.' Amerigo had poured two shots; one for Victor and one for himself. He pushed Victor's towards him and they chinked glasses before seeing the shots away.

Victor wasn't like his father at all, his father would never have shared a drink with the owner of a bar, nor would he have sat and spoke in the candid way that Victor did. He told Amerigo what had happened in the Isle Club. The building had started to collapse almost as soon as the earthquake had started and upon realising that their lives were in danger, the mercenaries lost all interest in keeping their prisoners and ran as fast as they could. Victor had grabbed Sofia's hand and they ran out together. Once out on the strip, Burns had attempted to regain control but too many people, including his own men, had gone. It hadn't been long after that soldiers began to swarm the strip. Burns was one of the last to surrender but nobody really put up a fight and after the building collapsing, there had been no further deaths.

A tear seemed to form in Victor's eye. He felt responsible for everything that happened but Amerigo reminded him that it wasn't in any way his fault. He had no way of knowing that Svoros and his father were even planning anything until it was far too late. 'You know Amerigo, the one thing that makes me feel at all for my father's loss is the fact that he wanted to protect me. I was to be locked in Svoros' cellar until it had all blown over. I suppose that no matter what he became involved in, how many deaths he had on his conscience or how many people he had betrayed, he still cared about me.' Amerigo agreed, it was well known amongst the islanders that Giorgio Corzones had always cared greatly about his son. 'I think he created this place for me. He had no interest in clubs and what went on here but he thought that it would make me happy,' Victor glanced over to Sofia, 'and perhaps it may turn out to in the end. I'll keep this place alive Amerigo, as long as there are people like you to help me.' Amerigo nodded.
'Don't worry Victor, I shall be going nowhere.'

Sofia rejoined Victor, kissing him as she returned to the bar.
'Are you alright?' Victor nodded in response. Will also returned, along with Lucy.
'Are you not playing anymore, Amerigo?' The barman smiled and shook his head.

'I have no idea where my ukulele went,' he looked over at the multitudes of people who were still playing music and singing along, 'but somebody there is enjoying it and that's good enough for me.'

A few minutes later, the last person Amerigo expected to see in a bar walked in. Keryn was still dressed in her uniform, even though Amerigo knew full-well that she wasn't a real soldier. She walked straight to the bar and looked at Will.
'We need to talk,' she said before turning to Amerigo. 'But first I need a drink.' Amerigo smiled and began to make her a cocktail. Once it was ready he handed it to her. 'Is there somewhere quiet we can all talk?' Amerigo nodded and walked with her, Will and Lucy towards the storage hut.

The music and singing were slightly quieter from a distance but they all found that they had to speak loudly to be heard over it.
'I need to be quick, it can't be discovered I'm a Super but I need you three to help me.' Amerigo, Will and Lucy all nodded simultaneously.
'What is it?' Will asked.
'The Professor isn't dead, simply a prisoner in the same place as Velza. We can get him back.' Amerigo felt his face light up and watched as Will and Lucy produced the same expression. 'Before he jumped into that portal, Professor Loch whispered to me that it would be possible to get him out while keeping Velza a prisoner. All we have to do is find out how.'
'Can't you get some of your Super friends on it?' Lucy's question seemed perfectly valid to Amerigo, why was Keryn sharing this with them?
'No,' Keryn shook her head, 'the other Supers would consider it too risky.'
'Then why do you deem it to be alright?' Keryn looked at Amerigo and sighed before she responded.
'The Professor taught me everything, he got me into this job and trained me. I've never seen him get anything wrong and I trust him completely. If he says that rescuing him is possible then I intend to do it, even if I don't have permission.' Keryn turned to Will.
'You're the archaeologist,' she said, 'you will have to be in charge. I can give you almost unlimited funds, equipment and any information that is gathered. Between us we can bring Julius Loch back, what do you say?'

Will hesitated and looked to Lucy for her thoughts. She smiled. 'Unlimited funds and equipment, that's your dream Will, that's everything you've wanted for your work. And at the end of it all you can save the Professor, I know you can do it.' Will smiled and nodded in agreement.

'Alright Keryn, but I have no idea where to start.'

'Just wait, I'll have the information you need very soon. There are many mysteries that need solving before we can find out exactly what to do. It won't be on this island though, that portal was completely destroyed but there will be others and they won't be blood locked, there will be a way of bringing him back.'

Keryn said her goodbyes, insisting that she had to return to her soldiers, they had a lot of work ahead of them but she promised that she would be in contact soon. Will and Lucy seemed happier and Amerigo had to admit that he did too. He'd assumed that the Professor was lost for good but even if there was the tiniest chance of saving him then it had to be explored. He promised Will that he would be there when it was time to bring the Professor back. The knowledge that he was only a prisoner as opposed to dead was a great relief. They all promised to keep it amongst themselves, after all it was just possible that some of Svoros' supporters had escaped. Before Keryn left she warned as much, she informed them that Doctor Sorn had vanished completely. They'd found her laboratory, complete with machinery that couldn't be identified immediately but the Doctor herself was nowhere to be seen.

The night had run its course and as the sun started to rise, Amerigo found that his bar was still as full as it had been in the middle of the night. The songs continued and the atmosphere was one of celebration. The day that was beginning would be the last that anybody apart from residents would be on the island, the final ferries were to depart and they would take Will, Lucy, Steve, Sofia, the man who arrived to write music, the girl who was now playing the ukulele and all others with them.

Victor Corzones was to stay on the island for a few more days, he wanted his father's funeral to take place there and had arrangements for a memorial to make. Will and Lucy had promised to meet up with each other as soon as possible once they were home, Amerigo even thought he'd seen Will use his phone to book

318

a train ticket to Manchester. Victor had invited Sofia to join him at his mansion in Cambridgeshire, he even offered to pay for her plane ticket from Barcelona. Steve spoke to Amerigo and assured him that despite his experience, he would be back the following year working as a rep yet again. Powell and Harry continued to speak and drink throughout the night and by the end of it, Harry had been offered a job on the island. He would have his summer-long holiday paid for if he were to keep an eye on things when there weren't any Security Officers around. Harry didn't seem to object to the offer.

It was about nine in the morning when the last few people left. The sun was high in the sky and emitting a great deal of heat. It didn't bother Amerigo, after so long on the island he was used to the warmth. His bar was the messiest it had ever been after a night. Bottles of beer and wine were scattered all over but he didn't mind picking them up. This was the first day of a different Corzones Island, one that wasn't plagued by old legends or bizarre cultists. This new version of the island would exist purely for people to enjoy themselves. Amerigo ripped open the first bin bag of many and began to clear his bar. It wouldn't open again until the next year and he didn't really know if it would even be half as busy when it did. He was happy though, everything was right for him and he knew that Corzones Island really was his home. As he waded through the mess and placed it in the bin bag he gave a smile. Left propped up against one of the ancient temple walls was his ukulele. He picked it up, sat down in one of the wicker chairs and began to play a song to himself. The island truly was quiet and he intended to enjoy it.

Epilogue

The air was clear and warm, a pleasure to breathe for Franko Young. He savoured every breath that he drew whilst looking out over the sea. It was dyed a magical orange by the picturesque sunset and for a short moment he appreciated the beauty that the island contained and how it was so hard to notice with everything else that usually went on.

The whole place was quiet for the first time since he'd arrived, so long ago. The clubs were closed and most people had left at the earliest opportunity. Freedom knew that he should have done the same but off the island he had no real life, no identity. He was just another fool who had taken too many drugs and hoped that the effects would make his life better. Maybe they did on a very temporary basis but the truth was that he had worked on the island for so long because he found that he was appreciated there in a way that nowhere else seemed able to offer.

If only Zoë were with him. He still didn't know what the reason for everything was. The deaths, the gunmen and the earthquakes. "Very few" people had died according to the news, which had reported that the gunmen were trying some illegal drilling technique under the island and thus caused the earthquake. Franko wasn't convinced that it was even scientifically possible and thought that it sounded more like something from a James Bond film. He didn't care though. Since the moment he had lost Zoë, the one thing on the island that brought him genuine happiness, he hadn't cared about anything. Having a gun pointed at his head had made him realise one thing: his life meant nothing to him. He hadn't achieved anything and if that man had chosen to pull the trigger it wouldn't really have made any difference to the world, or even the island for that matter.

Argyll had been arrested. Franko knew that he'd never really been a fan of DJ Freedom but he always pulled in a good crowd which meant money, as good a reason as any to keep him around. Obviously Argyll's dislike of Franko stretched even further than that and to hurt him the choice had been made to have Zoë killed. Franko couldn't believe that Argyll was involved with whatever conspiracy had taken place but the fact that he was alive when so many were dead wasn't close to justice in Franko's eyes. Justice was never going to be a strong point in this case though, too many secrets and cover-ups and allegedly the real people behind it had been buried below the island in a sudden and sandy grave. What their aims were would never really be revealed. All that death and now at the end it seemed to be so pointless.

The Isle Club had gone. The damage done by the earthquake had been so severe that it had been deemed unsuitable for repair. Victor Corzones had taken over control of the island and had already started to make arrangements for its full demolition. Offers had been flying towards Franko from the other clubs through the whole day, all of them convinced that the island would return to usual business the following year.

There would be a memorial wall for the victims of the conspiracy and the resulting earthquake, that was all. Those lives would simply be reduced to names etched into a stone, all because they were on the wrong island at the wrong time. It seemed that the authorities showed as little regard for their lives as the conspirators had. People had lost their sons, daughters, brothers, sisters, cousins, friends and even lovers but at least on an island full of lost souls and lost hopes there was a lump of stone containing their names.

Corzones Island was Franko's world and that world had been pulled apart over the previous few days. The greatest drug of all in Franko's life was the island, it doomed him but it was a habit that he would never be able to kick. It was part of him to the point where it defined him and even dominated him. It was all the life he had and after the events of the previous few days he no longer wanted it.

It was a wonderful spot that he had found, a rock that stuck out over the edge of a cliff, causing a heavenly echo every time a wave struck below. It was where Franko wanted to be, alone and looking out into the infinite sea, full of possibilities and hopes. The sun had lowered considerably and its reflection over the water was no longer beautifully orange, it had become a dark, harsh and bloody red. Even the sea was angry now and would soon be consumed entirely by an unforgiving darkness that couldn't possibly be negotiated with. After that, another day would dawn and more

321

people would leave the island. The whole place would be entirely empty by the time the sun set again. It's rebuilding and restructuring would begin and the new regime would come into power. It would never be the same, no matter what they did. What had happened would be remembered, it would stay with everybody and taint every second of their lives.

Franko had lived a tainted life for a long time but it was one that he was content with. Even that had gone now. Zoë was gone, his place of work was in ruins and his boss had been arrested for murder, amongst other things. The truth was that now he was alone and he realised that he had been all along. In the club he was surrounded by hundreds of people who all loved him because of what he was doing but that wasn't true really. They didn't know him, let alone love him and standing on this rock facing out to sea on Corzones Island, Franko felt as complete as he ever would do.

The light was fading entirely now, the ocean had turned black with only a thin red line reflecting from the last bit of the sun pointing towards him. All he could hear were the waves crashing against the rock. No music. No constant thumping of sound that had been such a large part of Franko's life for such a long time. There were no happy people, no couples rushing to a place where they thought they were alone. Even the gunfire that seemed to have become an integral part of the island had ceased. This was a new Corzones. Franko's drug no longer existed and nothing in the world could ever replace it.

His thoughts returned to Zoë, she really had cared about him and he about her. He thought about something she had said to him on the morning of the day she died, "I don't want to see you destroy yourself". She was gone now and therefore her fear would never be realised. The sun was gone and the final hints of light were hurriedly fading away. The dark sea looked inviting, like it would be warm and enjoyable but the drop looked significant so it was possible that Franko would never find out if he was right about that. He was three steps away from oblivion, just three. He took a deep breath and took the first step. This was real now, he was doing it to end his addiction to the island. Second step. That one was for Zoë, he was now one step closer to her. He looked down over the edge of the cliff and saw the beautiful white spray of a wave hitting the rocks below. He allowed himself a final smile and then knew that it was time to take the final step.

Coming Soon
'Hopes And...'

Thanks to...

Nick, Carol & Carly for reading the early drafts and Sarah Miles for doing the final proofread. This would simply not have been possible without you.

Steve Thornhill and Carol Hutchinson (again) for providing the cover art as well as Simon for the photo of me.

Pete, Jane, Chris and anybody else working in MASH while I was writing this. Best writing spot in the world!

Adam, Mike, Phoebe, Gareth, Spencer & Beth for putting up with me constantly writing while we were on holiday and Rosie for some great advice.

Mum, Dad, Nick (again) and Carly (again) for providing a great deal of extra support.

(Photo by Travelling Simon Photography - http://www.travellingsimon.com)

Johnstone is a Scriptwriting graduate and DJ from and currently living in Macclesfield. He has always written and plans to keep doing so.

@JohntyMacc

Made in the USA
Charleston, SC
01 November 2015